Love

C000125292

Emma Rae graduated from Plymouth University and joined the Foreign Commonwealth and Development Office in 2003, working in British Embassies across the globe. She writes both new adult romance and thriller novels, and is a graduate of the Faber Academy and Curtis Brown Creative. She now lives in Guildford with her husband and two children.

EMMA RAE

Love GAME

hera

First published in the United Kingdom in 2024 by

Hera Books
Unit 9 (Canelo), 5th Floor
Cargo Works, 1–2 Hatfields
London SE1 9PG
United Kingdom

A CIP catalogue record for this book is available from the British Library.

Print ISBN 978 1 80436 785 8
Ebook ISBN 978 1 80436 787 2

Look for more great books at www.herabooks.com

Printed and bound in Great Britain by Clays Ltd, Elcograf S.p.A.

1

Love game: *Noun.* Tennis. When a player wins a game without their opponent scoring a single point.

~

'I am no bird; and no net ensnares me; I am a free human being with an independent will, which I now exert to leave you.'

from *Jane Eyre*, by Charlotte Brontë

Chapter One

I'm faking another orgasm because I'm late for a job interview.

I made a vow to myself not to do this again. And yet, it's so easily done. Some well-timed murmurs, heavy panting, a dramatic moan and my boyfriend's none the wiser. I'd go so far as to say that I've honed my performance.

Jamie's been sleeping around for months. He thinks I haven't worked that out by now, but three weeks ago, I caved. I looked at his phone whilst he was asleep, only to discover several different message threads confirming my all-too-real suspicions.

Two of the girls I knew personally. Granted, I didn't know what their naked body parts looked like. I do now.

I don't know which hurts more: that I know the truth, or that it took me so long to realise what was going on, or, worse, that I'm still here, my simulated efforts serving only to massage my boyfriend's already inflated ego, creating an illusion of sexual satisfaction. They say people can get too comfortable in relationships. The truth is, I feel like I don't have anywhere else to go. Jamie's paid my rent for the last three months, and I'm flat broke. So, here I am, breaking my vow, too afraid to walk away. It's true to say that my self-esteem at this moment – or any other moment in my current life – is at rock bottom.

Today, Jamie's working from home. In our bedroom, at our shared flat in Earlsfield, in south-west London, once he's finished having sex with me, he collapses onto our bed sheets with a grunt. I shoot up off the mattress, whilst he's doubtless congratulating himself on another job well done.

'Oi, what's the hurry?' he raises his voice after me.

'I've got to be in Wimbledon Village in less than an hour, remember?' I squeak back, switching on the hot water for the shower in the en-suite bathroom, catching sight of my reflection in the mirror. I try not to be disappointed in the person I see looking back at me: brown eyes, dark brown shoulder-length hair, average build. Most days I feel like the embodiment of average. 'For the interview. I haven't even looked up which bus I need to take from the station.'

He's quiet for a moment, his brows drawing together. ''93 towards Putney Bridge. Get out at Parkside Avenue; you'll be round the corner. Only take you a few minutes.'

Yes, he's a cheat. Nor does he excel at the art of giving pleasure, or indulge in any foreplay for that matter. But the man is an encyclopedia of London's bus routes.

So at least he's good for something.

Sixty minutes later, I'm standing outside a pair of cast iron gates on leafy Parkside Gardens in Wimbledon Village. Most of the properties on this road are behind walls. The house I'm looking at is grand, three grossly expensive cars parked in neat formation on a driveway.

I breathe in. Even the air is better in this part of the city.

'Good morning,' a leggy woman trills as she emerges from the front door, holding a set of keys. Her neatly weaved braids are tied back and almost reach her waist. She looks a little younger than my own twenty-six years, though she's taller, with long, agile limbs, dark eyes, and pouty lips. She's wearing sports leggings and Lycra t-shirt, a beaming smile on her face. She speaks with a slight lilt from the American south.

'Elle Callaway?' she asks from the other side of the iron railings, the soles of her trainers crunching against the pebble stones.

'Hello,' I say. '*Uhm*, it's Caraway. Like the seed, not the golf equipment.'

'Oh, I am so sorry.' She double checks her piece of paper. 'Elle Caraway, yes, of course. I'm Sydney… Sydney Swanson.

You can call me Syd. Great to meet you.' She opens the gate using the keys, ushering me inside the property, and we shake hands. She escorts me directly to the kitchen, which contains a large marble-topped island backed by two oversized sash windows, and an impressive range cooker.

'Have a seat,' she says, indicating to a stool next to the island. 'I apologise; I would offer you a coffee but the cupboards are practically bare.'

'Really, don't worry, I'm fine.'

'So,' she continues. 'I'm delighted to tell y'all that the agency confirmed you passed all the relevant background checks.'

I force a smile. The agency contact didn't tell me the reason for requesting I submit a photocopy of my passport. For the last couple of weeks, I haven't been offered any work and I'm despairing.

'And the agency explained about the job, correct?'

'Uh... yes,' I nod. 'That it's a personal chef role... that the hours are variable. That it's a live-in position and...' I click my fingers under the table. 'There was one more thing but I've forgotten it.'

She's beaming. 'Don't worry, you got it. The last point was about full discretion. It's absolutely essential for this role.'

I nod. 'Happy with that. They said I may have to cook in the middle of the night, is that right?'

When the agency stipulated this as a job component, I thought I'd misheard. 'That's right,' Sydney confirms. 'This job requires a certain amount of... resilience. The hours are not always the most sociable.'

I try not to snort. 'I'm a chef, I'm used to that.'

'Good, good,' she grins. 'So... to explain, Nicky has an unusually high metabolism.'

'And... Nicky is who I would be cooking for?'

Sydney throws up her palms. 'Of course, I'm sorry, the agency wouldn't have mentioned that part. Yes, yes, absolutely, you'd be personal chef to Nicky. Nicky Salco.'

My face falls. 'As in the tennis player?'

'Yes, the tennis player.'

I paste on my best smile, swallowing my nerves. 'Okay.'

It's late June. The agency stated that the job was for three weeks, so I had a hunch there might be a tennis element involved, given that the Wimbledon Tennis Championships are just around the corner. Nicky Salco, on the other hand, is a gorgeous specimen of masculinity, the kind of man I don't think I can even look at without turning a cherry shade of red, let alone have a conversation with. He's tall, broad-shouldered, known for being moody as hell on court, but off court, for having women swoon all over his model looks. And now I would be expected to cook for him. Alone. In the middle of the night.

Sydney is still talking. 'Anyway, that's what the doctors say. His metabolism is a little haywire. It means he gets ravenously hungry at night, even if he eats, like, a huge dinner. Because he's constantly on court, he burns, like, super high amounts of calories. He can't seem to sleep through 'til morning; it's like his body is on a clock. The only way he can go back to sleep is if he eats a meal. For most of us it's a bizarre habit, but… there it is. He's like a plant that needs continual watering in order to thrive.'

'He really needs a chef in the night?' I blurt out. 'He can't just put something in the microwave? Eat a banana?'

My hand shoots to my mouth on realising that not only am I being rude, but that I could be doing myself out of a job. Sydney laughs, as though it's not the first time someone has made such a suggestion. 'It's outlandish, I know. But Nicky's pathologically incapable. We tried. Left to his own devices, he'll order 24-hour fast food and gorge on burgers and fries at three a.m. Not ideal for a sports pro. Coach has decided that this is the only way forward for our time in London. And that's where *you* come in.'

I stare at her, somewhat bewildered. 'I thought this was just an interview?'

4

'Oh, for sure,' she says. 'It is.'

A moment of silence passes between us. Sydney bites her lip, a self-conscious look flitting across her features. She leans forward and lowers her voice. 'Look. I'll be honest with you. We went through two agency chefs already. Neither made the cut. Don't tell anyone this but I'm desperate. The job's yours if you want it.'

'You don't want to ask about my experience?'

'I've seen your resume. You worked in a local bistro for the last three years. It shut down some months ago. Before that y'all was a teacher.'

'That's right.'

'Why'd you stop being a teacher?'

I wince, but I already feel at ease with her. 'Honestly? They said I wasn't dynamic enough to deal with thirty raucous children.'

Sydney waves her hand like she couldn't give a damn. 'So, what kind of food did you make at the bistro?'

'A bit of everything. The lasagna was always a favourite.'

'Well, the good thing about Nicky is he eats anything and everything. Man is many things; a picky eater ain't one of them. But if y'all can't get up outta bed and cook for him in the night... well then, that's where we run into problems. That's why I need someone resilient.'

Resilience is staying with my boyfriend when I know he's sleeping with other women. Resilience is not having a permanent job for the last twelve weeks, relying on agency work, trawling the classified ads, getting perhaps one interview per sixteen applications if I'm lucky. Resilience is sometimes feeling so alone and unappreciated that I could die, yet forcing myself out of bed every day.

'Getting up in the night is not going to be an issue,' I say with a nod, though, if I'm honest, I've never actually done it in practice.

I grin. In that moment, we seem to have established that I've got the job. Excitement surges momentarily in my veins.

Sydney claps her hands together and gets to her feet. 'So… you would be expected to make lunches and dinners every day for four to five people during normal and weekend hours, except Sundays. You'll then be expected to cook a meal for Nicky at approximately one thirty to two a.m., in time for an approximately two thirty a.m. sitting. And that would be every night of the week until your services are no longer needed.'

When I cock my head to one side, she must realise I don't quite understand her meaning. 'I mean, if Nicky gets knocked out of the Championships,' she corrects herself. 'Then your contract would come to an immediate end. But we would pay you for the full duration no matter what happens, of course.'

I nod in understanding. 'So, no breakfast?' I ask.

'Breakfast they mostly sort themselves out.'

'Right.' I'm still looking around and nodding my head. It feels surreal just being here. 'Do I get told what to cook in advance?' I ask.

'No, you have pretty much free rein to choose, so long as the food is fresh and reasonably healthy. Like I said, Nicky burns super amounts of calories on court and weight training during the day. I should mention that he's a total dessert hound, so Coach would say you need to go easy on the sugar. In the night, once you've made him something, you can slip away and go back to bed. He doesn't require conversation.'

'I see.'

Sydney points to a door leading off from the kitchen. 'You'd sleep through there. So as you can see, you wouldn't have far to walk to work. You wanna take a peek?'

I get to my feet, following her through the door that leads off the kitchen. I take in the cosy little room, containing one single bed, a fireplace, a wall-mounted bookshelf packed full of novels, and a set of French doors leading out to the garden. Outside I can hear the persistent *thwock* of a tennis ball hitting a racket.

'And you're Mr. Salco's assistant?' I ask her.

'I am. He's currently ranked in the top fifty players on the tour. That comes with sponsorship deals, so I manage travel, bookings, logistics, communications, any staff. Also here are his coach, Ragnar Norddahl, from Sweden, his training partner and physio, Tag Holström. Tag's also Swedish – we call them Rag and Tag, not that they find that funny – and finally, Nicky's fiancée, Mackenzie Scheffler. She's upstairs right now, working. You can call him Nicky by the way.'

I'm nodding so much I'm like one of those dog toys people put on their car dashboard. Of course he has a fiancée. I tell myself she probably looks like Victoria's Secret model.

'I'll introduce y'all later. Also, if you don't mind,' she continues. 'I need you to sign a Non-Disclosure Agreement. Anything you see or hear in the confines of these walls needs to stay that way. Any conversations you are part of or overhear. That okay?'

'Of course,' I smile.

'I took the liberty of printing off the paperwork, so let's get that signed.'

'Can I tell anyone I'm here?'

'A partner, close family members or friends, they can know, that's fine. It's mainly to protect Nicky from any negative press, so you can't say much more to them than that.'

'Understood,' I nod.

'Great,' she grins at me again. 'Welcome to the team, Elle.'

Chapter Two

'All done. Let's go meet Nicky.'

I put down the pen, having signed two copies of both my employment contract and the Non-Disclosure Agreement at the kitchen table. My heart starts to clatter in my chest as I follow Sydney out into the garden through the French doors. High hedges are on all sides. I spy a grass tennis court further down the lawn, surrounded by a high chain-link fence.

'This house is most coveted by all the players on the tour,' Sydney explains. 'At least the top ones. There are very few houses around here with a full grass court in the back yard and so much privacy. I started negotiating to get this house more than a year ago.'

'It's beautiful,' I comment, amazed at the softness and colour of the spongy grass, though I'm not giving her my full attention because my pulse is pounding in my ears as we approach the court. I don't follow tennis, per se, but due to my flat being in fairly close proximity to the All England Lawn Tennis and Croquet Club – home to the Championships at Wimbledon – I pay attention every summer when the tournament takes place. I've never actually been inside the famous complex, but like most people I've watched the matches on TV. The rest of the year, I'll give the sport a cursory glance, usually during the well-known Grand Slams. I could probably name half a dozen male tennis players, and Nicky Salco would definitely be among that number. Yes, he's known for his tennis prowess: but mostly I would associate him with being one of the best-looking and most desirable sportspeople walking the planet. And honestly, it occurs to me, who doesn't?

We stop at one corner of the fence. Already I'm mesmerized, watching him through the wire. Nicky Salco is at least six foot three, with long, powerful thighs and arms that are muscular, but not in a bulky way. His figure is lithe, with strong, broad shoulders. He's wearing a navy blue kit. His chestnut hair is longer at the front, pushed out of his face by a matching bandana. He has his back to us, so I can only picture his face from pictures I've seen on the internet. I know he's roughly in his late twenties. His movements are lightning fast as he zips about his half of the court, the immense power with which he can return a ball spat out from a machine on the other half of the court and make it look effortless leaving me quite out of breath. Opposite him, on the other side of the net, Tag is of a similar height and build, but he's older, closer to thirty-five, with wavy dark brown hair, a longer face and thinner jaw.

'It's different seeing them in the flesh compared to watching the Grand Slams on TV, ain't it?' Sydney says after a moment of watching them in action. 'You realise how talented they are. Nicky has one of the best returns of service in the game. On a good day, nothing gets past him.'

I can't drag my eyes from him. His movements are so quick, yet so graceful. I make a muffled hum in agreement.

'Nicky!' Sydney calls out. 'Can I borrow you?'

He doesn't even pause, nor does he cease hitting the balls that are firing at him from different angles, smashing each one back with precision. He just keeps on going until they stop. 'Not now, Syd,' he calls in an even baritone, a little out of breath. 'I'm busy.'

I force a smile through thin lips. Sydney shrugs off any embarrassment she might have felt. 'Try getting him to do anything, honestly, it's impossible,' she whispers to me with a roll of her eyes. 'Soon as the tables are turned, and you say no to him, he can't stand it. Come on, I can introduce yall at lunch.'

9

'Should I prepare lunch?' I ask, still struggling to tear my eyes away.

'Lunch would be good. I'm afraid the fridge hasn't been well stocked. That might have to be your first job after throwing a meal together.'

I glance back at Nicky Salco. He's still hitting balls with his back to me. It doesn't escape my notice that my pulse is still racing, my breathing still not back to normal.

In the kitchen, I stare at the contents of the open fridge, panic flooding my chest over what to prepare. I've just over an hour to concoct something from scratch.

'Is there any bread?' I ask Sydney.

'Oh, I – honestly, I don't know,' Sydney responds, looking around a little hopelessly.

'How far away is the nearest shop?'

'Not close. At least there's nothing around here that I could find. Have you got enough to whip something up do you think?'

'I'll think of something,' I breathe, closing the fridge and attempting a smile.

'Well, if you need anything, just holler. I'll be upstairs.'

In my new bedroom, I shut the door behind me, rummaging around for my mobile phone in my bag. Nerves cause my chest to tighten, making it hard to breathe. I dial Josie, my elder sister, who lives in Barcelona. She has the opposite of my personality, and tends to blurt out that first thing that pops into her head. She's the extrovert to my introvert, and the person I most trust in the entire world. A chef's working hours often make friends hard to come by. Temporary though it might be, now that I have this job, I don't want to mess it up before I've even started.

'You literally never call me,' Josie exclaims as she answers, as I breathe a sigh of relief. 'Something must be up.'

'I've picked up a job for three weeks,' I whisper. 'It's a personal chef role.'

'Sounds fancy,' Josie coos. 'Who is it for? Are you cooking for a celeb?'

Josie has always been a little obsessed with celebrity, regularly pouring over the weekly gossip magazines whenever she comes back to England.

'Well, you'd definitely recognize who it is.'

'Oh, it's like *that* is it?' she responds, matching my hushed tone. 'Alright, yes no game. Is this person a film star?'

'Jose,' I hiss. 'I have to be careful what I say. That's not why I'm calling.'

'You're not telling me anything: you're just saying *yes* or *no*. Film star, yay or nay? Come on, I'm intrigued.'

I sigh. 'Nay.' I keep my voice low.

'TV?'

'No.'

'Sports personality?'

'Yes.'

'Ooh Lord! Footballer? Oh, it's not to do with Wimbledon is it?'

'Yes.'

Josie squeals. 'British player?'

I rub the bridge of my nose and wish I wasn't having to do this right at this moment. 'No.'

'American?'

'Yes.'

'Male?'

Masculine, I want to correct her. 'Last time I checked.'

Josie gasps. 'Oh, is it what's-his-name? The guy who does that little bum wiggle before he serves the ball?'

'No. Isn't he retired?'

'*Oooh*, who else is there? I don't know any other American players. What about the one who rants and raves like McEnroe. Nicky Salco?'

I am silent for a moment. I know I'm allowed to tell her, but I'm in unfamiliar territory.

'Oh my God, it *is* isn't it?' Josie squeals. 'Holy shit. Did you meet him yet? What's he like?'

'No, I haven't met him yet,' I whisper. 'I need your advice on what to cook him and his coaches for lunch. I'm so used to you being told what to make; so now I'm looking at a half empty fridge and trying to find inspiration. If I cook the wrong thing, they might send me packing.'

'What's in the fridge?' Josie asks, sobering.

'*Uhm.* Smoked salmon, some cream cheese, heavy cream, a few veggies, milk, eggs, butter, that's about it. The last two chefs didn't last.'

'Did you check the cupboards?'

'Staples. Pasta, some different types of flour, dried herbs, not a lot else.'

'What are you thinking?'

'Frittata. It's not too basic?'

'Not if you make it well. And I know you, Elles, you make a mean frittata. Is there any chocolate in the house? Whip up a batch of your brownies for dessert? Your brownies are legendary.'

I'm pacing about the room, peeking out of the French doors. I can just see the corner of the grass court behind the wire mesh fence. Nicky Salco is still training.

'Okay, that sounds good.'

'If you're still worried, do what you do best. Sounds like you need a meal plan. Is the pay decent?'

'Yes, it's decent.' I don't mention about the need to work after hours, or the extra money that's been offered for that part of the job spec.

'Good. They'll love you. Make sure you get me an autograph.'

I get to work, slicing and peeling, scouring the cupboards for whatever I can find. Whoever this house belongs to appears to be a lover of baking, at least.

Sydney comes back downstairs just before twelve.

'Something smells good anyway,' she says. 'Nicky and Tag will get showered. Then I can introduce y'all properly.'

'Let them eat first, maybe,' I suggest. 'If my cooking's not up to scratch, then you might not even need to bother.'

Sydney looks at me, wide-eyed, as though I'm crazy for saying such things. But then she looks lost, her expression crumpling. 'I shouldn't say this,' she mumbles, 'But you are kind of my last hope, so if y'all get fired, I might not be long after.'

I'm glad I haven't cooked too much in advance, because showers seemed to be followed by some kind of physical therapy. When the group is ready, I serve smoked salmon frittatas with roasted vegetables on warm plates, allowing Sydney to carry them through to the dining room. Placing some of the dirty dishes into the sink, I wait, sat on a stool beside the kitchen island, hands clasped in my lap, still with my chef's apron on, listening to the sounds of the lively conversation in the other room, including another woman's voice.

When the clatter of utensils suggests the meal is over, Sydney comes scurrying back through to the kitchen with a broad smile on her face. My heart leaps in my chest.

'I think you very much passed the test,' she whispers with a grin, beckoning me to follow.

My stomach a maze of nerves, I follow Sydney into the dining room.

'Everybody, meet Elle,' Sydney says, holding out her arms towards me. I twist the material of my apron in between my fingers. 'Elle, this is Nicky, Ragnar, Nicky's coach, Tag, his training partner and Mackenzie.'

'Mackenzie, Nicky's *fiancée*,' the woman confirms drolly. She's blonde and exquisite with all pointy features and elegant make-up, with a colossal diamond on her left ring finger. 'Don't forget that part.'

'Sorry,' Sydney swallows. 'Of course. Mackenzie, Nicky's fiancée.'

I've never been good with an audience, or receiving attention for that matter. Blending into the background is where I'm most comfortable. As I feel all eyes on me, I sense the base of my neck grow warm, heat creeping up to my cheeks.

'Hello,' I mumble. 'Nice to meet you.'

'That was delicious, Elle, thank you,' Ragnar says, with a strong accent.

'Thank you,' I stammer. 'There wasn't much in the fridge. I made brownies too, if you'd like dessert. I halved the sugar content and used almond flour, so they're gluten-free. I'm sorry, I didn't have many ingredients to work with.'

No one responds. I keep my eyes down as much as possible. When I look up, Nicky Salco is watching me from the head of the table. I can't read his expression, perhaps because I'm distracted by how magnificent he is. This time I get a good look at his face. There are reasons people don't just talk about Nicky Salco's tennis ability. The man seems to have been born a heartbreaker, with dark, smoldering eyes, a well-defined jaw and a full mouth. And right now, his languid stare is sending my pulse rocketing.

'Well, this is a first,' Mackenzie continues talking. 'I've never had Nicky getting up in the night to a woman before.'

'I don't think you've got anything to worry about,' Nicky drawls, taking her hand and sending another wave of heat to my mortified cheeks. 'I hope you've set an alarm,' he says sharply in my direction.

'Nicky, Elle doesn't even have her stuff here yet,' Sydney reminds him.

'Elle, you know you'll be feeding a future champ,' Mackenzie says in my direction. She reminds me of a pouty, blonde high school cheerleader. 'Nicky's here in London to kick some grass court ass.'

I'm not entirely sure how to respond to her statement so I force another smile.

Mackenzie turns her attention to Sydney. 'You did get her to sign all the forms, right, Syd?'

'Yes,' Syd confirms. 'Elle's signed the contract and the NDA.'

'Good,' Mackenzie says, jutting out her chin and giving me a once over. 'Discretion in this business is *so* hard to come by.'

I look across at Sydney, whose gaze is now fixed assuredly on the carpet.

At the other end of the table, Tag is laughing, shaking his head. 'Next time, can't we just fly Alonzo out here?' he says.

Nicky is quick to respond. 'He won't do it. You know I've asked him a million times.'

Sydney begins to clear the lunch plates. I assist, while the conversation turns back to tennis.

I'm at the kitchen sink when Nicky Salco enters the room behind me. I can feel the heat of his presence yet I daren't turn around.

'You know, you can't just tempt a man with the promise of dessert,' he drawls, 'then keep the brownies all to yourself in the kitchen.'

I flinch, taking it as a criticism even if it's not meant as one, turning and wiping my hands on my apron. I force a bright smile, yet underneath I'm flustered. 'Of course, I'm sorry. I wasn't keeping them to myself,' I say, darting towards the plastic container on the end of the kitchen island, the sides all steamed up from the still warm batch of brownies I'd put in the oven just before lunch.

'Relax, I'm kidding,' he smirks, just as I open the container for him. Nicky Salco takes a step closer towards me, within touching distance and I can feel my muscles tensing up. 'Holy shit, those smell amazing,' he says as he helps himself to the biggest one. 'Don't tell Tag, okay, I'm in no mood to share.'

'Share what?' Tag asks as he enters the kitchen, his eyes lighting up at the sight of the open container. 'Oh no, my friend, no you don't.'

Tag helps himself too, Nicky biting into his brownie, making muffled noises of approval. He chews for a moment, and I realise I'm holding my breath. When he's finished, he helps himself to two more.

'I think Nicky might decide you can stay,' Tag chuckles at me with his mouth full.

'Was I wrong to make brownies?' I ask, worried.

'Oh, I wouldn't say that,' is Tag's response.

'Yeah, well, let's see if she can lift her pretty little head off the pillow when it's after midnight,' Nicky shoots back in his direction, without looking in mine.

I snap the lid back onto the box of brownies. 'I am in the room, you know,' I mutter under my breath. Okay, so he's a little rude, but Nicky Salco doesn't seem to hear me, his concentration focussed purely on his two remaining slabs of gooey brownie.

My job secured, in the afternoon I put together an internet order for food, leaving instructions for Sydney to pay for it before I return home to fetch my things.

I walk the long way back to the bus stop, stopping on route to linger beside beautifully designed shop windows and outside chic-looking cafés in Wimbledon Village. The later I arrive home, the sooner I'll have to leave to come back.

The rain is pelting down by the time I reach Willow Tree Close. Jamie is on a team call talking about mortgage rates so I make myself scare in the bedroom. On the floor, the bed sheets are still piled up in a heap.

'Alright, babe?' he says when he enters. 'How'd it go? What's the job?'

'It's a personal chef role for a tennis player. I start immediately. I have to live over there for two to three weeks.'

'What?' he blurts. 'Over where?'

I shrug, relieved. 'Wimbledon Village. It's part of the job spec.'

'So, it was a tennis player then?'

'Yes,' I say, because Jamie's not exactly the jealous type but the fact that I'm getting up in the night for Nicky Salco is not going to go down well. 'I'd never heard of him.'

'Guess I'm cooking my own food for a while then. Right. Well, I'm off out tonight.'

'What for?'

'Jonesy's birthday celebrations.'

'I thought that was last week,' I query, because despite what he might think, I pay attention.

'Yeah, well, you know how he likes to drag these things out,' he says, and starts fixing his hair in the mirror, slick with the usual amount of gunk.

Whilst he's finishing preening himself, I wonder if he's seeing one of the same girls he's cheated on me with, or maybe a different one, or whether he's even seeing Jonesy at all. Before I discovered the messages on his phone, I found condoms in his wallet when I was still taking the contraceptive pill. Things were good for a short while, when we'd first moved in together. He even supported me when my mother died suddenly in her sleep, and my father of a heart attack two months later. Yet at this moment, despite my desire to leave, I know that, financially, he's keeping me afloat, paying my rent and buying all of our food and supplies. I've contributed precisely nothing. In the last two weeks, the times I've thought about confronting him about his behaviour always leave me paralysed – the idea of the subsequent argument and the result being me left with nowhere else to live. I daren't ask my former colleagues if I can sleep on one of their sofas. Like me, they're all trying to find a permanent gig.

'Right, best get back to it,' Jamie says. 'You got time to make us a sandwich before you go, yeah?'

As I watch him leave the room, the image of Nicky Salco floats into my mind. I think about getting out of bed for him tonight, the idea of him eating something of my making almost giving me butterflies. Yet, here I am, my cheating boyfriend asking me to make him a snack.

I long for a different life. One away from Jamie.

In my heart, I want this to be the last sandwich I'll ever make him.

Shortly after, I head back over to Wimbledon with a packed suitcase, picking up enough food to cover dinner along the way. I make a reduced-fat lasagna, which seems to go down well.

Before heading to bed, I navigate to my alarms on my phone, making sure two are set to go off in the night. I tell myself that my pretty little head will be up and about and cooking at least an hour before he's due to get up, and – in my mind at least – Nicky Salco will be forced to eat his words.

By one a.m., I'm wide awake, not even needing my alarm to swing both feet out of bed and onto the floor. Getting myself dressed, I move to the kitchen, having left everything out in preparation. Looking at my workspace, I am reminded that this is where the real test starts.

I'd settled on a butternut squash fresh ravioli, served with a sundried tomato pesto cream. Everything prepared and ready to be heated, I realise I still have forty-five minutes to wait before half past two finally rolls around.

I sit back down on my bed, puffing out my cheeks, thinking I'm going to need to plan my time better during the nights to come. The minutes tick by. I freeze when I finally hear the creak of the floorboards above my head, the sound of his footsteps padding against the carpeted stairs as I scurry back over to the stove.

When he enters the dimly-lit kitchen, I don't know where to look. I straighten, both horrified and exhilarated that he's wearing a pair of low-slung jogging bottoms, with nothing on top. The under-cabinet lighting casts shadows across his powerful torso, defined abs and ludicrously muscular triceps, accentuating his chiseled, athletic shape, a thin white line of skin peeking above his waistband, emphasizing the depth of his tan. Compared to Jamie's mound of patchy hair on his chest, Nicky doesn't have a strand in sight, his skin ridiculously smooth. He gives a grunt in what I presume to be a greeting, pulls out a stool at the kitchen island, before he sits down, resting his elbows on the surface whilst he stifles a yawn.

I decide very quickly I'm not going to be able to do this without severe mortification, or without his bare chest making me imagine things I definitely shouldn't be imagining about my new employer.

'What's for second dinner?' he asks, his gravelly, half-asleep voice doing odd things to my stomach.

'I've made you fresh ravioli,' I respond.

'Nice.'

'It'll just be a minute,' I say, checking the saucepan. 'Would you mind... would you mind putting a shirt on?'

He rubs one hand across his rib cage. I'd love to know what that feels like. Then his hand goes to the back of his neck. 'Is the sight of my chest offensive to you?'

It's because I find you preposterously attractive, my internal monologue is screaming, as I grapple to come up with a valid reason. 'If I turned up here, tonight, to cook for you without my shirt on, wearing just my bra,' I shoot back, 'it would be deemed inappropriate. This is my workspace. Why should it be any different for you?'

My words come out more forcefully than I was aiming for. His lips twist, as though he's mulling the idea over that I might have a point. Getting up off the stool, he leaves the room, walking back upstairs, coming back down a couple of minutes later wearing a fitted white t-shirt. *Preposterously sexy he might be, but that's a bad colour for ravioli*, it occurs to me as he reclaims his seat.

'You're the first female chef I've had doing this for me,' he says, 'I'm sorry, I didn't mean to cause offence. I'll make it a policy that I wear a shirt from now on.'

Despite being the one to tell him to cover up, I feel a pang of disappointment wash over me that I might not get to witness the glory that is his physical form again.

'You got out of bed then,' he says at length.

I lift the ravioli out of the pan of boiling water with a mesh spoon, transferring them to a plate. 'Would you have fired me on the spot if I hadn't?'

In the shadows, his eyes glimmer. 'Those brownies might have been enough to give you a one-night reprieve.'

'I'm amazed you're allowed to eat them. I thought you'd survive on a diet of... protein shakes and kale.'

He pulls a disgusted face, shaking his head. 'Put me on a court four or five hours a day, I'll eat what I damn well like.' He pauses. 'Actually, that's not entirely true. Ragnar wants me to eat less sugar. Problem is, I like all the guilty pleasures, if you know what I mean.'

He holds my gaze for a fraction longer than is necessary, causing me to question exactly what guilty pleasures he's referring to. For a split second, impure images of Nicky Salco flit through my mind.

Adding the sauce and a garnish to the ravioli, I slide the warm plate to the opposite side of the kitchen island, between the knife and fork I've already laid out for him, along with a glass of water.

'Wait,' I order him, going to the fridge and retrieving the hunk of Parmesan I'd picked up along with the lasagna ingredients. Grabbing a hand grater, I grate a sprinkling of cheese over his dish. I feel a pulse of electricity go through me, standing so close to him.

'Thank you,' he says, picking up the cutlery. 'It smells delicious.'

Backing away to my side of the kitchen, I turn away, piling up the dirty dishes whilst he eats. Outside the window, the garden is pitch black.

He's finished within minutes.

'Any more where that came from?' he asks, wiping the corner of his mouth.

I turn, giving him a wide-eyed stare. 'You're asking me for seconds at a quarter to three in the morning?'

'Uh-huh. Future tip, you might wanna adjust your portion sizes.'

'Noted,' I swallow. 'I can offer you a banana?'

'Got any more brownies?'

'You and Tag polished them off already. Tomorrow I'll make more brownies.'

He gets off the stool, and I notice a tiny sundried-tomato pesto mark on his white shirt.

'Guess I'll be going back to bed again then,' he says with a jaunty smile. 'Thanks for the food, Elle.'

'Sleep well,' I mutter, watching him leave, having to pinch myself that I've just been alone in a room with Nicky Salco at almost three o'clock in the morning.

Chapter Three

I wake early to meet the food delivery driver at the front gate. Once the produce is all packed away, I shower and get to work on one of my specialties: a simple white sour dough loaf. Making breakfast may not be a requirement of the job, but I'm keen to make a good impression. I'm just removing the loaf from the oven when Tag appears, Nicky following him shortly after, both dressed for another court session.

'Coffee's on,' I say, pointing to the percolator. 'Are you allowed to drink coffee?'

'I am,' Tag says, helping himself to a mug. 'Nicky avoids caffeine.'

'Would you like some bread?' I ask. 'It's sour dough. Low salt. Tastes nice with jam.'

Nicky is looking at me, smiling. He shakes his head.

'What?' I ask.

'Nothing, I'm impressed. Did you even go back to sleep?'

'For a couple of hours, I think. Did you?'

'Nicky sleeps like a machine,' Tag chuckles. 'If he didn't get so hungry all the time, I doubt he'd wake up.'

I slice into the loaf, steam rising from the inside. Nicky draws up a stool and sits down, his focus on the bread. I pass him the butter and a pot of strawberry preserve.

'So how do you spend your day?' I ask Tag, who leans against the kitchen counter, sipping his coffee whilst Nicky eats.

'In the build-up to a tournament, we do two to three hours on court in the morning, followed by a warm-down session, followed by lunch, followed by weight training, strength and conditioning, followed by more court time, followed by a relaxation massage. The day before Wimbledon starts, we do only light training.'

'Do you know who you'll be playing yet?' I ask Nicky.

He has his mouth full. He nods. 'The opening match, we know,' Tag completes for him. 'He's a qualifier.'

'So, you should win?' I ask.

'And after that, win another six times,' Nicky responds with a shrug. 'Simple, really.'

I open my mouth to say that isn't what I meant. Instead, I lapse into silence, and get out of the way.

'You know, if you want her to stay, you should probably lose the sarcasm,' I hear Tag reproach Nicky once I'm in my room.

'What? I didn't say anything,' Nicky grumbles in response.

The kitchen tidy, and preparation for lunch complete, I take a wander out into the garden. On the bookshelves in my room, I've found a copy of *Jane Eyre*. I've never read it. I'm getting used to the constant sound of balls being thwacked by tennis rackets, along with the chirruping of birds in the surrounding trees and hedges.

I turn the corner, pausing momentarily when I realise Nicky is training with his shirt off. Lowering myself down onto a wrought iron bench on the far side of the court fence, I open the novel, enjoying the sunshine. I read from the first page, Bronte's opening lines: *There was no possibility of taking a walk that day*, yet I already feel my gaze being drawn upwards to Nicky's lithe figure, and the majesty that is his thumping serve, where he hits the ball so hard it isn't possible to follow it with the naked eye as it rockets across the grass court. Perhaps it's because he's well-known, but a part of me feels powerless, as though I'm being pulled into Nicky Salco's own personal vortex where nothing matters but him.

I force my nose back down to the novel.

'What're you reading?' Nicky calls out through the fence.

'Jane Eyre.' I raise my voice slightly, holding up the book. 'I found it in my room. Must belong to the owners.'

23

He walks nearer to me, resting one arm above his head against the chain-link fence. At the other end, Ragnar and Tag collect up tennis balls. I balance the book spine up next to me, getting up off the bench to approach him. His skin glistens in the sunlight, drenched in sweat, and he wipes his forehead with a sweatband attached to his wrist.

'Would you rather I put a shirt on?' he says, cocking his head.

'This is your workspace,' I nod, a smile playing on my lips in a kind of acceptance. 'That's really up to you. Do you mind me watching you play?'

'Not at all,' he says, and backs away again, but for a split second, I swear his eyes don't leave mine, and it makes my heart flip over.

I turn and go back to my book, only to find Sydney approaching from the house.

'That bread you made tasted *incredible*,' she grins, and lowers herself into the seat next to me.

'I'm glad you liked it. Was there enough for Mackenzie?'

Sydney rolls her eyes. 'Oh, Mac doesn't really eat breakfast. The only reason she's eating carbs is because we're away from home.'

There is another stupendous *thwock* from on court as Nicky thunders another ball down the central line, Ragnar applauding his attempt.

'How long have Mackenzie and Nicky been together?' I ask.

'They've known each other since they were young. Her parents are Florida elite. Her father once ran for State Governor, but he wasn't elected. He still holds a lot of sway in Miami. She and Nicky went out in high school, but they broke up, then they got back together after he won the Australian Open six years ago.'

'How long have they been engaged?'

She thinks about it. 'Maybe two and half years? Give or take. Nicky's mom Libby is getting impatient. The wedding is scheduled for early next February, right before the Rio Open, to allow time for a couple of days honeymoon, so that Nicky can get back to training in earnest for the European tournaments. Everything revolves around the timing of the Grand Slams. Honestly, I don't know why they're doing it that way. There's plenty more time at Christmas but Mackenzie's parents wouldn't stand for it because all their rich friends will be skiing in Colorado.'

'You said Mackenzie was working. What does she do?'

'She runs a chain of boutique stores in Miami and L.A. They sell dresses and bikinis mainly. She designs her own swimwear; Nicky's modelled the men's styles in the past. Did you see them? The pictures that came out last year almost broke the internet.'

'No, I didn't see them,' I say, but I can imagine, and I vow internally to look them up. 'What's the brand name?'

'Casa Gables,' Sydney confirms. 'Named after Coral Gables in Miami, where Nicky's crib is. How about y'all? You said you have a partner?'

'Jamie,' I say, realising I haven't thought about him since I left him at the flat.

'And is marriage on the cards anytime soon?' Sydney asks.

'I'm not sure he's the marrying kind,' is my reply.

We watch together as the practice session continues. Nicky seems to be growing impatient, his serve not landing where he wants it to, and Ragnar admonishing him for it.

'He hasn't won a Grand Slam since Australia,' Sydney sighs under her breath. 'Not really gotten anywhere close since. In Melbourne, he won at twenty-three, that was six years ago. He was an overnight sensation. Every sponsor wanted a piece of him. But since then, he's gotten through five coaches, and a bunch of psychologists, most of whom now refuse to work with him. As a coach, Ragnar's fairly new, and even then, they've had their moments already. Nicky can be... what's the word? *Idiosyncratic*. He doesn't even own a cell phone.'

'He doesn't own a phone?'

'Nup.'

'What about social media, things like that?'

She shrugs. 'I do it all for him. I mean, he has friends, but his regime doesn't allow for much down time. On the tour, he keeps his distance. He's not wildly popular amongst the other players 'cause he doesn't tend to hang out with anyone. Keeps himself to himself.'

We continue to watch the session. Nicky is certainly unique. 'What about Tag?'

Sydney's eyes go to the far side of the court, where Tag is shouting encouragement at Nicky, clapping his hands together.

'Tag's a former pro. Never moved mountains. I think his highest ranking was about thirty-six on the tour, so he was top fifty for a short while. Persistent knee injury ended his pro-career. Torn meniscus that was operated on, but never left him where he wanted to be. He met Nicky on the circuit and they just hit it off. Unlike Nicky, Tag's a popular guy on the tour. But he understands the pressures, you know. Plus, he doesn't take any of Nicky's shit.'

'How old is Tag?'

'Thirty-five.'

'Does he have a partner?'

'A wife back in Sweden. They're going through a divorce. No kids though.'

From the bench, we then watch Nicky and Tag in a prolonged rally, and I blink every time Nicky wallops the ball over the net, a grunt emerging from his mouth on each occasion. There's something hypnotic about the back and forth.

I lower my voice further. 'The noises they make... they're almost...,'

'...sexual?' Sydney finishes for me, and we burst into fits of shared giggles.

I wake with a jolt in the darkness, disorientated. Above my head, there are raised, muffled voices: Nicky and Mackenzie in the midst of an argument. Grabbing blindly for my phone, I check that I haven't slept through my alarm. I haven't: the clock reading just after midnight. My eyes narrow as I lie there, trying to decipher what's being said in the room directly above, but this is an older house and the walls are too thick. After a few minutes, their voices die down and the house is eerily silent once more.

Except that I can't sleep.

I pick up my phone, typing 'Casa Gables and Nicky Salco' into the search screen. I select the 'images' tab. The professional pictures I find there show Nicky reclining beside an aquamarine pool, head tilted up to the sky, wearing a fitted pair of short black trunks, skin a golden brown, the rest of him a living advertisement for biological perfection. *No wonder the ad caused such a stir*, I think to myself, selecting the picture and pinching the screen to make it several times bigger, moving it around so I can enlarge different portions of the image. I come to the conclusion that Mackenzie Scheffler is one lucky fiancée.

It doesn't stop there though. As it turns out, despite not posting anything himself, Nicky Salco has a vast, devoted following on social media. I discover accounts dedicated solely to Nicky, endless Instagram and Tik Tok videos dedicated to the appreciation of his torso, slickly-edited videos that splice together footage of him getting riled up on court with images of his naked chest, all coming from dedicated fan accounts that, when it comes to Nicky, seem to relish in the liberal use of flaming heart emojis. I look at the comments. There are literally thousands of them:

> @salcobabe *Angrier he gets, sexier I find him*
>
> @nickyfan2000 *hottest guy in sports… makes me so damn thirsty*
>
> @salcolove92 *would divorce my husband 4 one night with angry Nickyyyy*
>
> @elliealamo *Loving the Nicky torso appreciation on here #nickysalco*

When Nicky comes padding down the stairs at half past two, I'm plating up a pie, cooked with homemade puff pastry, served with freshly steamed vegetables and buttery mashed potatoes. The moment he sits down, I skate the dish under his nose, setting it down on the placemat. I want there to be no room for error. Nicky makes a humming sound in approval.

'There's gravy if you want it,' I say. 'I never know if Americans like gravy or not.'

'Sure, I'll take gravy,' he responds, and I move the jug across the surface of the island. 'What's in the pie?'

'Steak and ale,' I murmur. 'It's classic British fare. I challenge you to still be hungry after you've eaten all that.'

He raises his eyes, and I feel my pulse quicken under his gaze, all those fan-made videos of his sculpted torso still fresh in my mind. After watching them, it's hard to grasp the fact that I get to talk to the real thing. I straighten, clearing my throat, remembering that this is the job at hand.

'I never back out of a challenge,' he states matter-of-factly.

'Yes, well I thought you'd say something like that; that's why I made dessert just in case.'

A smile tugs at his lips. 'You came prepared tonight; I'll give you that.'

He pours the gravy, before cutting into the pie crust, the steaming contents oozing out all over the plate. He then lifts a forkful to his mouth, tasting it. I press my fingertips together, awaiting his verdict.

'Are you just gonna stand there and watch me eat?' he questions with his mouth full, at which point I jump, startled, looking around me before moving to the sink and clearing some of the dirty dishes.

'Dessert is in the fridge,' I stammer when he's polished everything off. 'A fruit salad. Only if you want it. I guess I'll... I'll go back to bed now.'

'Stay a while,' he says, still eating. I stop in my tracks, feeling the blood rushing to my cheeks and thankful that he isn't able to see in the dim light.

'Did you need something else?' I ask.

'Company's always nice,' he says between mouthfuls.

I turn to face him. 'Tell me something about yourself,' he says. 'Where did you learn to cook?'

I'm staring down at the floor. 'A few years ago. I was training to be a teacher when I realised that I wasn't going to be a very good one. Then both my parents died in quick succession, and I came out the other side not really knowing what I wanted to do with my life.'

'Sorry to hear about your parents.'

'They were older... they had children later in life. My mother died peacefully in her sleep. I should be thankful really.'

'So what happened after that?'

'I got a job as a waitress in a local bistro. But they moved me to the kitchen when I showed an interest in learning how to cook. The head chef there trained me up from nothing. I worked there for almost four years, but it went out of business over three months ago, so I've been applying for jobs ever since, working on and off for the agency. It's competitive out there. Lots of chefs like me; all looking for work.'

'Well, I consider their loss is my gain. And you can really cook, Elle. This is delicious.'

I grin at his compliment. 'Yes, but this job is only for three weeks.'

'Doesn't have to be,' he counters flippantly, in a heartbeat.

I feel my stomach do a little cartwheel at the idea of being able to stay with him longer than the Championships. 'Who gets up and cooks for you at home? I mean, where *is* home for you?'

'Miami, Florida. Coral Gables. Same place I grew up. I have a Cuban chef living in one of my pool houses. His name's Alonzo; we call him Lonzo. Usually, I can persuade him to get up in the night. Either that or I go pounding on his door.'

29

He's smiling as he says it, as though it's something to be proud of. 'Why *do* you get up at night?' I question him. 'Why not just have a snack before you go to sleep? Then you wouldn't have to get up out of bed at all.'

'When I was a kid, the docs questioned whether I had an attention disorder. I had what they called 'excessive restlessness'. Couldn't sit still. Eventually, they told my parents they didn't think I had one, and to just get me out every day; let me run around until I crashed. That's when I got into tennis. Later, when I was older, they ran some tests. Said I had an unnaturally high metabolism. It means I burn calories faster than most, so, I wake up hungry. Can't seem to kick the habit.'

'I've never met anyone like you. Someone who eats a full meal in the middle of the night as if it were the most normal thing in the world.'

'It *is* the most normal thing in the world,' he argues. 'It is if you're me.' He takes another bite. 'Being restless isn't always conducive for the level of focus required in tennis. And I shelled a helluva lot of money out on psychologists, only for them all to tell me the same thing.'

'So now you have to manage your own frustrations?'

'I'm not proud of it, but I'm currently the ATP player with the most code violations to their name. I've fallen out with more umpires than I have personal chefs.'

'Sounds like you need to calm down,' I murmur.

I'm cursing my blabbermouth even before his eyes shoot up, his expression a fraction accusatory.

'I'm sorry, I didn't mean—' I stammer.

Nicky finishes his meal, pushing back his stool, getting to his feet. 'I'll tell you what. When you're a top-flight tennis pro with a Grand Slam win under his belt, then I'll let you be the one to judge.'

The feeling is akin to having my skin catch fire. I open her mouth to speak, terrified that I've messed everything up in a matter of milliseconds. It's too late though – because Nicky has already left the room.

Chapter Four

The following morning, after breakfast, I'm still mortified. I take my copy of *Jane Eyre* out to the garden bench again, hoping to catch Nicky's eye so I can offer him an apology. He's out on court with Ragnar and Tag, his shirt on today. I still haven't made it past the opening page of the novel.

Forcing myself through the first chapter, I allow my gaze to flit up occasionally, to check his position on court. Nicky doesn't look my way, a machine at one end lobbing out balls that he can smash down to the other side. When there is a natural lull in play, Nicky indicates to Tag that he requires a water break. When he walks to the fence, I take the opportunity to get to my feet.

'Morning,' I say to his back as he guzzles water, squirting fluid all over his face.

Nicky wipes his forehead, glancing back at me. I feel my cheeks flush hot again. 'I'm training,' he says flatly.

'I know, I'm sorry,' I stutter. 'I don't mean to disturb. I just wanted to apologise for my comment last night.'

'Which comment?' he asks.

'About you... you know... needing to calm down a bit. I wanted to say that I didn't mean to cause offence. I don't even know you.'

One corner of his mouth tilts up. He takes another drink. 'You English people always worry so much.'

'So, you're not angry with me?'

'Why? You worried I'll fire you?'

'I really need this job,' I breathe.

'Mac wants you,' Nicky says.

'What?'

He cocks his head in the direction of the house, putting his water down. I follow his glance, seeing Mackenzie making tracks over the grass towards me.

'Word of advice,' Nicky says, picking up his racket. 'Don't ever try telling *her* to calm down.'

My mouth opens but no sounds emerge. He's walked back to his previous position on court to resume play.

'Elle,' Mackenzie is saying as she reaches me. 'Shouldn't you be in the kitchen?'

'Breakfast is over. I was just—'

'I'm craving an omelette,' she interrupts. 'Can you throw something together for me? I want egg whites, no meat, no dairy. Some salmon and capers would be just fine. Slivered onions.'

'Of course,' I falter, gripping my copy of *Jane Eyre* to my chest. 'I'll do it now.'

'You know, Elle, it's best you don't disturb Nicky when he's training. I mean, I'm his fiancée and *I* don't sit out here and watch, you know. I'm sure you're a little bedazzled, I get that, he's a celebrity and you've probably not met one of those before. But next week, he's gonna be back in the fish bowl of Wimbledon Centre Court, with the whole world staring at him, so I think he would appreciate not having anyone watching him at this particular time, *hmm*? Do you understand what I'm talking about? If you're not required in the kitchen, you do have your room. There's also a little gazebo on the other side of the house. You can read your book there. You wouldn't be disturbing anyone. Please remember that your position here is temporary.'

As she speaks, humiliation washes over me in waves. I feel my neck and cheeks burn hot, rendered mute by her reprimanding me. Nicky is too far away from me to hear her. I'm mortified; Sydney hadn't said anything about not being able to come into the garden.

'I apologise,' I choke out. 'I didn't mean—'

She's pursing her lips. 'Don't forget my eggs.'

I nod, ducking my head down, making my way back up the garden to the house, Mackenzie following behind me, like I'm being frog-marched across the lawn, away from her fiancé.

Inside, Sydney is in the kitchen sipping coffee, leaning up against the countertop.

'Hey, Elle,' she says, straightening when she sees who is behind me. I offer her a swift nod, dropping the novel in my bedroom before entering the kitchen and pulling on my apron.

'I am so *beat*,' Mackenzie yawns, stretching her arms above her head and addressing Sydney. She then takes a seat on one of the stools. 'My. God.'

'Bad night?' Sydney ventures.

'Nicky forgets that when he gets up at night, I'm in a deep slumber. Like, when he's done eating, he just throws himself back into the bed, creating this tsunami with the sheets. And, boom, I'm awake. And he wonders why I sleep with a mask and ear plugs.'

Hearing Nicky talked about in such personal terms sends a different sensation through me, but one that still makes my cheeks burn. I'm desperate for some kind of off-switch to prevent blushing. Impure images of Nicky flit through my mind, like the ones I witnessed on social media, not helping the situation. I go to the fridge to fetch everything I need for the omelette, glancing to my right to see Syd's also a little embarrassed at Mackenzie's outburst. I lay everything out on the countertop and begin slicing a red onion.

'And the other night, that *hangry* performance at three a.m.,' Mackenzie continues, massaging her forehead. 'When he realized that chef you hired for him hadn't got outta bed. You would think the world was ending because someone didn't make Nicky Salco a plate of pasta. Then he got all terse with me for suggesting he just eat a bunch of breadsticks.'

I'm guessing she's referring to a previous pervious chef who didn't last in the job. Syd looks like she doesn't know what to say, Mackenzie letting out an exacerbated sigh.

'Like, does he not realise what an inconvenience this is to *my* business,' she continues, 'coming here in the middle of June? It's practically the height of bikini season and he's brought me to the shitty weather capital of Europe. I had to reschedule two design consultations to drag my ass to London. Syd, I'm telling you, a *little* appreciation from Nicky wouldn't go amiss right now.'

Out of the corner of my eye, I see Syd swallow. 'Do you want me to drop a hint?' she asks.

Mackenzie wafts her hand back and forth, rolling her eyes. 'God, no. Sometimes you just need to vent. Right now, I'm like, *whatever, Nicky, go run along and play your sports.*'

A moment later, I feel her sharp eyes on me.

'Sydney, we did get her to sign *all* the forms, right?'

'Yes. Elle's signed everything.'

'Good. Elle, how long until my eggs are ready?'

'Coming now,' I mumble, and double the speed of my movements.

—

I'm standing in the centre of the spongy grass, feeling the spiky sensations of cool blades pushing up between my toes. It's a clear night. I crane my neck, hugging my waist, just able to make out Ursa Major above the roof of the house. A security light at the far corner of the garden has detected my presence, casting shadows into the high hedges. I spent the afternoon in my room, keeping out of the way, absorbing myself in *Jane Eyre*, before preparing the evening meal. I'd sent Jamie a message, asking how he was doing. He'd replied that he was in a meeting and would call me after work. He hadn't.

'What are you doing out here?' a voice says in the darkness, making me jump. He's standing ten feet from me with bare feet, and I realise that he would have had to walk through my bedroom to exit the house through the French doors. He's wearing grey jogging bottoms with a dark t-shirt.

'You're early,' I blurt. 'The food's not ready yet.'

I still can't see his face. Nicky moves closer. 'It's okay,' he says. 'I can wait. My body clock must be out tonight.'

I look down, abruptly conscious that I'm only wearing a strappy baby pink camisole with baggy pyjama bottoms, my nipples standing to attention through sheer material in the chilly night air. I cross my arms over my chest, trying to look casual, hoping that he hasn't noticed.

In the darkness he moves closer, until his face catches the far reaches of the security light. The sight of him makes my pulse throb at the base of my neck, sending a warm glow spreading out from my core. I can't handle what he does to my insides.

'Did you need some air?' he asks.

'I like the softness of the grass,' I respond. 'It's like a carpet. I don't have a garden where I live.'

'No? Where do you live?'

'Not far. It's a bus ride from here.'

'Do you live alone?'

I blush. 'I live with my boyfriend.'

'You have a boyfriend?'

'Don't sound so surprised.'

'I am surprised. You never said. Thought you would have mentioned him by now. What's his name?'

'Jamie.'

'What does he do?'

'He sells mortgages.' *And chases tail.*

'And what does Jamie think of you getting out of bed at night just to make me something to eat?'

I look at him, as if Jamie is supposed to be bothered somehow by my role as a personal chef. 'I didn't go into specifics about the role's requirements.'

'Oh, so he doesn't know how you spend your nights with me.'

I think I see a smirk cross his features in the shadows at the implication.

'It's only an hour, sometimes less,' I point out. 'You eat like you play tennis. With precision.'

'I can't work out if you're trying to compliment me or not.'

'It was just an observation. Eating is a... systematic requirement for you.'

'So is winning.'

He's stepped a little closer still, and I'm able to make out his cocky, almost wolfish smile. 'Shall we go inside?' I ask, still conscious of my rock-hard nipples.

'I thought that was the idea in the first place. Unless you're planning on making me a picnic.'

Minutes later I've pulled on a sweatshirt, plating up a tennis pro-sized portion of Chicken Fricassée with rice, garnished with thinly sliced spring onions and chives. Sliding it over to the other side of the kitchen island, Nicky tucks in hungrily, his fork at the ready. Occasionally I take a glimpse at him from underneath my eyelashes, coming to the conclusion that I draw satisfaction from watching him devour a dish of my making, though mostly it's because if I had to look at one thing for the rest of my life, I think I would choose Nicky Salco. Maybe it's because he's from Miami and that's desirable somehow. Maybe it's because it's hard not to fantasize about being kissed by him. Maybe it's because he's so unavailable.

'So, how old were you when you started playing tennis?' I ask at length, not wishing to return to my bedroom, beginning to savour our time alone together after hours, to the point where I've started to look forward to it.

Nicky finishes his mouthful. 'Four. My parents joined the local club. It was a good way to expend all my energy. Plus, everybody soon realized I was pretty decent at it, so they just let me play.'

'Do you have siblings?'

'No. Only child.'

'Oh,' I grin. 'That explains a lot.'

He raises an eyebrow. 'What's that supposed to mean?'

'Nothing. Everything about you screams only child.'

It takes a moment for him to respond, taking a mouthful. 'Would you care to expand on that?'

'You know... bossy...used to getting what you want... socially a little maladjusted...'

He drops his fork. It lands with a clatter, but he's smiling. He wipes his mouth, still smirking. 'Hold up... yesterday you were apologising to me for saying I needed to calm down... now you're calling me bossy and socially maladjusted. I'm sensing a pattern here. Anything else you want to get off your chest before the inevitable back-tracking that's gonna take place tomorrow morning?'

'I didn't say they were *bad* qualities,' I say with a pout. 'I think they're qualities that will win you a championship. Your ambition and your talent weren't born out of being conventional, or conformist, or *ordinary*. Being an only child has helped shaped who you are. You're a lion, not a sheep.'

'A lion not a sheep,' he repeats with a nod. 'What does that make you?'

'Oh, I'm a sheep all the way. Just following the herd. Prey for the wolves lying in wait.'

He shakes his head. The smile lives on. 'I don't think so. I'd categorize you as a little bird. Waiting to spread her wings. Definitely not a sheep.'

I feel my cheeks grow warm again, turning my back to clear away some of the dishes.

'What about you; do you have siblings?' he asks.

'An older sister. She lives in Barcelona. We see each other when we can.'

He's cleaned his plate in record time. 'That was incredible, thank you.'

'Do you have room for dessert?' I ask, taking the dish and wishing he didn't have to go back upstairs. 'There's low-fat yogurt and fruit in the fridge.'

Nicky places one hand on his stomach and rubs it, then stretches his arms above his head, yawning. 'I'm good, thank you. Save it for tomorrow. I'm gonna go back to bed.'

I nod, quelling the feelings of disappointment. However much I like spending time with him, I can't change anything about our situation. 'Good night, then,' I say.

'See you in the morning, Elle,' he responds over his shoulder.

I watch him go. I hope he goes on to win Wimbledon. Selfishly, I want him to remain in London for the longest possible time. I know it's only been a few days, but I also know after tonight, because of the butterflies in my chest that develop whenever he's around, that the hardest thing is going to be finishing this job, and walking away from him.

Chapter Five

On Sunday, the day before the start of the Wimbledon Tennis Championships, I take a bus home, telling Jamie in advance I'll be back by ten.

It's clear on arrival he's been up, cleaning, the carpets vacuumed, and whatever takeaway boxes there had been left inside put out into the recycling. The windows are open, sending a cool summer breeze around the flat.

'Alright, babe,' Jamie says, and I allow myself to be swept up into his embrace. 'I missed you.' He presses a dry kiss against the side of the mouth.

'I missed you too,' I lie, but staying in Wimbledon with Nicky and his team has a surreal quality to it. Being back in the flat makes me feel grounded, like an ugly dose of reality, reminding me that my time in Wimbledon Village will come to an end eventually.

'How's job going?' Jamie asks.

'Fine. Fine. It's good. The house is nice. I mean, it's a lot of cooking.'

'But decent money, yeah?'

I nod.

'Want a cup of tea? I went out and got milk. Fridge is a bit empty, mind.'

'Have you literally had takeaway for every meal?'

He laughs. 'Pretty much, babe, yeah. I need you here to keep me fed. Fancy making me some lunch?'

I've literally just spent my entire week in front of a stove; chopping, peeling, slicing, dicing, stirring, whisking, serving and washing up, and now I've come home to a man who wants exactly the same treatment. I should have made my excuses and just stayed in Wimbledon.

Half an hour later, Jamie clears his plate in minutes, letting out a loud belch, giving his chest a thwack before knocking back the remainder of his beer.

I'm at the sink when he pushes himself up against me, and I can feel his erection pushing into my behind. I wince.

'Come on, babe, don't do that now,' he rasps, biting kisses down my neck, his hands skating over my hips, his tongue sliding over my flesh. 'I haven't had sex for more than a week.'

My gut instinct tells me that that's not true. I know in my heart I should push back, say no if I'm unwilling. His hands are invading the waistband of my jeans, so instead I reach up and place one hand against the back of his head as he mauls me.

'Don't leave marks, alright?' I say awkwardly. 'They'll see.' Because in my mind, I don't want Nicky to know that I've been used.

'Well, come get your knickers off then,' he says.

I let myself be led to the bedroom, all the while my mind trying to come up with excuses that my mouth refuses to verbalise. My compliance both angers me yet keeps me silent. Recently, I've done this more times than should have, faking noises that should come naturally at this moment. I try to empty my mind of all other thoughts, knowing that this was what Jamie would likely want to do with our time together, despite my own reservations. I can't remember when I stopped enjoying sex with him, though for the longest time the act itself has never managed to leave me feeling remotely satisfied.

In the bedroom, his kisses feel sloppy and wet, his tongue burying itself inside my mouth, his hands yanking at my clothes. He gropes hard at my breasts, simultaneously undoing the zip on his jeans, dropping them down, his arousal springing forth and poking through the hole in his boxer shorts. I close my eyes, desperate to conjure some feeling of stimulation or delight in what he's doing. His excitement is palpable as he grabs my hand and places it around his swollen shaft, letting out a groan of pleasure as I comply with his wishes and stroke him out of some twisted obligation.

'Oh, that's good, babe, *so good*, yeah,' he mutters, his voice thick with tension.

When I'm undressed, he guides me to the bed, turning me and easing me forward onto all fours. I've been here before.

'Condom,' I remind him, knowing he's not going to wait.

'Come on, do I need one?' his voice grates.

'I'm not on the pill anymore, remember?' I say. I stopped taking it when my libido dropped off a cliff and a nurse recommended that I might want to try a different form of contraception. It's hard to get aroused when you know your boyfriend is screwing around. 'In the draw by the bed.'

I feel the mattress shift underneath me as Jamie gets up with a huff and goes to the bedside cabinet. I hear the crackle of a foil packet being opened. He has his back to me as he fixes the condom in place himself then returns to his original position on the bed. I wince as he eases himself forward, my channel feeling too tight and narrow to accommodate his length. He's undeterred. Once he's buried himself, I feel his wiry hands grasp my hips, feeling the beginning of his sharp, stabbing thrusts, each one producing a grunt from the back of his throat.

'Oh fuck, yeah,' he rasps, increasing the intensity of his thrusts.

Numb to any arousal, it's out of pure habit that I let out a moan that sounds as much like pleasure as I can muster.

'God, I hope you're close, Elle, 'cause I'm about to blow,' Jamie breathes, his hips bucking against my bare behind.

My eyes drift shut. To my surprise, Nicky Salco is staring back at me, shirtless, and I want to immerse myself in his image. He's everything I want, and everything I'll never have. Reaching up between my thighs, I touch myself, supporting my weight on all fours with one arm, and picture myself with

Nicky. What it would be like to be naked with him. As I do, I can feel my own arousal blossoming, and suddenly there is altogether less friction. Jamie's grunting rhythmically now yet, the thought of Nicky easing himself inside me brings me to the brink of a climax. Slowing my movements, I explore him in my thoughts, imagining the weight of him on top of me, my legs wrapped around his waist. Behind me, Jamie gives one last powerful thrust and comes with a snarl, and I allow myself to unravel, for the first time in months the ecstatic moan emerging from my lips entirely genuine as I ride the long, slow contractions of my orgasm. When they subside, I breathe in and out, my chest rising and falling, feeling the heat rise to my cheeks because I know exactly how I made it to this point.

When Jamie backs away from me, I'm still thinking about Nicky. About how I want to return to the house in Wimbledon. I feel no guilt. Jamie slumps down next to me, peeling off and disposing the condom by dropping it onto the floor next to the bed.

'So which tennis player is it?' he asks. 'The one you're cooking for. Anyone famous?'

I've decided I don't want Jamie to know anything about Nicky. 'No,' I lie. 'He's just some random Bulgarian player.'

'He like a top seed or somethin'?'

I shrug, giving the impression that I don't care. The only truthful thing I add is, 'He's got a fiancée who doesn't like me much.'

'Well, it's not like your making 'em Michelin-starred cuisine, is it? Do tennis players even eat Shepherd's Pie?'

'Turns out they do,' I say, getting up to get dressed again. *And they like it too.*

'So, what happens if he doesn't make it very far at Wimbledon? Do you still have to cook for him?'

'I don't know,' I lie again in a quiet voice, because the truth seems devastating to me.

'D'you still get paid for the full three weeks?'

'Yes,' I say, though even as the words are coming out of my mouth, I know full well that isn't what I care about.

-

Nicky's opening match at Wimbledon on the Monday is on No.2 Court, at one p.m.

At the house, I watch the coverage on the owners' wall-mounted wide screen TV, listening to the commentators making all kind of judgments about Nicky, everything from "*Is he still capable of winning a Championship?*", to "*That's why they call him the Triple Salco; you just never know what you're gonna get*", to "*Can he put a lid on that famous fiery temper and go all the way?*"

He's greeted on court to rapturous applause, Number 2 Court packed by tennis fans. He wears all white, as per the uniform requirement for the All England Lawn Tennis Club, the clean shade of the material in striking contrast to his Florida tan. Underneath his white cap, he looks calm and collected. His opponent is a young Australian qualifier. Occasionally, the camera pans to Tag, Ragnar, and Mackenzie sitting courtside in the stands. Nicky wins the coin toss and opts to serve first.

His first service is an ace. The crowd goes bananas and I find myself clasping my hands together in a prayer position. When he breaks his opponent's service on the fourth game, I feel my heart swell.

'One down, six to go,' Tag announces jovially when he enters the kitchen with Sydney later on that same evening, rubbing his hands together, and I'm already hard at work feeling like I'm making a celebratory meal.

'Did you manage to watch it?' Sydney asks me.

'I did. He looked good out there,' I smile, just as Nicky enters the kitchen, still wearing all white, the sight of him making me light up from the inside.

'Don't get too excited,' Nicky half-smiles. 'Got a long way to go yet. Easing myself in.'

43

'Congratulations,' I grin at him. 'Are you hungry?'

'Always,' he winks at me.

'I made celebratory brownies,' I point to the plastic container on the countertop.

Nicky pulls it towards him, snapping off the lid. 'Can't say no to *celebratory* brownies, right?' he says, helping himself to one and taking a bite, Tag following suit. 'Holy hell, these are always so good,' Nicky hums.

Tag is laughing through his mouthful when Ragnar enters. 'Nico,' he chides in his characteristic breathy voice. 'Go easy on the sugar. Tomorrow we begin again. Tonight, rest.'

'Yeah, yeah,' Nicky says, concentrating on inhaling his brownie.

'Dinner will be on the table soon,' I add.

'I need five minutes with you,' Ragnar says, and it's a moment before I absorb that his comment is aimed at me, and the others are all filing out of the room, still talking animatedly.

Ragnar closes the door behind him, leaving us alone. I wipe my hands, switching off the hob as a wave of nervousness makes my stomach clench. Up to now, Ragnar and I have only had a few cordial exchanges. He always seems too busy for someone like me. When he turns, removing his cap, the light from the windows emphasises the myriad of lines on his older face and greying, unruly hat hair. He's wearing a grey tracksuit with a red stripe.

'Is it the brownies?' I ask. 'I can stop making them. I've cut the sugar content right down. The almond flour gives them extra flavour.'

'No, no,' Ragnar says in his Swedish accent with a wave of his hand. 'I have no problem with them. No. But I do have a special request.'

'What can I do?'

'At night, when you make him something to eat... I believe Nicky likes to talk to you. Am I right?'

I can't look at him, feeling that same warm sensation creeping up from the base of my neck. I can hardly lie to Nicky's coach.

'Sometimes, yes. He talks to me.'

Ragnar takes a step forward. 'I thought as much. I can tell that he likes you, Elle. He is… enthusiastic about your cooking. But. And I am asking this only with Nicky's interests in mind… I need you to try and refrain from any conversation. He comes down, he eats, he goes up back to sleep. I need him to sleep as much as humanly possible. This waking up in the night… I wish I could break him out of this habit. It is not ideal. For now, you can help by remaining in the background. So, please. Try not to engage him.'

I nod in understanding, which he seems to take as my taciturn agreement. When Ragnar leaves the room, I let the disappointment crush me.

'Ragnar says I'm not to talk to you,' I say in muted tones as Nicky pads into the kitchen in bare feet at half past two in the morning, pushing the hair from his eyes. I try not to make eyes contact and my body aches from broken sleep. 'Here's your food. If you need anything… please come and get me.'

I leave the kitchen, entering my bedroom and push the door closed. On the bed, I sit on my hands, pressing my heels together, feeling that I can't very well switch the light out until Nicky has gone back upstairs.

A minute later, I hear a noise, before there's a tapping sound at my door. I get up and open it.

'It needs a little salt,' Nicky sighs, leaning his head against the door frame and I swear he's never looked sexier.

My lips twist into an involuntary smile. 'You never take salt.'

'Well tonight I really need salt. Get me some?'

'How about you have a look in the cupboard?'

He gestures with his right hand. 'I checked already. Couldn't find any.'

I push past him. It doesn't escape my notice that once he has me back in the room, he closes my bedroom door, leaving the kitchen in virtual darkness.

'Salt,' I repeat, locating an open box of rock salt and sliding it across the surface of the kitchen island.

'Thank you,' Nicky says, taking a pinch and tossing it over his shoulder.

'Happy now?' I ask.

'More than.'

'Okay, then.' I make moves back towards my bedroom.

'Maybe some pepper too,' Nicky says, stopping me in my tracks.

'Pepper?'

'You really do have excellent hearing,' he smiles, his hand sliding around the back of his neck. 'Some pepper would be just wonderful right now.'

'Ground black pepper?' I query, crossing my arms over my chest.

'I'll take it any way it comes,' he says. 'Just some pepper.'

'Nicky Salco,' I hiss. 'I'm not supposed to be talking to you. I promised your coach.'

Nicky sits back down at the kitchen island, taking another mouthful of his food. I storm over to the cupboards, bringing out a pepper grinder, pushing it in his direction across the island surface.

'Thank you,' Nicky hums, not touching it.

'Can I go back to sleep now?' I shoot back. 'Or are there other seasonings you have a craving for? Any condiments?'

'Maybe some ketchup?'

I close my eyes. 'You're eating risotto.'

'Who doesn't love little ketchup with their risotto?'

'Uh… those who believe in sacrilege? Nicky—'

I glare at him. His eyebrows perform a devil-may-care double bounce. 'Tell you what. I happen to know that Ragnar sleeps deeper than a hibernating bear that popped a dozen diazepam capsules before retiring to his cave. I won't tell if you don't.'

My glare morphs into a glower. 'You'll get me into trouble.'

He carries on eating. 'If anyone's gonna get into trouble, it's me. Besides, he doesn't pay your salary, I do. Technically he can't stop you from talking to me. Did you watch the match today?'

'I did.'

'Yeah? How'd I look on the big screen?'

Handsome, I want to say. 'Very… pristine. And tall.'

'How'd you think I played?'

I nod. I know nothing about tennis. 'I thought you seemed… relaxed out there. You never looked in any trouble. Will the next match be as straightforward?'

'I'd like it to be. He's got a low ranking but recently he's won some tough matches. On paper, I should win. But that's never a given.'

Recently, I've had to fight the urge to fidget in his presence, unable to control the crazy pounding of my heart whenever he fixes his eyes on me. Even now, I'm grappling to control my breathing. 'I heard a commentator today refer to you as Triple Salco. Why do they call you that?'

Nicky finishes his food, pushing his empty plate to one side, leaning his elbows against the countertop. 'Some asshole commentator coined it a few years back, then it just stuck. He said I have three personalities. Which one ends up on court dictates whether or not I will end up victorious.'

I pull a disapproving face. 'What are the three personalities?'

'First is relaxed, confident Nicky. Nicky who breezes though a match in style. Second one is frustrated, unfocussed Nicky. Guaranteed to produce a lot of unforced errors and has a fifty fifty per cent chance of losing. Third… third is…'

He shakes his head, like he's not proud of it. 'It was something like spoiled brat Nicky, or angry, impulsive Nicky. Guaranteed to explode at the umpire and gets riled up for the smallest

reason when things don't go his way. Generally loses his cool…
and the match.'

'Is there a dominant personality amongst the three?' I ask.

'My efforts to banish all but the first one haven't exactly been
successful. Dealing with what happens when things don't go my
way never was my strong point.'

Despite my opinions, I stay quiet, unwilling to give them a
voice.

'I should probably stop talking,' I say. 'You should go back
to bed.'

He gets to his feet.

'You know, you shouldn't listen to those commentators
giving you labels,' I blurt. I don't know where it comes from,
the words just emerge, untethered. 'Putting you in a box like
that. You should treat the Triple Salchow akin to what it is. A
complicated ice-skating manoeuvre that has nothing to do with
your tennis game.'

He's staring at me.

'Also,' I add hastily with forced laughter, 'You shouldn't listen
to the opinions of a person who only knows about food, and
who doesn't have the first clue about professional tennis. Sorry,
I'm doing it again.'

There's a pause and I want the ground to swallow me up. I
don't know what possesses me sometimes. He places two hands
inside his pockets. 'Thanks for the food, Elle,' he smiles, then
goes back to bed.

Chapter Six

On the Wednesday at one o'clock, I watch the Wimbledon coverage alone on TV, as Nicky loses the first set of his second-round match. Watching him, my fingers balled into two fists, I am coming to understand the theory behind the 'Triple Salco' nickname. Both commentators can't help but refer to it, several times, until I am irritated on Nicky's behalf. A couple of unforced errors, giving his opponent the advantage, and suddenly Nicky out on court is a man plagued with pent-up frustration. Nothing is going his way. A heated second set means he's given a verbal warning from the umpire for bad conduct, throwing his racket in exasperation at losing an advantage point. He claws points back, winning the tie-break to take the second set.

For the duration of the third set, I pace the room. His opponent breaks Nicky's serve early on, before Nicky immediately breaks back, saving his own skin, the crowd whooping and applauding the high standard of tennis on display. His opponent not backing down, the sweat-covered strain on Nicky's face is palpable, infuriation etched into his features. He loses the tie break, meaning he's down one set to two.

I watch the fourth set through my fingers, shoulders tensing as Nicky falls apart, broken twice in a row to finally lose 6-2 and the match; the commentators, despite their apparent neutrality, seemingly revelling in his loss, putting it down in part to what they perceive to be an unsportsmanlike attitude.

When the match is over, I sit in silence. His defeat causes my selfish heart to ache, the sensation weighing me down.

Nicky losing his second round match means he's crashed out of Wimbledon earlier than anticipated. My contract has come to an end. I wonder how quickly they will move out of Wimbledon Village or for how much longer my services will be required. Having watched him sitting alone in his chair in between sets, drinking some vile looking pink fluid and eating half a banana, I know I'm not ready for my time with Nicky to come to an end. I knew that eventually our time *would* come to an end – even if he won the entire Championships – and my life would go back to what it had been before, but it's something I'm not yet willing to contemplate. In my mind I look forward to the midnight hours, the ones where I have him all to myself.

I return to my bedroom, checking my phone. A message from Sydney reads, *Can we talk when I get back?*

I stay out of the way, waiting in my room for their inevitable return. When I hear the gate opening outside, I get to my feet, nudging my door open a fraction to allow the sounds of any conversation to drift through. In one of my more hopeful daydreams, I wonder whether they might stay, due to the fact that the house has been paid for up front, for the full three weeks.

In the end, there's no conversation, the mood subdued. When Sydney knocks on my door, I wait beside the bed to hear the words that I already know are on her lips.

'We'll pay you for the full three weeks, of course,' she says, looking forlorn. 'But tomorrow the plan is to head back to Miami.'

I prepare a simple dinner, a protracted silence hanging over the house. I can't bring myself to be around whilst the group eat, leaving instructions for Sydney and asking if it's alright if I go out for a while.

'I don't think anyone's that hungry anyway,' Sydney sighs. 'I'm sorry, Elle. I know it means you gotta move to another job. I think we all hoped… or expected… Nicky would last at least until the second week.'

'What will happen to the house now? Will it stay empty?' I ask.

'No, we'll need to be out by noon tomorrow,' Sydney confirms. 'They'll send a team in to prepare the house for whoever is next in line.'

I take a bus home. I don't even know why. I can't let them see me this way. Outside, on foot, I allow the tears to fall, at the same time telling myself that I have no right to cry, that my role in Nicky's life was always meant to be short-lived, and chastising myself for being immature. He's a world-class tennis star, and I'm someone who cooks food for him in the middle of the night. There are plenty of other people who can perform that function. I have developed a crush on him, pure and simple, like some pathetic, innocent, starry-eyed teenaged girl. The agony of saying goodbye will pass. Except that I knew in my heart that the pain will stay with me for quite some time.

At eight o'clock I enter the flat on Willow Tree Close, gliding the door closed behind me. As I enter the living area, I hear sounds emerging from the bedroom. My skin begins to prickle as I survey the carpet where articles of clothing are strewn haphazardly, leading all the way to the bedroom door, not all of them Jamie's.

My eyes slip shut. I've known for a few weeks that this day might be on the horizon, though his timing could not be less ideal. Tears well up again, but I resolutely push them back down, swallowing down a lump of anger and regret in my throat.

I think about barging in on them. Seeing who the unfortunate female is, whether it's someone I know. Whoever it is has lilac-coloured lace underwear. I taste bile at the back of my throat, angry for allowing Jamie to push me into sex at the weekend only three days earlier. Sex I hadn't wanted (again), but had submitted to anyway. Yet barging in on him is acutely not my style.

I creep closer to the bedroom, the door partially open. Light floods in from the windows inside. No mood lighting then, just stark, light of the evening sex. So Jamie. Tilting my head, I realise that I can see the inside of the bedroom via the mirror on the wardrobe door.

On the bed, the blonde female is on her hands and knees, doggie style. He's barrelling into her from behind, causing her plentiful breasts to slap together with each of his enthusiastic thrusts. He's talking non-stop, the filthy diatribe that I've heard before leaving me stone cold. I've spent too many years listening to him believe he's some kind of porn king, only thinking about his own sexual needs. Witnessing Jamie having sex another woman on our bed (a bed that I bought, when I actually had a disposable income), beside a photograph us together, and one of my sister in Spain, means I can no longer live in blinkered denial. Relief, replaced by anger, washes over me.

Turning, I leave the flat, slamming the door hard as I go.

Walking away, I feel surprisingly relieved. I no longer care that, in my own mind at least, I should be somehow indebted to Jamie for paying my rent these last few months. His actions tonight have obliterated any residual guilt I might have felt by leaving him.

I walk back towards Wimbledon Village, hands pushed deep in my pockets, still crowds of people leaving the All England Lawn Tennis Club complex after 8 p.m. I take in their faces. It doesn't matter to any of them that Nicky's been knocked out. It doesn't make a single jot of difference to their everyday lives. He's just another showcase. To me, despite my short time with both him and his team, it feels like everything has come crashing to an end and the loss weighs heavy on my shoulders.

Arriving back at Parkside Gardens, I let myself in through the front door. In the entrance hall, I can hear two raised voices upstairs, once more muffled behind closed doors: Nicky and Mackenzie.

Sydney is waiting for me, her chin tilted upwards, listening to the sounds.

'Are they arguing about the match?' I ask, keeping my voice low.

Sydney shakes her head. 'Uh-uh,' she says.

'So, what are they arguing about?'

Sydney looks at me. 'You,' she states matter-of-factly.

My stomach rolls over. 'Me?'

Sydney takes a step forward, giving an elongated a sigh. 'Look, you might as well know. Nicky wants to ask you to come to Geneva for the Swiss Open, then with us back to Miami. To work as his personal chef full-time. Rag approves. I took the liberty of making a few calls. The lawyers think we can get you onto an O-2 visa scheme. It covers essential support to an athlete or sportsperson, so you'd only be able to work in the U.S. under Nicky's direct employment.'

'I'll do it,' I blurt, before she's even finished. 'I'll come to Miami. If I'm needed.'

'You're sure?' Sydney asks, a smile dancing across her lips. 'You should know that Mackenzie is most definitely *not* happy about it. As you can hear...'

We both look up to the upstairs floor, drawn to their raised voices. I can't hear Nicky, but I can clearly hear the outrage in Mackenzie's tone as she appears to be questioning why it has to be me who accompanies them.

A small part of me understands her position. I wouldn't want my fiancé getting out of bed in the night to another woman, no matter who she was, or what she looked like. Yet I've done nothing wrong. I've done my job, and frankly, the prospect of letting Nicky go leaves me wretched.

'I don't care,' I respond, without hesitation. 'I'll do it anyway.'

'What about your boyfriend?' Sydney asks.

'He'll be fine with it.'

Sydney raises her eyebrows. 'Are you alright? You're trembling.'

I put my shoulders back, tucking my hair behind my ears. 'I'm fine. Please tell Nicky that I said yes.'

'I will,' Sydney replies, her smile growing into a huge grin. 'For the record? I'm so happy that y'all are coming too.'

That same night, I'm unsure whether Nicky will get up as he usually does. I get up anyway at one thirty, having tossed all the ingredients for a Cassoulet into a slow cooker before I'd gone to bed. Lifting the lid, I inhale the delicious aroma of pancetta, cooked with sausages and beans, leeks, rosemary and garlic, before getting to work on some roast potatoes. At three a.m., Nicky is still a no-show. I'm about to switch off the light when I hear the creak of the floorboards upstairs.

When he comes into the kitchen, he's shirtless, seemingly half asleep. He's wearing his usual loose pair of jogging bottoms. Wordlessly, he pulls up a stool at the kitchen island. I drag my eyes down and dish out a plate of food, sliding it across the table, as has become our nightly ritual. I pass him a fork and watch him dig in. On the first mouthful, he lets out a low hum of approval, devouring the entire plate. I stand by the sink, watching him, gripping the countertop, tracing my gaze over the rippling contours of his chest, the curve of his collarbone and biceps, attempting to emboss the images on my brain so I can revisit the memory later.

When he's finished, he puts the fork down, the self-pitying expression on his face accentuated in the dim light. I go to the fridge, reaching for the Banoffee Pie I threw together after my return. I know I'm supposed to limit sugar his consumption, but something told me he wasn't going to be in the mood for following the rules following his defeat. This is meant as commiseration food. Setting the dish down on the kitchen island, I take a bowl and spoon and served him a reasonable-sized portion. Sliding the bowl towards him, Nicky raises his eyes to me. There is hurt behind them, an almost childlike sense of failure maybe. Leaning forward, he first takes the spoon on offer, before returning the smaller bowl to me and reaching for the larger dish. Head down, he digs in, demolishing the pie in large, voracious bites, whipped cream all around his mouth. I press my lips together, concealing a smile, pulling a spoon from the drawer and dig into the smaller bowl.

When he's finished the entire dessert, he pushes away the glass pie dish that's been scraped clean, resting his elbows on the table, lowering his head onto his forearms, and running his hands simultaneously through his hair. He remains motionless in the same position for some moments. I swallow. It feels like an acceptance of his defeat.

He inhales shortly after, pushing up with his hands, rising to a standing position. Looking across to me, his palpable disappointment sends little daggers into my chest.

He gives me a nod, and then looks to the empty dishes, as though in wordless thanks.

Then he's gone again.

Chapter Seven

In the late July mornings, I like to pinch myself. There's a reason Americans like to retire to The Sunshine State. During my two weeks living in southern Florida, I've reached the conclusion that persistent sunlight is like a magnificent shot of adrenaline to the soul. It's an addiction, and I'm well and truly hooked. Grey, rainy Great Britain, this is not.

In the neighbourhood of Gables By The Sea, a small, private enclave just outside the southernmost borders of Miami, part of Coral Gables, lies Nicky's substantial, exclusive private compound, complete with outdoor swimming pool, a veranda, four pool houses for staff, a fenced-off hard tennis court, a separate basketball court, a garage, a gym, an immaculately maintained garden, and a grandiose two-story house, all protected by a ten foot wall, cast iron gates, and a sign that reads 'Keep Out – Private Property' in red lettering. Or, as Sydney likes to call it: 'Nicky's fire crib'.

The pool houses – single story bungalows painted white – are taken by staff. Ragnar's building adjoins Tag's, towards the rear of the garden, behind a row of palm trees. My own pool house, with a windowless ensuite bathroom, adjoins the house taken by Alonzo Cabrera, Nicky's chef of Cuban origin, who lives there off and on. His wife and children live in the Miami suburb of Little Havana, about ten kilometres directly north of here. Sydney has her own, what she deems modest apartment, in West Miami, where she grew up with her dentist father and receptionist mother.

It's a thirty-metre walk from my pool house, along paving slabs nestled in the grass, to the ground floor of the main house and the expansive kitchen, blessed with its own side entrance through a set of French doors. The kitchen extends out from the ground floor, has its own pantry and a substantial kitchen island in the middle, with an induction hob and a range cooker under an awning. As I walk, I savour every moment, met with the sounds of sprinklers and the constant pop of tennis balls being walloped back and forth over a net on the other side of the garden, part of the ritual that is Nicky's training regime. In the Swiss Open, he reached the third round, before losing to a seasoned German player.

'*Buenos dias, Lonzo,*' I smile as I enter the kitchen, '*Cómo estás?*'

I already know that I adore Lonzo. The Cuban native has been nothing but kind, and welcomed me into his kitchen from the moment I'd walked through the door, somewhat unexpectedly, following Nicky's trip to London. I think he likes me too, because it no longer means he has to drag himself out of bed in the middle of the night to whip up a plate of something to satisfy his hungry boss. In his late thirties, he has caramel Hispanic skin and full lips, a gently rounded middle, with tattooed arms wide as tree trunks. His culinary skills are second to none, and it seems every day I'm learning new techniques and ways of cooking. He plays a Spanish radio station – Tú 94.9, introducing me to a raft of popular Latin music, despite Mackenzie coming down from her office and complaining about the noise on occasion.

I feel inspired.

I feel free.

I love it here.

'*Elllla,*' Lonzo grins, waving his knife in the air in a non-threatening circular motion. '*Buenos días. Eres muy linda hoy.*'

I squint at him, tilting my head sideways. 'Did you just call me pretty?'

'*Siiiii*,' Lonzo winks at me and I punch the air, because it means I've translated correctly, rather than this being some misguided attempt to flirt with me. '*Hoy* means what?' Lonzo says, in a pronounced Cuban accent.

'Today,' I say with confidence, because I'm satisfied with my miniscule amount of Spanish progress.

'*Correcto*,' he replies, rolling his r's. '*Mañana les daré una nueva frase*.'

I laugh and shake my head. 'Okay, I didn't get any of that last bit.'

'I said, tomorrow I will give you a new phrase.'

'*Gracias, acere*,' I grin, emphasizing my pronunciation, fetching my apron. 'What's on the menu for today?'

'For lunch, Paella Valenciana,' he replies.

'Sounds delicious. Want me to dice some onions and peppers?'

'*Por favor*,' he nods and I go to the gargantuan American-style fridge, complete with double doors. Even my knife skills have improved after two weeks under Lonzo's tutelage.

'All okay in the night?' Lonzo asks.

He's referring to my nighttime role. 'Fine. He came, he ate, he went back to sleep.'

It's a lie, or a half-lie. Nicky kept me up, wanting to talk to me endlessly, and, guiltily, I let him.

'Sydney says she's going to talk me through the travel schedule today. Everything that's coming up for the tour.'

Lonzo seems to have an exemplary knowledge of the ATP tennis tour already. 'Nicky's skipping the Canadian Open this year to recuperate, so Cincinnati's next, later this month. Before Flushing Meadows.'

'He plays a lot of tournaments.'

'He's a top fifty player. Has to play four grand slams, eight out of the nine masters, four ATP 500s and two ATP 250s during the year. Before Ragnar came along, Nicky was playing twenty-two tournaments and taking two ice baths a day, by order of his previous coach. Ragnar came along, scrapped the ice and brought the number of tournaments down to eighteen.'

'Wow. I had no idea. And did you accompany him for all those?'

'No, no. Just to the important ones. But he knows I'd prefer to be here with my family in Miami. That's where you come in.'

A smile touches my lips.

'I didn't go to Cincinnati last year,' Lonzo says. 'I regretted it after.'

'Why?'

'Nicky crashed out first round. Complained he couldn't sleep he was so hungry all the time.'

He says that last bit with a wink. 'Oh,' I grin back.

Lonzo waves his knife blade in the air again. 'Like it was all my fault! No matter. This year Nico has you as his lucky charm.'

'Not sure I'm all that lucky. But at least I can make sure he's not hungry.'

Mid-morning, Sydney picks me up from the kitchen. We sit on metal chairs near the blue hard court, watching Nicky and Tag slug balls at one another from their respective baselines whilst we sip coffee. I've already decided I will never get bored of watching Nicky Salco play tennis.

'So,' Sydney sighs, 'You'll head to Cincinnati next week in advance of the WSO.'

'WSO?' I repeat, trying (yet mostly failing) not to be distracted by Nicky's shirt riding up every time he smacks the ball, to reveal his toned abs underneath.

'Western and Southern Open,' Sydney confirms. 'Hard court ATP Masters 1000 tournament in Mason, a Cincinnati suburb. Played at the Lindner Family Tennis Centre every August as a prelude to the U.S. Open. You'll fly with Nicky, Rag and Tag.'

'Wait, you're not coming?'

'No, but I'll come to Flushing Meadows.'

I swallow. 'Is Mackenzie coming along?'

'No. She says it's the height of summer so her bikini business is thriving. She'll be here in Miami mostly. Most of the players stay at the Marriott but I've booked you guys into a five-bed house on the borders of Mason and Loveland.'

'*Loveland?*' I chuckle.

'Don't get any ideas,' Sydney winks. 'It's got its own practice court.'

'Who pays for that then?'

'Nicky does.'

'How much does it cost?'

'About six grand for the month. Again, all paid for out of Nicky's endorsement and sponsorship fees. Now that you're here, he's gonna need another deal.'

'Wow. How the other half live.'

'You'll have your own room. I'll give you a credit card so you can get supplies in. I was thinking you could fly up a little earlier to prepare. I'll give you the taxi fare from the airport.'

'Of course. I can do that.'

At that moment, Nicky saunters over, his shirt drenched in sweat, his cheeks puce, resting one arm on the fence that separates us. I watch him as he picks up his water bottle and downs about half the contents, the same bizarre-looking translucent pink fluid, that looks revolting, contained within.

'S'up, ladies?' he says, wiping his mouth just as Tag comes over and joins us.

Sydney seems to straighten. 'I was just saying to Elle that it would make sense for her to go ahead in advance to Cincinnati... you know, access the house, sort out food supplies, that sort of thing.'

'How advance are we talking?' Nicky asks with a frown.

'I don't know, maybe the day before?'

Nicky shakes his head. 'It's not necessary. Elle can fly with us.'

'You're sure?'

'We can look after ourselves without you, Sydney,' Tag laughs. 'Even if Nicky does require a nursemaid to make him something to eat in the middle of the night.'

'I am not a nursemaid!' I blurt in mock outrage, at which point both men are already grinning.

'But it does get you a seat on the plane,' Tag smiles, squinting in the sun.

I look across to find Sydney's lips have puckered, her gaze staring down Tag.

'Excuse me for not serving a *higher purpose*. I'll just make the bookings, shall I?' she snaps as, abruptly, she gets up off her chair and storms off, leaving me confused as to what has just taken place.

'Hey, Syd!' Nicky calls after her.

'What?' she shouts back.

'Elle can go business class too, alright?'

Sydney waves her hand in confirmation, still marching back to the house. When I glance up, I find Tag has his head turned, watching Sydney go, his fingers gripping the wire of the fence. When I look at Nicky, he's already staring back at me.

'Everything okay?' he asks.

I finger my earlobe. Sometimes when he looks my way, he robs me of the ability to think in a coherent fashion. 'Think I'll just go and see if Sydney's alright,' I excuse myself, wobbling to my feet. It takes all my might not to look back, to see if Nicky's still watching me.

–

'My sister told me she's worried about me being here,' I tell Nicky at 2.45am as he demolishes a plate of medium rare rump steak paired with rosemary potatoes, vegetables and a peppercorn sauce, all accompanied by a tall glass of milk.

We're in the kitchen, through the windows the darkness of the garden surrounding us.

'Oh yeah?' Nicky questions with his mouth full, twirling his fork expertly between his fingers like it's his own tennis racket. 'The one who lives in Spain?'

As part of the move, I've signed a new employment contract, and am now on a two-year conditional resident green card, allowing me to work and travel with Nicky both in and outside of the U.S. I'd double-checked with Sydney that it was alright to tell my sister who I was working for.

'Her name is Josie,' I say. 'She couldn't quite believe it when I said what I was doing.'

He cocks an eyebrow. 'Had she heard of me?'

'I think I can safely say that most people have heard of you.'

'No, they've heard of Triple Salco, and that's not necessarily the real me. Is she frightened I'm not gonna watch out for you?'

'I think she thought it was... out of character. A little too spontaneous for someone who's usually so cautious. She's threatening to come and visit me.'

Nicky carries on eating. 'I think I'd like to meet Elle Caraway's formidable sister. Tell her she's very welcome. And what about the boyfriend? He gonna make an appearance anytime soon? To check up on you?'

I turn my back, clearing away some of the dirty dishes. I'm yet to tell anyone about Jamie, and despite his increasingly desperate calls to my mobile phone in the days that followed my discovery, I am yet to speak to him, other than to tell him, via a message, that I was going to Miami and that I didn't wish to see him again. Not knowing exactly what I knew (or had witnessed), Jamie had played things innocently from the start, questioning my motives, until after two weeks, he caved, asking me if I'd been the one to slam the front door that day. A straightforward 'yes' answer from me had elicited a simple 'I'm sorry' from him, at which point all communication has ceased. That was three days ago.

'I don't know about that; he doesn't like to fly,' I lie, still with my back turned.

Nicky clicks his tongue. 'For the woman he loves, that guy needs to man up. Get on a plane.'

'Would you like anymore?' I ask, changing the subject, offering him some more food. 'I was going to ask you how you proposed to Mackenzie.'

Nicky downs the glass of milk, shakes his head and wipes his mouth. 'I'm good. How I proposed to Mac? It was at a dinner, in Coconut Grove. Her parents were there. So were mine.'

'You proposed to her in front of her parents?'

Nicky gives a shrug. 'Sure, why not?'

'But what if she'd said no?'

'If I thought she was gonna say no, I wouldn't have asked her in the first place. I'd already asked her father. Why are you shaking your head?'

'Nothing, I'm not.'

'You are... you're doing that thing you do when you don't quite believe the words coming out of my mouth. Spit it out.'

My lips twist involuntarily. 'No one's ever really said 'no' to you before, have they?'

He sits back a bit, crossing his arms over his chest, his tongue going into his cheek, before he says, 'Is this one of those occasions when you call me... what was it... socially maladjusted?'

I give a shrug. 'I'm just saying that your confidence is... maybe that's why you're a pro tennis player and I'm a chef... You've never questioned your own abilities and neither did your parents. You literally haven't one iota of self-doubt.'

He's shaking his head. 'Ask me to cook a meal, or climb a solid rock face, or... run a marathon. I'd have plenty enough self-doubt outside of my tennis swing.'

'But not when it comes to proposing to your beloved in front of her parents. And yours.'

'Come on, I've known Mac since we were kids. She was in my high school class. Me proposing to her eventually was inevitable.'

'So does that mean you've never had any other girlfriends?'

He raises an eyebrow. 'You're asking about my history of girlfriends now?'

I give an ungainly snort of embarrassment, trying to find something to do with my hands. 'I'm sure I could look it up on the internet.'

He fixes my gaze. He possesses an intensity that I suspect he likes to use to intimidate his opponents, if only for his own amusement. 'You probably could. Mac and I have had our fair share of bumps along the road. Especially recently. But she's not the only woman I've been with, no.'

I feel mortification rise all the way up from my toes to the base of my throat at the thought of him with other women. I push a carnal image of him from my mind and once more I'm thankful for the dim light in the kitchen. I take his empty plate and place it in the sink. 'I just wanted to ask how you got engaged, that was all. Anyway. I'm… going to go back to bed now.'

He hasn't moved. 'So, what, I don't get to ask you the same question?'

'What question? I've never been engaged. No man ever asked me.'

'I mean about how many boyfriends you've had.'

'I don't believe you went into specifics.'

He's smiling again. 'So, you're not gonna tell me?'

'Oh, I imagine it's substantially less than you've had girl-friends.' I indicate to the upper section of my body, moving my hands in a haphazard semi-circular motion. 'I don't think all this possesses your same level of appeal.'

He does something unexpected by rising partially out of his seat, leaning his torso forward across the kitchen island towards me, resting his hands on the flat surface. He keeps his voice low and steady. 'I'll tell you something,' he says, 'If I was your boyfriend, and you'd have told me you were flying halfway across the world to cook meals for an American pro-tennis player, I would have done *anything* in my power to keep you at home with me.'

64

Then, as if he's said nothing at all, he gets up fully and walks away. 'But I guess that makes me the lucky one, doesn't it?' he says without looking back. 'Goodnight, Elle.'

Chapter Eight

On Sundays, Nicky belongs to Mackenzie. That's her rules. Sunday is a non-training day. According to Sydney, everyone either has to remain out of the way inside their accommodation, or vacate the premises entirely, at Mackenzie's behest. On Friday nights, Lonzo returns to his family's apartment in Little Havana, returning on Sunday night. I'm not sure what Rag and Tag do, though on this particular Sunday in early August, Tag doesn't seem to be around and Rag is either hiding out in his room or has followed Tag's lead, unwilling to risk Mackenzie's ire.

I leave early when the sprinklers are still on. The preceding Sunday, Mackenzie caught me sauntering towards the gate at around 11 a.m., after a lengthy lie-in. Rather than say anything – especially when it feels like Mackenzie prefers not to even acknowledge my existence – she pushed Sydney to have a conversation with me about making myself scare on Sundays, under the strict understanding that this means *for the full day*.

My eyes still tired, I leave via the gate, first walking just under a kilometre north to the farmers market at Pinecrest Gardens. I arrive so early they're still setting up. I spend an hour browsing, purchasing some produce before walking around the gardens themselves, admiring the posturing peacocks before following a leisurely route around the lake, my skin already glistening with sweat, the back of my neck tingling with sunburn. By ten a.m., my water bottle already emptied, I begin to wish I'd just stayed in my room.

My phone buzzes in my bag. I have a message from Sydney. *Just checking you OK??* she says. *Would have invited you 4 lunch but somethin came up last minute, sorry.* Sitting on a bench overlooking the lake, I type my response. *Don't worry. You don't need to babysit me, but thx for the invite :) Heading to the beach. Wouldn't want Medusa to turn me to stone if I dare get caught in the garden again...*

Sydney replies with, *LOL ;) Head to North Beach, not South Beach if you're going that far. Less tourists. Tho Crandon Park beach is nearer. Enjoy your day x*

From Pinecrest, I take an Uber to Crandon Park beach. Sydney has loaned me a bikini. Renting a sunbed and umbrella for an extortionate amount of dollars, I settle myself in for the day, a gossip magazine in my bag, along with a sandwich lunch from Pinecrest Farmers' Market. I'd meant to order myself a new copy of *Jane Eyre*. I'd had to leave the previous copy at the house in Wimbledon so never had the chance to finish it.

By eleven thirty the beach is becoming crowded. My concentration on the magazine is waning, my attention drawn to the eight shirtless men playing four-a-side football nearby on the sand. It's not long before a wayward shot sends the ball directly into my face, bouncing off my nose, knocking my sunglasses underneath the sunbed.

'Sorry, so sorry,' a deep voice says. As I'm clutching my nose a male in low-slung grey denim Bermuda shorts approaches, grabbing the ball and kicking it back to his companions. 'Are y'alright?'

I give a sniff, pressing the cartilage on the bridge of my nose and concluding that no real damage has been done.

'I'll live,' I say, glancing up into the sun, squinting to try and see his face.

'You don't sound like you're from around here,' he says immediately, as half of his compatriots are trying to call him back, the other half wolf-whistling and egging him on.

'I'm not,' I say. 'I'm from England.'

He moves into shadow and I swallow. He has an impeccably muscular chest, even more so than Nicky's, and his skin is a deep golden brown, surfer blonde hair too long at the front sweeping into his eyes, which are blue as the ocean.

'England?' he repeats. 'Y'all just visiting?'

'I, uh—' I begin, unsure exactly how I can describe my role. 'I work here. I'm a personal chef.'

His companions give up yelling at him and return to their game. 'A personal chef? Is that for someone with money?'

I nod. I would never say who, imagining Mackenzie tearing shreds off me if I do. 'Over in Coral Gables.'

It's his turn to nod. 'That makes sense. I'm Oliver, by the way.'

'It's nice to meet you, Oliver,' I reply, too nervous to even give him my name.

He's tall. Not as tall as Nicky. He lingers for a moment, a slight smile on his lips. 'Guess I'll get back to my soccer game then.'

'Football, you mean,' I smile. 'Where I come from anyway.'

'Football,' he repeats, backing away. 'If you say so. We'll try to keep the ball away.'

I pout, give him a nod. From the short distance I admire his powerful shoulders and the curve of his back. I lean down, picking up my sunglasses from the sand, watching the rest of the game through sideways glances though the lenses, pretending to be lost in my magazine.

An hour later, he wanders back over.

'I hope you don't mind,' he opens with, hooking his thumbs into empty belt loops on his shorts. 'But my friends and I, we're heading home now, but they're not gonna let me get in the car unless I get your number first.'

I try not to smile, but it's impossible not to feel my lips twitch.

'That is, unless you're already spoken for,' he adds candidly.

The one man I want, I can't have, I think to myself, before glancing behind me, only to see we have an audience. I feel myself blushing. 'Well, that depends on how far your friends are going to make you walk?' I ask.

He puts his head down and grins. I glimpse two glorious dimples. 'Oh, I live a *really* long way away from here,' he smiles. 'I mean, I couldn't even contemplate walking it. It would take me forever.'

'Too far for an Uber?' I quip.

'It's funny, they always refuse to take me… 'cause my place… would you believe, I live on this really obscure road, the sat nav never picks it up. Confuses the hell outta the Uber drivers. So, you know, I gotta rule that option out.'

'Right,' I nod. 'No trains then, I take it?'

He runs his hands through his hair. 'I'd have to walk all the way back along the causeway just to get to the nearest station.'

I look back at his friends. They're enjoying seeing Oliver squirm.

'Guess I'll have to give you my number then,' I say.

There's relief in his eyes. 'That's very good of you, er—'

'Elle. My name is Elle.'

'That's a really nice name.'

'Do you have a phone? I'll put my number into it.'

He reaches into his back pocket, unlocking his phone and passing it over to the sounds of distant wolf whistles and rapturous applause from his friends. He looks like he wants the sand to swallow him up as I enter my number.

'It's a British cell phone,' I say, giving him back the handset when I'm done. 'In case you don't recognise the number.'

'I'll be sure to give it a try.'

'I hope you don't have to walk home now.'

'Thanks for saving my ass. Maybe I could call you sometime? I mean, should the call actually connect.'

I nod. 'I'd like that.'

When he's gone, I feel flustered in the heat, the ability to absorb anything going on in the gossip pages back down to zero. Being asked for my number is flattering, and it feels nice to be flirted with, but it's sent me into a spiral of panic should Oliver decide to pick up the phone.

By mid-afternoon I'm thoroughly bored. I've been absent from the house for almost seven hours. Puffing out my cheeks, I decide to run the risk of returning to my room in the vague hope that Mackenzie won't witness my return.

Back at the house, punching in the security code, I wince as the access gate squeaks, announcing to anyone listening that I've come back. Following the path with my head down, my beach bag slung over my shoulder, I don't allow myself to look at any part of the house or garden, the peaceful chirping of the birds broken only by my name being called out.

I stop in my tracks, raising my head a fraction, checking I haven't misheard.

'Elle,' Nicky calls out again from the far side of the pool.

I stiffen, glance over. He's relaxing on a wide two-person sun bed in a black pair of swimming shorts. Reclining next to him, Mackenzie wears a hot pink bikini and shades, her hand resting on his thigh.

He beckons me over. I wait, checking for Mackenzie's reaction. There doesn't seem to be one.

Reluctantly, I make my approach, my stomach turning over.

'You been out?' Nicky asks casually, Mackenzie suddenly aware of my presence, and I realise she's got Airpods in her ears. She slides her hand from his thigh, straightening, as I stop a couple of metres from the foot of the sunbed.

'I went to the beach.'

Mackenzie pulls her sunglasses down her nose, 'We can tell, sweetie. You're really rocking that lobster look. Is it because you don't really have much sun in England, or you didn't use any sun block?'

'Mac—' Nicky interrupts in a warning tone before she's even finished speaking.

'Sorry,' Mackenzie laughs. 'I have sun block Elle can borrow.' I feel her critical stare scour over my clothing for a second time.

'For today you might wanna use some aloe on that skin. Were all the parasols taken?'

'You should have just stayed here by the pool,' Nicky says.

I produce a thin-lipped smile. 'I didn't think that was an option.'

'And you are a smart girl, Elle, because it's definitely not an option,' Mackenzie says tersely, looking towards Nicky as she raises her voice. Nicky shakes his head. 'Sunday is *our* day, Nicky, I'm not changing that ruling just because Elle can't amuse herself for eight hours straight.'

'Jesus Christ,' Nicky snips. 'She's not disturbing anybody.'

Mackenzie pushes her sunglasses back up her nose, getting up off the sunbed, swiping up her phone and walking back indoors.

'I don't mean to cause trouble,' I mutter.

'You're not, ignore her. She can't handle that you're female. Did you enjoy the beach?'

My mind flits back to Oliver asking for my number. I find myself wishing that it was Oliver who would leave me breathless, who would leave my chest feeling constricted, like I can't eat for longing. I wish I could say Oliver's the one who leaves me with a heavy throb of desire between my legs. Seeing Nicky lying relaxed on a sunbed, watching me, I feel that same heat returning, my tongue thicker in my mouth.

'I'd better go,' I manage. 'Lonzo told me Mackenzie's cooking for you guys tonight?'

'She is. You can have the night off.'

'And what about… later?'

'I'll get Mac to make extra and put leftovers in the fridge. Don't worry about tonight. Get some rest before Cincinnati tomorrow.'

The disappointment, that I won't get to see him in the night, slaps me hard in the face. 'You're sure? I don't mind getting up.'

'I'll manage. I'll see you tomorrow. Syd's booked a driver for nine o'clock.'

I nod, wishing him a good evening. Walking away feels like a special kind of torture, the knowledge that Nicky will be spending the evening with a woman he will one day marry – a woman who is as spoiled as she is rich – eating away at me.

My phone vibrates. Oliver has sent a message already. I won't open it straight away. When I reach the door to my pool house, I turn, glancing back, checking what Nicky is doing on the far side of the swimming pool. I watch as Mackenzie walks back out of the house, easing herself into Nicky's lap. As Mackenzie leans down, puts her arms around him and kisses him, the sight makes me feel physically sick.

–

A little like the journey out of London, Nicky receives special VIP treatment when we travel. On arrival at Cincinnati Airport, there's no queuing for a taxi or hire car. Sydney has arranged everything in advance. Tag only needs add his signature to a few forms and the vehicle pulls up outside arrivals, just as we're being escorted through. It doesn't escape my notice that our group attracts a lot of stares. Outside, a porter loads our suitcases and the racket bags into the boot of the 4x4. Tag plugs the address of the rental house into the vehicle sat nav, whilst Nicky climbs into the front passenger seat, having signed some impromptu autographs, his face mostly concealed by a branded cap worn low. I sit in the back with Ragnar, who's barely said a word for the entire journey. According to Nicky, Rag rarely makes small talk.

'Give me an update,' Sydney says over the phone after four days of concentrated training for Nicky, mostly on the hard court at the back of the house. 'Nobody's talking. What's the house like?'

'Honestly,' I whisper from my room on the ground floor, peering out of my window, allowing me an excellent side-on view of the tennis court at the bottom of an expansive garden, where Nicky and Tag are running fitness drills. 'The house is great. Though, if I'm not cooking, I'm trying to stay out of the way. Things have been feeling, well, a little... tense, lately.'

'I *knew* it,' Sydney breathes. 'Is it Rag? Have he and Nicky fallen out?'

'They eat dinner in silence. You can hear a pin drop.'

'Shit. Rag is his fifth coach in six years.'

'I've not heard them argue. I think he's trying to ensure Nicky remains focussed. Ragnar asked me again not to talk to him at night when he gets up. Just leave the food in the oven and get out of the way.'

'And how's that working out?'

'Four nights now and I've not seen him. I hear Nicky eat then he goes back to bed. I think Rag gave him a lecture about not punishing his body. He's worried he'll get tired.'

'What about Tag?'

'Seems quieter than usual. They're working hard though, every day. Nicky seems keen for the tournament to get underway.'

On the Saturday night – or very early on the Sunday morning – I place a plate of hot food in the oven, my robe hanging open. Closing the door, I adjust the temperature a fraction. When I turn around, I gasp when I see Nicky lingering in the doorway, leaning one shoulder up against the solid frame.

'You scared me,' I say. 'You're not supposed to see me.'

'What can I say, I miss your company,' Nicky replies, in a low and lazy tone so that Ragnar won't hear him, tilting his head. 'These late-night hours can get lonely sometimes.'

'Rag still thinks I'm a distraction.'

His eyes move down to where my robe has slipped off my shoulder, to my strappy pyjama top, sliding lower still to the cut-off shorts I am wearing, moving to my bare legs. Adjusting my robe to cover myself, I sense a shudder travel down the length of my spine, my nipples hardening underneath my sheer top at the lack of attempt to conceal his gaze, which verges on brazen.

He moves closer. 'He's not wrong; you can be very distracting sometimes.'

I swallow, looking to the floor. 'Then I should probably go back to bed.'

'Stay with me awhile,' Nicky says softly. 'Just for tonight. Please.'

That last 'please' hammers down the last of my resistance, and I find myself nodding, turning to retrieve the plate of food from the warm oven, with my free hand switching the unit off.

There's no table in the kitchen, so he eats in the dining area around the corner, and I take a seat adjacent to him at one end of the table. My breath hitches in my throat when my bare knees brush against the fabric of his cotton sweatpants under the table surface. I draw away immediately, instead curling my legs underneath me, averting my eyes as he digs hungrily into two bountiful beef enchiladas. Once more, peering out from underneath my eyelashes, I am granted an intense feeling of satisfaction watching him devour a dish of my making.

'Is it good?' I find myself asking.

'It's always good,' Nicky hums between mouthfuls.

'Not too much spice?' I ask.

'Too much spice is never a bad thing.'

I bite my bottom lip, trying not to laugh. He's chuckling as he takes his next bite, wiping his mouth with the back of his hand.

'What?' he says.

'It's nothing.'

'Tell me.'

'Rag spends all his time getting you focussed, to the point of peak mental performance. I sometimes think that I come along and wreck it all after dark.'

'By doing what?'

'You know what.'

His eyes light up. He lowers his voice. 'Does that mean you did what I asked?'

Yesterday, at lunch, when Rag and Tag had gone back out into the garden, Nicky came and requested that I make him a dessert: without cutting out the sugar, saturated fat, carbs, or anything else that he's not meant to consume in excess. Just something calorific and delicious. His words.

'I'm serious,' I whisper. 'I don't want to be the one who undoes all of Rag and Tag's hard work. You're so focussed right now—'

He looks pleased with himself. 'I'm gonna take that as a yes.'

'I'm turning you into a rule breaker.'

'You think you have that much power over me?' he says with a smirk. 'You flatter yourself, Callaway.'

My eyes go to slits. 'Caraway, thank you very much.'

'Like the seed, not the golf equipment,' he grins, and takes another mouthful of enchilada.

I'm well aware that we have strayed into flirting territory. It's why every nerve ending in my body right at this moment is standing on end.

'Don't change the subject. I think you need your sleep. As does Ragnar.'

He puts down his fork, leans back and clicks his fingers. 'The moment my head hits the pillow again, it's done, I'm out.'

'You're lucky. It takes me ages to drift off again.'

'What do you think about?'

You, I want to say. *I lie there thinking about you.* 'Nothing really. I try to empty my thoughts.'

I watch him finish eating in silence. When he's done, he puts his knife and fork together.

'So can I go get it?' he asks after a moment.

'I'm going to pretend like *it* doesn't exist. If Rag asks me, I'll deny all knowledge, I swear it.'

'I love that you'd lie to Rag for me.'

I offer him a withering look. He's excited. 'Is it in the fridge?'

'I haven't the first idea what you could be referring to.'

He rises out of his chair, taking his plate back to the kitchen. I listen to the muted sounds of him moving around, his bare

75

feet against the tiled floor, opening the fridge. There's a pause. Then he's pulling out the cutlery draw. He comes back around the corner holding the entire dish, grinning like the Cheshire Cat, before he digs in with a spoon.

I shake my head, rolling my eyes. '*Uhm*, Mr. Caveman? You're supposed to cut yourself a slice.'

'Oh man, I've died and gone to dessert heaven,' he manages with his cheeks already stuffed full, closing his eyes, still standing up and ignoring my comment.

'Passionfruit cheesecake. It's one of my specialties.'

It takes him some moments to reply because he's still shovelling spoonfuls of cheesecake. It occurs to me that Rag is going to kill me when he finds out, but right now, Nicky looks so happy that I don't care. 'I think Elle's brownies just lost their place at the top of my favourite dessert list,' he enthuses. 'Why am I only just tasting this now?'

I give a shrug. 'I couldn't find any passionfruit in Miami.'

'They sell it at Whole Foods,' he exclaims, again with his mouth full. He points to the dish with his spoon. 'When you get back, you gotta show Lonzo how to make this. Actually, scratch that, you can stay until I'm bored of eating this, which will be never.'

He's walking back over to the table, and I'm all too aware that we've never spoken about how long our arrangement might last. 'Seriously, tell your boyfriend I said you're not allowed to leave,' Nicky says as he reclaims his seat. 'He's got an issue with that; he can take it up with me.'

My fingers go to the back of my neck, playing with some loose strands of hair.

'Seriously,' he continues, 'I can increase what I pay you. I know we didn't discuss it, but... You think he'd mind?'

I've been scared to tell Nicky the truth about Jamie. He's always seemed respectful of Jamie's existence, despite knowing nothing about him. In my mind, me having a boyfriend keeps things safe between us. I don't know if Nicky feels about me the way I feel about him. This way, I can fantasise that he does, without ever having to deal with the truth of the situation: that all I am is his personal chef.

'Oh, he'll be fine with it, I'm sure,' I say, trying to conceal the tremor in my voice.

'I'm not looking to break up a relationship here. What I mean is, you're a great chef, Elle, and if you wanted to stay working for me—'

'I would,' I nod, feeling my cheeks flush. 'I would like to stay.'

He stops then, his cheeks once more packed full of cheesecake, his lips smeared with passionfruit coulis and mascarpone cheese.

Under his intense stare, I feel the need to flee. Standing, I pick up his glass and a spare knife, because they're the only things on the surface of the table that I can clear away, allowing me to escape back into the kitchen.

At the sink, I hold on to the metal surface for support, my breathing uneven. Nicky appears behind me moments later, holding onto an empty dish and his spoon, his mouth wiped clean. He's consumed the entire cheesecake.

'I'm sorry, I didn't mean to embarrass you,' he says, taking a step closer.

'You didn't.' I fix my stare on the floor tiles then turn around to face him.

'What's going on, Elle?' he asks, sliding the empty dish onto the kitchen surface nearest him.

'There's something I should tell you,' I whisper. 'I didn't really know how to say it before.'

He seems to baulk a little. 'You didn't know how to say what before?'

'At Wimbledon… the day you didn't make it through. Last month. I walked home to my flat… I mean, my apartment. I found my boyfriend with another woman. They were… He hadn't been expecting me. So, whilst I *had* a boyfriend, I don't have one anymore.'

I press my lips together, gripping the sink, unable to make eye contact with him, tears gathering at the corners of my eyelids. Nicky's presence in the kitchen makes my every nerve ending tingle. He bears down on me, his body inching closer.

'I'm sorry to hear that,' he says at length.

I shake my head frantically, using tiny movements. 'That's why I'm glad that I'm here. And not there.'

He's even closer now, his proximity sending my pulse racing. He's closer to me now than he's ever been, so close I can smell his earthy scent.

'I'm glad you're here too,' he says, his tone so achingly soft it causes a ripple in my chest, so powerful I can barely contain my longing for him. When I raise my eyes, he's there, inches from me, his gaze searching my face. My lips part yet I can hardly breathe.

Nicky lifts one hand. It comes to rest against my left hip. He might as well have lit a match, because my skin prickles under the fabric of my shorts as the tip of his thumb grazes the curve of my hip bone through the thin material. Suppressing a gasp, I feel my chest rising and falling. When he lowers his head, I think for one blissful moment that he's going to kiss me, but at the last moment he tilts his chin, his forehead coming to rest against the bare bone of my right shoulder, where my robe has once more slipped down to the crook of my elbow, leaving the skin exposed. I feel the softness of his breaths against my collarbone. His fingers brush mine, the electricity almost causing my knees to buckle.

'You know this changes everything, don't you?' he finally says.

I nod my head in some kind of acknowledgement, yet I haven't quite absorbed what he's saying. I'm still focussed on the torture of having him so near me yet so out of reach. Desire throbs in my veins. 'You should get some sleep,' I whisper, knowing it's the right thing to say but, in my heart, praying he disagrees.

He raises his head, his face in touching distance. I wish I had that confidence some women possess of taking control in a moment like this, of summoning my inner seductress, like I could have him if I wanted to. It occurs to me that all I have to do is raise myself up on tiptoes and I'd be able to touch my lips to his. Is that what he's waiting for?

Fear and lack of experience easily best me. I might be available, but Nicky Salco most definitely is not. My feet remain flat on the floor.

The moment he steps back, cold air rushes between us. An appropriate employer-employee distance resumes.

'Sleep well, Elle,' he whispers, and backs away.

Chapter Nine

> Wondered if you'd wanna hang with me today?

I sit on my bed, staring at the message from Oliver on my phone. Last night I couldn't go back to sleep, and my eyes feel hollow.

I was kept awake wanting to know what Nicky meant. That my being available changes everything. There was a moment last night when I thought he might kiss me but I've questioned over and over whether I imagined it.

Kissing Nicky would mean crossing a red line.

I start typing out several different responses to Oliver, all of which involve me turning him down. Part of me thinks I must be insane to even be thinking along those lines. He's single, handsome as anything, and keen on taking me out. So why isn't he the one who fills my thoughts twenty-four-seven?

Another message pops up unexpectedly. *You figuring out how to blow me off?*

I smile. *Trying to let you down gently*, I type.

Don't gimme excuses, Elle

I would, but I'm not physically in Miami. Another time?

His response takes a few moments to come through. *Let me know soon as u back x*

I remain in the kitchen and my room all day on Sunday; Nicky, Rag and Tag undertaking some light training and physical therapy. Nicky takes a nap. Tag stops by the kitchen for coffee, but Nicky steers clear. I leave a meal out for the night-time as usual, lying awake, listening out for him, but on the

Monday morning, I find the plate of food untouched, tepid and dried out in the oven.

When the official car arrives to collect them early on the Monday morning, I go out into the main hallway. The atmosphere is muted. When Rag comes downstairs, I offer him a limp smile.

'Feeling ready?' I ask.

Ragnar rubs his hands together. 'He's ready.'

'I was going to wish him good luck.'

'I'll tell him you said so, of course,' Rag says. I give a self-conscious nod, ducking back into the kitchen. Instead of seeing them off, I watch them all leave through a crack in the door, wringing a tea towel in my hands.

Later, I flip through the TV channels in the house, attempting to find coverage of The Western & Southern Open. Frustrated, I check Google, only to find that coverage is on the Tennis Channel, which the house TV doesn't seem to broadcast. Instead, I am confined to getting live updates of the score for Nicky's match online, but with no visual.

Sydney calls me from Florida twenty minutes later. 'Are you watching this?'

'I'm watching score updates on my phone,' I groan in the garden, sat in the sun with my phone and a mug of coffee, a chorus of birds chirping in the trees. 'Refreshing the screen every few seconds. That's the best I can get.'

'You're kidding! I'm sorry. Nicky playing so good. His opponent's gone to pieces already. He looks relaxed. Must be whatever food you're giving him.'

I laugh, but it's forced. 'I highly doubt that.'

'I thought by now they would at least take you along to watch. That's it, I am organising a ticket for you for the next match. To hell with what Mac says.'

Sydney told me before we left for Cincinnati that Mackenzie didn't want me attending any of Nicky's matches in person, should the presence of another female alongside his coaching team become an unwanted source for gossip.

81

'I should be able to get you a spot in open seating,' Sydney adds. 'I'll make some calls this morning. There's no way Nicky's not going through based on the last twenty minutes of play.'

I somehow doubt Ragnar will want me tagging along to Nicky's next match. 'Where's Mackenzie now?'

'At the tennis club, watching the match on TV with her parents and Nicky's.'

'Cosy,' I say, blurting my thoughts out loud.

'Break point,' Sydney cuts in and we both go quiet. I refresh my phone screen.

'He's got it,' Sydney states assuredly. 'Seriously, Nicky's in annihilation mode.'

When they return in the late afternoon, the buoyant sound of their collective voices echo through the hallway, in direct contrast to the muted conversation during the morning's departure. I resist the urge to run out and offer my felicitations. I am surprised when Nicky is the first person to walk into the kitchen.

'I spoke to Syd; she said you couldn't watch,' he says, without offering any form of greeting.

'Oh, I watched the score changing on my phone,' I grin. 'Congratulations.'

He's nodding, hair still damp from his shower. His gaze doesn't leave mine. 'You should come along next time. I should have thought; I'm sorry.'

'It's fine. I'm fine. The important thing is that you won. Syd said you looked really good out there.'

There's a moment where neither of us speaks, the electricity of two nights' earlier still palpable, another delicious shiver running down my spine.

'First round, early days,' he shrugs. 'The usual.'

Ragnar enters behind him, clicking his tongue, and I instinctively turn my back and return to my food preparation. 'Nico,' he scolds, clicking his tongue in disapproval. 'Tag. Go, go.'

They've left the room, still discussing the match whilst Tag joins them in the hallway, the sight reminding me once more that I'm not part of that world, I'm just an accessory. And to Ragnar, at least, I'm still Nicky's biggest distraction.

At one forty-five a.m., sleep tugging at my eyelids, I switch on the light in the kitchen, followed by the oven, pulling out a lamb curry from the fridge to reheat. Reaching for a bag of rice in the cupboard, I turn and gasp, almost jumping out of my skin at the sight of Nicky sat in the corner on a chair, resting his elbows on his knees.

'You scared the bejesus out of me,' I breathe, clasping my chest, my heart beat racing.

His expression is sombre. 'Couldn't sleep,' he mutters, raking a hand restlessly through his hair. 'My mind's going in circles.'

I put down the rice. 'Are you worried about your next match?'

'That's just it. Not for a minute.'

I look at him, unsure how to respond. A moment passes before Nicky gets to his feet. He keeps his gaze on me, taking four steps forward before taking my hand, sliding his warm fingers between mine. At first, I stiffen at the thrill of physical contact, but then relax a little and follow his lead, through to the dining room and in the darkness, to the spacious living area, where he goes to the curtains, pushing them aside, silently turning the key in the door lock. Opening one side to the double doors, he leads me outside into the night air. I don't argue, my pulse still racing from the moment I'd turned around to find him waiting for me in the chair.

He's still holding my hand when he eases the door closed behind us, clicking it shut, guiding me along across the paving stones and moist grass, heading for the trees at the far end of the garden, beside one end of the tennis court fence. I don't ask questions, matching his brisk pace. Under a clear night sky, after spongy grass, I feel the sharpness of woodchip under my bare feet, cool air making my skin prickle. In the shadows, the only light from the house comes from my bedroom, where the curtains are open a fraction. Nicky slows when we're far enough back, out of sight of the main house. Letting go of my hand, his fingers go to my waist, positioning me so that I'm stood with my back up against a tree. My heart is racing. I allow myself to be maneuvered, the power of his touch exhilarating. He holds me there wordlessly for a moment, his breathing laboured, before he steps away from me. I grip my fingers into fists, my knees weak, sweat breaking out along my top lip. He's pacing, his mouth moving, as though he's trying to form words, but none emerge.

'I can't—' he begins, before he stops himself.

'What is it?' I breathe. *Why have you brought me out here?*

He paces some more. 'You're so... you're so quiet. Unassuming. This little bird who never whines or complains about anything.'

I clasp my fingers together. It's some moments before I can respond. 'That's just who I am.' I shrug. 'I'm an introvert.'

He stops pacing. 'That winning shot today. At match point. I wasn't thinking about any of it. All I could think about was getting back here so that I could see you again.'

My lips part. In the shadows of the trees, I blink in the darkness, taking time to absorb the words that have just come out of his mouth. Somewhere deep within my chest, my heart is bursting into song.

'Ever since you told me there was no boyfriend... that you were... I couldn't...—'

He takes a step closer. His hands go to my face, the backs of his fingers caressing my cheek, the same electricity I felt the previous night, whenever he's close to me, exploding in my gut.

'Tell me I'm not imagining things,' he whispers. 'Please tell me it's not just me.'

I raise my eyes to him. 'It's not just you.'

He gives a quiet sigh. His fingers journey into my hair, bringing his face so close in the darkness that his breath is mixed with mine. I tilt my chin, inviting the kiss I already know is imminent, yet craving it sooner. He takes his time. Our lips touch once, briefly, before he pulls away, one hand sliding downwards as he gently rubs his thumb across my bottom lip. When he lowers his mouth again, his lips are soft and inviting, tender yet insistent, capturing mine and drawing a whimper from me, my enflamed sigh only serving to encourage him further. When he fully claims my mouth, my world comes crashing down. His arms go around me and I feel my body being lifted and crushed to his chest, a throb of need ballooning between my thighs, and evidence of his own arousal pressing into my belly button. His tongue probes forward, testing me, and I allow it to meet my own, causing a low growl to emerge from his throat. Still kissing me, his left hand slides down my thigh, finding the crease of my knee and lifting my leg, pressing me back against the tree trunk. I slide one hand around his neck to maintain balance. Hooking my right ankle behind him, I feel the fingers on his left hand in a lazy crusade, sliding down the underside of my thigh, all the way up to the curve of my bottom, and cupping it. I let his mouth go in surprise as his fingers continue onward, sliding inside the material of my shorts and skimming the lace hem of my underwear.

'Why can I not stop thinking about you?' he whispers against my lips, his tone thick with desire, his fingertips searching, seeking to gain entrance. 'You're everywhere I look.'

A sound from the garden next door – a bird flapping from a tree – brings reality crashing down around my ears. I lower my leg, breaking our kiss, and his fingers slip away. Words rattle through my mind in incoherent sentences, his kisses having left me feeling heady and intoxicated. *What about Mackenzie?* I want to say, regret scratching the walls of my throat.

Nicky looks down, his hands having moved to cradle my hips, his legs spread apart, the lower half of his body still pressed fully into mine, so that I'm well aware of his very rigid length. As his palms traverse my hips to rest on my behind, he lets out a weary sigh, stifled only by the breeze in the trees above our heads. I wriggle then, taking his wrists in my hands and moving them away from me. Nicky steps back. It's too dark to read his gaze.

'We shouldn't do this,' I swallow, despite every fibre of my being crying out to the contrary. 'You should try to get some sleep.'

He laughs gently, shaking his head. 'How am I ever going to sleep now? When you just kissed me back like that?'

'Nicky. This is wrong. I shouldn't be out here. *We* shouldn't be out here. You have Mackenzie. And I won't be a distraction for you.'

'Then you should leave now.'

Tears sting the corners of my eyes. 'Do you mean that?'

He comes back to me, his hands sliding back into my hair. 'I will never mean that,' he says, kissing me with a gruff sigh. Thoughts of Mackenzie melt away as I kiss him back with equal intensity, this time feeling his hands snake underneath my top, his palms scaling my rib cage, brushing against the slippery crease of both breasts, damp with sweat, making my skin tingle. His left hand feels softer than his right.

Almost as quickly, he's gone again, pulling away, air rushing in between us.

'I'm sorry,' he says tersely, adjusting himself, wiping his hands through his hair. 'You're absolutely right.'

I straighten my clothes, making myself presentable, shaking off the woodchips that are still pecking the bottom of my feet. This time he doesn't take my hand. Instead, we walk side by side at an appropriate distance back over the grass, back through the double doors, back to the kitchen, as if our interaction was merely an interlude: a water break.

'Are you hungry?' I ask him in the kitchen, the question so heavily laden with subtext that it makes me want to cry.

'Thanks, I'll manage without tonight,' is his muted response. 'Save it for me for tomorrow?'

I nod my head but look to my hands, not knowing quite what to do with them. He lingers for a moment, as though trying, and failing, to make a pleasant or inoffensive remark following our garden exchange, so instead he says nothing at all.

'I'll see you in the morning,' I say, as though filling in a blank. Nicky gives a curt nod, and I watch him walk back upstairs.

Chapter Ten

'Elle?'

The voice comes from a distant place, as if through thick fog. Try as I might, I can't raise my eyes to see where it's come from.

'Elle?' it says again. 'Is there more coffee?'

In an instant, the real world — the one where I am not in Nicky Salco's arms — comes rushing back.

'Oh!' I exclaim at Tag as he lingers in the kitchen doorway, a hopeful smile on his face, 'Sorry, I was miles away. Let me just grab it.'

Tag thanks me and goes to sit back down. I move to the coffee percolator, pulling out the still warm jug and walk back round to the dining table in the room next door, Rag and Tag facing one another at the breakfast table.

'Still no Nicky?' I ask innocently.

'Let him sleep,' Tag says. 'Did he get up last night?'

'I left him out some food,' I reply, the memory of Nicky's touch threatening to send my mind into another delicious spiral, 'but it was still there this morning. Maybe he decided he wasn't hungry.'

Rag is looking through some kind of tennis brochure, not listening to either of us.

'Sometimes all that adrenaline, it's hard to stop it from pumping, you know. After yesterday's win, he was on a high. Victory can do that to you. His body needs to recover. Sleep will play a big part. We can ease him into training today.'

After breakfast I clear away the dishes, finding myself increasingly desperate to catch a glimpse of Nicky, to tell myself that

I haven't imagined the events of last night. When he'd left, I'd put the food away and gone to my room, and sat on my bed and for a long time re-lived those moments with him in minute detail, questioning whether it was possible that I was kissed by *the* Nicky Salco, and that *he can't stop thinking about me.*

He's out on court by twelve, after a swift sandwich lunch. I'm peering out of my bedroom window, weary from lack of sleep as he walks down to the court alongside Tag, seemingly all smiles, the sandwich followed by an apple that Tag retrieved from the fruit bowl in the kitchen. My gaze journeys to the right, to the group of trees that border one edge of the court's chain-link fence, my teeth sliding over her bottom lip in remembrance. Watching him warm up on court, it's like nothing has changed, yet my world has shifted on its axis. No matter how many times Jamie kissed me, he never once kissed me like Nicky Salco kissed me.

Mid-afternoon, Tag comes to fetch more snacks from the kitchen before the two disappear for a recovery session. Holding him out a full bunch of bananas, I begin to feel that Nicky is avoiding me.

As I'm preparing dinner, Nicky enters in his sweatpants and a plain white tee, clutching a laptop which he sets down on the dining table around the corner, proceeding to conduct a video conference call with Mackenzie, Mackenzie's parents, and his own parents. I listen to a conversation about the match the day before, the next one to come, and, to perhaps rub salt in my wounds, a conversation about wedding planning.

That night, I wait, darkness outside, a plate of food in the oven, but there's no sign of him.

~

In my second-tier seat of the Grandstand Court at the Lindner Family Tennis Centre in Mason, Ohio, the sun is beating down. The venue is full to its five-thousand capacity. Everyone is here to see Nicky play his second-round match against a Russian player named Stepanovich. On the opposite stand, I can see Rag and Tag taking their seats in one of the dedicated boxes.

A people carrier brought us to the venue. I sat in the furthest back row, my knees squashed into the backs of the seats in front, looking at the back of Rag and Tag's heads. Nicky sat in the front next to the driver. On arrival, he was swamped by eager fans and autograph hunters.

'Are you gonna be alright?' Tag asked me, helping me from the back of the car, as I attempted to get my bearings at the vast tennis venue.

'I'll be fine. I can get an Uber back to the house when the match is over.'

'Give me your number; you can message me. You can grab a lift with us after.'

I offered Tag a smile, Nicky still standing near me still signing autographs and talking with the fans. 'I'll be fine, don't worry,' I told him, excited to be free of the house for a morning. 'Tell Nicky I said good luck.'

In the Grandstand Court, cheers go up from around the packed court as the players enter, carrying their racket bags. I watch Nicky closely. He's not looked my way, not since our moment in the garden. I heard him up last night, but I steered clear, hoping he might knock on my door, only to be left disappointed.

It's obvious he regrets what happened between us. That much is abundantly clear; in the last thirty-six hours, he's avoided me at mealtimes and any other opportunity.

On court, Nicky has taken his seat, preparing himself with his back to me, one of his knees jigging restlessly up and down. He's wearing navy blue; his favourite shade. I want to know his thoughts. Whether our kisses the night before last have ended any fascination he may have had with me, however fleeting. I'd be lying if I said I'm not worrying that our brief physical interaction – however electrifying it might have seemed to me – was something of a letdown to him, as though my lack of experience quickly became apparent. I'd tried to wriggle out of coming along to watch the match, only for Tag to be the one to insist I accompany them in the car, Nicky keeping silent. But my biggest fear is that, having kissed me, Nicky will decide that he doesn't need me as his chef anymore.

As Nicky starts to warm up, my attention is drawn back to Rag and Tag's viewing box. Both men are on their feet, greeting the four additional bodies who are joining them. I recognise Sydney immediately by her Glamazon height and her mounds of dark braids. The next two people look to be Nicky's parents. The last to enter the box is Mackenzie, wearing a stark white skin-tight dress and a pair of sunglasses. I look down, feeling a barb pierce my heart as it sinks.

-

I'm the first to arrive back at the house, having taken an Uber alone back from the venue, Nicky winning his second-round match in straight sets. I'm busy slicing onions in the kitchen, wearing an apron when I hear cars in the driveway, before there's a commotion at the front of the house. The sound of Mackenzie's high-pitched voice cuts through the air, causing a jarring spike in my heart rate. Putting down the knife, I wipe my hands.

'There you are!' Sydney squeals as she enters the kitchen, coming over to me and wrapping me in a comforting embrace. I hold onto her tight. I feel the need to confess everything, immediately, so to keep it all from spilling out of my mouth I bottle my feelings tight.

'I couldn't pick you out in the stands,' Sydney says. 'Wasn't it a good match? That atmosphere was electric! Come and meet Nicky's parents.'

I freeze and grip the countertop. 'I don't know about that—'

Sydney's dragging me from the room by my wrist. 'Come on, they've heard *all* about you.'

Out in the entrance hall, Rag is heading upstairs. Mackenzie has her fingers wrapped around Nicky's bicep. Up close, her dress is low-cut.

Syd says, 'Ben, Libby, meet Elle Caraway. Elle, these are Nicky's parents, Ben and Libby Salco.'

'Hello,' I smile brightly, shaking their hands. 'It's nice to meet you.'

'Oh, you are just a *doll*, look at you,' Libby Salco exclaims in a strong southern drawl. She's taller than I imagined she would be, with hair that's been highlighted ash blonde. 'That beautiful British accent! It's lovely to finally meet you, Elle. You're the poor girl who's toiling away in the kitchen.'

'Luckily the kitchen is my favourite room in the house.'

'Well, thank you for getting up at night for my Nicky. Honestly, sweetie, you deserve a medal.'

Mackenzie gives a snort. 'Lib, it's a privilege Nicky pays her handsomely for.'

Ben Salco nods his head, seemingly in muted agreement. He has a severe expression, a long face, dark hair slicked-back with tanned skin. He's wearing a suit and has the look of a lawyer-type, nothing like his son. I hold my smile like I've just had botox. Part of me is disappointed when Nicky says nothing.

'Congratulations on your win,' I force myself to say in his direction, but any eye contact between us right now is impossible.

'Thanks,' Nicky responds stiffly.

'Libby and Ben are staying in a hotel the next couple of nights,' Syd addresses me back in the kitchen. 'I'll stay over there with them but I'll stick around for dinner. Mac will stay with Nicky so it's two extra place settings, is that okay?'

'No problem, of course,' I manage, my stomach still churning.

'Y'alright? Girl, you look exhausted. Has Nicky been keeping you up?'

I feel my cheeks warm. *You have no idea*, I want to respond. 'No, no. Everything's been fine.'

'You managing the time difference with London?'

'What do you mean?'

She raises her eyebrows. 'You know... with your boyfriend?'

'Oh. He's not my boyfriend anymore.'

Her eyes go wide. 'Say what now?' she breathes. 'When?'

'Turned out he was seeing someone else behind my back.'

'You're kidding me! I hope y'all kicked his ass to the curb?'

'Most definitely. I'm fine. Really.'

She puts her arms around me. 'You sure?'

'Very.'

She pulls back, placing both hands on my shoulders. 'Elle, when we get back to Miami, I'm gonna find you a guy, and I'm gonna hook you up.'

I force a smile. *But not with the man that I want*, is my only thought.

Dinner consists largely of detailed tennis talk, going over the finer points from Nicky's match. I potter about in the kitchen, keeping my distance, turning down Sydney's entreaties to eat with the group. I can't bear to be in the same room as Nicky, the memory of his kisses still too potent. The idea of sitting at the table with his laughing fiancée would be a unique form of torture.

Sydney leaves the house around ten p.m., bidding me farewell. Tag goes upstairs, coming back down in his running kit, informing me he's going for a late-night jog before slamming the front door behind him. Nicky, Rag and Mackenzie have moved to the living area, the muffled sounds of their conversation drifting through to the kitchen. I'm dicing ingredients for a Cobb salad: chicken breast, hard-boiled egg, blue cheese, avocado, chives, tomatoes and salad greens, when I feel a presence behind me. I glance up to find Mackenzie is leaning her elbows against the countertop, her eyes glassy.

'That all for Nicky?' she asks, slurring her words.

I nod, a knot forming in my stomach. 'I was planning on leaving it in the fridge for later. Did you need more wine?'

'It's sweet how you take such good care of him.'

My skin prickles. 'I just cook for him. That's all.'

She cocks her head to one side and her question causes a streak of panic to pulse through me. 'Do you find my fiancé attractive, Elle?'

'No,' I lie. 'I mean—'

'You mean what?'

'I mean he's an attractive man, of course.'

She's levelled her eyes on me, a lazy smile on her face. I keep chopping food into even cubes.

'You'd think I'd be intimidated by the number of fans who thirst over shots of his torso on social media. But then I remember that *I'm* the only one who gets to touch him in the flesh.'

'I'm not attracted to your fiancé, Mackenzie,' I state emphatically, my knife blade hovering over the board.

'Then it's a good thing you're definitely not his type, huh?' she counters.

Heat burns through me. Mackenzie straightens, shouting out towards the living area. 'Nicky! Baby, isn't it time we went to bed?'

Her eyes return to mine. She slides her empty wine glass along the countertop by its stem. 'Wash that for me?'

When she's gone, the tension in my shoulders eases and I allow myself a breath.

Chapter Eleven

At sunrise, I sit with my toes pushed into the soft, pale yellow sand of Ocean Beach on Fire Island. I breathe the dawn sea air, barely a ripple out on the water, soft waves lapping calmly on the shore. Situated on the south side of Long Island, the beach feels like an idyllic slice of paradise. I doubt Nicky sees it that way, or has time to. We have moved on to the next stage of the tour, and his next Grand Slam: the U.S. Open.

The tournament in Cincinnati ended in a crushing third round defeat, in a controversial match that saw Nicky get riled up and swear at the umpire, not once but twice, and – in what Sydney dubbed an epic temper tantrum – lob his tennis racket across court in protest, gaining himself a point penalty. It had all gone downhill after that.

Taking a photograph of the sunrise, I send the picture to Josie in Spain. When my phone vibrates moments later, I expect some kind of shocked emoji face as my sister's response.

Yet the message that comes through is from Oliver in Miami. I haven't messaged him since our last exchange. Today's message reads: *So am I being ghosted, or what?*

Reading his words feels like the first time I've smiled in a while. He's up early. I tap out a reply. *I'm sorry. Still not back in Miami. I've been really busy.*

So where are u now? his reply reads.

I was in Cincinnati. Now I'm in Long Island.

I regret my last message when he writes, *So you're personal chef to a tennis player?*

Dammit. I couldn't possibly say…

How long you in Long Island? Or does that depend on how long it takes Salco to pitch a hissy fit at Flushing Meadows?

I stare at the screen in alarm, wondering if I've just inadvertently violated the terms of my non-disclosure agreement. *I don't know what you're talking about.*

His response reads, *Once he crashes out and you're back in Miami, will you go out with me?*

I like that he's persistent. I type, *I'll give you a shout when I'm back x*

In which case, Oliver replies, *I hope he gets knocked out first round.*

The house where we're staying, booked by Sydney, is fifty metres back from the beach front: a two-story rustic property with five bedrooms, its own private pool on a vast upper deck and an outdoor shower. Four of the bedrooms are downstairs. I took the bedroom adjacent to the kitchen on the upper level, where it's lightest. The property is costing Nicky more than a thousand dollars a night, despite the organisers of the tournament wanting us all to stay in an official tour hotel in Manhattan.

From the beach, I enter on the ground floor, the bedroom doors still all closed. It's not yet six. Ragnar has banned Mackenzie from accompanying us to Long Island, partially blaming Nicky's failure to get through to the fourth round in Cincinnati on her arrival with Nicky's parents, though I'd only heard that from Sydney, who in turn had heard it from Tag. Climbing the stairs, I go to the kitchen, switching on the coffee machine and preparing breakfast al fresco.

Ragnar is first up, admiring the view, followed by Nicky, already dressed for training, his hair damp from the shower. The pair of them exchange conversation on the terrace with their backs to me through the bifold doors. We arrived at the property late last night, Nicky asking me to make him a sandwich if he woke up hungry. It was still there, untouched, when I got up.

Sydney is next up, bounding up the stairs. She's clutching what looks like a pile of swimwear.

'Mac let me raid her stash,' Sydney says, once we've exchanged good mornings, throwing the pile of bikinis on the kitchen countertop. 'So now you've got no excuse.'

She's determined to get me in the pool, or failing that, for a dip in the ocean. I grin at her then roll my eyes. 'I'll take a look.'

'I totally dig this sunflower one,' Sydney replies, holding up the top half, two frilly layered triangles held together with bright, yellow-coloured string fabric. 'It would look hot on you.'

I reach for the top, holding it up to the light. It is the definition of skimpy. 'This is Mackenzie's bikini brand?'

'That's two-hundred-dollar beachwear, right there,' Sydney winks.

My eyes widen at the price tag. 'I'll try it on,' I concede. I'll admit; I'm used to wearing something a little less flashy and a lot more boring.

Sydney nods towards Rag and Nicky outside. 'Those guys are gonna be out all day. I think you can give yourself a couple hours' away from the kitchen at least.'

'Good morning, ladies,' Tag smiles as he makes it to the top of the stairs, freshly shaved.

'Morning, Tag,' Sydney smiles, and I follow suit, 'what's on the schedule for today?'

'Go hit some balls around I guess,' Tag replies. 'You girls going for a dip in the ocean?'

'Jealous much?' Syd grins.

His lips twitch. 'I'll be in there myself before the sun goes down.'

'How's Nicky doing?' Sydney mouths, lifting her chin to towards the terrace.

I pay attention. I haven't been able to gauge how Nicky is feeling after his most recent defeat, and we've barely exchanged words. Tag's gaze flits outside. He rubs his jawline and gives a shrug. 'Onto the next challenge. Try put some reins on his mood. Not always easy with Nicky, you know? He's frustrated, for sure.'

'What about you?'

I watch the two of them interact, detecting something that I haven't picked up on before, yet unable to put my finger on exactly what. 'You mean, am I frustrated?' Tag questions with a smile on his lips.

My eyes go between them, and I suddenly feel like I'm getting in the way of two people who so badly want to flirt with one other. The moment is broken by Ragnar and Nicky walking over to the table on the deck, chair legs scraping over the wood. Tag goes and joins them.

I pick up the coffee jug, heading for the table, not without witnessing the exasperation in Sydney's expression.

'Please don't feel the need to answer this,' I say to Sydney once the men have all left for the training courts, lying out on the deck on a sunbed next to the small pool under a cloudless sky. I'm wearing the sunflower yellow bikini from Mackenzie's collection. 'But is there something going on between you and Tag?'

Sydney takes a sip of her drink. 'I am pleading the fifth on that.'

I smile. 'Okay. Then I should tell you I might have a date lined up for when I get back to Miami.'

Sydney bolts upright. 'Shut. Up. Girl, that didn't take you long! Who is he?'

'His name's Oliver. He came over to talk to me at the beach, the day before we left for Cincinnati.'

'Wait, you got hit on at the *beach*?!' Sydney makes a point of high-fiving me. 'Is he cute?' she adds.

'I think so. Nice hair. Kind of bleach blonde. He was playing football... I mean, soccer, on the sand. I think he might be a little younger than me.'

'Nothin' wrong with a toy boy, sister. So, when you gonna go out with him?'

'I haven't arranged anything yet.'

Sydney waggles her finger in the air. 'Moment we get back to Florida, girl, be sure to hit him up.'

I giggle; as does Sydney. 'I will.'

We sit in comfortable silence, soaking up the sun's rays, listening to the rhythmic sounds of the ocean, and I'm relieved in a way that Nicky is spending the day out of my company.

'Alright, alright, *something* is going on…' Sydney confesses at length.

It's my turn to bolt upright with a gasp. 'I knew it!' I squeal. 'I saw it, this morning, at breakfast, in his eyes, the way he was looking at you!'

She covers her face with her hand. 'Honestly, I don't know what it is, but that man blows hotter than the Sahara and in the same minute colder than the Icelandic Fjords. I'm figuring it's a Swedish thing.'

'So, what, is it just flirting?' I ask.

Sydney bites her lip and I find myself grinning again. '*Liiiittle* more than just flirting. The day Nicky crashed outta Wimbledon at the end of June. It was late, like, after midnight. I'm awake and I hear this tapping on my door. So, I open it, and he's there, holding an open bottle of wine asking if I wanna keep him company. His eyes are partially bloodshot and I can't tell he's already drunk, but… one thing led to another… *aaaand—*'

I let out another little squeal. 'Are we talking a one-night stand?'

Sydney seesaws her head, stifling another giggle. 'I mean, it was meant to be. Can I call it a one month stand? On and off?'

'You are not serious! Does Nicky know?'

'Nobody knows. Except you now. And y'all can't tell anyone either. That's part of the problem, he thinks Ragnar will see it as unprofessional and that Nicky won't approve. Plus, he's getting a divorce.'

'What's the divorce got to do with anything?'

She lets out a deflated sigh. 'His wife instigated the separation. Due to the amount of time he spent away from home. I can't help feeling like he's holding a torch for her, like, if she called *off* the divorce, he'd be back together with her inside of a minute. Like I'm just the fill-in. The substitute warming the bench.'

'I don't believe that for a second. I mean, look at you.'

'You're sweet, Elle. But shit keeps happening! Like we can't resist one another. I love this job. I wouldn't wanna have to choose between the two.'

'What if Tag spoke to Nicky?'

'I don't think it's Nicky he's worried about.'

We're quiet for a moment. I consider telling her that Nicky kissed me.

'Is he good in bed?'

She bursts out laughing. 'I'm telling you, girl, the man is *athletic. Mmm-mm.*'

At one a.m., I switch off my alarm. I lie under the sheets in the darkness for a moment, pushing my toes into the cooler, unoccupied parts of the bed. I yawn. Sydney's revelation about her evolving romance with Tag kept me smiling all afternoon, especially the detailed accounts of the sex, Syd's theory that she's benefitted from going to bed with a man who's been schooled by a former wife on how to please a woman. Over lunch, I came close to telling her about Nicky. It took good deal of effort to stop the words from spilling out of my mouth, yet a kiss was all it was, and categorically not going to happen again, so instead I remained silent.

Under the kitchen lights, the windows shielded by roller blinds, I'm plating up a two spiced salmon fillets with buttered potatoes and creamy, homemade coleslaw when I hear the sounds of Nicky's bedroom door downstairs. Panic hits me and I feel the need to scurry back to my room; he's earlier than expected.

I keep my gaze down when he arrives at the top of the staircase, taking a moment to pull a t-shirt over his bare chest. He stifles a yawn. 'Smells good,' he says throatily, squinting, his voice still thick with sleep.

'It's almost ready,' I say, adding some lettuce leaves and tomatoes on the side as a garnish. 'I can get out of your way.'

He takes a step forward. 'You don't have to go. Really. Unless you want to.'

I produce a thin-lipped smile. I want to find a way to forget that he ever kissed me.

'I know, I know, we need to clear the air,' he says, holding up his palms, as though reading my mind.

'What happened in Cincinnati—' I begin, my voice trailing off.

'It was a mistake,' he finishes for me. 'Pure and simple. It was my fault. It won't happen again.'

I know he's right, yet disappointment swells dull and heavy in my chest.

'We should pretend like it didn't happen,' he says. 'That's my suggestion.'

I shift the plate to the breakfast bar, trying to remain focussed on the job at hand. 'You taking the blame makes it sound like I wasn't a participant,' I state, before taking a step back and wiping my hands on a towel.

'I was the one who led you out into that garden,' Nicky replies, without taking a seat, and my mind can't help but go back to that blissful moment. 'I was the one who instigated... what happened after.'

In recent days I've fed off the memory of his kisses, the intoxication of the moment his mouth had fully found mine. It crushes me that he was now saying it had all been a mistake, despite me knowing that it's the truth, because when I dwell on it too much, I always end up feeling guilty. I've just come out of a relationship with a serial cheater, and I can't bear to put Nicky into that same bracket. 'We can pretend like nothing happened,' I force out. 'That's fine. Go back to how it was before.'

He gives a single nod in agreement. 'Thanks for cooking for me.'

'Do you need anything else? Otherwise, I might go back to bed.'

'I'm good. You go. Thank you, Elle.'

I compel my legs to back away towards my bedroom. Once inside, I lean against the back of the closed door in the darkness, tears threatening to spill out over my cheeks. I swallow hard, grappling to control my breathing. He'd called it *his mistake*. Of course, it's right that he would regret kissing me. I crawl back between the sheets, still hearing the muted clatter of his knife and fork against his plate, just outside the room. When the tears come, I don't wipe them away, allowing them to soak into the fabric of my pillow. Hatred for my own self-pity surges in my veins. I remind myself again that he isn't even available. Tortuous though it is, I'm going to have to accept that there will be no further kisses between me and Nicky Salco. Despite my every justification, that part feels worst of all.

The following morning, Nicky has a fitness test booked for eight o'clock, the kind where he's hooked up to treadmill, where specialists monitor his oxygen consumption and cardio capacity, or so Tag explains to me over breakfast. When Nicky comes upstairs, he helps himself to a bowl of cereal, and I avoid making eye contact.

'I don't understand; how does that help his tennis game?' I ask Tag.

'It doesn't,' Nicky grumbles behind me with his mouth full.

Tag rolls his eyes. 'The science people, they like to do it. It determines the maximum amount of oxygen he can absorb for aerobic exercise. You know, the kind that gets your heart pumping.'

'So, it's like, measuring his stamina for the longer base line points?'

'Kind of,' Tag smiles. 'It's basically a test of how physical he is.'

Annoyingly, my mind drifts back to the image of Nicky pressing me up against a tree back in Cincinnati, practically lifting me off the ground, his hands exploring my body. I'm fairly sure that if I got to speak to the science people, I could answer that question.

'Basically, I'm a lab rat,' Nicky says, swallowing down a glass of orange juice and placing one hand on Tag's shoulder. 'You ready to hit the road?'

Tag swallows the remainder of his coffee, getting to his feet.

'Have a good day,' I smile at Nicky.

I feel his gaze linger on me for a moment. 'Thanks, you too, Elle,' he says.

Mid-morning, once I've cleared the breakfast things away, I'm back on the sunbed in the sunflower yellow bikini, my head tilted back to alter the angle of the sun on my face.

'You've never told me how you started working for Nicky,' I say to Sydney, as Syd dries herself off following a dip in the pool.

'Actually, I was working for Mac's company before I started working for Nicky,' Syd says, rearranging her towel and taking her seat again on the sunbed. 'In one of her boutiques. Just on the shop floor to start with, then she moved me into a more logistical role which I was more suited to. She came in one day and said Nicky was looking for an assistant and would I be interested. He interviewed me the next day.'

'Have she and Nicky always been together?'

'On and off. They were high school sweethearts, though because of the tennis, Nicky mostly had private tutors to work around his schedule. His in-person attendance was minimal. She told me they broke up when Mac went to college and grad school to study for her MBA. Nicky had some girlfriends on the tour, but none of them serious. Mac's got her claws into him, you know. I mean, you've seen them together. I don't think Mac would let him go without a fight. Nicky is her territory; it's like she's peed in a circle all around him.'

'Do you think he feels the same way?'

'Honestly? If someone gave him a choice between Mac and tennis, I think tennis would win, hands down. Besides, he's always out on court, and he now distances himself from the rest of the tour, so how else is Nicky gonna meet someone if he doesn't marry Mac?'

'That's true,' I mutter.

Sydney sighs. 'If he could just get back to his winning streak. It feels like... I don't know... he's distracted.'

'Distracted with what?' I say, a tight coil forming in my stomach.

'Maybe he's tired. I don't know. Does he talk to you? In the night I mean? When he gets up?'

I swallow. 'Rag always gives me strict instructions to leave him alone. Occasionally we exchange a few words.' *And kisses*, I think.

We graduate from the sun beds to the pool and back again. I throw together some lunch from leftovers in the fridge, the sun's rays dappling my shoulders and the back of my neck.

'Is that the door?' Sydney says, whilst we're at the table.

I hear voices from down the stairs, in the bowels of the house. 'I thought they weren't due back until later?' I say, only to find Sydney looking as confused as I am.

'Guess they decided to come back early after Nicky's fitness test,' Sydney shrugs, getting to her feet.

Panic swells in my chest at the idea of Nicky seeing me relaxing when I should be working, and not only that but I'm wearing a bikini of his fiancée's design. Tag is the first to reach the top of the stairs, followed by Ragnar, then Nicky, carrying his racket bag and a second bulky bag of kit.

'Ladies,' Tag smiles. 'How's the water? You not go in the ocean yet?'

'Pool's good, we just ate,' Sydney replies. 'We were going to do the ocean later. Did you guys have lunch already?'

I remain in my seat, glancing around frantically for a towel. There isn't one nearby.

'We ate at the venue. We're gonna take a break, it's too hot outside for practice. We'll go back out later on,' Tag confirms.

I feel Nicky's presence. I rise to my feet, starting to clear away the used lunch plates on the table.

'Are you sure I can't make you anything?' I ask, as Sydney falls into conversation with Tag.

'I'm fine,' Ragnar says, stretching out his back. 'It's pleasant here. I'm going to walk along the sand.'

My eyes flit to Nicky. 'How about you?'

I swallow as I feel Nicky's gaze burn a trail of heat down my figure, a look so visceral it almost makes me tremble. 'I'm good,' he says in a low pitch. 'Thank you.'

'I'm gonna hit the pool,' Tag says to Nicky. 'You coming in?'

'Sure, in a minute,' Nicky says stoically. 'I gotta drop all this downstairs first.'

He disappears down the stairs as I push the hair behind my ears, carrying the plates through to the kitchen sink, thinking I should probably throw on a cover-up now that Sydney and I are no longer alone.

'You want any help, Elle?' Sydney shouts back.

'No, no, you guys get in the water,' I say. Despite this being paid employment, it often doesn't feel like it.

I peek through the windows at Tag kicking off his shoes and unbuttoning his shirt, hearing the sounds of Sydney shriek as they splash about in the pool, moving out of view. I smile, thinking that they make a cute couple. Down the staircase, I glimpse Ragnar leaving for the beach via the front door.

Returning outside to the table, I clear the rest of the lunch supplies, placing most of the leftover food back in the fridge and wrapping up what's left of the crusty French loaf I purchased in the village this morning. Walking around the corner to my bedroom to locate a cover-up, I open the door and freeze at the sight of Nicky sitting on my bed, resting his elbows on his knees.

'Oh,' I exclaim, behind me still hearing Sydney and Tag laughing in the pool. I don't move.

105

His eyes are on me again, sliding from my face down to the yellow bikini top then continuing their determined path further south to my belly button, then lower still. Slowly, he gets to his feet, stepping forward until he towers over me. He nudges the door closed behind me.

I feel my heart begin to gallop, pounding my ribcage, my skin prickling with goosebumps. Nicky's arm is still resting against the door, over my head. 'I really am trying,' he mutters under his breath, sounding annoyed with himself, his brow furrowed into a deep frown. 'Really, I am.'

My breaths quicken, catching in my throat. I swallow. His gaze is still on the yellow bikini. One hand goes to my hair, guiding a loose tendril away from my forehead, before it travels lower to my chin, cupping then raising it gently until I have no choice but to meet his stare. His eyes are ablaze. I don't move, a shudder passing through me causing my nipples to harden underneath the lycra material.

When he lowers his head, my constant, nagging sense of guilt melts away. In this moment, nothing else matters. At first, his lips are warm and tentative, brushing over my own, tenderly grazing the sides of my mouth. I raise myself up onto tiptoe, which brings me into closer proximity to his mouth, my lips rubbing against his. Nicky takes his time, stealing chaste kisses, until I'm clamouring on the inside for him to claim me.

'I tried to stay away,' he breathes against my mouth. 'But I can't stop. I can't. You're in my veins.'

He breaks away an inch. I open my eyes to find him gazing down at me with an intense, heat-filled stare from underneath heavy lids. No man has ever looked at me that way. And I know how badly I want him.

I reach up, grasping the fabric of his sports shirt in my fingers and twist it, tugging him closer. He doesn't need any further invitation. This time, when he captures my mouth, he doesn't hold back, imprisoning me against the door, his hands purposefully exploring my bare flesh, his mouth insistent, his tongue demanding. I feel devoured by him, wrapping my arms around his shoulders, shuddering with the burning sensation that travels from my stomach to surge between my thighs, all the while trying to keep silent for fear of being discovered. I pull away, breathless, realising he's lifted me up again, almost off the wooden boards, and that mine aren't the only breaths coming out in gasps. Nicky lowers me down a fraction, so that my toes touch the floor, his hand moving to my chest. With a single finger he teases aside the fabric on one side of my bikini top, exposing one full breast. A heavy sigh escapes his lips; a sound I equate with longing, because I've made that sound before. I feel his palm graze the tight bud of my nipple, brushing his thumb over the tip. It's my turn to sigh, arching my back at the exquisite sensation as he caresses me. Nicky groans, lowering his head again, returning his mouth to mine, with purposeful lips, his movements deliberate.

'You destroy me,' he whispers between kisses, his tone laced with torment, before he seems to waver. He eases himself away from me, re-covers my breast with my bikini top. 'And I... I shouldn't be here,' he mutters, the words catching in his throat. He looks to the floor. 'This isn't fair to you, I'm sorry.'

I want to tell him I don't care. That I'm not sorry. Yet I know deep down that I've been in Mackenzie's shoes. What we're doing makes him a cheat, and though I crave his touch, I can't condone our behaviour, no matter how much I despise the woman he's chosen to spend his life with.

'You should go,' I whisper. 'Before you're seen.'

Nicky adjusts himself, his hands going to the door, opening it a crack.

'They're still in the pool,' he says, closing it again.

His fingers go to my face, tracing my jawline. He presses one final kiss to my forehead, before he slips away.

Chapter Twelve

I find myself craving the midnights, the hours when the house is noiseless, when the darkness is all-consuming, when Nicky comes to me alone and I can have him to myself. In the kitchen that night, I can't concentrate, the memory of his heated kisses that afternoon invading my senses, my knife blade coming to hover in the air as I get caught in a moment, whatever vegetable I am attempting to slice all but abandoned to impure thoughts of Nicky's fingers teasing my nipple, and how I'm yearning for it to happen again.

When he climbs the stairs, I feel lost for words. Nicky Salco, the world-famous tennis player somehow a different entity to, and at odds with, the Nicky who presses himself up against me and tells me he can't stop. So instead, I turn, offering him the best smile that I can muster under the circumstances, the agony of our situation leaving me with an aching heart.

'Hi,' he whispers at the top of the staircase, watching me.

'Hi,' I reply, and my throat is thick. 'I'm sorry, it's just pasta. Nothing special.'

'Pasta's good,' he mumbles in response, coming to rest beside me at the countertop, leaning his back up against it, crossing his arms over his chest, his gaze going to the floor. 'There's no hurry. I think we've established that I can't leave you alone.'

'You also have a fiancée,' I remind him, as though it's a stock phrase that I roll out every time we have a conversation, as though it's supposed to make a difference. Maybe we're past it making a difference. 'And I'm a mistake, remember? So, we can't do this.'

Nicky reaches out, taking my left hand, the one that isn't holding the knife, sliding his fingers through mine. I shudder. 'I shouldn't have said that. I know now that's not true. That said… I won't kiss you again if you don't want me to.'

I close my eyes, my head and my heart screaming too many different things. 'I want you to,' I whisper.

He straightens for a moment, inhaling, letting go of my hand, glancing to the windows, out towards an invisible ocean cloaked in pitch black. We're silent, absorbing my words, both accepting the impossibility of the situation.

'Look, things are complicated—' he starts, but in that moment, I don't want to hear it.

He doesn't continue and I finish what I'm doing, walking the plate of pesto pasta with steamed broccoli, garlic, sundried tomatoes and pine nuts to the breakfast bar, leaving it on the place setting and filling him a glass of water. I feel the heat of his stare, his eyes moving with me to the fridge and back as I grate some parmesan over the dish. Once I've transferred the dirty pans to the sink, I back away and return to my room.

I listen under the sheets as Nicky demolishes the dish, the clatter of his fork against the ceramic of his plate in the kitchen interrupted only by the sound of the ocean roaring in the near distance. My heart is hammering again. The orange flood-light from the garden below peeks through my blinds, casting opposing shadows.

The tap at my door is so quiet, I almost don't hear it. Crawling from my bed, I open the door a fraction. Nicky is waiting, his head bowed, one arm leaning against the door frame. When he raises his eyes to me, I urgently crave his touch, however much it seems that it isn't right or decent.

I open the door wider. He slips inside. Once it is closed behind us, Nicky folds me into his embrace with zero hesitation, his mouth finding mine in the shadows in an instant. His lips are commanding. Residual guilt gives out to primitive need. I taste a hint of the pasta I've just made for him when my tongue tangles with his. He pulls back, yanks off his top, then goes for mine, guiding my camisole over my head, his hands cupping my bare breasts before he eases off my shorts too, pulling down his own sweatpants and underwear as soon as he he's done so. Without even seeing him properly, I can tell that he's big. That we've gone from just kissing to both stark naked in less than a minute takes me by surprise, but in a good way, feeling the white heat curling between my thighs, yet I'm thankful that it's still so dark in the room. I allow him to lower me back down to the bed, covering me with his hard body, his arousal now pressing against the doughy part of my thigh, the size of him giving me slight cause for alarm. I draw breath as his mouth seizes my right breast, sucking tautly on the nipple, teasing it out further so he can lavish it with attention, as his right hand strokes my thigh, traversing the soft valley. He shifts himself partially off me so that he can guide my thighs apart. Lifting one of my knees, his movements are quick and decisive, driven by the same urgency I feel, though my desperation is increasingly mixed with feelings of dread.

Everything happens fast. I gasp for a second time as two of his fingertips find my centre, sliding confidently down my damp folds until he's parted me, releasing molten liquid that has pooled inside my core, causing a low groan of desire to escape his lips as he makes circular motions with his fingers, stroking me, moistening me, readying me, finding the exact spot that makes me shudder. And suddenly it's like nothing I've ever done sexually can match up to the feelings blossoming down my thighs and inside my stomach right now, purely from his fingertips. As the pressure builds, I'm straining, my hips bucking beneath him, feeling as though I might unravel, but my squirms only seem to encourage him. Before I know it, his lips have begun a tantalising journey south from my breasts, travelling down my abdomen, his mouth ebbing closer to my most intimate part.

I emerge from an intoxicating fog of pleasure as panic explodes in my chest. It's as though I've only just got up to speed that this is happening, grappling with the sensations shooting around my body, before I've realised what he is mere inches from doing. So, I clamp my legs together. 'Wait,' I hiss quickly, twisting away from him, trying not to squeal. 'Wait, wait, wait, *wait*.'

In the darkness, I feel his body stiffen. 'Are you alright?' he whispers. 'Did I do something wrong?'

'No, no, I just—' I squeak out, trying to keep my volume levels to a minimum.

'Am I going too fast?' he asks.

I nod frantically. 'A little, m–maybe.'

'I'm sorry. I can slow down.'

When he lowers his head again, the touch of his lips achingly soft, I still feel my body go rigid, my breathing ragged.

'It's just—' I choke out as Nicky moves back up, hovering above me, his features now searching mine in the shadows. Embarrassment washes over me.

'Tell me,' he urges me, the soothing tone in his voice lessening my mortification, but only by a fraction.

I struggle to find the words. 'It's been a while since anyone… did that to me.'

After a moment, I feel Nicky's body lift as he twists away from me, switching on the lamp on the nightstand, reminding me in such a stark fashion that I'm lying in bed naked with a perfectly sculpted Nicky Salco. His face comes back to mine, his hand stroking my hair. He's frowning.

'I thought you had a boyfriend until recently,' he says under his breath.

I feel heat racing to my cheeks for a second time, thankful that the light still is too dim for him to detect it.

'I did… he just… he wasn't…' I stop and take a breath, trying to force the words out. 'What I am trying to say is… he never liked… to…'

'Elle—'

'To go down on me,' I finish with mortification, covering my eyes with one hand.

Nicky moves my arm out of the way. 'What the hell?'

'Wasn't really his thing.'

He shifts his position. I glance down, allowing me to sneak a look at his glorious contours. 'Okay,' he murmurs matter-of-factly. 'I mean, but he still... made you climax, right?'

I feel myself sinking into difficult waters, both our voices having to remain at a strained whisper. I bite my lip. 'No, not... not frequently, no.'

'Hold up, what does that mean?'

'I mean, a lot of the time, I... you know.'

'I don't think I do.'

I roll my eyes. 'I may have...' I mouth. I feel myself sinking. 'I may have... faked it.'

Nicky's eyes go wide. 'Are you kidding me?' he asks, in all seriousness.

'No.' I shake my head. 'It was just easier that way.'

'*Easier?*' he blurts out, as though he can't quite believe what I'm saying. 'So, when was the last time...you know... a guy made you come?'

I wince, but holy hell I love hearing him talk like this. 'I – I don't remember exactly.'

'Like how long are we talking? Months? Years?'

'You don't have to make a big thing of it.'

'I'm not. I'm just... surprised is all. Elle, you're beautiful. Desirable.'

When he doesn't say anything else, I'm immediately worry he's judging my lack of experience. But he hasn't moved, and instead he seems to be contemplating something.

'Can I make a suggestion?' Nicky says after the lengthy silence, cradling one hand against my cheek. 'Will you let me try? Just by touching you. I won't do anything that makes you uncomfortable, and you can tell me any time you want me to stop.'

Leaning down, he places a tender kiss against my lips. I sink lower into the pillow so that he can lie by my side, his upper body covering mine. I nod my head in consent and he strokes my hair. Then he lowers his mouth again, increasing the intensity of his kisses, and I feel my body's voluntarily response; I'm getting even wetter and the coil of intense pressure is mounting again between my thighs. He kisses me for some minutes until I can't even think, taking his time, before one hand drifts lower again, caressing my breasts and my stomach in an idle excursion, until his fingers come to rest against my upper thigh.

'Okay, we need to remove the manacles from these legs,' he whispers against my mouth in a half-laugh. He moves the same hand lower, hooking his fingers behind one of my knees, guiding it upwards and urging me to lift it upright. 'That's it,' he says, directing my knee outward, opening me wide, before he does the same with the other.

'Can we turn out the light?' I ask, my shrill voice coming out as a strained whisper, my nerves getting the better of me, my heart beating so fast I feel as though it might explode.

In one swift movement, Nicky twists his body, switches off the lamp, and returns to his position. When we're back in darkness and shadow I feel my confidence returning, enough so I can guide his hand back into the desired position between my legs. His fingers slide against my flesh, teasing, gentle. He mumbles something about me being perfect but I don't hear it because his mouth is on mine and I'm holding onto him as though the world might end any second. When I pull back I'm panting, desperate for his touch.

'Is this alright?' he asks, stroking me.

It's just the right pressure. It's everything and more. Is this proper foreplay? My voice quivers as I gasp out, 'Yes... Yes.'

He adds another fingertip, sliding against my glistening warmth, caressing me, working his way up the plump folds. When he reaches the point that gives me the maximum pleasure, he massages it, using circular motions, slowly at first but increasing the intensity. Then he relaxes into an exquisite rhythm and I let out a deep sigh.

'Does that feel good?' Nicky rasps.

I can't respond for the throb pulsing through me, yet a whimper in confirmation escapes my lips. He knows what he's doing. The coil tightens; I can feel how close I am, and how swiftly he's brought me to the brink. Nicky increases the tempo of his movements, quickening then slowing the rhythm, lowering his mouth and kissing me deeply until I'm digging my nails into the contours of his back.

Delicious sensations build from deep inside me, sending me hurtling towards an eruption over which I have no control. Still Nicky caresses my clitoris with his fingers, quickening his pace before slowing it right down, torturing me, teasing me, the pleasure causing my thighs to quake as in my head I beg him to let me crash over the edge.

'Relax and let yourself go,' he urges me, the moments passing in a blissful haze until I feel a rushing sensation, another whimper escaping my lips as long, slow, deep contractions explode between my thighs in wave after wave of ecstasy. The moment I come, Nicky's mouth collides with mine, smothering my cries as my hips buck under his hand, my world crashing apart at the seams. Nicky holds fast as I shudder and tremble, his fingertips never losing rhythm to ensure I grasp every last peak of pleasure.

When the sensations subside, my body goes limp, sinking into the sheets. I grip onto him, breathless, floating back down from a place I never want to leave.

When I have strength, I roll my body into his, trailing kisses across his clavicle, my thighs coming into contact with his substantial erection. Nicky's warm hand traces down my spine, his fingers still wet with my arousal, coming to rest on top of my hip.

'That didn't feel like there was any faking involved,' he whispers at length, his voice gravelly.

I can barely form a response before he's kissing me again, ousting any rational thoughts from my mind. I'm eager to explore him. Yet when I go to touch him, he pulls back and mutters, 'I should probably go.'

Blissful elation is trounced by bitter disappointment. I raise my head to object. 'Stay,' I say, not bothering to lower my voice.

In the shadows, he strokes my cheek, and mutters words I dread hearing. 'You should get some sleep.'

Frustration surges in my chest as he untangles his limbs from my embrace, getting up to walk to the other side of the bed and collecting up his clothes. I wait for him to get dressed in the darkness.

What *was* that? I have questions. So many of them; all jumbled up together in my brain. How do we go back from this? What happens tomorrow, and the day after that, after what just took place? What about Mackenzie? Is this all my fault he ended up in here?

I cover myself with the top sheet. Back in his clothes, Nicky sits back down on the edge of the bed, the frame sinking under his weight. He leans down, drawing me in for one final kiss, which both lessens my panic but makes me more eager for him not to leave.

'When you're ready to progress things,' he whispers. 'I got you covered.'

I'm confused as to what he means. My mind's still reeling, too full of questions to form a coherent response, the implication being that what just happened between us is destined to occur again, and at my bidding, and that, by telling me *I got you covered*, Nicky apparently means he is willing to service me for a second time, should I so desire it.

He pinches my chin lightly between his thumb and forefinger. The mattress shifts from under me again as Nicky gets to his feet. Seconds later, the door clicks shut behind him.

~

By morning, it's stormy outside and I'm filled with self-loathing, the events of last night leaving a bad taste in my mouth. Guilt swells in my stomach; my eyes leaden from lack of sleep. In my mind, I'm no better than Jamie was, only this time Mackenzie is the one who suffers, as I'm the one cheating with Nicky Salco. It's occurred to me multiple times that maybe sex is all that Nicky's interested in. The worst part is that I wanted more. *So much more.* I keep picturing Mackenzie, thinking that she doesn't deserve him, yet it doesn't make any of the blame go away. This wasn't just a simple kiss. What we did was duplicitous, and wrong.

Overnight, Oliver's sent me another couple of flirtatious text messages. In any other moment, I'd be flattered, plus, half the world doesn't know his name. He's handsome, sweet, uncomplicated, and – more pertinently – single. It's easy enough to flirt back on the phone, when we're not face-to-face. Yet still my mind is cluttered with thoughts of Nicky's fingers trailing down my naked thighs, making me wet with anticipation. This morning I'm left wondering whether, if it was Oliver who'd touched me so intimately, would I have experienced the same reaction?

Given the choice, I know who I should pick.

In the kitchen, I'm peeling a large beetroot, two oranges and a kiwi, and there's a broccoli stem waiting to be sliced. Apart from Nicky, everybody is out of bed. Rag, Tag and Sydney tuck into cereal and cinnamon pastries on the sofas in front of the TV on the far side of the staircase, outside the rain hammering against the glass panes of the bifold. The news is on, both men already dressed for a day's training.

I'm slicing the beetroot into chunks when I hear Nicky's footsteps. I stiffen as he reaches the top of the staircase, his imposing presence still sending me into a tailspin. I glance up, our eyes meeting as he flashes me a brief smile, but I look away. He's dressed for training, wearing shorts, a black long-sleeved top with a zip, and a brand-new pair of trainers.

'Good morning,' he says as he saunters over.

'Morning,' is my curt response.

'How are you?' he asks, pulling out a stool, taking a seat.

'Fine. You?'

'Good,' he says, then lowers his voice. 'Had to take a cold shower after last night.'

I say nothing in return, ejecting the images of our naked, entangled bodies from my brain, continuing in my task without looking in his direction, instead checking that the others are still engrossed in the CNN headlines.

'What're you doing?' he asks.

'Yesterday I found this juicer at the back of a cupboard. I washed it. Seems like it still works.'

Nicky looks at the bulky metal device sitting on top of the countertop. 'Looks a little decrepit,' he comments, his gaze shifting to the pile of fruits and vegetables. 'Is all this meant for me?'

'It is.'

He turns in his seat, checking the others are still concentrating on the TV, now showing the latest news in American football. I feel him lean closer, crossing his arms on the surface. 'Can I see you again tonight?' he asks in a low tone.

My eyes immediately flit to where Sydney, Rag and Tag are sitting. None of them pay either of us any attention. I panic for a moment, then point with my knife blade. 'Did you know that beetroot is a superfood?' I say, speaking normally, 'So's broccoli. You should eat way more of both than you do. Both are rich in antioxidants. Studies suggest they both have natural anti-inflammatory properties. They can also support your energy levels.'

A smile creeps onto his features. Nicky keeps his voice close to a whisper, his lustful gaze making my nerve endings tingle. 'We could leave the light on. I wanna see your face this time when you finish.'

A rush of heat mushrooms between my thighs. Quickly dicing up the broccoli, I pile everything into the funnel of the juicer. It's already been plugged in so I switch it on. It's loud – going off like a rocket, the motorised whooshing sound filling the entire room. Everyone looks over but they soon lose interest as I press the metal pusher down through the funnel, purple and green juice spurting out into a waiting jug through a spout. Loudly, I say, 'Oranges makes the juice more palatable. Gives it a natural sweetness. Good for vitamin C also.'

I look to Nicky. 'I want you,' he mouths emphatically at me.

I switch the unit off and it takes a moment to power down, leaving us in silence again, only the sounds of the rain audible against the glass panes. 'Kiwis are meant to improve sleep onset, quality and duration,' I say. 'Some people say that kiwis are the true superfruit.'

He feigns interest, but his eyes dance flirtatiously. I fill him a tall glass with the juice from the jug, sliding it across the countertop. 'Drink,' I instruct him.

Nicky's watching me, like he cannot understand my resistance. Without argument, he picks up the glass and downs the entire contents in one, doing as he's told. Putting the empty glass back down on the countertop, he wipes purple stains from his lips with a grimace.

'Happy now?' he asks.

'Do you have a juicer back in Florida?'

'Don't know. Ask Lonz. Can we leave out the broccoli in future?'

I ignore him, instead scraping together all the leftover peelings.

He glances over his shoulder again before the same, shameless look returns to his features. He's whispering again. 'Let me show you how good it can be. Let me show you what you've been missing all this time.'

My stomach clenches. I've run out of random fruit facts. I avoid eye contact. 'I don't think that would be a good idea,' I respond.

'Why not?'

'You know why not,' I hiss. 'Now, please. Stop it.'

His whisper is strained. He looks almost hopeful, not like a man who's recently cheated on his fiancée. 'Tonight, Elle. Please.'

I stop moving, the stoney, exasperated look I finally give him conveying my true feelings: that his current situation means there is no possible way this can continue.

'No,' I say, my tone shaky. I grip the countertop. 'We can't.'

Then I turn, return to my room, closing the door behind me.

Chapter Thirteen

I sit in silence in the back of an official Miami yellow cab next to Syd, the journey from the airport whisking us south from the airport towards Coral Gables. The mood is subdued. About half way through the journey, Sydney's phone starts to pulse, several messages coming through all at once.

'They're quoting four hundred dollars to replace the broken mirror,' Sydney sighs, clicking her tongue, referring to the wall mirror Nicky smashed at the Fire Island property, after he'd crashed out of the U.S. Open in the first round, losing badly to an unseeded, low-ranked qualifier.

'That sounds like a lot,' I murmur. 'It's just a mirror.'

'That's the cost of the replacement. I don't think we can really argue it.'

'I suppose not.'

I look out of the window as we speed down a five-lane freeway. The size of American roads never ceases to amaze me. I'd heard the sound the mirror made as it smashed, Nicky cutting his fingers on the shards when he'd punched it.

'Oh God,' Sydney groans.

'What is it?'

'Mackenzie wants to talk to me when we get back. Says she wants to see you, too.'

My eyes widen. 'Why does she want to see me?'

'Says she wants to have a *re-think* after Nicky's defeat.'

I feel sick. Sydney reaches over and pats my arm. 'Don't worry; she's not gonna fire you. At least, I hope not, as I'll be toast also.'

I swallow, already picturing myself on the next flight back to London.

When we reach Nicky's house, there are two cars parked in the driveway.

'That's not good,' Sydney hums in a cautious tone as she walks through the gate, after she's punched in the code.

I follow, pulling my suitcase, to witness the bright red Porsche parked behind a white Range Rover Sport, as the taxi driver helps unload the last of our bags from the back of his vehicle. 'Whose cars are those?' I whisper.

'The white car belongs to Nicky's parents. The red convertible belongs to Francisco, Nicky's publicist. He'll have been sent here by his agent, no doubt.'

'Is that a bad thing?'

'Francisco only ever turns up in a crisis.'

Inside, the sprinklers are on, the gardener in the middle of trimming the hedges.

'When are we supposed to see Mackenzie?' I ask.

'Speak of the devil,' Sydney mutters, just as Mackenzie comes running out of the front door of the house, wearing a pair of bright green capri trousers, a low-cut, floaty white blouse and a towering set of heels.

'Sydney!' Mackenzie calls. 'You're here!'

Nicky's flight was full, so Sydney and I took one that departed three hours later.

'What's going on?' Sydney asks.

'There are reports in the press about Nicky's injury,' Mackenzie blurts, out of breath. 'And how he got it.'

I remain quiet, but my pulse rate rockets.

'How?' Sydney breathes.

'Nicky thinks one of the medical staff could have blabbed to a news reporter. Francisco's up there with him now; they're talking damage control. Ben's called his lawyers. The story is already circulating on some of the networks. Elle, don't you have to be in the kitchen?'

I literally just got here. I'm standing as an innocent bystander but suddenly I snap to attention. 'I thought you wanted to see me?'

'That was *before* the news about Nicky's hand,' she clips dismissively, shaking her head. 'I'll talk to you later.'

Mackenzie has already slipped her arm through Sydney's and is marching her towards the house. I puff out my cheeks, dragging my suitcase across the grass, back towards my side of the pool house.

Inside, the air feels cool. I'd left the curtains partially closed before we'd departed for Cincinnati. It feels like so much has happened since that day. Pulling them aside to let in some light, I check my phone, searching for headlines relating to Nicky. There are four or so news reports, all relating to his injured hand:

Tennis Ace Nicky Salco's Injures his Hand Reportedly Punching a Mirror, Following Shock Early Exit at U.S. Open; Requires Hospital Treatment

Nicky 'Sulko': Tennis Champ Fails to Get Past First Round of U.S. Open, Smashes Mirror and Wounds Hand

Tennis Star Nicky Salco Takes his Frustrations Out on a Mirror and Injures Hand After Crashing Out of U.S. Open

Curse of the Triple Salco: Moody Tennis Champ Continues Disastrous Losing Streak

Whilst I am reading each of the reports, my phone vibrates with a message from Oliver. *Did you make it back to Miami?* he asks.

A smile touches my lips. *How did you guess?* I type back. Oliver's reply reads, *Told ya he'd pitch a hissy fit. So can we go out on that date now?*

I wait a moment, before replying, *Maybe.*

The idea of going out on an actual date with him makes me excited with nerves. *As in maybe next Tuesday night at 7? Coconut Grove?* Oliver asks, and I type back *Can I think about it?*

His reply is immediate: *Unfortunately, this is a one-time only offer! Expires midnight tonight!*

Fine, I say, *then I'll give you my answer by midnight ;)*

I go back to reading about Nicky when there's a knock at the door.

'Come in!' I raise my voice and Sydney enters.

'What's going on?'

Sydney shakes her head. 'It's all coming out in the press.'

I lift my phone and gave it a little shake. 'So I'm reading. Do they know who leaked the story?'

'One of the nurses who gave Nicky treatment put something on Twitter, and it snowballed. She deleted the tweet later, but that seems to be the origin of all this.'

'Will Nicky be penalised for it?'

Sydney shakes her head. 'For punching the mirror? No. It didn't happen on court so I doubt the ATP would take any action. There's a surgeon coming later to look at his hand. Nicky has only himself to blame for any negative press.'

'What does Tag think?'

Sydney rolls her eyes. 'Don't know. Can't seem to get him alone. And if Ragnar is even anywhere close, he pretends not to notice me.'

I pull a face. 'I'm sorry.'

'Anyway. I came to tell you Mackenzie wants see you now.'

My stomach rolls over. 'Right now?'

It's Sydney's turn to pull a face. 'Don't worry. She can't fire you.'

'She can't?'

'At least I don't think she can. Why, are you worried she might try?'

I get to my feet and shake my head. 'No. She just doesn't like me very much. Where do I go?'

'Up the main stairs in the house. Take a left. That's Mac's office.'

I walk up the path to the main house on jelly legs. The front door is already open. The red Porsche has left, but Nicky's parents' white Range Rover Sport is still parked in the driveway. When I enter, I spy Ben Salco pacing in the living room, wearing a suit like the first time I met him in Cincinnati, his phone glued to his ear. Loud rock music emanates from upstairs, muffled through closed doors.

I take the wooden stairs, clinging to the banister, sweltering in the August heat and thankful for the air conditioning that's pumping through the house. I am anxious that Nicky has somehow confessed to Mackenzie what's been going on. Nicky being in my room in Fire Island feels like a dream – I've barely seen him in nine days, every now and then the ache in my chest swelling, until I can distract myself and push the memory of our exchanges from my mind.

When I reach the top of the stairs, I hear Mackenzie on the phone, the music coming from the other side of the house, presumably where their bedroom is situated. The bedroom door is firmly closed; Mackenzie's office door wide open.

I linger outside for a moment. I can hear Mackenzie on the phone. She appears to be giggling, yet not outwardly so, in complete contrast to her mood in the garden half an hour earlier.

I poke my head inside. Mackenzie looks up from her desk, startled, offering me a severe frown. Her hair and make-up are immaculate; her false nails freshly applied.

'I have to go, I'll call you later,' she mutters into the handset and I can't help but feel like I'm interrupting something.

She hangs up, placing her phone face down on her desk before beckoning me inside. I swallow and do as I am asked, guiding the door closed behind me.

'Elle,' she then says in a severe tone, leaning back in her leather chair. 'Take a seat. If you can't hear yourself think, it's because Nicky is sulking.'

I sit down on the opposite side of her desk. 'How's his hand?'

'He'll be fine to play tennis again in a few days once the stitches are out.'

'Does he even want to play tennis right now?'

Mackenzie stares at me for a moment then lets out a snort. 'It's not about *wanting* to play for someone like Nicky. Tennis is his entire life. He's been training for these moments since he was four years old. You've only been here five minutes, so I wouldn't expect you to understand that.'

I stiffen in the chair. It hasn't taken long for her to draw first blood. 'You wanted to see me?'

'Yes, I did. I talked to Nicky, and to Ragnar. Nicky still wants Rag to coach him, despite the recent... setbacks. But some things will need to change if Nicky is going to return to winning form. We've drawn up a list of adjustments to make. This whole business of getting up in the night, of disrupting his sleep, of eating at all different hours, it has to stop. Nicky knows that. He's agreed to try and slowly phase it out as part of his routine.'

I grip the sides of my chair, thinking I *am* about to get fired.

'Now, as much as I would like Lonzo to leave him something in the fridge, we also can't have Nicky falling back into his old habits of ordering pizza at three in the morning. Nicky therefore wants you to stay on, and Ragnar agrees with him.'

I let out a sigh of relief, loosening my shoulders, though there was nothing in that sentence about Mackenzie wanting me around.

'But,' Mackenzie snips, 'I feel now is the time to remind ourselves of the ground rules.'

I give a single nod.

'From now on, at night, there is to be *zero* contact between you and Nicky. You will get up and make him something to eat as per the arrangement. You will leave it covered in the kitchen for him, or in the oven. You will return to your room before he is even out of bed. There will be no discussions, no exchanges between you both, is that clear? No conversation whatsoever in the middle of the night.'

'I understand,' I murmur, and I wonder if she's heard us speaking at night before now.

'You will continue to assist Lonzo in the kitchen, preparing meals throughout the day, serving and clearing away the dishes. During your free time, you will stay in your room, or you will leave the premises. Other than the kitchen, you should treat the house and the garden as off limits, unless you are working. Understood?'

I stare at her slack–jawed for a moment. I know perfectly well that Sydney has full run of the house, as do Lonzo and his family, whose children sometimes have use of the pool after school hours. Rag and Tag regularly use the courts outside of training sessions, as well as the pool. And Mackenzie knows it.

'Is there a reason I'm being singled out?' I manage, my voice hitching in my throat.

'You are a distraction for Nicky,' Mackenzie states. 'If it was up to me, we would have left you in London.'

Tears spring to my eyes. I fight them back. 'Then why not tell Nicky to fire me?' I choke out. 'If I'm so unwelcome here.'

'Unfortunately, Elle, even I don't have that kind of sway with my future husband. You're what some would consider a necessary evil.'

My throat has gone dry, the urge to get up and flee the room almost overwhelming.

'Is there anything else?' I ask.

'No, we're done here,' Mackenzie says. 'You can go.'

I get to my feet, clasping my fingers together, realising that music has ceased.

As I open the door to Mackenzie's office, I emerge into the hallway to find the door on the opposite side is wide open, granting me a view all the way down a corridor to the master bedroom. Nicky and Mackenzie's bedroom.

'Mac, can I borrow your laptop?' Nicky's voice drawls from somewhere unseen. 'I gotta send an email.'

I freeze, just as he rounds the corner, wearing only his underwear and a white bandage covering the fingers on his right hand, his hair and sculpted torso still damp from a very recent shower. His eyes flash when he sees me.

'Sure, it's downstairs,' Mackenzie's voice floats out from behind me in her office. 'But I need it in a half hour.'

I swallow. Nicky does the same. He moves a few steps closer. I feel the urge to go to him, to put my arms around his neck. I hear Mackenzie move behind me and I snap back to reality, turn on my heel and flee back down the staircase.

–

Before midnight, I lie in bed in the darkness, unable to sleep and devoid of all tears, questioning how I have managed to find myself in such a position, and with no one to talk to about it.

I know three things for certain:

Number one; Mackenzie Scheffler loathes me.

Number two; despite number one, my position as a personal chef to Nicky appears to be safe, for now.

Number three: I am hopelessly in love with Nicky Salco.

I have questioned so many times in the passing days whether it is love that I feel, and not some kind of misguided crush, or primal lust, pure and simple. Mackenzie summoning me to her office to lay down a new set of 'rules' has also confirmed two things: firstly, that the only person barring me from being sacked, is Nicky. Had Nicky been ambivalent, Mackenzie would have been free to fire me on the spot. But Nicky appears to be standing his ground, showing loyalty to me, which clearly pisses Mackenzie off. Secondly, Mackenzie banning me from any nighttime contact with Nicky demonstrates a kind of nervousness on her part, that perhaps she's picked up on a connection between us that concerns her. This, in turn, worries me: Mackenzie finding out that her fiancé has been in my bed would definitely put me on the first plane back to London.

Yes, he's physically attractive. Yes, his kisses make me melt. But he's kind to me too, and considerate, when he isn't being distracted by being a World-Class Tennis Star. The jury is still out on whether he's interested in me, and not just my body. Jamie never showed that level of interest. For a while at the beginning, I was frightened to lose my job on the basis that I'd be out of employment again. Only at Fire Island, I realised it wasn't the job I now fear losing.

And yet.

I cannot have him. However things pan out, I cannot picture any possible route that he can be mine. I pictured the headline: *Nicky Salco dumps fiancée for personal chef*, feeling my cheeks warm at the sheer unlikelihood of it ever happening. And however much I don't like Mackenzie; I still can't get past the deceit that goes with a cheating behind someone else's back.

Lying in the darkness, I convince myself that having limited contact with Nicky can only be a good thing, despite the ache in my chest that accompanies being apart from him.

On the nightstand, my phone lights up. I pick it up, staring at the screen. A message has arrived from Oliver. It's 11.58. *That offer's about to expire…*, it reads.

I find myself smiling. He's tenacious. My distraction: from everything that is going on. I type my reply, knowing that if I'm going to move on from Nicky, I have to start somewhere. *You've persuaded me*, I type. *Tuesday night at 7. I'll be there (wherever there is) x*

Chapter Fourteen

In the rum bar the wallpaper has a tropical print, cheese plants and vines embossed with images of parrots and monkeys. I stare across our table, thinking it's a small miracle that Oliver Davenport doesn't already have a girlfriend, given that he resembles an Abercrombie & Fitch model, complete with an expensive smile. For the duration of our date, he seems, so far, at least, to be a perfect gentleman.

He's talking about his time at college when I suddenly blurt out, 'Can I ask you something?'

His cheeks flush red, swallowing another mouthful of cocktail. 'Sure, go ahead.'

'How is it you are still single?'

He starts chuckling, bobbing ice cubes up and down in his drink. 'I don't know, I guess. My friends say I'm too *particular* when it comes to women.'

I grin. 'So, you're fussy?'

He gives a shrug, squirming a little in his seat. 'Fussy? You mean, like, picky? No, not picky. My mom says it's because I get bored easily, that I can never just stay in a relationship. I keep telling her it's because I haven't met the right girl yet.'

'Come on then, how long did you stay with your last girlfriend?'

He thinks about it. 'Three, maybe four months?'

After a couple of cocktails, I find I'm enjoying watching him squirm. 'And what was wrong with her?'

'That's just it, nothing!' he blurts. 'She just wanted more than I was willing to give.'

'What did she want?'

'The usual stuff. To meet her parents, her sister, her cousins, hang out with all her friends...'

'That all sounds pretty acceptable to me.'

'It's all good if you're... you know... in love. And I wasn't in love with her. So, I told her she should go out in the world and, you know... find a guy who loved her.'

'And how did that go down?'

He winces. 'Not all that well. We were in a bar up in South Beach at the time. She marched out, not before she'd tipped her drink over my head.'

I bite my lip, failing to keep the laughter from escaping my lips.

'It's fine; she's with somebody new now!'

'And are you alright with that?'

He gives another shrug. 'Sure. She's happy. Meanwhile, I'm still on the lookout for Ms. Right.'

His eyes twinkle, surfer blonde hair falling into his eyes. I take another hasty sip of my drink. 'Turns out I think I like British girls,' he adds. 'Who knew?'

'Oh? And how many British girls have you met?'

He laughs. 'Just the one.'

'That's casting a fairly big net, based on your opinion of one individual.'

He rubs his chin, trying to suppress his smile. 'I have good instincts. I guessed you were working for Salco, didn't I?'

My smile fades, Nicky's image taking up prime position back in my mind.

He senses my reaction. 'I'm sorry,' he says. 'I didn't mean to sound rude.'

'No, no, it's fine. I do work for Nicky Salco,' I concede.

He still manages to look surprised, perhaps even disappointed, nodding his head. 'I guess I was still hoping you would say I was wrong and that you were working for someone else.'

'Your messages gave me the impression you're not a fan?'

'Hey, this is Miami. Everybody loves Nicky Salco, apart from me and my family.'

'Why, did something happen?'

His expression sours. He puffs out his cheeks. 'Honestly, I've never met the guy. Seems like a chip off the old block to me though. Bad attitude. I'm sorry, I should probably explain. Nicky Salco went to high school with my cousin. His father, Ben Salco; he wrecked my uncle's marriage by having an affair with his wife, my aunt. They got divorced. Really fucked up my cousin. Ben Salco… his wife and family just turned a blind eye, like nothing had ever happened.'

I raise my eyebrows, surprised by the revelation. I cast my mind back to the two times I have seen Nicky's father. The first time we'd met in Cincinnati, he'd not said a word to me. He was a tall enough man, but not as tall as his son, who'd seemed to have inherited his height from his mother's side, Libby an inch or so taller than her husband. There's something severe about Ben Salco, as though he disapproves of everyone and everything around him, his manner consistently critical. The second time I saw him was last week, when news of Nicky punching a mirror was being leaked to the press. Sydney told me that Ben Salco had been furious – not with Nicky – but with the actions of the press for tarnishing Nicky's reputation, and had spent hours on the phone to his lawyers to see whether he could have the story quashed: by which time, it was already too late.

'That's terrible,' I breathe. 'How old was your cousin at the time?'

'Fourteen. Same age as Salco, but Salco was well on the way to going pro at that stage. Probably too focussed on his serve to worry about his dad pissing all over someone else's marriage.'

'Were your cousin and Nicky friends?'

'Not really. At high school, Nicky was one of the in crowd; at least when he was around and not out on court. My cousin remembers his girlfriend though, the current one. Said in high school she was a real bitch.'

'Mackenzie Scheffler. She's still a stone-cold bitch. They're getting married early next year.'

Oliver finishes off his cocktail. 'So, what's he like? Salco. Is he a total asshole? Like, do you ever talk to him?'

I falter, the image in my mind of Nicky undressing me at Fire Island, yet the voice I hear belongs to Mackenzie, reminding me that I've signed a non-disclosure agreement. 'I've talked to him a little… he seems… pleasant.'

Oliver chuckles. 'Pleasant? Now that I can't imagine. So, he's not a total prima donna?'

I clam up, not exactly sure what I can get away with.

'Oh, Jesus, I'm so sorry,' Oliver interjects. 'It's none of my business. It's you I should be asking about.'

After drinks, we're walking out on the streets in the pleasant evening air. It's already dark outside. We pass a bookstore that's still open, and I ask Oliver if he minds if we go in.

'You after something in particular?'

'A copy of Jane Eyre. I need to finish it.'

'What is it with that book?' is his response. 'My ex had a thing for it too.'

'It's romantic,' I sigh in jest, wandering the shelves and searching for the section covering classical fiction.

He stops, shelves of paperbacks both sides of him. 'She made me watch the movie. It's depressing. Obnoxious dude hires an ugly duckling to educate his daughter, gets the hots for the ugly duckling then it turns out he's hiding his crazy ex in the attic.'

I tap him on his arm. 'Don't ruin it for me!' I exclaim. 'And it's never said expressly said that Adele is Rochester's daughter. She is his ward.'

Oliver raises a dubious eyebrow in my direction, poking his tongue into his cheek. 'You think that if it makes you happy.'

'I like it. I like the story. I identify with Jane. She's lonely. She has to fight to exercise control over the decisions that concern her own life. And I can't believe I'm discussing Jane Eyre with you.'

He laughs at that. I'm still searching when Oliver rounds the shelves, clutching a copy of Bronte's classic tale.

'Let me buy it for you,' he says, holding it up for me to take.

'Of course you can't buy it for me.'

'Go on. Chivalry might be dead, but you can at least let me buy you cheap a slushy novel.'

'Slushy novel indeed,' I repeat, rolling my eyes. 'And it might be cheap, but Charlotte Bronte's words are as beautiful as diamonds. It's easy to forget the value of the written word.'

He smirks. 'You gonna let me buy it for you, or what?'

'If you insist,' I sigh.

Oliver drives me home. Outside the entrance to Gables by The Sea community, I sit in the passenger seat of his car.

'I had fun tonight,' he says.

'Me too,' I say, biting my lip. He's my distraction, but he doesn't know that.

Without warning, he leans forward, stroking my hair with a warm hand. 'Can we do it again sometime?'

I am nodding my head because I genuinely like spending time with him. I want to like him more than I do. I don't want my head filled with thoughts of someone else.

'You're cute, Elle, you know that?' he grins.

He hovers for a moment. It's obvious he wants to kiss me. I hold my position, his leather seat crunching underneath him when he leans forward.

His hand goes to my cheek. I daren't breathe. The pressure of his lips on mine sends a small shiver down my spine, but when my eyes close, Oliver is not the man staring back at me, despite the fact that I want him to be.

He pulls back. For a brief moment, it feels awkward, though in any other world, his end-of-date kiss would have been perfect. 'Thank you for my copy of Jane Eyre,' I smile, and yank the door handle. 'And all those rum cocktails.'

'Get home safe,' he says. 'Be sure to tell Nicky Salco I called him a douchebag.'

'I won't,' I laugh, and get out of the car.

—

The following day Lonzo and I are serving lunch on the veranda in the sun when Sydney decides to bring up my date with Oliver in front of everyone.

'So, Elle, you haven't told me how it went last night,' she hums over a salad starter, at a point when there is a natural lull in the conversation.

My cheeks redden as I pour drinks. Ragnar is speaking to Ben Salco, who's been dropping by the last few days with Libby whilst Nicky isn't in full training mode.

'How what went last night, sweetie?' Libby enquires, looking to me.

I shoot Sydney a look and she grins. 'It was nothing exciting,' I mumble.

'Oh, come on,' Sydney grins. 'Elle had a date yesterday.'

Firstly, I'm aware of Nicky shifting in his seat slightly at the table, but I daren't look his way. Our exchanges since our return to Miami have remained minimal. I'm getting up to cook for him in the night, but, as per Mackenzie and Ragnar's orders, we are not interacting. Nicky has been holed up with a physical therapist, from what I've heard.

'Oh, a date?' Mackenzie croons, as though we are best friends, except nothing could be farther from the truth. A part of me thinks she must be glad. 'You kept that very quiet, Elle.'

'It was nothing, really.'

'Is he from Miami?' she asks. 'How did you meet him?'

'She met him at the beach,' Sydney answers for me.

'The beach? God, he's not a tourist, is he?'

Tag comes to my aid. 'How about we stop embarrassing Elle; it's obvious she doesn't want to talk about it.'

I'm not exactly sure what the status of their current relation-ship is, but I'm picking up on a definite frosty vibe between

Tag and Sydney. Still, I'm grateful to him for shutting down the conversation about my date.

'I'm sorry, Elle, it definitely wasn't my intention to embarrass you,' Sydney chimes in and I offer her a forgiving smile. 'I'm just excited for you. He sounds cute.'

Lunch over, I'm starting work on dinner when out of the corner of my eye, I spy Nicky enter the kitchen alone. I stiffen. Lonzo isn't in the room, though he's due back any second.

Nicky approaches, seemingly with caution. He helps himself to an apple from the fruit bowl right next to the stove top, where I'm frying some sliced onions and peppers in garlic and oil in a pan. He takes a bite into it using his good hand. There's still a bandage on the fingers of his right. Eyes down, I try to concentrate hard on what I'm doing. Nicky lingers, a fraction too close to me, and I feel the intensity of his stare.

'Can we talk?' he asks.

'I'm working,' is my reply.

He eats his apple. I keep my eyes on the pan.

'Who'd you go on a date with?'

My breath catches in my throat. 'Nobody you'd know.'

He edges closer, lowers his voice, avoiding eye contact. 'Did he kiss you at the end of the night?'

I reach for the salt. 'That's not any of your business.'

I hear the sound of air rushing through his nostrils. He glances over his shoulder, checking that no one is within earshot. 'I need to see you.'

The pan sizzles. I still refuse to make eye contact. I raise my chin a fraction. 'Mackenzie and Ragnar have banned me from communicating with you.'

'Not during daylight hours,' he counters, biting again into the apple.

'Mackenzie will fire me if she sees us together.'

'Mac can't fire you. Only I can do that. Besides, I pay you. You're my employee.'

On the one hand, that he confirms my thinking gives me confidence. On the other, that he has reminded me I'm his employee makes what's happened between us that much more improper. He might be the one protecting me, yet at the same time, he's purposefully making this harder for me. 'You see,' I hiss back at him, removing the pan from the stove, 'that makes it more inappropriate... after we... after what's happened between us.'

He shifts his position, leaning closer to my ear. 'I need to be alone with you, Elle. I miss you. I need more of you. Please.'

Heat rushes to my cheeks. Before I can form a response, Lonzo enters from the garden.

'*Acere*,' Lonzo grins at Nicky, '*Qué bola?* How's the *mano*?'

Nicky raises his bandaged fingers. '*Quebrado*,' he says.

'What's *quebrado*?' I ask.

'Broken,' they say in unison.

'I thought it wasn't broken,' I say.

'It's not,' Nicky says. 'Just sounds more impressive than *rasguñada*, which basically means scratched up.'

He shrugs, and I'm quite taken aback by Nicky's knowledge of Spanish.

'Saw your opponent got the shit kicked out of him yesterday,' Lonzo comments, looking to Nicky, the conversation quickly moving on.

'Quarter finals though,' Nicky muses, and I keep my eyes back on my pan. 'Boy did well. Least it wasn't second round. Don't think I could have handled the humiliation.'

Lonzo makes a sound, dismissing Nicky's concerns with a wave of his hand. 'Next year, *'cere*. You'll be back.'

'Nico,' Ragnar barks sharply from the hall, and Nicky rolls his eyes, taking one last bite of his apple before leaving the remaining core on my chopping board.

Later, Lonzo and I drive out to the supermarket. In the car, I talk to Lonzo about increasing Nicky's consumption of superfoods, when he comments on the number of beetroots, broccoli stems, oranges and kiwis I've put into the shopping trolley.

'Sure, we got a juicer,' he tells me. 'Hasn't been used for about a year. Mac went through this phase of juicing as a form of dieting. You know, juice for breakfast…healthy lunch… juice for dinner… she lasted about a week before she asked me to make her a bacon double cheeseburger with all the extras.'

He cackles with laughter in the driving seat and I laugh along with him.

'Nicky's not so keen on beets, far as I know,' Lonzo continues once he's composed himself and honked at the car in front for braking too suddenly. 'Or broccoli. Not even sure he likes kiwis much either.'

'Well, he was drinking them all in Long Island,' I argue. 'And I'm not sure it matters if he likes them or not, it's what they do for his body that counts.'

Lonzo shrugs, offering me a grin. 'You're the boss,' he smiles.

I glower at him. 'Actually, I think you are.'

'But Nicky listens to you. And you've got the knowledge on all this stuff.'

In the kitchen, I run a whole beetroot, two thirds of a broccoli stem, two oranges and a kiwi through the juicer, filling Nicky a tall glass, giving it a stir.

I carry it through the house, with the aim of delivering it in person.

'They're in the gym,' Syd tells me in a whisper, pointing outside and pacing in the living room, her phone glued to her ear.

I know where the gym is, on the far side of the compound. It's not somewhere I've spent any time. In the blazing Florida sun, I carry the glass down the path, past the pool and the hard court, to a small white building near the far outer wall. I linger nervously in the doorway, poking my head inside. The room is full of equipment. Nicky sits with his legs dangling over the side of a massage table, in front of a wall-length mirror with his shirt off, his fingers still bandaged, Tag putting him through some shoulder stretches, making him wince.

I enter, walking over the floor mats. Nicky looks up when he sees me.

'Hey,' he smiles, though his expression collapses into a frown when he sees what I'm holding. 'Oh no.'

Tag looks up and grins.

'That for me?' Nicky asks.

'It is.'

'Got broccoli in it?'

'I'm afraid so.'

He grimaces. Behind me, at the door, Sydney appears out of the blue. 'Tag,' she says in a tone laced with irritation. 'Your phone is going off non-stop in the house.'

Tag lets go of Nicky, looking over. 'Yeah?' he questions.

'It's your *wife*,' Syd adds tersely, then disappears.

Tag puffs out his cheeks, cursing and muttering something incomprehensible in Swedish. He heads for the door, leaving Nicky and I, somewhat unexpectedly, all alone. I come to stand in front of him.

'What's up with her?' he frowns.

'No idea,' I lie with a shrug, holding out the glass.

He eyes it. 'Can I drink it later?'

'No. The orange juice will spoil. Come on. Down the hatch.'

His expression is back to being playful. 'Are you enjoying torturing me?'

'Now that you mention it, a little.'

Nicky takes the glass and necks the contents. When he's finishes, he wipes his mouth and makes out like he's gagging. My lips twist in mock annoyance.

Handing me back the empty glass, I notice that he's missed a tiny purple juice stain on his upper lip. 'You missed a spot,' I say, and without thinking, reach out to wipe it away with my thumb. Nicky's gaze shoots to mine, heated yet tender.

'You didn't answer my question earlier,' he says.

'Which question?' I ask, knowing perfectly well which one he means.

'Did he kiss you? Your date.'

'Why'd you need to know?'

'Because I'm insanely jealous. Why else?'

'Nicky,' I begin, my tone unsure.

'I know. I get it. You're my employee, and I have a fiancée. It's not appropriate. But just so you know… it doesn't make me want you any less. There are some things I need to explain to you—'

He reaches for my free hand, caressing my knuckles with his fingers. Heat pulses through me before there's a sound of footsteps and Tag re-enters the gym. I snatch my hand away, Tag's still muttering under his breath in Swedish.

'All alright?' Nicky asks him as I take a step back.

'Nothing a decent lawyer can't fix,' Tag mumbles, his mouth set in a grim line as he goes back to his position behind Nicky.

'I'll let you two get on,' I say, and I can read from Nicky's pleading look that he doesn't want me to go.

At two a.m. I'm back in the kitchen, cooking undisturbed. I am following Ragnar and Mackenzie's decree that I should stay invisible and not interact with Nicky. Plating everything up, I cover the dish with aluminum foil and leave it out. Checking I've left everything tidy, the dirty dishes I've used piled next to the sink as normal, I return to my room.

I can't sleep. His words have plagued me for the rest of the afternoon and all night: *It doesn't make me want you any less.*

I can't stop fantasizing about what that means.

Sexually speaking, I was a late bloomer, the shy girl at the back of the class who usually ran the other way if a boy even tried to speak to me. I lost my virginity at twenty-one, and Jamie was only my second serious boyfriend. How was I to know Jamie would possess precious little sexual prowess, despite him believing the total opposite? I spent a year of our relationship trying to summon the courage to say what I wanted in the bedroom, only for me to lose confidence when I began to suspect that I was no longer the only woman in his life. After that, it was a matter of feigning interest. That I didn't walk away sooner angers me now, yet that anger melts away to a heady mix of fear and excitement at the idea of Nicky desiring me.

Yet still, I have to remind myself constantly...

Nicky Salco is off-limits.

Chapter Fifteen

I'm sound asleep when I hear the gentle tapping at my door. I bolt upright in the bed, rubbing my eyes, thinking I've imagined it. I check my phone: it's 3.10 a.m. There's a set of sheer lace curtains over the glass-paned entry doors, a spotlight from the garden highlighting a shadow underneath.

Then it happens again. Tap, tap, tap.

My heart races. I know it's him by the height of the shadow. A thrill runs through me, followed by a panic that I'll get found out. I switch on the bedside lamp, throwing back the covers and cross to the door. I peek through the curtains to find Nicky waiting on the other side of the glass.

I slide the key around in the lock, opening the door, allowing him to duck inside. In the semi-darkness, he clicks the door closed behind him. He's wearing sports shorts and a white Miami Dolphins t-shirt, his feet bare. Even without shoes on, he towers over me.

'What are you doing here?' I whisper.

'What the hell was that I just ate?' he says in his normal tone.

'*Shhh!*' I hiss, knowing that Lonzo is asleep in the room next door, in the adjoining pool house. 'Someone will hear you.'

'I said what the hell was that I just ate?' he asks again, this time in a whisper.

I bite my lip and sigh. I had an inkling he might take issue with the dish, but I certainly didn't expect him to turn up in my room in the middle of the night. 'It was quinoa. It was a quinoa salad.'

'No offence, Elle, but I didn't like it.'

'Will you *please* keep your voice down?'

'Sorry. What happened to my Elle would made me the nicest food ever? I'm still hungry after that. And don't tell me quinoa is a superfood.'

'It *is* a superfood.'

'Superfoods can kiss my ass. I'm already chugging that vile juice concoction you keep giving me. I'm a guy. I want steak.'

I cross my arms over my chest. 'I had a feeling you'd complain.'

He grins. 'I've never complained about your food before, have I?'

It's impossible for me not to smile. 'No. Never. Do you want me to make you something else?'

'No. It's fine.'

There's a silence. I've barely seen him for three days. I glance down at the bandages.

'How's the hand?' I ask.

'Getting there.'

Another silence.

'I miss you, Little Bird,' he says tenderly.

I shake my head. 'Don't call me that. Mackenzie will find out you've been in here and I will lose my job.'

'I don't know where you've got this idea from that you're somehow gonna lose your job just by talking to me,' he says, stepping forward and reaching for me. 'And Mac's dead to the world.'

Since the events of Long Island, I've tried to do nothing to provoke him. To invite an interaction. But, as with everything with Nicky, he's not making it easy to resist.

'She's banned me from the garden when I'm not working, did you know that? Practically everywhere but the kitchen.'

He holds up his hands. 'I gotta pick my battles, okay? I had to make some concessions in order to keep you.'

'You're admitting that your fiancée hates me?'

'She doesn't hate you.'

'No, she despises me.'

'She thinks you're… surplus to requirements. Look. Things between Mac and me. It's complicated. There's history you don't know about. We go back a long way. I know things have been weird lately.'

'You punched a mirror. You didn't like losing.'

He takes a step closer, sliding his hands in mine. I stiffen. 'I didn't punch that mirror because I lost the match.'

'No? Then why did you do it?'

He lets out a sigh. 'Losing was a part of it. It was. It was my fault. I didn't play well. They all think that's why I lost my temper and punched that mirror. But there was more to it than that. Mac was berating me over the phone for losing, and all I could think was how fucking trapped I am in this life… with tennis… my relationships… and all the time… my mind keeps going back to you.'

He swallows, his head going back. 'And worse, I come back to Miami and find out you're kissing some other guy and I swear to god, Elle, the thought of it is just killing me.'

He lowers his chin again, his eyes boring into me. My heart is thundering. He really is jealous. And the idea that I have that much power of him makes me feel… good.

'He kissed me. My date. At the end of the night.'

Nicky's lips twist into a grimace.

'Can't blame the guy, I guess,' he whispers stiffly. 'If it was me, I would've done the same.'

'How would you have kissed me?' I ask, feeling daring. 'Mouth or cheek?'

He seems to register the uptick in mood. 'Mouth. Gently. No tongue. Not on a first date. Not if I wanted to see you again. Which I definitely would.'

Maybe it's because this conversation is making me feel warm inside. Maybe it's because he's given me a confidence boost, but I say, 'Show me your first date kiss then.'

Nicky practically beams at me. 'Right now?'

'Right now. I want to know how Nicky Salco kisses a girl at the end of their first date.'

He inhales audibly, as though psyching himself up. 'This is hard to do when I'm having to whisper.'

'Do it anyway.'

'Well, uhh, first I'd tell her... *you*... what a great time I'd had. Then, you know... if you said the same back, I'd probably ask if it would be alright if I kissed you.'

'And if I'd said yes?'

He takes a small step forward, until I can feel the warmth of him, bathed in the light from my nightstand. He looms over me. 'I'd move nice and slow, then put one hand right here...'

He puts his bandaged hand on my cheek, sending bolt of electricity down my spine. With the same hand he raises my chin a fraction. 'Then I'd do this.'

Achingly slowly, he lowers his mouth, and grants me the sweetest, lightest kiss, brushing his lips against mine. Before it's barely even begun, he steps back. It's quicker than Oliver's kiss was. A fraction more chaste.

Nicky smiles, looking embarrassed, wiping a hand around the back of his head. 'How'd I match up? Would you want to see me again after that?'

'Definitely,' I whisper.

The heat between us is undeniable. Yet I sense Nicky is holding back.

'What's his name? Your date,' he asks, looking to the floor.

'Oliver.'

'And do you like this... Oliver?'

'He's nice. And he's available.'

'Well, I hate the sonofabitch,' Nicky says, his volume raised with another grimace.

I squeeze my lips together, stifling a laugh. Nicky smiles, but it seems to mask some kind of misery underneath.

'I should probably go,' he mutters grimly.

I nod. He should. But I wish he didn't have to. I love being alone with him like this.

'Goodnight,' he says and backs away to the door.

When I see his hand go to the door handle, I can't stop myself. 'Nicky, wait—' I blurt out and he turns. I cross the floor in a second, my arms going round his neck as I feel his arms going around me, his mouth capturing mine with a groan in a burning kiss that has no place on a first date. It's a kiss that tells me how much he's missed me. My heart swells with the knowledge as I kiss him back in the shadows, wanting him to know that I've missed him too. Before I know it, he's swept me fully into his arms and is walking me over to my bed, lowering me down, the back of my head resting against his right wrist.

Lying down, his lips explore mine for some time, as though we're making up for lost ground, our tongues sliding together: open-mouthed, intimate, risqué kisses meant for lovers, the kind that precede wild, sensual lovemaking. The kind of kisses Jamie never gave me, or I him. Kisses I didn't think were possible until Nicky Salco came to my room. Liquid heat floods through me, desperate and yearning, and I gasp as the fingers on his left hand slide underneath my top, caressing my stomach, working their way up to my breasts.

Nicky lifts my top, taking one nipple in his mouth, licking and sucking it until it's taut and I'm arching beneath him. With his right hand he caresses the other, the rough fabric of his bandages increasing the friction, my nipple standing to attention as he moves across to devour it with his mouth.

Perhaps rashly, I lift my shoulders, removing my top, allowing him better access. I tug at the cotton of his Dolphins t-shirt and he follows my lead.

He goes back to kissing me, warm skin against warm skin, his bandaged right hand taking an expedition away from my breasts, south past my belly button, skating past the lacy hem of my underwear, sinking down into the curve of my thigh, then up again, cupping the cotton of my knickers between my legs. I don't need to use my fingers to know that the material is already drenched with my own enthusiasm for him. Beside me, through his shorts, I feel his erection twitch. Nicky rubs me through the material and I moan into his mouth.

'Elle,' he rasps. 'Woah.'

'It was all that talk of first date kisses,' I whisper, at the same time trying not to laugh.

'I didn't know I was turning you on so bad,' he grins wolfishly. He uses one finger to hook the hem of my underwear aside, before two fingers slide against my molten, swollen folds, a groan escaping both of our lips. 'Holy shit,' he mutters, caressing me, before he pauses.

'Technically my fingers are out of action, I'm sorry,' he whispers when he raises his head. 'I'm under strict orders. I could use my left hand, but—'

I feel a cold sensation as he removes his hand, replacing the damp cotton material, moving his moist fingers over my thigh. 'It's okay, we don't have to do anything,' I whisper, nerves making my stomach clench.

He looks down at me, his good hand stroking my hair. 'You're kidding me, right? You're doing that British thing again, where you don't say what you want. A woman doesn't get that aroused without needing to come.'

Before Nicky, it was the kind of word I could never utter out loud. He kisses me and it feels like I've been sucked into a sexual haze, where all my inhibitions have melted away. 'I need to come,' I whimper, words those brazen never having escaped my lips before.

'Then let me go down on you,' he breathes, 'Please.'

Mild panic sets in, just the idea of me letting him do just that. 'I... I'm nervous,' I choke out.

He strokes my cheek. 'Tell me what you're scared of. I'm not gonna do it if you're not comfortable with it. I would never.'

'Nicky—'

'Tell me,' he urges me in a whisper.

For a moment, I'm lost for words.

'Earlier today,' he says, his tone low and rough. 'Rag was making me watch some of my past matches. Picking apart my performance on the screen. Telling me what I'd done wrong, all that. And you know what I was thinking of that whole time I was in front of the TV?'

'What?' I ask.

His fingers return to the damp material between my legs. 'My mouth. Right here. Making you say my name.' He applies gentle pressure right where it counts and warm sensations zing up my spine. 'So don't think it's because I don't want to do it, because, believe me, it's all I can think about,' he breathes. 'But you have to want it too.'

'Is that true?' I ask, about his story.

'It is. Couldn't stand up for about ten minutes after. I needed an excuse to see you tonight. Thank the good Lord for *quinoa salad*, huh?'

I let out a giggle.

His hand comes back to my cheek, all serious. 'We could have a system. Tap me twice on the head if you want me to stop, or any time you wanna pause, or if you're not feeling it. I swear to god, I'll stop right away.' He bites his lip. 'It's not just your cooking I want to taste, Elle.'

He's smiling. I relax. After a moment, I nod my head. 'But Lonzo's right next door,' I add.

Nicky seems to ruminate on this fact for a moment. Then he gets to his feet, guiding me upwards from the bed to a standing position. He takes my hand and walks me from behind to my en-suite bathroom, the entrance beside the front door.

Inside, he switches on the light above the mirror cabinet then closes the door behind us. The only thing I can hear is the gentle whirr of the extractor fan.

In a split second, Nicky draws me close and is kissing me deeply, at the same time grasping my hips and guiding me backwards, so that I'm standing against a patch of cold marble wall next to the shower and the toilet. Then he slides his fingers into the waistband of my underwear, gliding my knickers over my bottom and down my thighs, so that once more I'm fully naked in his presence.

'You are too damned beautiful,' he mutters, his gaze roving appreciatively over my body, every fibre inside me tingling.

Once more, his shorts remain firmly still on. Yet I'm so turned on at this moment that I don't pick an argument with him. All I can focus on is what happens next.

Nicky looks around, and tugs a towel off the shower pane. He drops it to the floor, then, to my surprise, he sinks to his knees in front of me, his face almost level with my sex. I feel myself blush. With his bandaged hand, he nudges my thighs apart, and I comply with his wishes, not sure how exactly this will work in practice. I'm barely clinging to rational thought before his lifts his left hand and parts me, sliding two fingers against my wet folds, drawing a gasp as those same two fingers slip all the way inside me, simultaneously working my pleasure spot with his thumb.

'Oh, Jesus, Nicky,' I mumble, my legs trembling. Against his onslaught, my head goes back and my knees buckle.

'Hold onto me if you need to,' he whispers.

My hands slide into his hair. I only partially hear him, and before I know it, he's removed his fingers and is lifting my right leg up, positioning it over his shoulder, so that it's resting down against the powerful, muscular length of his back. I rise up on tiptoe with my other foot on the ground, grabbing a nearby towel rail for support. It allows him greater access. Nicky dips his head further, and the next sensation I feel is his hot tongue licking my wet flesh, sweeping over my folds, and causing a low growl of pleasure to rumble in his throat. I stop breathing for a moment for the shock of the sensation, then have to wildly draw breath.

Nicky pulls back for a moment, his lips glistening. 'You all good?' he asks.

'Don't s-stop,' I manage to choke out, and I think I hear him let out a chuckle, before he claims me again with his tongue, licking me, sucking me, dipping inside of me, tasting me and *holymotherofgod* doing all manner of things that Jamie would never even have considered doing. Nicky's tongue is firm as it pulses against my core, in a perfect rhythm that liquefies me, and I want to stroke his hair but don't want him to misconstrue that with a signal to stop doing what he's doing. So I grip the rail as he moves upwards slightly, finding my clitoris and increasing his pace so that I'm moaning, thrashing the back of my head against the marble and chasing the climax that is already escalating between my thighs.

'Oh, Jesus, Nicky,' I gasp out again and his fingers grip me more tightly. He can tell how close I am to exploding in his mouth and he's giving me exactly what I need, yet he slows his tempo, leaving me suspended, as though floating, straining and desperate for release. My moan tells him how badly I'm chasing it, and, as though obeying my wishes, his tongue returns to its prior rhythm, flicking repeatedly over my pleasure centre, pulsing against my delicate nerve endings until I can't take it anymore, before he sends me over the edge, keeping his tongue in position but sliding his two fingers back inside me, withdrawing and thrusting them gently. The explosion begins and I unravel, feeling myself come against them, the walls of my channel squeezing him in long, slow contractions, ripping his name from my lungs as at the same moment he sends me into orbit with his mouth. With his bandaged hand, Nicky holds me in place whilst I ride out the shattering orgasm he's giving me, my vision blotting, until finally, breathless, I sag back against the wall.

For a moment, neither of us moves. I catch my breath, pressing my palms into the cold marble. Nicky shifts my leg, sliding out from under me and gets to his feet, subtly wiping his mouth before wrapping me in an embrace, holding me whilst my breathing stills, trailing kisses along my neck.

'You taste better than passionfruit cheesecake,' he whispers, pressing his face into my hair, and that draws a laugh from me.

I curl my arms around his shoulders. For a moment we just stand there, holding onto one another. I can feel the extent of his arousal pressing up into my abdomen. I trace my fingers downward, traversing his rib cage, sliding my fingers into his waist band of his sweatpants, perhaps just to see how he'll react.

Gently, he eases away from me, and my fingers are released. 'I should probably be getting back,' he says.

It hits me then. Nicky Salco is emotionally unavailable.

'Of course,' I say tersely, once more going from being in a state of post-orgasmic bliss to acutely aware of my own naked-ness in a nanosecond, bending and swiping up my underwear from the floor. 'I mean, heaven forbid you should want me to touch you.'

Nicky looks embarrassed, one hand going to the back of his head.

'Didn't I just make you—' he starts.

My underwear back on, I cover my breasts with both hands, feeling idiotic. 'Yes, yes, you did,' I huff in an exaggerated whisper. 'And yes, it was probably the best of my life.'

His lips twist into a wry smile at the compliment. 'I don't understand. So, what's the issue?'

'The issue, Nicky, is that I am not your plaything. I'm not your hamster wheel that keeps you amused for ten minutes.'

'Hamster wheel? What are you even talking about?'

If the mood's soured, it's because I'm angry with him. Despite the mind-blowing oral sex, I once again feel dirty once he's lavished his attention on me and now it's all over because I can't reciprocate.

I move one hand between us, back and forth. 'Whatever *this* is, it's starting to feel very one-sided. You seem to be using me for your own gratification.'

He frowns. 'How does that work when I'm not the one having the orgasms?'

'You tell me,' I say. 'You not allowing me to touch you, it still constitutes you cheating on your fiancée. In case you thought it gave you some kind of free pass to do whatever you want. Your mouth and your hands and your *tongue*, they're still cheating, even if other parts of you aren't.'

I look down pointedly at the distinct mound in his shorts. He puffs out his cheeks, as though wordlessly thanking me for the reminder that he's cheating, but also taken aback that I would say such a thing. Well tonight I'm no longer feeling quite so *three-bags-full-Nicky*, even if he did just go down on me and blow my mind.

He shakes his head again. 'You can't ask me to break up with Mac, Elle. Not right now.'

I stare at him, aghast. So that's the truth of it. It has never even occurred to him that he *could* break up with Mackenzie to be with me. Because clearly that's never been his intention, despite our bedroom exploits. 'Congratulations,' I say. 'You just reinforced the case that I *am* just your plaything. Well, for *Mackenzie's* sake, I refuse to be so *compliant* and so *complicit* in whatever this is. It's not fair to her. I'm here to cook, Nicky, not to provide you with sexual entertainment.'

'Elle, that's not how I... is that what you think this is?'

It's hard not to raise my voice, but I'm still able to convey the bitterness I feel right now. 'You should go before Mackenzie realises how long you've been out of bed.'

He's still shaking his head, as though puzzled by my reaction. He backs away, opens the door to the bathroom, then turns and leaves without another word. I hear him walk to the bed, presumably to fetch his t-shirt, before I hear my front door open and click shut behind him.

When he's gone, tears splash down onto my cheeks.

Chapter Sixteen

In the morning, on the Friday, I ask Lonzo if I can go on an outing to stock up on produce again. He's more than happy to drive me, so we throw together a lunch of cheese, cold cuts and leftovers for the house, and take Nicky's 4x4, with storage containers for fish and meat in the back. For the duration of the morning, Lonzo takes me on a tour of some of his more specialist suppliers, and then on to Miami's Little Havana, where over a lunch made up of traditional Cuban dishes, he introduces me to his cousin, Ramón.

'Ramón owns a café that only makes dessert,' he says in the car as we park in the Cuban neighbourhood. 'He couldn't get the capital together so we asked Nicky to invest.'

'Wait, so Nicky's the part owner?'

'Nah, he just gave Ramón the cash on the condition that he got free food for life.'

'Nicky's all about dessert,' I chuckle.

'Right?' Lonzo laughs, switching off the engine. 'That passionfruit cheesecake you made him was a real hit.'

And you have no idea what it started; I think to myself.

Ramón is the spitting image of his cousin, except Ramón has a bigger, rounder belly. His family welcomes me with open arms. As chefs, we spend an unsurprising amount of time reeling off our favourite desserts and talking about food, Lonzo sweetly singing my praises when it comes to my cheesecake. Ramón even asks me to send him the recipe.

I feel nervous when Lonzo pulls the car back into Nicky's driveway. The place is oddly quiet, no one on the courts.

We're in the kitchen, unloading, when Sydney appears. 'No dinner required tonight, guys, you can take the night off, Elle,' she announces.

'How come?' I ask.

'Nicky and Mac are last minute gala guests; Rag got invited to some art show in Brickell and Tag's out with a friend.'

Lonzo disappears inside the pantry with his arms full.

'Tag's out with a *friend*?' I query.

'He's taking me to dinner,' she whispers gleefully, swinging her hips and performing a little dance move.

I grin. 'I didn't know if things were good between the pair of you or not.'

'We had a little fight. His wife's been calling, giving him shit. Now it seems he just wants her to sign the divorce papers so we can all get on with our lives. Dinner is his way of apologizing to me... And *hopefully* he's taking me to more places than that.' She gives me an exaggerated wink. Lonzo reappears just as we burst into fits of girlish giggles.

'Whatever it is, I'm closin' my ears,' Lonzo says, picking up more food.

I don't ask any more about the gala. I didn't sleep much after Nicky left my room last night, worrying about everything I'd said. I'm desperate to speak to him again.

'Do I still need to get up for Nicky tonight do you think?' I ask Syd.

'They'll be back late. Girl, I got zero idea.'

Around six that evening, I'm in my room with the TV on when Sydney pokes her head around my door.

'Hey. Y'all got five minutes for a quick meeting?'

I pick up the remote control and switch the screen to mute. 'Sure. I thought you and Tag were off out?'

Sydney puts a single finger to her lips. 'We're leaving separately and rendezvousing at the restaurant.'

'Romantic! You know, I still think Rag and Nicky would support you guys. If you told them.'

She sighs. 'I know, they probably would. But Tag is freaky about it, so I'm not gonna be the one to come clean.'

I get up off the bed, pushing my bare feet into my shoes. 'What's the meeting about?'

'Tennis.'

I roll my eyes playfully. 'What else?'

'A booking fell through; I gotta tee something else up asap.'

In the main living area of the house, I enter to find Ragnar standing like an army general, feet slightly apart, dressed in a smart suit, his hands behind his back, looking impatient. Tag is sitting down on the sofa wearing jeans and a striped shirt open at the collar, with his legs crossed at the ankles. Lonzo has gone home to Little Havana for the weekend.

'Where's Nicky?' Syd asks as she walks in behind me.

'Upstairs, still getting ready,' Tag replies.

I take a seat next to Tag. Ragnar looks at his watch, clicking his tongue.

'You're looking very dapper, Ragnar,' I say to him and he grants me a smile.

'Thank you, Elle. Though it will all be for nothing if I am late.'

I hear footsteps on the stairs outside in the hallway.

'He's coming,' Sydney says.

When I see him, it takes a moment for me to realise that my mouth has fallen open. Nicky is wearing a dinner jacket over a white dress shirt, elegant suit trousers and a pair of shiny black shoes. His collar is pulled up and a loose bow tie hangs from his fingers. When he enters, Tag gives a mock wolf whistle.

Nicky shakes his head with a grin.

'Lookin' fly *Señor* Salco!' Sydney exclaims, looking him over. 'Nice tux.'

'Mac picked it out. This is a rare occasion that I wear a goddamned outfit like this.'

I squeeze my hands between my thighs, keeping my gaze on the floor, sneaking glances at him from under my eyelashes.

He doesn't look my way. Nicky Salco in a dinner jacket is devastatingly handsome. For the first time since last night, I regret the way I spoke to him.

'Sydney, my Uber is coming in five minutes,' Ragnar states, checking his phone.

'Okay, I'll make this quick. So, Shanghai Masters, the house I booked six months ago has fallen through. Some kind of flood situation. I can't get anything else decent, not at this late stage, the Rose Garden Resort near the venue can do us a deal, and the ATP is encouraging all players to stay at official tournament hotels. I explained the situation; the hotel can provide you with a personal chef for the nights. It just means there's no point in Elle going with you, not all the way to Asia anyway.'

I look up, feeling everyone's eyes on me, except Nicky's.

Nicky shakes his head, rubbing his forehead. 'What about Tokyo?'

'For the Japan Open, we had that hotel booked anyway, remember? Because the houses were all too far away from the venue. I mean, if you want, I can find a space for Elle—'

'Fine, fine, Elle can stay here,' Nicky says. 'Last year the sashimi was amazing. I'll just eat that.'

'And what about Paris? Do you want Elle coming to the Paris Masters?'

Nicky sighs heavily, as though he doesn't want to be talking about this now. I want to talk to him before he makes any decisions. I hate that I left things unresolved with him. 'Come on, Syd,' he groans, 'I don't know.'

'We have a house booked for Paris but they want final confirmation otherwise we can't get a refund.'

Nicky closes his eyes. I'm not sure if it's because of what I said to him last night, but he mutters, 'Just cancel the house in Paris. Take the hotel and make sure they provide someone.'

Sydney turns to me. 'Is that okay with you, Elle? It just means you won't have so much to do. Mac will still be here, so you can assist Lonzo.'

'How long will you all be gone for?' I ask.

'Depends,' Sydney shrugs. 'If all goes well, we'd be back early November.'

My throat constricts at the thought of Nicky being away for nigh on six weeks. 'Of course. I'm happy to stay here.'

'Sydney, my Uber is here,' Ragnar pipes up.

'We're done,' Syd replies, clapping her hands together, and Ragnar bids us all a good night.

When Rag has gone, Nicky dangles his bow tie from one finger. He looks to Tag. 'You know how to fasten one of these things?' he asks.

Tag frowns and shakes his head. 'The one I have is on elastic. You just button it at the back.'

'Mac doesn't know how to tie it either. I don't know why she got me one. Syd? You know how to tie one of these things?'

'No,' she laughs, already typing into her phone. 'You're on your own with that one.'

I wait to be asked, but he doesn't ask me. When he finally looks my way with questioning eyes, I get to my feet, walking over to him. 'Here,' I say, sliding the bow tie from his grasp, smoothing it out with my fingers. Normally, if we're standing in this position, facing one another in close proximity, it's because he's kissing me.

'You know how to do this thing?' he asks me, his face so close to mine that I'm scared of how it looks to others. His arms remain at his sides. My fingers tremble as I draw the material around his upturned collar.

'You need to fasten your top button,' I instruct him, as he does as he's told.

'Not gonna strangle me with it, are you?' he mutters, so no one else can hear. Tag is on his feet and Syd is now making a phone call.

'No,' I swallow, the air between us feeling too thick.

I begin to tie the tie. 'In the bistro where I worked before, we used to have these James Bond theme nights,' I tell him, in an effort to dismiss any kind of atmosphere. 'All the waiters would be wearing dinner jackets and carry silver platters with martinis on them. I used to have to help them all with their ties. I learned how to tie one by watching YouTube.'

A smile tugs on one side of his lips. 'Yet again, their loss is my gain,' he says in a low tone.

I know that Nicky has one week left of training in Miami. It actually hurts me to know now that I won't accompany the group to Asia and Paris Masters. Standing there, fixing his tie, it feels for a moment like he's all mine, like I'm the steady girlfriend, the fiancée. When I raise my eyes to his, I know that this electricity between us is genuine. I sense the heat of his stare, images of last night flashing through my brain. When I'm finished, I fold down his collar, resisting the urge to slide my fingers down the front of his dress shirt. I want to know what he's feeling.

I check my handiwork. My heart in my throat, I stand back. I can hear Mackenzie coming down the stairs.

'Looks good,' Tag says from behind me.

'Thanks,' Nicky says, pressing his fingertips to the tie, his gaze locking with mine for one last fleeting moment.

Mackenzie sweeps into the room in a stunning emerald green evening gown, paired with a silver pair of towering, strappy high heels, her blonde hair elegantly styled in a side chignon, with impeccable nails and immaculate make-up.

Sydney gasps in dramatic fashion. 'Make way for my Queeeen!' she trills.

Mackenzie gives a twirl. 'Oh, Syd, you're a honey. In case you didn't notice, I haven't eaten in like a month. I suspected they would ask us last minute.'

'You look beautiful,' I say, through the lump that's blocking my throat, thinking if her waist gets any thinner, she might snap in half.

'Thank you. Oh, sweetie, your tie is done!'

'Elle did it,' Nicky deadpans.

Mackenzie's smile evaporates. She pauses, cocking her head in my direction. 'My, my, aren't we full of surprises,' she adds drily, and somewhere in my head I hear a cat yowl. 'Can you do something else for me, Elle?'

'Sure, no problem.'

'I'm going to New York next week for three nights. Can you let Lonzo know for the catering?'

'Which nights?'

'Away Tuesday through Friday.'

'Of course, I'll tell him.'

'You didn't tell me you were going to New York,' Nicky cuts in.

'Potential big European deal came up. Just received the email. I'll need some preparation time with the team before Thursday's pitch.'

'We fly to China a week Sunday,' Nicky says.

She puts one hand on his arm. Jealousy explodes in my chest, but I hold it in. I have no choice but to hold it in.

I want her life. I want her fiancé.

I squeeze my lips together, biting my teeth into my own flesh, the resulting pain reminding me that he's not mine, and never will be.

'Then we'll have the Sunday, hon,' Mackenzie says to Nicky, planting a kiss on his cheek as she tucks her arm under his, guiding him towards the door. 'Come on, we need to get going.'

I forget to ask Nicky if he wants me to cook for him in the night. I do anyway, my brain fuggy with sleep, but I don't hear anyone come back. On Saturday morning, the once tasty-looking dish of pan-fried mackerel in a tamarind sauce with fresh egg noodles and sliced spring onions is now congealed in the oven. I remove the plate, scraping the contents into the food waste bin, thinking of hungry, poverty-stricken children and wondering why I even bothered. I puff out my cheeks, glancing out at the sun shining on a pristine swimming pool that I'm not allowed to use, and question why I even took this job in the first place. Because only an idiot would have said yes to a gig like this. Except I'm double the idiot because I fell for my boss, who isn't even available.

I return to my room to find two separate messages on my phone.

The first is from my sister, Josie, and is a reply to my message from the night before, telling her that Nicky was going to Asia, but I wasn't accompanying him and would she come and visit me in Miami. It reads, *Er, yes?! Send me the dates and I'll book a flight asap x*

The second, from Oliver, reads, *Wanna hang today?*

After lunch over cheeseburgers in Five Guys, Oliver buys me an iced coffee and we walk north from South Beach, parallel with the ocean. Outside, it's twenty-eight degrees. Technically, as it's Saturday, I'm meant to be working, and Syd mentioned to me before departing for her date with Tag that today was also Nicky's first full day of proper training after damaging his hand in Long Island. Therefore, in preparation, I spent my morning baking a dish of minced beef cannelloni with creamy tomato béchamel sauce, to be served alongside an Italian arugula Parmesan salad with sun-dried tomatoes and figs, leaving the former warming in the oven, ready to be devoured by three hungry men, and Mackenzie, provided she can get past the fact that the key ingredient in cannelloni is a complex carbohydrate.

Walking down Sunset Boulevard with Oliver is really the first time I've witnessed the lavish architecture in Miami, and I adore the Art Deco style of the buildings. We stop at the museum to mooch. Conversations with him are easy. He talks about his job helping to manage his father's boutique hotel business, and I hear about his upbringing, in an upmarket area of town, and how generations of Davenports have lived and worked in this city.

I let him talk, asking a few questions here and there. I know he can tell I'm distracted. By the time we reach the North Shore beach, the sun dipping a fraction in the sky, the heat notionally less oppressive, he suggests that we rest on the sand.

'I had this whole big plan to ask you out on another date today,' he says suddenly, hugging his knees, squinting at me.

I smile at him. 'You did?'

He sucks air through gritted teeth, then looks to his fingernails. 'This is the part where you tell me you're not that into me.'

My mouth falls open and I find myself looking at the grains of sand between my knees.

'It's okay, you can be honest,' he adds.

I pause. He's bathed in hazy, late afternoon sunlight, the sound of the seagulls squawking overhead. Oliver Davenport is unbelievably good-looking, considerate, kind, and a gentleman to boot. He's the perfect catch.

'I like you a lot,' I say. 'I'm attracted to you.'

'You are?'

'Who wouldn't be? Look at you. You're gorgeous.'

His lips twist in grim acceptance. 'So, what gives? Why do I get the feeling I don't have a shot with you?'

I look out to the ocean. It's beautiful here but somehow, I don't feel present, like I can't appreciate it because I feel dragged down with the weight of longing. And I hate myself for that.

'You know what I realised about today?' Oliver says when I say nothing.

'What?'

'That we haven't talked about Nicky Salco. Not even one mention.'

I push my toes deeper into the sand, where it's cooler. Even the mention of his name sends me on a downward spiral. 'What if I don't want to talk about Nicky Salco?'

'I mean, you know I think the guy's a total douche, but just now you let me talk about everything. You're a good listener, Elle, but every time I try to turn the conversation around, you turn it back to me.'

It takes me a moment to respond. 'Nicky Salco is a dull and turgid topic of conversation,' I state emphatically.

That gets me a laugh, before he adds, 'Come on, what d'you really think of him?'

I go silent. I have no idea what to say.

'This isn't one of those clichés, is it, where you say you've fallen for him?' he asks.

'Because that would be really stupid,' I scoff.

'I mean, looks-wise, I get it. A lot of ladies seem to get it, but when it comes to personality, I hate to be the one to say I thought more highly of you than that, Elle.'

I'm still lost for words.

He winces. 'How bad is it?'

Tears sting the corners of my eyes. 'It's bad.'

'Like, bad, as in, it's just a little crush? Does he know?'

My shoulders droop. I pick up a handful of sand, letting fine grains run through my fingers. I picture Nicky in my bathroom, and I'm naked.

Oliver shakes his head. 'I'm sorry; it's none of my business.'

'No, no, I'm the one who should be sorry. I don't have anyone I can talk to about what's been going on.' I keep my eyes on the sand. 'And things have been going on.'

It's Oliver's turn to remain silent. Perhaps because I'm being ambiguous.

'I know you don't like him. I know I'm stupid to get involved. I wish I didn't feel the way I do about him, but I do. So, I could leave... before I'm in too deep... but I don't want to leave. I have nothing to go back to. No job. Nowhere to live. I like it here in Miami.'

'He's got a fiancée,' Oliver says, running his teeth along his bottom lip. 'What you're doing is technically an affair.'

I swallow the brittle lump in my throat. 'I know that.'

Oliver gives a shrug. 'Like father, like son, I guess. One day he'll end things. And he'll break your heart in the process. If you stay.'

'I know that,' I whisper again.

I force a smile. Oliver leans closer to me and rubs my arm. 'Wanna go get ice cream? Or get wasted. You choose, either way, it's my shout.'

Chapter Seventeen

Oliver pays for my Uber back to Nicky's House. I feel like a prize idiot for rejecting such a nice guy, but I feel a weight has lifted, having told someone my secret. As I slip through the gate, I spy Nicky and Mackenzie sat at the table on the veranda, the sun causing long shadows to stretch across the garden. As I approach, I see Nicky has three tennis rackets piled up on the table surface, one in his hand, and is diligently wrapping new tape around the handle, his focus purely on what's he's doing. Mackenzie sits with her back half to him, a cocktail in front of her on the table, hugging her knees, and before either of them notices me I watch as she puffs out her cheeks, knocking back another mouthful of drink out of boredom.

'Hi,' I say, and both their eyes shoot up. Only Nicky offers me a smile.

'Hey, Elle,' he says, though I detect a faint note of trepidation in his tone.

'I won't bother you,' I say, approaching the table, Mackenzie giving me her usual contemptuous once over, so blatant now that it doesn't even bother me. 'I just wanted to ask whether it would be alright for my sister to come and visit me whilst Nicky is away.'

Mackenzie glowers. Sydney advised me to ask Nicky in Mackenzie's presence, so there was no chance that her ladyship could turn down my request.

'Of course,' Nicky says, cheerfully. 'You didn't even need to ask.'

'This is our house, Nicky, Elle's asking out of *respect*,' Mackenzie responds, masking her irritation by taking a drink. 'Elle, we'd be delighted to have your sister come stay. What's her name?'

'Josie. She lives in Spain. Barcelona.'

'Lucky girl,' Mackenzie croons. That she's being all pally with me I now find doubly irritating.

'Thank you. I'll confirm the dates when I know them. Have a nice evening.'

I turn to walk away to my pool house.

'Oh, Elle,—' I hear Mackenzie's shrill voice cut through the air behind me.

I turn back, the sun in my eyes. 'Yes?'

'Tomorrow morning. I'm thinking a romantic breakfast for two. Right here, for me and Nicky. Seeing as I'm going away this week and then Nicky's away a while. I'm thinking... waffles, pancakes, fresh fruit, pastries... maybe some eggs? Whatever you can throw together.'

'Mac, what the fuck?' Nicky interrupts her abruptly. 'Elle doesn't work Sundays.'

'Nicky,' Mackenzie breathes, her tone seductive, teasing. 'Baby, does it always have to be about the tennis? I'm not gonna see you. Elle's gonna have much less on her plate for the next six weeks. I'm sure she won't object to one itty bitty breakfast. You don't object, do you, Elle?'

I swallow the lump that has formed in my throat, just as Nicky's shaking his head. 'Of course not,' I manage. 'One romantic breakfast for two. Tomorrow morning. I'll have it ready for nine.'

At one a.m. on the Sunday, I'm awake again, walking along the path from my pool house to the kitchen, when I spy Nicky, sitting alone on the edge of the pool with the underwater lights on, his feet dangling into the water.

'Elle?' he says, his head turned towards me, arms by his sides.

'I was just going to make you something,' I say stiffly. My anger at him is irrational, because I want to feel for Oliver what

164

I do for him – yet I don't – and being here is starting to feel like a brutally emotional rollercoaster ride.

'Where were you today?' he asks.

'Over in Miami Beach.'

'Oh. Was that with—'

'With Oliver, yes.'

'Right.'

He turns his head back around. I stand there in semi-darkness, staring at his back.

'Are you hungry or not?' I ask him.

'Will you sit with me a minute?'

'Am I cooking or am I not cooking?'

'I'm not all that hungry.'

'Fine.'

I walk over to the pool, lowering myself down and sitting cross-legged, blowing out my cheeks in an exaggerated fashion, making sure I sit some metres from him. Nicky clocks the distance and rubs his eyes with his fingers.

'What is it?' I ask.

He looks across at me. In the light from the pool, his expression is pained. For some moments, he says nothing.

'I keep trying to convince myself that I should fire you,' he finally says at length.

I stiffen. My mouth falls open. Once more, I'm lost for words.

'I don't want to. But I probably should. It's probably for the best.'

I bite my lip, feeling tears surging again. I swallow them back. 'Then do it,' I dare him, thinking that it might end my agony.

His head goes back, his mouth open. It is some moments before he speaks.

'This house,' he says, 'this pool, this garden, that tennis court... that gym. I would have none of this without Mac's father. I sometimes tell people that this is the house that Mikhail Scheffler built.'

'I don't understand.'

He looks across at me. 'My parents gave up everything for me to play tennis. Every last drop of money they had, they spent it on me. When I was fourteen, my father lost his job. He couldn't pay the mortgage on our house, and he was so depressed he started cheating behind my mom's back. Their marriage almost imploded and we were out on the streets.'

He moves his feet, sending ripples out across the surface of the swimming pool. 'Mac was my first girlfriend; I was on a sports scholarship to her private school. When Mikhail found out about our situation, he paid my parents' mortgage in full, and he pledged to sponsor my pro career. He paid for my first ever coach, he paid for my parents to go to couples' therapy, he even gave my father a job in his company. He saved us. And he believed in me. I would be nowhere if it wasn't for him giving me that support when I needed it most. I would never have won the Australian Open without it.'

He pauses before he adds, 'I had to find some way to repay his investment.'

There's a tightness in my chest. 'By marrying his daughter?'

Another pause. 'I loved Mac once.'

'But do you love her now?'

He doesn't answer. Part of me doesn't want to know, because if he does, I don't see it. I see a spoiled, entitled bitch who keeps Nicky as a trophy to suit her extravagant lifestyle.

'I know I'm not obligated to marry Mac. But I owe it to her *and* her father.'

I nod my head in understanding at his meaning. Though I don't understand marrying anyone if it's not for love. 'Then I have a solution,' I say.

'Don't say it involves you leaving.'

'Nicky, I *have* to—'

'No,' he says, shaking his head.

'How can I possibly stay?'

'I'll work it out. In my head, I'll work it out. Stay a little longer. Please. Then I'll come back and we can talk. Please don't go anywhere.'

I say nothing, instead getting to my feet. I tell myself that life will be easier if I remain angry with him. 'If you're not eating then I'm going back to bed,' I declare.

'Elle,' he says when I start walking, and I turn to face him.

'Nicky, I'm tired.'

He keeps talking, like he doesn't care who hears him. 'I've tried to tell myself it's the right thing to do. To cut you out of my life. Ever since you walked in, I... haven't been able to think straight. The other night, when you accused me of using you... of all this being one-sided... Elle, I don't think you understand that... I'm not allowing you to touch me because the moment you do, I will lose it. I will lose myself in you. And I won't be able to stop.'

I stare at him, hardly believing the words that have come out of his mouth.

'Please,' Nicky continues. 'Don't make this breakfast in the morning. I'll square it away with Mac.'

If I don't make them their 'romantic' breakfast, I consider that Mackenzie might suspect something. Or she'll use it as ammunition against me. If Nicky is never going to be mine, I have to find ways to accept that I must give him up.

'I have to,' I whisper, and I walk away.

On Sunday morning, at eight a.m. I lay the table for two on the veranda, using a tablecloth and pristine white plates. I seek out red hibiscus flowers from the garden, and place them in the tops of two clean, empty glasses. I find actual rose petals and sprinkle them where I can find space. I juice a dozen oranges and make a fruit salad. I even craft a little handwritten menu. Using the lever, I wind up the parasol.

It's the best fucking romantic breakfast for two I can produce.

When Nicky appears, he looks glum. Mackenzie, on the other hand – possibly for the first time since I arrived in Miami – looks in good spirits.

'I will please have a whites-only omelette with finely-sliced zucchini and a dash of onion and Monterey Jack cheese,' Mackenzie orders as I pour them both their freshly-squeezed orange juice.

'I'll have the eggs Benedict,' Nicky mumbles under his breath.

'Coming right up,' I say, injecting an extra dose of cheerfulness into my tone.

Once I've served their orders, I leave them alone.

In the kitchen, I escape to the pantry, and have to wait there in the dim light until I can swallow my tears, and stop myself from trembling.

Chapter Eighteen

On Tuesday morning, I watch Nicky loading Mackenzie's suitcase into the back of a cab in the driveway, through the long kitchen windows. I watch him put his arms around her, and as she raises herself up on tiptoe, leaning in to receive his goodbye kiss. It makes me crave the softness of his lips on mine.

'All okay there?' Lonzo asks me from the other side of the kitchen island. 'Those onions not gonna peel themselves, *cariña*.'

I feel myself go bright red, almost tossing a half-peeled onion in the air.

'Sorry,' I say, clearing my throat, hearing the cab pull out of the driveway behind me.

Lonzo lifts his chin towards Nicky, standing and watching the vehicle leave. 'You think they'll last?'

'What do you mean?'

'Mac and Nicky. You think they'll go the distance? Once they get married?'

'Why wouldn't they?'

'I dunno,' Lonzo muses, rinsing some vegetables under the sink tap. 'She can be a princess, you know? She got that entitled thing goin' on. If you take away the tennis, Nicky's a pretty low-key guy.'

'I guess it all boils down to how much they love each other,' I say, sounding more bitter than I had intended.

Lonzo thrusts out his bottom lip. 'She don't look after him.'

I glower at the Cuban chef. 'Oh, because that's a woman's job. To look after the men.'

'*Mi mamá*, god rest her soul, woulda said *men ain't no good at looking after theirselves*. Except she didn't speak no English.'

I smile at Lonzo, rolling my eyes in a playful way, and glance out of the window again. Nicky has gone.

Later, I go outside to the courts. Syd is on the bench, on her phone, but Nicky and Tag are trying to outdo one another in base line rallies. Ragnar is nowhere to be seen.

Sydney hangs up and beckons me over. There's not a cloud in the sky today.

'You've potentially got a whole month or more without having to get up in the night, or in the morning,' Syd grins. 'How does it feel?'

'I think… *weird* more than anything else?' I say as I take a seat next to her, watching Nicky race to the back of the court for a lob and cursing when he misses it, crashing into the fence instead, Tag bursting into laughter. Both men are drenched in sweat. 'I'll probably wake up in the night thinking I have to make something.'

We watch Nicky and Tag in the rally, Tag giving Nicky pointers and Nicky swearing back at him. The balls are hit harder and faster as Tag makes Nicky work the width and breadth of the court. Every time he or Tag hits a ball they let out a masculine sounding grunt, the kind of sound that's almost carnal… animalistic…, the kind of sound a man might make when he –

'God, it's so sexual, isn't it?' Syd giggles under her breath, as though reading my mind. 'We say it every time, but it's true.'

We carry on listening, a smile on both our lips.

'And is Tag still… *impressing* in that area?' I ask.

'Giiiirrl, these noises… they're like the appetizer. I get the main course. My man is *vor-a-cious*.'

I'm giggling as I say, 'And does anyone know he's your man yet? I mean, apart from me?'

Her shoulders slump. She rolls her eyes. 'We're still working on that part.'

'I'll miss having you here,' I say, because I dread the thought of being left with Mackenzie.

Her phone rings in her lap and she blows me a kiss before she answers. I watch Nicky on court and Syd's conversation fades into the background. Nicky is still panting and grunting, wiping his forehead whenever there is a break in play. I know he wants me to stay, but staying means spending my days longing for contact with him, not just exchanging a few words in the middle of the night. I'm not sure how much more of this agony I can take. I want him; I can't have him, it's a simple enough dilemma. I've never felt this need with anyone before now. I look at him and I feel lust, but it's more than that. I want to feel loved by him too.

I know the solution is to leave. But he's captured me, and I'm grounded.

At 1.30 a.m., I'm in the kitchen when I hear footsteps coming from upstairs. Nicky enters barefoot, wearing sport shorts and a dusky grey fitted T-shirt. He grins at me all the way from the hallway, and my heart explodes at the sight, like somebody put it in a mincer, though my face gives nothing away.

'You're early,' I breathe stoically. 'Nothing's ready.'

He pulls out a bar stool from the kitchen island. 'Do you mind if I watch you work? What's for second dinner?'

I push the hair from my face. 'Uhh... braised duck with shallots and porcini mushrooms on a bed of polenta. Usually, I would prep everything before I go to bed but I was on the phone to my sister this afternoon and Lonzo wanted me to help with dinner... so, everything went out of the window today. You guys are so rigid with your training. You never seem to have that problem.'

'Sure, I do. Look at today. Couldn't hit a ball straight.'

'You look like you were trying hard enough.'

'Trying is not the same as doing. Much in the same way as I am *trying* not to be attracted to you.'

It's like he's pulled a pin and lobbed a grenade. After our exchange at the pool last night, he seemed to be mulling over the idea of sacking me, if only to get me away from his presence. Tonight's admission appears to confirm that he's done wrestling, and wants us to carry on down the road we've been walking for a more than a few weeks now. My eyes flit up from where I'm slicing the shallots on the chopping board. He doesn't avert his gaze, just watches me from where he's sitting.

'I think it would be easier if we didn't spend time together,' I state at length.

He keeps his gaze fixed on me. 'Are you saying that because you want to, or because you think it's the right thing to say?' he asks me.

I look down at my knife. 'It's not about saying the right thing. If I don't leave—'

'If you don't leave, then what?'

'You know what. Eventually...' My heart begins to thud. 'It's like you said last night,' I swallow. 'We won't be able to stop.'

His eyes go to mine. 'What if I don't want to stop?' he says.

My breaths come in small, shallow gasps. I put down my knife, nodding my head slightly, trying to say something but the words won't come. A second later, Nick gets up off the bar stool, walks around to my side of the kitchen island and wrenches me into his arms.

We clash together with messy, frantic, desperate kisses. We paw at one another hungrily, tongues tangling, palms groping, my mind spinning out of control with an indescribable onslaught of wild sensations. My core turns to liquid. Nicky thrusts the chopping board, the knife, and all the food out of the way and they clatter. He lifts me onto the flat surface, positioning himself between my open thighs. He immediately slows our kisses down, sliding his palms up from my knees, caressing me, brushing against my skin with his fingertips, sliding his hands around my waist. When his lips go to my neck, I whisper, 'Somebody could see.'

He draws away, cupping my face with both hands. 'Mac's gone. There's no one else in this house.'

He follows my gaze as I turn my head to the large bank of kitchen windows that look out to the garden in complete darkness, the only thing visible the lamps inside the surrounding hedges and the underwater lights of the pool.

'Come with me,' he whispers.

He eases me off the kitchen island, his hands sliding up the backs of my thighs as he does so. Taking my hand, he leads me from the kitchen, through the darkness of the entrance hallway and through to the living room area. We pass a long, formal, dining room table, which I've never seen used, as mostly everyone eats outside on the veranda, or in the kitchen. On the back wall is a door I've never walked through. Nicky opens it, guiding me out in to a small corridor, then opens a second door and still holding onto my hand, leads me inside. The room is almost pitch black, cooler than the rest of the house. Letting go of me, he walks a few paces then switches on a light.

I'm in a bedroom. The blinds are down. In front of me is a vast four-poster bed, with a high mattress covered with a cream throw. On the floor is an expensive looking faux-sheepskin rug, beyond it, in the shadows, an equally enormous desk, a low table with two chairs, and a tall cylinder vase containing some kind of artificial grass. The poster-sized picture on the wall is a photograph of Nicky as a young man, winning the Australian Open.

'I didn't even know this was here,' I whisper.

'It's where my parents stay when they come over. Tag's pool house is just beyond that window so we still have to keep our voices down.'

I go to the blind, pulling it aside and glance out. I can just about make out the white building at the back of the garden in the darkness, all the lights off.

Nicky pulls me back, grips my hands, planting a kiss on my forehead. 'Wait here,' he says. 'I'll be right back.'

He exits the room, turning left, leaving my heart fluttering in my chest. There's only one reason he's brought me to a bedroom. Every nerve in my body is on fire, a delicious tingling sensation making my skin prickle, my core beginning to throb. I will him to come back. I move to the sheepskin rug, feeling the soft hairs bristle between my toes.

When he returns, he closes the door behind him, sliding the key in the lock. He turns to face me, a small, square box of condoms clasped between his fingers. He drops it on the edge of the bed.

I am trembling as we face one another, something straining inside me. Normally I'm a passive person, but tonight, all my reservations are banished, and I need him to know that I want him. Crossing my arms over my waist, I lift my t-shirt over my head, unclasping my bra, allowing them both to drop at my feet. Holding my breath, I slide my fingers down to my shorts, nudging them at the waistband, pushing them over my hips and they fall to the floor. I step out of them, kicking the material away, and everything is gone, my chest rising and falling with nerves, all the while Nicky edging closer to me, his eyes roving over my naked body, seemingly captivated by the sight.

'I only brought you here to show you my trophy collection,' he smiles.

I purposefully cross my hands over my breasts, my lips twisting. 'Oh,' I say, tilting my head. 'For some reason I thought you were coming onto me.'

He stops in front of me, reaching up and untangling my arms. As I watch, he yanks his t-shirt over his head, tossing it at the wall, before dropping his shorts and sending them in the same direction. He stands before me, as naked as I am, and visibly aroused.

'I'm all yours,' he says softly, looking into my eyes. 'Touch me wherever you like.'

I raise my eyebrows at the nature of his invitation. The thought thrills me. *Finally.*

I feel wicked. 'Put your hands behind your back,' I instruct him.

For a moment, he frowns, but then his lips twitch. He obeys, his feet slightly apart.

'You're not allowed to touch me,' I say. 'Not until I say.'

I take a step forward, not so we make contact, but close enough that I can feel the heat emanating from his body. I reach out, tracing one finger across his torso, gaining confidence as I explore, before flattening my palm against the contours of his warm skin. He breathes out, flexing his muscles, making his already sculpted abdominals more pronounced.

'Are you trying to impress me?' I ask.

He's struggling not to smile. 'Is it working?'

I first explore his chest, then his shoulders, down his solid biceps, all the way to his fingertips before moving to his behind, sliding over his smooth lines. I then skate my fingers past his belly button, down the line of hair that runs south. Teasing him feels delicious.

'Do you want to touch me?' I ask.

'Very much so,' he chokes out.

I slide my fingers gently around the length of his swollen erection. He shudders as I do so, drawing a sharp breath as I stroke the tip. 'And what if I said you can't?'

I stroke him for a second time. He sighs, bows his head. 'It would be torture. It *is* torture. Can I please touch you?'

I move closer, so that we're skin to skin, and I keep one hand wrapped around his length between us. 'Definitely not.'

Nicky swallows, powerless, hands still clasped behind his back. 'Is this payback?' he asks with a smile.

'I like to call it sweet revenge,' I smile, sliding my hand up and down whilst simultaneously leaning up on my tip toes, my lips hovering over his, holding onto his shoulder with my left hand. I kiss him and he eagerly returns it, yet I pull back.

'*Now* do you want to touch me?' I ask, the words dancing on my lips and Nicky grins at my teasing him.

'Very, *very* badly,' he whispers.

'That's a shame,' I pout and he bites his lip.

'How much longer?' he asks, his tone gravelly. 'You're killing me, Elle. Please.'

I let him go, snaking both my hands around his neck, rising up on tip toe once more. 'Okay, you can touch me now,' I whisper, and he groans, capturing my mouth, deepening our kiss, his arms going round me, crushing me to his hard body. I've never been held like this, or needed like this. His hands slide everywhere, as though trying to absorb me.

When we break apart, we're breathless. 'Jesus, Elle, I'm not sure I'm going to last,' he confesses shakily.

'It's definitely your turn,' I say, glancing down. 'And I like the look of this rug.'

Nicky follows my gaze. 'I don't even know where the hell it came from,' he says.

'Then we'll christen it.'

He looks at me, the smile that spreads across his lips sending a rush through me. That we're actually going to do this. 'You're sure?' he asks, and I nod vigorously.

'I just need a second,' he says, and he turns back to the bed. Cold air rushes in as our bodies part. I lower myself down to the floor, out of sight of the window blinds. The soft hairs of the rug prickle up my spine, the chill making my nipples stand to attention. I hear the box being opened, the tearing of a foil. Raising myself up on my elbows, I watch him in the shadows, admiring his impressive rear on display, white against his tan lines, as Nicky fixes the condom into place, and I feel myself getting wetter with anticipation.

The weight of his body comes next and it feels glorious, pressing me down into the rug and making it hard for me to breathe. I open my legs around him, feeling his length press against the damp, engorged folds of my core, and all I can think is that I want to be filled by him. Nicky kisses me into oblivion, until I'm desperate and panting.

'I need you… inside me,' I manage, lifting my hips, increasing the friction, as Nicky sucks one of my nipples until it's taut.

We've stopped talking. The playfulness of our lovemaking has slipped away, giving way to tempestuous desire and desperate longing. Nicky groans, sliding his hand down my ribcage with purpose, his fingers sinking fully into my wetness, skillfully circling my clitoris before burying two fingers deep inside me. I moan against him, bucking my hips. He withdraws, going back to the point that gives me the most pleasure.

'There's so much I want to do to you,' he whispers and my head falls back as his fingers fall into a steady rhythm. 'I promise you next time, it won't be this quick.'

I want to tell him I understand, that it's okay, but my ability to verbalise anything has dissolved with the ache that now exists between my thighs. I feel Nicky shift his position. His fingers are gone, replaced by something much larger, hot and insistent at my entrance. I spread my legs wider, and marvel at just how gentle he's being with me, how courteous. Moving one hand between us, he eases forward as I feel myself opening up to him, stretching to support his size. Yet rather than burying himself in one swift movement, he takes care, pulsing inch by inch inside of me, as though savouring this blissful moment of my body gently accepting and accommodating him. And when we're finally joined, Nicky holds me there, one hand on my hip, lying fully on top of me, gazing down into my face, stroking my hair, his breaths as shaky as mine, sighing at the shared bliss of our union. Still, he doesn't move, resting his elbows on each side of my head. When he lowers his head and kisses me with such tenderness, I realise I've discovered what true intimacy is. And it makes me feel complete.

'You are perfect,' he says between kisses. 'So beautiful.'

'I've pictured us… like this,' I tell him, reaching for him. 'For a long time.'

Nicky groans again, a primitive sound that tells me that he has too. It's all the encouragement he needs. When he eases back for the first time, blissful sensations whoosh up my spine from my core, and at his first thrust, I think I might have gone to heaven. A second, and a third has me arching against him, my body encasing him, gripping him tight. In that moment, he seems to snap, to lose control, saying my name as he increases the tempo of his movements, taking us higher, the friction so achingly good, like he's fulfilling a need that I've had for weeks now in his presence. I've had quick sex, bored sex, uneasy sex... never slow, loving, passionate sex. No, I've never had sex like this before.

Above me, his breaths are short and sharp, like he's trying to restrain himself but can't, his mouth seeking out my neck, my lips, consuming me, whispering my name, our breaths intermingling, until he can't kiss me because above me, it seems like he's clenching his jaw.

'Don't hold back,' I whisper, and it's all he needs to let go, because he curses as he plunges into me one final time, burying his head in the curve of my neck. When he comes, it's the most satisfying sound I've ever heard. His hands clamp down on me and he growls, and I feel the length of him tremor and throb. He gives one final judder before his body gives out and he collapses down onto me, breathless, and I feel his heart pounding in his chest. I revel in being trapped underneath his solid length, my body still in flames and desperate for release, yet at the same time, I find myself smiling, because despite all those grunting noises he makes every day on court, none of them quite aligns with the sound of Nicky Salco reaching his climax.

'Is there something funny?' he asks, raising himself up, still out of breath, as I realise with mortification that I'm chuckling whilst he's still deep inside of me.

'Nothing,' I whisper back, stroking his hair. 'Nothing's funny.'

'Did I do something?' he asks, because I still have to bite my lip to make the laugh go away.

'No, not at all. It's just—'

'Tell me,' he urges me, sliding out of me, reaching down and sliding off the contraceptive. 'If there's something I did wrong, I need to know.'

'I can't say. It's too embarrassing.'

'Embarrassing for me… or embarrassing for you?'

'Me, of course.'

'Okay, see, now you're going to have to tell me.'

'I'll tell you another time, I swear.'

'Elle, no guy wants to be laughed at when we just did what we did. You're killing my ego here.'

I am flat out giggling now. 'I wasn't laughing at you! I'm sorry, I was curious to know if—'

'If what?'

I'm squirming. Then he does something I don't expect, by sliding his fingers down to my knee and then brushing his hand upwards between my thighs. I gasp as two fingers probe my entrance, finding my pleasure points again, before sliding back inside me. 'If you're not gonna spill, then I'm gonna have to make you scream it,' he murmurs.

'Sydney and I had a conversation…,' I manage, 'About the noises you and Tag make out on court… ahhhh we agreed they're almost… Oh god…mmm…'

'Primal?' he asks, rubbing over my sensitive nub with his fingers until I'm gasping, my hips rocking.

'Sexual…mmm,' I confirm as I shudder, my head going back, the sensations moving down my legs, making my toes tingle.

He lets out a deep laugh. 'That's very… *depraved* of you both,' he says, keeping up the rhythm with his fingers, but shifting downwards on the rug, skating kisses across my stomach, sinking lower so that his mouth is level with my hips. With his hands, Nicky guides my thighs further apart, until I'm spread wide for him, fully exposed.

He removes his fingers. Everything is pulsating. Everything is on fire and I'm gasping for release.

'Please, Nicky, don't stop,' I beg him.

'I like watching you like this,' he responds in a low tone, dipping his tongue in once, sliding it between my folds until I'm shuddering. 'So close. So perfect.'

My thighs are trembling. When he moves forward, his tongue making contact, I sigh heavily, because nothing is as good as this feels. He licks me, finding a rhythm until I'm squirming underneath him. Then he slides two fingers back inside, gently plunging in and out, still lapping at me with his mouth, until heat floods through me and I forget how to breathe. I murmur his name incoherently over and over as he edges me closer to the brink of ecstasy with his fingers and tongue working in synch.

'I can't, I can't...' I whimper, but it's too late, because I'm grabbing fistfuls of the rug hairs and seeing stars. The rushing sensation starts at the base of my opening, and it travels upwards until my walls are squeezing his fingers, my vagina going into spasm, blissful contractions exploding inside me as I come hard, Nicky's tongue still working me, my legs and thighs clenched tight as I soar against a tidal wave of pleasure, swallowing my own cries.

When my breathing steadies, Nicky gets to his feet. I suddenly feel exposed, lying naked on the rug in a post-coital haze, and something inside me makes me panic that he's leaving, that our time is up and that he plans to return immediately to his room. Lying on the rug, I experience an overwhelming irrational feeling of shame, not unlike the way Jamie used to make me feel when we were together. Sitting up, I watch in the darkness as Nicky stops beside the bed, before grabbing two pillows and throwing them down towards me. I am equally surprised to see him drag the quilt off the mattress and carry it over to me on the rug. He does some arranging, fashioning us a bed on the floor, positioning a pillow behind my head.

'Comfortable?' he asks as I sink my head into it.

'Perfectly,' I reply, and he's lying back down beside me, fitting his full form to me, covering us both with the quilt. Then he's back to hovering above me, lowering his head and capturing my lips. I'm still reeling that he's not going anywhere.

He lies down, rolling me into him, our legs entwined, and I lower my head to his chest. I'd stay like this forever if I could.

'You should eat something,' I whisper, trailing my fingers down torso.

'I thought I just did,' he chuckles, and my fingers ball into a fist, punching his side. He laughs, twisting away from me.

'You are so *rude*,' I say. 'I meant proper food.'

He goes back to cradling me, his arm around my neck, his fingers in my hair, tickling my scalp.

'How about I stay with you instead?'

I give him a squeeze. 'I'd prefer that.'

We lie there in silence before he says, 'Tag's sleeping with Sydney; did you know that?'

I raise my head in surprise. 'She told me, yes. Did he tell you?'

'He 'fessed up after I quizzed him on it. He's really into her. Did you tell Syd about us?'

'No. I wanted to. I don't think she suspects a thing. Did you tell Tag?'

He holds up his thumb and finger. 'No. I came this close to saying something after Flushing Meadows. No, I haven't told anyone about this. About us.'

'I haven't either,' I lie, failing to mention my confession to Oliver. 'What about Mackenzie?' I ask.

I feel him tense at the mention of her name. 'Mac's always so wrapped up in her business. I didn't know she was going away. But now I get to have you to myself for a few days... or nights, at least.'

He turns to face me, stroking one hand against my cheek. 'I shouldn't say it... but can we just forget about Mac for a few days? Because you're all I want to think about.'

When I kiss him, a sound emerges from the base of his throat. It's the sound of acceptance, of satisfaction, of a weight being lifted. As he rolls me onto my back on the rug, I cling to him, meeting his kisses with equal fervour. Until Mackenzie returns to Miami, I get to pretend that he's all mine.

Tonight, we've crossed a bridge. Except that, under the weight of reality, I know the bridge is unstable, and there is absolutely no turning back.

Chapter Nineteen

'Elle,' Mackenzie snaps at me on a Friday morning, when Nicky's been away for almost three weeks. I'm sitting at the kitchen island, lost in the memory of our three intense nights together, when Rag was reprimanding Nicky for being so tired prior to their trip to China, yet having no idea to the reason behind his general state of exhaustion.

Our goodbye was hurried, Nicky sending Lonzo on some spurious errand before he'd pulled me into the kitchen's pantry and crushed me to him, kissing me until we were both breathless.

'I'm such an idiot,' he'd murmured, resting his forehead against mine. 'Why didn't I tell Sydney to just find us a house? Why didn't I just insist that you come with us to Shanghai?'

'You said it yourself... changing your mind will look completely sus,' was my response, despite my anguish at his imminent departure, stroking my fingers through his hair. Part of me had wanted him to insist anyway, as some kind of red flag to Mackenzie to call off her own wedding.

Generally, I've been keeping out of the way, unless I'm required in the kitchen, staying in my room, finishing *Jane Eyre* and then reading it again because I adored it so much the first time. I've been getting up in the night still, partly out of habit, but partly to watch Nicky play his matches on the gargantuan TV in the living room with the sound down. It's the only TV that has the Tennis Channel. China is twelve hours ahead, so his afternoon matches started at 2 a.m. Miami time. He reached the fourth round of the Shanghai Open, and so far, he's reached the second round of the Japan Open in Tokyo. I get a thrill of excitement watching him play, but mostly I just crave the close-up shots, the ones where you can detect his mood by the look in his eyes. When I'm watching, I wonder if he thinks about me between shots, before telling myself not to be ridiculous. He's a professional. And then when whichever match it is I'm watching has come to an end, I slink back to my pool house, just as the sun's starting to peak over the horizon. I've never once seen Mackenzie get out of bed to watch him play.

'Yes?' I blurt out, realizing she's still waiting for an answer.

'I've got an associate coming for lunch today. He can't have gluten. Two salads will be fine. No egg though. And he doesn't like tuna.'

There goes my Nicoise idea, I think to myself, getting to my feet. 'What sorts of things does he like?' I ask her, moving to the fridge.

'I'm not a mind-reader, Elle, just throw me together two healthy salads for lunch. And don't dress them, I never like it when you dress the salad.'

I want to tell her it's Lonzo who always tends to dress the salads but instead I keep my mouth shut. 'Coming right up,' I say, forcing myself to sound upbeat.

The house is oddly quiet with everyone away, to the point that I can't wait for my sister's visit. Even Oliver is visiting California with his father; something to do with their hotel brand.

At lunch, I peek through the lace curtains of my pool house door as Mackenzie's 'associate' arrives in a swanky silver sports convertible with the hood down. He wears a beige suit with no tie and slicked-back hair; Mackenzie greeting him with a kiss on both cheeks. He looks like he's in his mid-thirties. They disappear around the corner to the veranda. The salads made; she asked that I make myself scarce so she could discuss 'business matters'.

I'm sitting on my bed when I hear her laughter carried across the garden. It doesn't sound like any kind of business meeting to me. An hour later, I puff out my cheeks, bored of staying inside with nowhere else to go. I open my door, creeping barefoot along the path towards the kitchen. Entering the kitchen from the side door, I hear loud, blaring music coming from upstairs, which strikes me as a little odd. Looking outside the kitchen windows, I spy their empty plates and glasses still on the veranda. Her associate must have brought with him a bottle of wine, because it's open and mostly empty on the table. I walk towards the hallway, realizing the front door is still open a fraction. Looking down, I see a wallet and a phone on the side table. My curious fingers hover over it, upstairs the music changing to a new track. Picking it up, I open it to find a Florida driver's license in the name of Bryan Dabrowski, the picture matching the man I saw get out of the convertible.

I know for a fact that Mackenzie will fire me if she finds me lurking, but I can't help myself. I follow the sound of the music upstairs, creeping against the staircase, which turns to the left and goes back on itself. Half way up I stop, clinging to the wall, tilting my head to one side, trying to filter out the overarching racket being made by the baseline of the Taylor Swift track. The music is coming from Mackenzie and Nicky's room. After a moment, I catch something, though instantly I wonder if I've imagined it.

I can't say for sure, but part of me thinks I just heard the very distinctive sound of a woman reaching her orgasm.

~

A week later, Josie is gaping at me in horror.

'I've been here for five days and you're only just telling me this *now*?' she blurts.

We're relaxing on white sunbeds in South Beach on a Tuesday morning at the beginning of November, laid back in the Miami sunshine. It's quiet. I can't look in her direction, and I've kept my sunglasses on. 'I couldn't find the words,' I mumble.

'I'm. Fucking. Nicky. Salco. There you go, that's four words.'

I look around, checking there's no one within earshot. I knew she would react in this way. My sister is the ballsy one who always says what's on her mind. She is my polar opposite. She's taller than me, thinner than me, with wavier hair and a pointier nose. 'It's not like that,' I say, under my breath. 'I knew you wouldn't approve.'

She looks like she might explode. '*Wouldn't approve?* Well, there's the understatement of the year. In case you hadn't noticed, you're living under the same roof as his fiancée! Who doesn't seem all that nasty, *by the way.*'

That's the other thing. Since Josie arrived from Spain, Mackenzie's been nothing but pleasant, inviting Josie and I for sundowners on the terrace, offering us unlimited use of the pool. Despite my horror stories, Josie seems to find Mackenzie completely charming, making what I'm doing with Nicky all that much worse.

I've decided ours is not quite like any other modern affair. For one, 92% of the world's population has a mobile phone, though Nicky Salco can't be counted in that bracket, so my contact with him whilst he's away is zero. All I have to feed off are the snippets of messages that come from Sydney, usually via Tag, on how Nicky's feeling, whether he's relaxed or feeling tense before a match, whether he's sleeping, how the hotels are handling his appetite for food after hours. My sister asked Mackenzie how she speaks to Nicky whilst he's away. Mackenzie replied that she spoke to Nicky on hotel phones, and only when he made the point of calling, which doesn't seem to bother her all that much.

I miss him so much it makes my chest ache.

At the beach, Josie has sat upright on her sunbed, hugging her knees in her bikini, her eyes blazing. 'You are going to get hurt, you know that, right? You are insane to get involved with him. These things never end well. Seriously, what are you thinking? What is *he* thinking?'

I snatch off my sunglasses. 'What, I'm not good enough for him, is that it?'

Her gaze softens. 'Elle. Of course that's not the case. He'd be the luckiest man in the world to have you, but he's not *available*. He's getting *married*. Has he told you that he's going to break up with Mackenzie?'

I remember his words. *You can't ask me to break up with Mac, Elle. Not right now.*

'No,' I swallow.

'So, what exactly does he think you're both doing?'

'I don't know! I've not asked!'

Josie throws her hands up in the air. 'Why the hell not? Why are you not demanding he break things off with Mackenzie if he's with you?'

I'm shaking my head, trying to hold back tears of frustration. *This is the house that Mikhail Scheffler built.*

'You are such a cliché,' Josie continues to rant. It's the same word Oliver used, only this time, it stings. 'Filthy rich, talented, good-looking tennis player starts screwing his personal chef in the middle of the night because he knows he can get away with it. And what kind of a name is Nicky anyway? Nicky is like a five-year-old boy's name. Why is he not Nick? Nicholas? That's a grown-up name. It's lust, that's what this is, Elles. Pure and simple. He just wants to hook up with you. You've got the hots for one another because you both were… or *are* in comfortable relationships.'

I've reached my limit. I get to my feet, pulling on my shorts and top, gathering my things into my bag and sliding my feet back into my flip-flops. Josie's still talking before she realises I'm heading off.

'Hey! Wait, where are you going?'

'Home,' I deadpan, and begin my trek back up the sand towards Ocean Drive.

'Elle!'

I keep walking, simmering anger I my stomach, annoyed that I ever said anything because I knew how it would be. I knew I would get a patronizing lecture.

Eventually, Josie catches up with me, half her possessions falling out of her bag, her towel dragging in the sand.

'Elle-Belle, stop, stop, wait.'

I come to a halt, gritting my teeth.

Josie places two hands on my shoulders. She takes off my sunglasses. She can see how angry I am. She squeezes her own eyes shut.

'Alright. I may have gone too far.'

'You think? Just a little?'

Her shoulders droop. 'I didn't mean to call you a cliché. I don't want to see you get hurt.'

'I don't have anyone else I can talk to about this. You think that I don't spend my whole day feeling guilty? That it kills me that he doesn't just break up with Mackenzie? That I could just be his girlfriend? That I don't feel shitty enough as it is without you telling me that I should know better? And, by the way, I never had a *comfortable* relationship with Jamie; I had a *bad* relationship with Jamie, but I never had the incentive I needed to leave. And yes, it's not an ideal situation, but Nicky cares about me.'

She raises her eyes a fraction. 'Cares enough to break up with his fiancée?'

I storm off again. She runs after me.

'Elllle!'

She grabs my elbow. 'I'm sorry. I'm sorry. I promise I'll stop saying anything disparaging. I will support you one hundred per cent.'

'You promise?'

'One hundred *per cent*. Whatever you decide to do. But, if he hurts you, I can't promise I won't chop his balls off. And by that I don't mean his tennis balls.'

My lips twitch. I try not to laugh. 'Fine,' I say.

Josie gathers up her things, pushing everything down into her bag. 'Hug?' she asks, holding out her arms.

I step forward. She wraps me in an embrace. 'I can't believe Nicky Salco is sleeping with my little sister,' she breathes into my hair.

'I know,' I mutter.

She giggles. 'You're sleeping with a celeb, Elles.'

'I know,' I try to laugh, but the ache in my chest returns, because with Nicky gone, and with no communication, our past transactions feel like a fever dream, out of reach and implausible.

She pulls back, placing one hand on each of my cheeks. 'I hope he knows how lucky he is. If I get to meet him, I *will* be telling him.'

'That's not the only thing...' I sigh.

Josie's eyes widen. 'What? Oh god, what else is there?'

'I met another guy. A nice, single one. His name's Oliver.'

'Oliver?' Josie questions. 'And is *he* single?'

I roll my eyes. 'Yes. And I think he really likes me.'

Josie performs a little seal clap. 'That's more like it! Who needs a Nicky when you've got an Oliver? Tell me everything.'

'Whose car is that?' Josie asks when we arrive back at the house after lunch.

A pristine white Range Rover is parked in the driveway.

'Nicky's parents,' I tell her warily.

It turns out, it's just Libby on her own. She and Mackenzie have just had lunch. Lonzo and his family have gone to Cuba for the week, including for Halloween.

'Elle! Hello,' Libby smiles.

'Hi, Libby,' I smile back. 'This is my sister, Josie. She's visiting from Spain.'

'How glamorous, dear,' Libby says, shaking Josie's hand. 'I went once, to watch Nicky play tennis. Didn't get much time to look around though.'

Josie is on her best behaviour. 'You should come to Barcelona; you'd love it.'

'I'm positive I would. Did you girls eat already?'

'Josie bought me an early lunch at Yard Bird,' I say, omitting the fact that I'd spent the entire meal giving her a full download on Nicky/Oliver/Oliver/Nicky. 'We ordered the ribs. So we're stuffed.'

'Oh well, perfect. Do y'all have plans for the afternoon? Can I ask for your help with something? We can watch Nicky's opening match in Paris at the same time.'

My voice tremors slightly. 'Of course. What do you need help with?'

'Wedding invitations,' she says. 'I need to get them all sent out this week, but we gotta get them *aaaall* in envelopes first. Maybe you girls could help out?'

Josie and I exchange glances.

Minutes later, we're sat around the TV on sofas, Nicky's Paris Masters opener about to start on the big screen, the one that I've been watching him on for all of his matches whilst he's been away, except nobody knows that but me. It's an evening start, 6 p.m. Paris-time. Mackenzie is on her phone, talking about her bikini business, not paying the screen any attention.

Josie and I have both showered and changed, and Libby is pouring us all a glass of champagne.

'Now, I've printed out a copy of the guest list,' Libby says, pointing to a piece of paper on the table, next to piles of invitations, ribbon, envelopes and address labels.

'How many people are coming to the wedding?' Josie asks, curling her feet under her.

'About two hundred,' Libby says, putting down the bottle.

'Two *hundred*?' I repeat, thinking the number is an insane amount, given Nicky doesn't appear to have any actual friends, apart from maybe Tag.

'Oh sure, once you count all of Florida's great and good, people from the tennis tour, high school friends, college friends, country club folk, Mackenzie's parents' friends and family. Y'all wouldn't believe how many cousins Mackenzie has.'

Mackenzie's eyes flit up, knowing she's being talked about. She gets up, still on her phone.

'Is Elle invited?' Josie asks and I shoot daggers her way.

'Oh sure, of course, honey,' Libby says, patting my knee, 'Elle gets a front row seat.'

'Thank you,' I whisper, a lump lodging itself in my throat, just as the screen fills with Nicky's face. *Lucky me.*

'Lord, he is *not* looking happy today,' Libby purrs in her Southern drawl.

He's really not. Even the commentators are mulling over Nicky's thunderous expression, before ruminating over his so-so performance of the tennis season so far this year. I hear the words 'Triple Salco' and my heart sinks.

I reach for my phone, messaging Sydney, who I know is in the crowd. They flew to Paris a few days ago. I type out, *What's up with Nicky?*

It doesn't take her long to respond. I glance down at the screen. *Tag says he's distracted. Doesn't want to be here. Practice sessions not good.*

'If I know my Nicky, this is not gonna go his way today,' Libby is saying as she takes her seat.

'Why's that?' Josie asks.

'Did they tell you why they call him Triple Salco?' Libby says to her, sipping her champagne.

Josie looks like she doesn't want to respond to Nicky's own mother.

'That look right there,' Libby sighs, looking to the TV. 'That there is impulsive Nicky. Or, as I like to think of it, *wild* Nicky. Something's bothering that boy today. I would not want to be the umpire for this match.'

Josie raises her eyebrows at me. I try to ignore her, not wanting to think about what may or may not be on Nicky's mind.

'Now, girls,' Libby says as she leans forward. 'I'm gonna write names on all these invitations. Then Elle, if you can please put each one into an envelope and Josie, you stick the label on with the address. Mackenzie's gonna tie the ribbon on each once she's off the phone.'

Gingerly, I pick up a wedding invitation. The card it's printed on is large and heavy, the font a shade of deep purple, in a classical style, embossed and swirling. Flowers surround the text. *Mikhail and Sara Scheffler request the pleasure of your company at the marriage of their daughter Mackenzie Natalie Sienna to Nicholas James Salco.*

Looking at it, I feel nauseous. The date is set for the second day in March, less than five months away. What happens to my relationship with Nicky beyond that date, I cannot tell.

'How old were you when you got married, Libby?' Josie asks, as my gaze once more goes back to Nicky on screen, where the match is about to start.

Libby gives a sigh. Her Southern accent makes everything sound like a lullaby. 'A baby. Not even twenty-one. I got married because I was knocked up and Nicky's grandfather, God rest his soul, was the religious type. Benji's parents hadn't even met me at the time he proposed.'

Josie looks surprised. 'And how many years have you been married?'

Libby holds up her ring finger with a smile. 'Thirty years strong.'

I started putting the invitations that Libby has written on in envelopes and think about what Oliver said about Ben Salco having an affair with his aunt, wondering if that was an isolated incident. When I've done five, I pass the first pile of invitations to Josie, who checks the names and sticks an address label on the front of the envelope.

On TV, Nicky's match begins. It's his service game. Mackenzie comes over and flops down into an armchair.

'Libby, I hope you're using your best handwriting,' she smirks.

'Of course, darlin', your mama would give me her stamp of approval.'

We lapse into silence, each performing our various roles, except Mackenzie who settles her gaze on screen.

'Did you talk to him today, honey?' Libby asks.

Mackenzie blows out her cheeks. 'Yesterday. He didn't have time to talk for long. He didn't like the bed in the hotel.'

'Well, kinda looks like dark clouds are swarming.'

Mackenzie clicks her tongue. 'You know Nicky, Lib. It'll all blow over.'

'You're not wrong, sweetie.'

'Do you miss him when he's away?' Josie asks Mackenzie and I feel my shoulders tense.

'I'm used to it. I mean, I do, of course, but I enjoy the space too, you know.'

'You're not worried about him being on tour, that he'll be surrounded by other women?'

Mackenzie lets out a laugh. 'All that man cares about is the tennis. And I mean, until he's back with me, tennis is *everything*. He could have Miss America out there as his goddamned ball girl; I still don't think he'd look.'

Libby is chuckling, as though in agreement with her future daughter-in-law.

Mackenzie sobers before letting out a snort. 'Nicky would never cheat on me. He wouldn't dare.'

I keep my eyes on the invitations, and placing them neatly inside the envelopes.

The match is a difficult opener for Nicky. The first set goes to a tie break, which Nicky loses on a controversial point. Nicky argues with a line judge, contests the decision with the umpire. He looks frustrated, annoyed by every little error in his game. At one point he is even booed by the crowd, my heart surging in my chest in his defense. Mackenzie puffs out her cheeks, losing interest, wandering into the kitchen to fetch a bottle of wine. At length, Libby follows her. With Lonzo on holiday, there is an expectation that I will make dinner.

We watch the TV. Nicky's about to begin another service game.

Josie moves to sit next to me, poking me in my side. 'Maybe you're getting to him,' she whispers.

I check Mackenzie's position then poke her back. 'If I am,' I whisper, 'It's not exactly doing him any good, is it?'

We watch as Nicky produces a disastrous double fault, hammering both balls out of bounds and visibly cursing on screen.

'Well, I hope he doesn't have sex like he serves,' Josie giggles and playfully, I land my fist in her stomach.

Chapter Twenty

Nicky loses his opening match at the Paris Masters. I feel an overwhelming sense of disappointment for him, but the excitement of him returning to Miami earlier than anticipated soon eclipses any other reservations I hold onto. I can introduce him to Josie. Everyone else views it as a disaster.

My sister and I are in the pool house, thinking about heading to bed when my phone buzzes, a message from Sydney popping up. I swipe up the handset. *Heading back tomorrow*, she writes. *Mood here not good.*

I'm not surprised, I type back. *You're up late. How is Nicky holding up?*

Honestly, I don't know, comes the reply. *He's quiet.*

–

'This is killing me,' I whisper to Josie the following evening, lingering beside the door to my pool house, peering out of the curtain. Josie's on the bed, her back propped up with pillows, reading an American gossip magazine. A few days ago, she tried reading *Jane Eyre* and couldn't get beyond the first chapter.

'Well, you can hardly run out there and throw yourself into his arms,' she comments drily, licking one finger and turning a page. 'One doesn't get to do that when one's boyfriend is engaged to someone else.'

I puff out my cheeks. By continually referring to Nicky as my *boyfriend*, she's trying to get a rise out of me. 'They've been back half an hour already.'

I'd watched the car arrived from the airport through the same gap in the curtains: the somber mood as Nicky stepped out, followed by Rag and Tag. The limp embrace that Mackenzie had given him before ushering them all inside the house. Nicky's parents are here too. And despite my desperation, all I can do is watch and wait.

Half an hour later, I'm still pacing beside the bed when there is a soft knock at my door. My head whips around as Nicky enters. He closes the door and walks in, his eyes only on me, a small smile on his lips. He's wearing his usual: navy jogging bottoms and a navy sports t-shirt, his hair partially in disarray. It's weird, to say the least, having spent the last month not seeing him in person but watching him on TV, only for him to now be here, in the flesh. It's a moment before he catches sight of Josie behind me on the bed, his pace slowing.

'Hi,' he says, faltering.

'Hi,' I say back.

There is a moment where it feels like time is suspended. 'This is my sister, Josie,' I blurt.

'Hi, Josie, good to meet you,' Nicky forces out with a slight wave.

'Hi, Nicky,' Josie purrs breezily, like she's known him all her life.

He looks to me, his expression containing so many words unspoken.

'It's alright, she knows everything,' I swallow. 'I told her about us.'

A weight seems to lift from him. 'Oh, well, in that case—' he begins, before stepping forward and confidently pulling me to him beside the bed, one hand going to my cheek before his lips find mine, gripping my cotton top in his fist. Amazed that he's made such a bold move, I wrap my hands around his neck, holding onto him, kissing him back with everything that I have.

We don't stop for some moments until Josie coughs, muttering 'Ugh, get a room you two.'

I break the kiss. 'This *is* my room,' I say, glancing back, his hands firmly grasping my waist.

Josie purposefully flicks another page on her magazine. 'Yes, well, tell your boyfriend he still has a fiancée.'

'Here we go,' Nicky grumbles, his head falling back.

'Well, you *do*,' Josie reminds him.

Nicky ignores her, his concentration on me. 'Did you miss me?' he whispers.

'Did you miss *me*?'

Josie starts making gagging noises on the bed when he says, 'You know that I did,' before he wraps me back in his embrace, capturing my lips again.

'*Fi-an-cée*,' Josie hums and I reach out, my lips still attached to Nicky's, and grant her a middle finger.

I agree to see him at two thirty in the morning: our usual time. Josie stirs as I rise from the bed, barely having slept. The idea of being alone with him again is too enthralling, knowing what's going to occur between us. A few weeks ago, whilst he was away, I shopped in Miami for sexy underwear, something I'm definitely not used to doing. As I slip into it, under my plainer clothes, I feel a shiver of excitement pulse through me.

In the kitchen the lights are dim, but when I arrive, he's already there, waiting for me, a smile on his face. I smile at him, but we don't talk as I take his hand and he leads me into the hallway. Nicky's parents are staying over, so I know that we can't use their bedroom. When he ushers me into the downstairs shower room, it doesn't feel all that romantic, barely enough room for us both to stand up. He switches on the small light above the mirror, but keeps the main light off, as well as the extraction fan, and I know that we're going to have to keep any sound to an absolute minimum. He closes the door, sliding the lock closed until we're alone, our chests rising and falling, heat and desire practically oozing out of our pores. His kisses are ravenous and greedy, as though he has to compensate for being starved of my presence for more than a month. I want to know what he's thinking, but now is not the time.

I slide my palms underneath his t-shirt, lifting it off, then follow suit with my own top, and hear him draw breath at the sight of my scarlet red push-up bra. His fingers trace the lacy edge, before sinking lower and inside the waistband of my shorts, guiding them down my legs, revealing a matching Brazilian style thong. I hear him sigh, as I lean back against the surface of the sink unit, the straight edge digging into my lower back, allowing him to trail hot kisses across my breasts, down the plain of my stomach, past my belly button, one finger hooking into the lace of my thong and sliding it down my thighs until I am naked but for the bra.

I pull him back upwards, his mouth clashing with mine, his kisses still insistent and demanding, my hands pushing into the waistband of his sweatpants. He helps me by grasping at the material, dragging them down, first removing a condom, still in its foil, from his pocket. I glance down at the massive bulge in his underwear and realise I'm panting with anticipation.

I reach behind my back, unclasping my bra, allowing it to slip away to the floor, the throb between my legs increasing as his eyes rove over my naked body in the shadows. I wait as he drops his underwear, opens the condom packet with his teeth. Instead of him doing it, I take the contraceptive in my fingers. Nicky's eyes flash as I move it to his tip and roll it down the entire length of him, fixing it in place. He groans appreciatively, before grasping my hips, guiding my feet back down to the floor and turning me around, so that we're both looking into the mirror, him behind me.

'Is this okay? Like this?' he whispers at me in our reflection and I nod my head.

He reaches down in front of me, indicating that I should lean back into him as his fingers slide down into my wet warmth. His lips go to my neck as I gasp, allowing him to caress me with one hand and cup my breast with the other, his lips licking and sucking and tasting, his stubble rubbing against my skin. It's a sensual onslaught that almost sends me to my knees.

'My god, Elle,' he whispers as I grind the contours of my behind into his erection, driving him wild. 'I missed you so much.'

'I missed you,' I say back. 'I need you.'

I lean forward, moving my face closer to the mirror. He moves one hand from my breast to his shaft, and, widening my stance, I feel his tip probing my entrance, the sensation sending tiny bolts of electricity through my core.

He raises his eyes to the mirror and we watch one another in the reflection as he slides into me. I'm so wet, my folds so swollen, that he glides in easily, not stopping until he reaches the hilt. When are bodies are joined completely, I let out a sigh, matching his own, feeling whole somehow. Nicky starts to move then, inching out but then filling me again, and I feel myself accommodate him. In the reflection, I see that same ravenousness in his eyes. My eyes slip shut at the sensuality of it all as his fingers return to rub me, taking me with him as he increases the pressure of his thrusts. But he remains focused on giving me the most pleasure, not allowing himself to lose control. I love watching us in the mirror, his hand covering my sex, his fingers probing me, until I'm quivering, desperate for release, tiny moans emerging from between my lips.

Nicky gently shushes me close to my ear as I feel my orgasm building between my thighs. His fingertips pulse rhythmically, pleasuring me. The explosion starts at the very base of my core before ballooning upwards as my walls contract, squeezing Nicky hard and I feel him groan with the sensations. I see white stars. I want to scream, to let him know what he's doing to me. My mouth falls open in ecstasy, but instead no sound emerges, my body juddering in silence as waves of sensations wash over me.

When they finally subside, I'm hazy, leaning back into him, conscious that he's still inside me. One look in the mirror gives him the go ahead to let go. I lean forward slightly again, until he's fully immersed inside me once more. We watch in the mirror as he thrusts in earnest, one hand covering mine on the surface of the glass, and it's so good I feel I might climax again. When he comes moments later, he buries his head in my neck, struggling to contain the insatiable groan escaping his gritted teeth.

When I slip back under the covers of my bed, I quickly become aware that Josie is awake.

'Did you ask him if he's going to leave Mackenzie?' she murmurs in the darkness.

I lie there in silence, already knowing my answer, yet scared of her judging me. 'No,' I say. 'It wasn't really a time for talking.'

'Do you love him?' she asks.

'Yes,' I say.

She rolls away from me, exhaling in a deep sigh of disapproval.

Chapter Twenty-One

I wake to the sound of cars in the driveway. I check the time; it's a little after six thirty. I look across at Josie, still fast asleep. When I get out of the shower, she's still in her pyjamas, peering out of the glass door.

'Well, something's going on,' she comments. 'Either that or your boyfriend just took delivery of a very expensive motor.'

I frown at the sight of the fancy-looking vehicle parked in the driveway. 'What kind of car is that?'

'That's a Bugatti. Retail value about three and a half million.'

I raise my eyebrows. 'Nicky's not really into cars; not that I know of. I'll go and find out.'

'Elle,' Josie says. 'You might want to do something first.'

'What?'

'*Uhm*, you might want to cover up the massive hickey on your neck?'

My eyes go wide. I dash into the bathroom, wiping steam from the mirror. On the right side of my neck is indeed a conspicuous reddish-purple mark. I touch it with my fingers, my mind flitting back to Nicky's trailing kisses and him sucking passionately at my skin.

Josie lingers beside the door, offering me a withering look. 'I'll get my foundation,' she sighs.

In the kitchen, Lonzo is stressed. I wear my hair down, conscious of the layer of make-up on my neck, and offer him a sympathetic look. I roll up my sleeves, ready to help out.

'Nobody says nothin',' he sniffs, throwing up his arms in despair. 'Breakfast for eleven? How about a little warning?'

'What's going on?' I ask. 'Why so many people?'

He nods towards the living area, where I can hear voices. 'Crisis talks,' he says. '*More* crisis talks...'

'Because of what happened in Paris?'

'Mackenzie's *papa* is here. Mikhail Scheffler. He doesn't think Ragnar is doing his job properly. Wants him—'

Lonzo slices an invisible knife blade across his throat.

I start breaking eggs into a bowl. 'Mackenzie's father? That's who the car belongs to? He has some sway in all this?'

'More that you would think. Like, imagine Nicky was the Dolphins; it would be like Mackenzie's father owning more than a fifty per cent stake. Nicky wouldn't be where he is right now without Mikhail Scheffler's investment.'

I nod my head, remembering Nicky talking about Mackenzie's father, and his sponsorship of his future son-in-law.

Before breakfast has been served, I hear raised voices from the other end of the house. It's hard to ignore, and I'm trying to pick out which individuals are speaking. Nicky's parents are there, as are Mackenzie's, plus Nicky's sports' agent, Ragnar and Tag, Nicky and Mac. I haven't seen Sydney since the group got back from Paris.

Lonzo is huffing in frustration when Sydney finally appears. I give her a smile but she doesn't look in the mood to grant me one back.

'Hey,' she says, gripping the sides of the kitchen island. 'It's like a pressure cooker in there. I had to get out.'

'I thought I'd see you yesterday,' I say.

'Plane landed; I went straight home for some zees.'

I lower my voice. 'What's going on in there?'

Sydney rolls her eyes. 'Mac's father Mikhail's deciding what's what. Wants Nicky to get a new coach. *Another* one.'

'What does Nicky want?'

'To end his losing streak? To actually reach a quarter or a semi-final, let alone win something? Only that sure ain't happening.'

'Does he want Rag to stay?'

'At this rate, he may not get a choice in it.'

'And how're you doing?'

She puffs out her cheeks. 'Girl, honestly… I feel like going to work in a bar. Or drive a boat. Or flip burgers. Anything but this bullshit.' She waits until Lonzo is out of earshot. 'Tag broke up with me.'

'*Why?*' I breathe.

She lowers her voice. 'Cold feet… doesn't want anything serious, doesn't want to be tied down, he needs to get divorced, Ragnar won't approve…, blah, blah, blah. Same shit.'

'I'm sorry,' I sigh.

'Don't be sorry. I'm not. I need a girls' night out. You down?'

I grin. 'I am *so down.*'

'Saturday night. You should invite Oliver. Tell him to bring his soccer team. You think he has any contacts… you know… anyone who can get us onto a list for a fancy venue downtown?'

'I'll ask him. His father owns a bunch of hotels, I think, so he might do. I can send you his number.'

She nods, looking pleased, then puffs out her cheeks. 'Girl, you and I need to have a little fun.'

Breakfast is almost a non-event. After the arguments, nobody feels like eating, and Lonzo storms out of the kitchen, tossing his apron and cursing in Spanish.

I am clearing up, Josie lying in the sun beside the pool when I am summoned.

Sydney enters the kitchen, a look of concern on her features.

'What is it?' I ask.

'They wanna see you upstairs in Mac's office.'

My heart starts to pound. 'Who is 'they'?'

'Mac, Nicky and Ragnar.'

Anxiousness explodes in my chest. I wipe my hands on a dishcloth, removing my chef's apron. I pile it up in a heap on the kitchen island, my mouth suddenly dry, questioning whether

Nicky has confessed to anything. I briefly touch my fingers to my neck.

'Do you know what it's about?' I squeak.

'They just asked me to fetch you.'

At the top of the stairs, the door is closed. Fearing I may be about to hyperventilate, I tap my knuckles against the surface.

'Come on in,' I hear Mac say from inside.

My fingers tremble as I push the door handle down. I picture myself on a flight back to Europe with Josie, perhaps after Mackenzie has left me with a bloody nose for stomping all over her relationship.

'Ah, Elle,' Mackenzie clips in a businesslike tone. She's stood behind her desk, Ragnar standing to the left of it, hands shoved inside his pockets. I take a step forward, revealing to my right that Nicky is standing beside the window, arms crossed over his chest, looking morose.

'Sydney said you wanted to see me?' I try to say, but my voice breaks, and it's obvious to them all that nerves have got the better of me. I feel the heat of Nicky's stare, but I keep my gaze locked on Mackenzie. Her look isn't thunderous, at least no more than usual, so I conclude that she doesn't know that I'm sleeping with her fiancé.

'We have something to discuss with you,' Ragnar starts but Mackenzie's terse look behind his back tells me she wishes to lead the conversation.

'A change to your contract,' she says.

'My contract?' I ask.

'From now on, you will no longer be Nicky's personal chef.'

The room goes silent for a moment. A bubble of panic swells in my chest, the question in my mind: *Is she firing me?*

'Before you jump to conclusions,' Mackenzie continues, 'You still have a job here. Nobody is getting fired. But the nature of your role will be altered to a degree.'

'Okay,' I choke out.

Ragnar steps in. 'Elle. Nicky is... exhausted. His body needs rest. Recuperation. We are wholly reevaluating his training regime. Part of that is dedicating serious effort to attaining a balance between the amount of sleep Nicky gets, versus the amount of time he spends out on court. The right amount of undisturbed sleep improves accuracy, reaction times, stamina, accuracy... I've been saying all along, we have to stop this business of Nicky getting up in the night. He must sleep. All the way through the night. He is not a small child.'

Beside the window, Nicky shifts. An image flashes through my mind of us together the night before, our naked bodies reflecting in the mirror. No, he's definitely not a small child. And seems to me, there's currently nothing wrong with his stamina.

'He has the greatest chance of success this way. Well-rested. Mentally, well-prepared.'

'I understand,' I say.

Mackenzie takes over. 'You will continue to work alongside Lonzo. To remain here working for us in Miami. Working for Nicky as and when, should there be a requirement. Your role will be expanded. Provided you're happy with the new terms.'

I know she wouldn't have put it so nicely, had it just been the two of us in the room. Faced with the alternative – of going back to England and resuming life as an agency chef – I know where I'd rather be.

'Of course,' I stammer out. 'I'm happy.'

'Plus, you no longer have to get up in the night,' Ragnar beams at me. 'This is a good thing, no? You get to work regular hours.'

My eyes flit to Nicky, for barely a second. He hasn't looked at me and is staring out of the window.

'Yes, of course,' I smile at Rag. 'Of course, that's a good thing.'

He's just asking me to give up the man I love. No big deal.

'Elle, I have another proposal,' Mackenzie pipes up, her breeziness sitting oddly with me, perhaps because it's so out of character, 'We had a cake designer booked for the wedding.

Somebody contacted me yesterday to say that they can no longer fulfill the contract, and I thought, since you make such delicious desserts, why not get Elle to design our cake? I mean, it would be the perfect solution. Lonzo's already working on the menu for the wedding banquet, so it makes sense to keep things in-house.'

An icy sensation travels through my veins. So *that's* why she's being so nice to me.

'Of course,' I manage. 'It makes perfect sense.'

'Have you ever made a wedding cake before?'

'No, but now I have plenty of time to learn.'

Mackenzie beams. 'Then it's settled. Isn't that wonderful, Nicky? Elle's going to design our wedding cake.'

I look over to the window. When he raises his eyes to me, I can't read his expression. I question whether this conversation is hurting him as much as it's hurting me.

Nicky lets out a sigh. 'Do we really need an enormous cake for the wedding?'

'Of course we need a *cake*,' Mackenzie retorts. 'A wedding isn't a wedding without cake.'

'Are we done here?' Nicky says moodily.

'Yes,' Ragnar replies. 'Everything is settled.'

'So, I can't even walk down to the kitchen at night and make myself a sandwich? Am I banned from even leaving my bed?'

I note that Ragnar doesn't seem to be going anywhere, at least not for the time being. 'For the next few weeks, Elle can make you a sandwich. You can take it with you when you go to bed. So, there will be no reason for you to move around at night.'

Nicky's shoulders droop. He's closer to me now, close enough that our hands are almost touching. I wonder if he shares my heartache at our time coming to an end.

'Fine,' Nicky says in a clipped tone, and he leaves the room.

My first instinct, once I've left Mackenzie's office, is to burst into tears. I manage to hold it together until I reach the pool house, where Josie is back from the pool and starting to pack her things, in preparation for her departure.

'Where did you go?' she asks.

'Mackenzie wanted to see me. Actually, it was Nicky and Ragnar too.'

Josie's face falls. 'Oh, holy fuck. They're onto you?'

I shake my head vehemently. 'No, no, nothing like that. They want to change my role. They don't want me making food for Nicky at night anymore.'

'But doesn't that mean...'

I can't hold back the tears anymore. 'I know what it means.'

'Oh, sweetie, come here,' Josie says as she steps forward an embraces me. I sob into her shoulder.

'I don't even know why I'm crying,' I say. 'He was never mine in the first place. It was just sex between consenting adults—'

I hear the words coming out of my mouth, as though trying to convince myself that they are true. Yet deep down, I don't believe them, because I still want to believe that Nicky and I share an emotional connection. That it isn't just about sex. That there *is* something more.

I step back, taking a deep breath and wipe my eyes. 'I need to pull myself together,' I say.

Josie stares at me with empathetic eyes, but she's nodding her head. 'You know it's for the best, right? He's cheating on her. With you.'

I nod my head, no matter what I believe, no matter the things that Nicky has said to me.

Josie grips my arms. 'If you can get through this, you can get through anything. It means you are free to walk away. If things get too hard, you can just walk away and leave it all behind.'

I look to the floor. 'There's something else. Mackenzie wants me to make her a wedding cake.'

The expletives that come out of my sister's mouth almost make me blush.

Later I'm in the kitchen, helping Lonzo put together some lunch. When Nicky enters, I stiffen. He should be training, but he isn't. I listen to him make casual conversation with Lonzo, but my mind is in a spin, and I can't focus on what they're saying.

Eventually, I hear Nicky say, 'Can you give me a minute with Elle?'

I put down my knife, placing my hands flat on the kitchen island as Lonzo makes himself scarce. I can't look at him. He comes closer to me, within touching distance, yet there is no physical contact between us. For a moment, neither of us speaks, the tension unbearable, and all I want to do is throw my arms around his neck. Instead, I keep my gaze fixed firmly on the pile of bell peppers I've just diced into little pieces.

'I'm sorry about earlier,' he says in a tone that's just above a whisper.

I nod my head furiously, wiping my hands on a nearby towel because it keeps them occupied.

'You understand? Don't you?' he says, his breath shaky, not completing the full question, perhaps because he can't bring himself to. *You understand that it's over between us.*

'I owe it to them to try this,' Nicky continues. 'They've all worked so hard for me; I owe it to them to give it all I've got. If I want to win a Grand Slam. If I want to get anywhere close.'

I nod my head again. 'It's what you should want. It's what you've been aiming for this whole time.'

'I'm taking some time out for the rest of November. There're no tournaments in December. I'll start again in January. They're gonna run some tests. There's some kind of sleep specialist coming this afternoon.'

'You think that'll help?'

'I'll listen to what they have to say.'

'You do look tired. What happened in Paris?'

He shifts his position, as though he doesn't want to talk about it. I feel that I've crossed a line, one that doesn't adhere to us keeping our distance.

'Nicky, if you think it's better that I leave—'

'I don't think that. I know we don't have a reason to spend time together from now on, but—' I glance up as he swallows tightly. His fingers lightly brush mine and I wallow in the agony of it for a moment.

'Josie goes back to Spain today,' I say, our hands shifting apart.

'Right,' he says. 'I'll be sure to say goodbye.'

'She thinks... *this*... our new arrangement. That it's for the best.'

'She's probably right.'

From outside the kitchen, Tag is shouting Nicky's name. 'I should go,' Nicky says.

'Wait,' I whisper. 'Why did Tag break up with Syd?'

'They broke things off? I didn't know that.'

'Then tell him he's an idiot.'

'I will.'

I watch him back away. It's inevitable, in a way, that it's easier talking about others' relationships than our own. I want to tell Nicky that I'll miss him, but he's already gone again.

I realise I'm staring when behind me, Lonzo clears his throat. I hadn't even heard him re-enter the room.

'Everything alright?' he asks, washing his hands.

I go back to dicing bell peppers. 'Everything's fine,' I reply, my smile as forced as my movements.

Lonzo gives a nod. We work in silence for some moments.

'Lonzo, can I ask you something?'

'*Siii*,' he remarks, pushing out his bottom lip.

'Would you be able to write me a job reference? I mean, like something on paper, in case I ever need to leave here at short notice?'

He stops what he's doing. '*Si, por supuesto.*'

I screw my face up at him. 'That means... of course?'

'*Siiiii.*'

'*Gracias, Lonzo.*'

He tilts his head towards the door, to the point where Nicky left. 'There a reason you might need to leave here short notice, *cariña*?' he asks.

'No reason,' I say, but my voice quivers and it's almost like he's worked it out for himself. 'I just like to be prepared. Plus, Mackenzie might really hate my wedding cake.'

He laughs at that.

–

Saturday night, and I'm under strict instructions from Syd. She's coming over to collect me before our night out. Yet I have to pretend to be running late, by lingering in my room past her supposed collection time. This will apparently allow her some time to strut around in her outfit in Tag's presence, before we then head out. At Syd's request, Oliver got us onto the guest list, along with a bunch of his friends, to one of the city's most exclusive rooftop bars in Downtown Miami. How it will work in practice I have no idea, yet I'm standing in front of the mirror, wearing the shortest electric green dress, the highest heels and the most blusher I have ever worn in my life, my hair straightened, and with pretty false eyelashes that Syd taught me how to apply. I've still needed to apply a layer of Josie's foundation to my neck. In truth, I look like something out of 'Selling Sunset'. I hardly recognise my reflection, but in a good way.

I hear her Uber pull up, and I know that's my cue to wait. Part of me hopes that Nicky will see me like this. Since Josie left, I've gone back to barely seeing him, plus the sleep doctor prescribed him a light sleep-aid, ensuring, for now at least, that Nicky makes it through the night without waking. I make a sandwich for him in the evening, and Nicky takes it to bed, in case he gets hungry, but the aim is for Nicky to wean himself off his nightly dining habits.

When I enter the house via the kitchen side door, I can hear Syd talking. I can hear other voices too: Nicky's and Mac's.

When I enter the living room, Tag is in there too, sitting down with Nicky and Mac.

'*Giiiiirrl*, you look dynamite!' Sydney shrieks at me as I enter, my heels making a clattering sound against the floorboards.

I instantly feel Nicky's eyes on me. Tag looks quiet and miserable, playing with a loose thread on his armchair, still in his sportswear. Nicky is in a t-shirt and long cotton shorts, Mac curled into his side.

'So do you!' I say back, and we grasp one another's hands, grinning. Sydney does indeed look breathtaking, in a sequin bodycon dress that contrasts starkly with her dark skin, and accentuates her every tiny curve. Her braids hang loose about her shoulders, her eye make-up sparkling. Even her toenails look glamorous.

'How are the lashes? Did I do them right?' I ask, raising my face to her.

Syd inspects them. 'You got it down,' she confirms. 'I'm calling the Uber. We are ready to kick it.'

'Oh my god, I'm almost jealous I'm not coming with you,' Mackenzie blurts. 'Have a Mai Tai for me, won't you, ladies?'

Neither Nicky nor Tag has spoken. I sneak a look at Nicky. Despite the cessation of relations, he still occupies my thoughts for an unhealthy amount of time during my day, and a part of me wants to remind him that I'm still here, still breathing, still deserving of his affection, yet tortured by wanting something I can't have. His expression is hard to read. Something about it seems infuriated.

'Okay, five minutes away,' Syd says, looking at her phone. 'Let's go wait out front.'

On the path to the gate, Sydney whispers, 'You think that got his Swedish attention?'

I let out a giggle in the darkness. I could have asked her the same thing about Nicky. 'He looked like he was about to cry.'

Oliver meets us in Brickell, at ground level, before we head up in an elevator to a high floor, to a rooftop terrace with stunning views of downtown and beyond.

'Girl, you'd better give Oliver a *big* thank you from me for tonight,' Sydney whispers in my ear as the lift door opens, winking at me as we exit. If only she knew the truth.

Oliver's bought a group of friends, and some of Sydney's girlfriends are also here. She takes time to introduce me. The music is loud, heavy guitar over a pulsating beat, all around; it seeps into the warm, slightly moist night air. Oliver pulled some strings to get us here and I still can't help wishing I found him more attractive than I do. Because, hell knows, he's divine.

The alcohol is flowing. Mojitos, mainly. Bodies are writhing to the music. I feel Oliver at my side for most of the night, making sure I'm looked after. I watch with a grin on my face as Sydney gets *a lot* of attention from his soccer friends, who cannot, it seems, get over her curves. She's having a blast, and it amazes me how she can pick herself up after a break-up. I envy that level of confidence she possesses.

Ninety minutes later, I'm more than just tipsy.

'Do you wanna take a seat?' Oliver asks me, taking my elbow.

I give a nod, swaying as he grabs my hand.

The circular booth under a black sail awning, near to the bar, is just being vacated, and Oliver grabs it for us. I have the perfect view of Syd dancing with all of her girlfriends, seemingly carefree, without dwelling on whether Tag Holström is missing her or not.

'Everything alright?' Oliver asks.

'Everything is good,' I reply, grinning and waving at Sydney.

'She seems over that dude already,' he remarks. 'Whoever he is.'

'I think she's good at hiding it.'

'Better than you are, maybe?'

I pull a face at him. 'That's all done now.'

'Yeah? With Salco? What happened?'

I wince. 'I don't want to waste any more breath on Nicky Salco. Not tonight.'

Oliver's expression alters. He's looking over my shoulder. 'Looks like you may not have a choice. 'Cause Miami Vice just walked in.'

'What?' I say, my head snapping around to where Oliver is looking. To my disbelief, Nicky and Tag have entered the rooftop terrace, along with Mackenzie, who has her arm hooked through Nicky's. Nicky and Tag are, somewhat unfortunately, wearing near identical outfits, light chinos with white t-shirts and dark jackets. You can tell they don't get out much, either of them, more comfortable in their sports attire. Mackenzie looks breathtaking in a powder blue skin tight bandage dress with a sweetheart neckline. Nicky is getting all the attention, glad-handing a bunch of strangers who've swarmed around him. Tag's face is serious. He's eyeballing the crowd, searching for something, or someone. I look over to Sydney, trying to get her attention. When she finally looks my way, I cock my head in an exaggerated fashion towards Tag. She follows my gaze and I swear I see a phantom smile cross her lips before she adopts a look of complete indifference. Her plan appears to have worked.

'How did he get on the list?' I ask, incredulous.

'This is Miami,' Oliver remarks. 'He's literally on every single list already. I see he bought the fiancée.'

I roll my eyes.

Oliver cocks an eyebrow. 'Want me to make him jealous?'

He looks mischievous. In the back of my mind, I know it's the mojito talking when I say, 'Jealous how?'

He slides around to my side of the booth, gliding his arm around my shoulders. My eyes widen with glee. Oliver moves his lips close to my ear, close enough that I can feel his breath on my skin. 'If I take it too far, squeeze my knee. If you want me to leave, squeeze my knee twice real hard.'

I level my eyes on his, bite my lip and nod my head. If it wasn't for the alcohol in my veins, it would feel unfair somehow.

'He might not even come over here,' I whisper.

Almost in answer to my statement, I hear Mackenzie's voice behind me. 'Well, hello, Elle.'

I do my best surprised face, leaning into Oliver. 'Mackenzie! What are you doing here?'

'When you left us at the house, Tag suddenly announced that he wanted to go out. And Nicky pushes Tag into telling me he's got a thing for Sydney. I mean, how did I not know this? Did you know?'

Ugh, she's being all faux-charming again. 'I thought they'd broken up.'

Mackenzie laughs gaily, though I detect a note of irritation in her tone, like she doesn't like to be kept out of the loop. 'See? Y'all *did* know. Anyway, Nicky offered to accompany him, and I thought… *I am* not *gonna be the one who stays home alone.* I don't remember the last time I got Nicky out to a bar.'

I look around. 'Where is Nicky?'

Mackenzie flaps her hand. 'Oh somewhere,' she says, looking to Oliver and holding out her hand. 'Mackenzie Scheffler, nice to meet you.'

'Oliver Davenport,' Oliver says coolly, shaking hands. 'Would you like to join us?'

'Sure,' Mackenzie says, taking a seat on the other side of the booth. She is studying us both, like she's trying to figure out if we're an item.

'Tucker Davenport is my cousin,' Oliver says to Mackenzie. 'You were in the same class at high school.'

Oliver's cousin's mother had an affair with Nicky's father. I presume Mackenzie knows this.

'That's why y'all look so familiar!' Mackenzie screeches. 'Oh my god, Tucker Davenport. Is he still in Miami?'

'Runs a catering business up in Fort Lauderdale,' Oliver replies.

'That's crazy. One of my girlfriends had such a crush on him.'

A shadow comes over the table. I look up to find Nicky has arrived, holding a bottle of beer and a cocktail for Mackenzie.

'Nicky!' Mackenzie blurts. 'This is Oliver Davenport. You remember Tucker from high school? This is his cousin.'

'We've met before,' Nicky says stoically, before shaking Oliver by the hand. 'Like fifteen years ago. You must have been about ten.'

Oliver removes his arm from my shoulders to shake Nicky's hand. The moment they let go of one another, Oliver's arm returns to its position. Mackenzie shifts over, allowing Nicky a seat. All around us, the music throbs.

'I remember,' Oliver says. 'It was at a junior tennis tournament in Olympia Heights.'

Nicky takes a large swig of his beer. 'I won it that year, I seem to remember.'

He sounds arrogant when he says it. His attitude irritates me. He is yet to look in my direction.

'So, Elle, is Oliver the same guy you met at the beach?' Mackenzie asks.

Oliver's arm tightens around my neck like a boa constrictor. I feel his lips pressing a kiss against my temple. Part of me feels like I'm cheating on Nicky, but then I remember there is no me and Nicky. There never was.

'Yes,' I smile, without looking Nicky's way, placing one hand against Oliver's chest.

'You guys are cute together,' Mackenzie remarks. 'Don't you think they're cute together, Nicky?'

I raise my eyes to his for the first time, as though challenging him. 'Very,' he says tightly, taking another swig of his beer.

Mackenzie starts talking about something when I feel Oliver's lips against my ear again.

'He can't stand it,' he whispers, in a way that Nicky won't hear. 'I'm gonna kiss your neck. Laugh at what I'm saying?'

I allow my lips to curl into a grin before a giggle escapes them. My eyes are on Nicky when I feel Oliver's lips caress the skin on my neck – to other side to where Nicky left his mark five nights ago. Nicky watches us, his gaze set like stone.

Two women come running up to our table and Mackenzie suddenly squeals. She knows them. She gets up, squeezing out from behind Nicky to greet them. I listen as she introduces him, before they beckon her over to another group on the other side of the bar. I'm left with Nicky staring at me, Oliver still brushing delicate fake-kisses up the side of my neck. Nicky looks like he might be about to commit murder.

Under the table, I give Oliver's knee a hard double squeeze.

He raises his head. 'Babe, I need the bathroom,' Oliver says languidly. 'Save my seat, okay?'

He slopes off. Moments later, here I am: alone with Nicky Salco, face to face on two opposite sides of the booth.

He's peeling the label from his beer bottle, a muscle pulsating at the base of his jaw. Hastily-put-together-Operation-Jealousy, it appears, was a resounding success.

'So that was Oliver, huh?' he drawls at length.

We don't move. My tone implies more than a little sarcasm. 'Yes. That's Oliver.'

Nicky touches his nose with his thumb. 'I remember him because Tucker's mom was the woman my dad cheated on my mom with. I remember my mom cried for weeks when she found out. My dad begged her not to leave, telling her that it would derail my tennis career if she did, because they didn't have any money left as it was. They couldn't afford to divorce. That's when Mackenzie's father stepped in and helped us out financially.'

Now I just feel guilty for provoking him. 'I'm sorry,' I say. 'Looks like Tag made up with Syd anyway.'

I look over to where he's looking. Tag and Syd are on the dance floor, their lips locked together, Tag crushing her to him in her sequin dress, her arms encircling his neck. I wonder what he's said to her to get her to forgive him. Their secret appears to be out at least.

Unlike mine.

Nicky catches my smile as I watch them. He swallows tightly, unable to look me in the eye, draining the last of his beer. 'So, are you sleeping with him?'

'Would it matter to you if I was?' I snap back.

'You know it would.'

I can't hold back my bitterness. 'I didn't realise our arrangement was exclusive.'

The truth doesn't seem to matter, of course, in this instant, with too much alcohol coursing in my veins. It's the *implication* that counts.

'I mean, it certainly wasn't from your side,' I add, just to twist the knife.

Nicky recoils, like he's been wounded. 'What are you doing?' he asks.

I frown, not understanding his meaning. He leans forward slightly. 'How am I supposed to resist you when you're dressed like that?'

'I didn't know you would be coming here.'

'Oh, so you dressed like that for Oliver?'

'I didn't dress like this for anyone. I can wear what I want.'

'You're not supposed to make it harder for me,' he says in a whispered hiss.

I stare at him, incredulous, his words making my jaw go slack. 'Harder for *you*? Harder for *you*?'

'You know that I want every inch of you. You know that I don't want any other man's hands on you but mine.'

My lips twist. It's still the mojitos talking but I no longer care. 'It's called having your cake and eating it, Nicky. I think you'll find you made your choice. Last time I checked, I wasn't your girlfriend.'

And for perhaps only the third time in our relatively short history, I'm the one walking away from him.

Chapter Twenty-Two

'Okay, you can look now,' I say.

In the kitchen, Mackenzie turns around. She's wearing a grey pencil skirt, a crisp white shirt and towering high heels, having come back from a visit to her boutique in Miami, though it seems odd to me that she would dress up for such an occasion. Lately, she's been disappearing a lot in the afternoons. Yesterday, she sent Lonzo and I on a last-minute trip to Whole Foods. As we were leaving, I noted that her 'associate', Bryan Dabrowski, with the slicked-back hair, was just pulling up outside the house in his plush silver convertible.

Today, Mackenzie's gaze settles on the three-tier cake on front of her, of my making. She lifts her chin, walking around it in a slow circle with her arms crossed, inspecting it from every angle.

'Well, it's certainly an improvement,' she says drily.

I marvel at her lack of enthusiasm. This cake is a masterpiece, if I do say so myself. I decide to ignore her comment. 'Absolutely everything is edible,' I say, 'Apart from the ribbon around each tier. It's the same vanilla sponge with the lemon buttercream inside.'

It's taken me almost three days. My first three attempts at a wedding cake were not bad in my eyes, but the moment Mackenzie said she'd prefer fondant for the icing was the minute I knew I was in trouble. In early January, I took a three-day course run by a bespoke cake shop in downtown Miami, specifically for fondant design. As it turns out, I have quite a knack for fashioning flowers out of sugar paste and gel food colouring, using just a toothpick as a crafting tool. I've surprised even myself.

Though I wouldn't say she's been nice to me over the past few weeks, something has definitely changed in Mackenzie's demeanour. Neither Lonzo and I can work it out, though Lonzo thinks it's because the wedding is fast approaching, and finally, Mackenzie will be legally bound to the man she sees as her property. Lonzo believes she's practically rubbing her hands together at the prospect, though I remain unconvinced.

Mackenzie's verdicts on my wedding cake attempts have been – unsurprisingly – brutal. The first she lambasted as 'terrible', to the second she simply said 'go again'. She said my third attempt wouldn't look out of place at a seven-year-old's birthday party, despite Lonzo calling it the most impressive wedding cake he'd ever seen. At first, I saw it as a form of torture, making a cake for Nicky's wedding. But then, like my love of concocting desserts, I began to enjoy the process, and it became a personal challenge to create something spectacular.

I haven't seen Nicky since before Christmas. I flew to Spain for a week, staying in Barcelona with Josie and Gideon, and when I came back, Nicky had already flown to Australia with Rag and Tag. Before I left, Sydney reeled off a list of all the tournaments he was set to play in: Adelaide first, followed by the Australian Open, then Rio de Janeiro, followed by Indian Wells, the Miami Open before the big Europeans: Monte Carlo, Madrid, Rome, Roland Garros and Wimbledon. The wedding is to take place in the brief gap between Rio and Indian Wells, played in California. So, Nicky will be home for that. That and the Miami Open, his favourite tournament, on home soil. Those are the only times he will likely spend any significant time in Florida. When Sydney told me, I did my best to conceal my disappointment.

The latter part of November he spent at some special sports facility for 'targeted recuperation', including sleep monitoring. In early December, he was mostly out on court and we succeeded in avoiding one another's company altogether. The day times were fine. I got used to going almost an entire twelve hours without thinking about him. Yet the nights are when I miss his touch. When I fantasize about us together. When I exist in my own little dreamworld, living in my version of the story where he chooses me over Mackenzie.

Yet that's all it is. A fantasy.

Every day that passes by brings us closer to his wedding. A wedding for which I am making the cake. Almost like my gift for the golden couple.

It hasn't stopped with the cake either. Mackenzie's got me involved in everything from table design to the choice of flowers for the bridal bouquet. And not in a good way: mostly I have become her personal assistant, fetching things from across town, or making phone calls on her behalf. I feel seeped in it, to the point where I feel dirty, like I can't rub any of it off. The lie sticks to everything.

Mackenzie's taking some pictures of the cake on her phone, which I take as a positive sign.

'You think Nicky'll like it?' I ask, mostly because it's a chance to say his name out loud.

'Lord knows, if it's got sugar in it; he'll devour it. These flowers here, they're too small. I want it with slightly bigger flowers.'

'You want me to make another?'

She gives me a look like I'm an idiot. 'Yes, Elle. Isn't that what I just said? I'm thinking... it also needs to be more pink. Maybe a strawberries and cream-themed cake? Try that instead.'

I sigh inwardly, but outwardly I'm nodding my head. The problem is – as with every version I make for her – we now have a three-tier cake that requires eating, and I refuse to let the whole creation go to waste.

In the afternoon, and for the fourth time this month, Lonzo and I deliver four boxes of sliced-up wedding cake to a homeless shelter in downtown Miami.

It's eleven p.m. on a Monday night in mid-January. I've finished doing the dishes as Mackenzie's parents and Ben and Libby Salco gather in front of the television for Nicky's opening match of the Australian Open. Mikhail Scheffler is entrenched in the biggest armchair, a large man with a rounded stomach, a deep tan, glasses and curly grey hair, wearing jeans and a shirt that's open at the collar. He cradles a large glass of red wine. Mackenzie is upstairs in her office.

Melbourne is fourteen hours ahead. Expectations are high. Nicky has just come off the back of a quarter-final place at the Adelaide International, and the Australian Open is his only previous Grand Slam win. It's the best Nicky's been playing in a while, and from the conversations I've been overhearing all day, Ben Salco is declaring his son 'fixed'.

'Elle, please honey, stop what you're doing and come sit with us,' Libby says to me, patting the vacant seat next to her as Ben Salco paces in front of the TV, unshaven and with a stern glare in his features. 'Come watch Nicky play. If I need more wine, I can go to the kitchen.'

I offer her a smile. My eyes go to the TV screen. Nicky is warming up. He looks focused, less tired. No matter how much I try to put a stop to it, my heart still lurches in my chest whenever I see his image, my pulse quickening uncontrollably. Libby covers my hand with hers when I take a seat, rubbing my knuckles. I quickly realise I've sat on someone's phone, stuck in the material folds of the sofa.

'Is this yours?' I ask Libby, holding out the handset.

'I think that's Mackenzie's, sweetheart, just leave it there.'

I move the handset to the armrest. 'See that's much better,' Libby says. 'He's looking much better, don't you think, Mikhail?'

Mikhail Scheffler shifts in his seat. 'We'll know in the next few hours.'

We lapse into silence. The American commentator starts talking about 'Triple Salco', about how Nicky once won this tournament as a twenty-three-year-old, raising the question of both his current form and focus.

I sit with my back straight, wishing I could retreat to the kitchen.

Next to me, Mackenzie's phone buzzes. I glance down as a message pops up on the screen. The message is from 'Bryan' and reads, *When can I see you again? x*

The message disappears on screen as fast as it arrives, but I stiffen. That Bryan has followed his question with a kiss makes their relationship more intimate than I would imagine an 'associate' relationship to be. It makes the whole nature of their involvement unclear. It makes me question what I heard that day, when her music was blaring loudly upstairs.

Is Nicky not the only who's been one cheating?

I'm still pondering what it means when Mackenzie enters the room from upstairs, wearing a cut-off pair of denim shorts, and swipes up her phone, unlocking it.

'Did I miss the beginning?' she asks nonchalantly, and I watch as a smile dances across her lips when she reads the message from Bryan.

'No, sweetie, but they're about to start,' Libby hums. 'Did you want another wine?'

'I can get it,' Mackenzie says, walking towards the kitchen. I lean back in my seat slightly, watching her walk through to the hallway, stopping to lean her back against the wall outside the kitchen, bending one knee underneath her bottom as she types a response into her phone.

I watch as Nicky takes the first set comfortably. In the second set, one of his returns goes awry, hitting a ball girl at the net in the face at some speed. She covers her face, bent double. He apologises, but it appears the girl is in some pain.

Go over to her, Nicky, I think, echoed by Libby who says to the television, 'Oh Lord, Nicholas Salco, I raised you better than that, go over to her.'

'It's a hazard of being at the net,' Ben Salco grumbles in disagreement. 'They should just carry on.'

On the TV, Nicky's opponent has gone over to the ball girl, checking if she's alright. Nicky's already walked back to his position, looking annoyed. It doesn't go down well with the crowd, which is packed to the rafters. Someone appears to jeer him, Nicky irritated by the gesture. It's a moment before Nicky moves to go to the ball girl, but by then it just makes him look bad. By the time he's reached her, she is being soothed by an official too. The impact has caused her nose to bleed, a ripple going through the crowd as she raises her head, blood gushing down to her chin. Play is halted whilst she is replaced and walked off court with her head tilted back and a towel pressed to her nose.

Though a relatively small incident, things go downhill immediately after.

When Nicky loses his opening match of the Australian Open, Mackenzie is incensed. I'm desperate to leave the room but I feel rooted to my seat. The camera focusses on an increasingly dejected Nicky.

'I do not understand it,' Mackenzie rants at her father and Ben Salco, pacing back and forth across the rug. 'Ragnar has got to go. He cannot carry on like this! Honestly, what else can he have on his mind? What is so wrong with him that his game has been shot to hell? I do not understand what else we can do here. Maybe *both* Rag and Tag need to go. We re-group. We start again. A different coach. A different training partner.'

'I'm in agreement,' Ben Salco states grimly.

'Honey, you know how much Nicky likes Rag. He's already refused to fire him,' Libby says.

Ben Salco then gets to his feet. 'Then maybe it shouldn't be up to him anymore. We all know he can play a lot better than this. Ragnar has not proved his worth. Nicky was playing better than this last spring. His performance has been poor since last summer. Mikhail, wouldn't you agree?'

My eyes on the TV, my heart aches for Nicky. He's sitting courtside, alone in his chair, elbows rested on his knees and his head down, reeling at his first round defeat, his expression a mixture of frustration and disappointment. The commentators are once more ripping into him, remarking on his demonstrably below-average tennis game, and how his form has never been worse.

Mikhail also gets to his feet, stretching out his back. 'I'll go back to the list of coaches we put together a few weeks back. Maybe make some calls.'

I lean over to Libby. 'They can't really do that without Nicky's say-so, can they?' I ask.

Libby's shoulders droop. On the TV, Nicky is leaving the court, not stopping for any of the autograph hunters.

'Technically, no,' she whispers back. 'But Nicky can be stubborn. We might just need to give him a little push in the right direction. I know my boy. Something is not right with him.'

Later, in my room, getting ready for bed, I google 'Bryan Dabrowski Miami'. It turns out he works as an estate agent, or realtor as they call it in America.

Once again, I question their association, because on the surface, it seems he doesn't have anything to do with Mackenzie's bikini business.

The next morning, a photograph of the ball girl with a bloody nose makes the front page of the Miami Herald. And with it, Nicky's first round defeat at the Australian Open brings about a change of plan.

'We'll need to stock up again,' Mackenzie addresses Lonzo and me in the kitchen. 'Nicky arrives back this evening. They're already in the air. They'll stop over here for a week before heading down to Rio. Be warned, there may be some paparazzi snooping around the walls.'

I accompany Lonzo to the markets, stocking up on fresh produce. Lonzo talks the whole way about his dislike of Mackenzie and her father's involvement in making decisions that involve tennis on Nicky's behalf.

Throughout the journey I'm quiet. I'm still pondering the idea that Mackenzie could be in a relationship with another man, someone who isn't genuinely her associate. I have zero idea about how to find out the truth. In addition, the knowledge that Nicky's coming back to Miami has unsettled me. More than that: I'm a nervous wreck. Lonzo doesn't comment on my subdued mood, just keeps talking. It's been thirty-nine days since I last saw Nicky, and up until today I thought I was coping with his absence. My stomach churns with a desperation I haven't felt for some time and I'm bursting to see him again.

When we arrive back, sure enough, a group of photographers are gathered on the opposite side of the street.

I'm still awake at 2 a.m. when I hear the vehicle gate. I know from my continual checking of the arrivals board at Miami International on my phone that their flight from Qatar has been delayed. I creep out of bed, peering out of the curtain that covers the glass pane on my door. I hear voices, witnessing Sydney getting out of the back of the white van in the driveway, followed by Tag. Tag puts his arm around her and takes her bag. My heart pummels my rib cage when I see the back of Nicky's head as he carries his bags to the front door of the house, the lights still on. Ragnar is behind him, retreating to his pool house at the far side of the garden. As the van departs, I see Mackenzie opening the door in her white silk robe, witnessing yet another lackluster embrace that she gives him, and Nicky's brushed kiss against her cheek. I want to go out there and show her how it's done, but he's already gone inside and the night is quiet again.

It takes me a long time to fall asleep.

Chapter Twenty-Three

A loud blast of music from outside wakes me, a mash-up of heavy guitar with rap vocals and a throbbing base line. I rub my eyes and check my phone. It's 6.00am.

I dress quickly and go outside into the garden. There's mist in the air, the temperature around fifteen degrees, the sky gloomy and overcast, the sun not yet fully up. The music is coming from the tennis courts, beyond the pool. I pull on a pair of trainers and make my way slowly past the house, checking for signs of life. There are none.

Rounding the far side of the house, hugging my waist, I find myself staring at Nicky alone on court, shirtless, a basket of balls by his side, racket in hand as he wallops serve after serve after serve to the far side of the court, taking his frustrations out on his invisible demons. He doesn't see me, and I can't see his face, only the glistening sweat across the line of his back. The music comes from above me in the house above my head, from some kind of amp. I want to go to him, but at that moment I daren't move, enthralled by his movements. The thing that's stopping me is fear. Fear that I he'll tell me I have to keep my distance. Fear that I won't be able to hold back. Fear that he'll reject me outright. I turn to go back to my room, but I stop in my tracks, realizing I want him to know that I'm here.

I edge closer to the fence. Still his back is to me. I stop for a moment, admiring the sheer power of his serve.

When I draw level with him, he spots me, coming to a halt. I keep moving another six or seven metres forward to the open gate, level with the net, where my fingers cling to the chain link wire mesh. For a moment, he just watches me. I can't read his expression, though he looks exhausted. All I know is that I ache for his touch.

Nicky walks over. I enter the court. I see the hurt in his tired eyes.

'Hey,' he says.

'Long time, no see,' is my response.

We stand there, the futility of our situation lingering around us in the haze. There's so much to say, but we're trapped. I glance back at the garden. There's no one there. Nicky edges closer to me. Unable to resist, his recent absence playing on my mind, and combined with my desperation to see him, I feel emboldened to a risk. So, impulsively, I step forward, raise myself up on tiptoe and press my lips to his. It's an awkward kiss: a meld of a brief peck on the lips and the kind of smooch one might give their husband or wife before departing to work. Either way, it's more fleeting than I would wish for, armed with the knowledge that we are exposed, and that absolutely anyone, including some journalist with a long-lens camera lingering outside the walls, could see us. Still, the unexpected nature of it causes Nicky to drop his racket to the hard court, where the graphite frame bounces off the concrete and clatters to the ground.

'You call that a kiss?' he smiles after a moment, his fingers going to his lips.

I raise my eyebrows at him. 'Well, it's all you're getting. I shouldn't even be out here.'

'But you are. Out here. And nobody else is.'

'How are you?' I breathe.

It's obvious that the sting of his defeat, and the fallout that has come with it, still pains him. 'Feels like I'm letting everybody down.'

'You're not.'

He sighs, raises his eyes to me. 'Australia was hell without you.'

It's not what I expect him to say. 'I wish I could have been there,' I respond.

He rakes one hand though his hair, checking we're still alone, gritting his teeth. 'I can't hide it anymore, Elle,' he says. 'I don't *want* to hide it anymore. I want us.'

I stare at him, hardly able to comprehend the words that have just come out of his mouth. 'You're still getting married,' I finally choke out.

He shakes his head. 'I'm crazy about you, Elle. It's you that I want. Alright? I miss you so goddamned much when you're not with me. I'll make it right. I just... I need a little time to straighten some things out. I'm not gonna marry Mac; no matter what she might think. I swear to you.'

My heart has gone from thundering in my chest to border-line exploding. Tears splash onto my cheeks as I process his words. I glance over at the garden, breathless, checking no one is around. It's the first proper conversation we've had in weeks. I want to throw my arms around him, yet I know we need to be cautious. To do things properly. He needs to end things with Mackenzie first. I nod my head furiously in his direction, biting my lip, stifling a grin, the words robbed from me as I acknowledge his promise: that he is willing to break off his engagement for me. In my smile is the hope of something that before this second, I considered an impossibility.

Nicky breaks into a broad grin, squinting in my direction. 'Is that a yes? We're gonna do this?'

I nod vigorously, backing away. He bends to pick up his racket.

'By the end of the today, Elle,' he says, his gaze fixed on mine as I go. 'I'll fix all this by the end of the day, I swear.' Walking backwards, I grant him an ecstatic smile in return, before turning and making my way back to the house, the morning mist dispersing all around me.

And just like that, everything has changed.

~

'Elle.'

I look up from my chopping board. It's after breakfast. Mack-enzie approaches me, an odd, haughty expression on her face, lips puckered. She stares at me for longer than is necessary, her look sending a shudder down my spine.

'A favour,' she breathes, holding out a piece of paper with something scribbled on it. I take the handwritten note, containing an address. 'Get Lonzo to drive you. You may need help getting it into the car.'

'What are we collecting?' I ask, but she's already walking away.

'You'll see,' she hums back.

Lonzo parks the car outside the address in Coconut Grove. It appears to be a couture bridal boutique.

'This is it,' he says, puffing out his cheeks. 'Did she say what it was we're supposed to pick up?'

There's a horrible feeling swirling in the pit of my stomach, despite Nicky's pledges to me this morning out on court. An odd sense of foreboding.

'I'm guessing it's the dress?' I swallow, my voice rising with uncertainty.

Lonzo mutters something in Spanish, and I can tell by his tone that it's derogatory.

'I'll go in, shall I?' I say, opening the passenger side door.

A few minutes later, I re-emerge. Though it comes sealed inside a zipped cover, I struggle to carry the dress back outside due to the sheer weight of it, squeezing my frame out of the door to the boutique, cradling its hefty bulk in my arms.

Sydney is in the driveway as we return. She greets me with a bear hug.

'Where'd you go?'

'Mackenzie sent us to fetch her dress. When we're not in the kitchen, Lonzo and I make excellent errand boys.'

Lonzo throws Sydney a look as he walks back in the direction of the kitchen.

'You want help bringing it inside?'

I nod, opening up the boot of the car.

'What's the latest?' I ask under my breath as she moves closer, bursting to tell her about my exchange with Nicky this morning, though holding back, mostly because part of me is still wondering if I imagined it.

Syd rolls her eyes. 'Endless arguing? Nicky caught in the middle of it all? He doesn't want to give up Rag and Tag. And hell, I certainly don't want to see either of them go.'

Because Nicky losing Tag means Sydney more than likely losing Tag too.

'So, what's the consensus?' I ask.

'Ben and Mikhail have given Nicky the Rio Open to pull things out of the bag. If he doesn't perform in South America, Ragnar's out. Gone. Nicky's back is against the wall.'

We both grit our teeth in realization at the ultimatum, which seems absurd to us both.

'And what about Tag?'

She swallows tightly. 'I don't know yet.'

'What does Rag say?'

'That's just it. I don't think he's had any kind of say. They've cut him out of the equation.'

It's then that I realise the garden is quiet. 'Where is everybody?'

'Nicky just left for a round of golf with his sports agent. Up north of here, in Jupiter.'

'Golf? Now?' I question.

'Something about getting everybody to cool off. Take a step back. Discuss Nicky's options informally. Plus, there's a potential sponsor gonna be there, I think.'

Sydney helps me unload the dress from the car, and I wonder what it means for Nicky's promise to me at dawn.

The afternoon is uneventful, though there's no sign of Nicky's return. I am uneasy, a permanent lump in my throat as a result. Sydney comes into the kitchen when Lonzo and I are in the middle of cooking dinner.

'Lonz, can I borrow Elle for five minutes?' she asks. Lonzo nods his head, humming along with the upbeat Latin tune on the radio.

She looks to me. 'Mac wants to see us.'

'What does she want?' I ask, moments later, following Syd through the ground floor of the house.

'I have no idea; she just messaged me.'

My pace slows for a moment, as I realise we're walking through to the guestroom at the back of the house, where Nicky's parents usually stay. The room where Nicky and I first made love on the rug on the floor.

When we enter, Libby herds us quickly inside and shuts the door. Inappropriate memories fill my vision for a split second. My legs freeze up when I see Mackenzie is stood in her wedding dress, the couture gown I lugged into the back of the car, with the photograph of Nicky winning his first Grand Slam as a backdrop. She's covered head to toe in elegant lace, the off-the-shoulder design complimenting her décolletage, a sumptuous skirt, with her bare feet nestled in the hairs of the sheepskin rug peeping out at the hemline. The rug issue would have bothered me more if my breath hadn't been stolen away by how incredible she looks.

'Well,' she questions, sashaying in a circle, holding out her arms. 'What do y'all think of the gown?'

Sydney has let out a serious of rapturous gasps. I slap a grin on my face, trying hard to empty the panicked thoughts from my brain.

'Do y'all like it?' she says.

'*Giiirl*, Nicky gon flip his lid when he sees you,' Syd enthuses. 'You look a million bucks.'

'You look absolutely stunning,' I say, with as much enthusiasm as I can manage, Nicky's voice in my head telling me, *by the end of today.*

'It's not too much lace?'

Libby starts shaking her head.

'The lace is perfect,' Syd enthuses and I keep nodding, else I might cry.

'Elle, what do you think?' Mackenzie asks me pointedly.

'The lace is lovely.'

'You think Nicky will like it?'

'I'm sure he'll love it.'

'I designed it with him in mind. The man who very soon I'm gonna call my husband. I wanted a dress that reflected our history together. Everything we've gone through over the years. It's important to have history, don't you think, Elle?'

Her eyes are on mine as she speaks. I detect something in her Southern drawl. As though, by showing me her wedding dress, she's somehow stamping her authority.

Panic explodes in my chest. I start to wonder if Nicky has said something to her. I question whether she saw us this morning out on the court.

Because in her tone, there's something that sounds strangely to me like malice.

It's a pleasant evening, the sun stretching long across the surface of the pool and the veranda, and onto the tennis courts, the early morning mist long forgotten.

And yet still, there is no sign of Nicky.

'Elle, you sit here, by me,' Mackenzie says before we've sat down.

It's a bizarre request, given her usual desire to keep me out of her sight, but I comply without objection.

'Right, settle down, everyone,' Mackenzie says. 'I've got a bunch of wedding-related questions to ask y'all, just so I can check we're in good shape.'

For dinner, Lonzo and I made a large vat of chilli con carne, served with tortillas, rice, sour cream and Monterey Jack cheese, with diced jalapeno peppers as the garnish. Rag starts doling it out onto individual plates.

'Tag, you first,' Mackenzie says and Tag's eyes widen in jest. 'You think you can get those nets down before you go to Rio? So the guys can come and build the marquee? Like, I could leave it to the construction guys to do it, but I'm convinced they're not gonna know how and they'll break them or something.'

'Yes, ma'am,' Tag nods.

'Lib, did you call the florist?'

'I sure did, honey. Everything is locked in.'

'Good,' Mackenzie continues. 'Ragnar, did you try on your suit pants like I asked?'

Ragnar raises an eyebrow. 'The legs are too short.'

'Did you give them to my mom to be altered?'

'I did,' Ragnar hums.

'Syd, I'm not gonna ask you anything, 'cause I know you're all over it.'

Sydney grins sweetly.

'Benji, did you call the DJ back?' Mackenzie continues.

'I did.'

'Good,' Mackenzie says, though the smile on her face doesn't reach her eyes.

'Just like I thought. I just have one more question. It's for you, Elle. Did you really think you were gonna be able to steal my fiancé away from me?'

A breeze goes through the air, just as a hush descends over the veranda. My chest restricts. Somewhere, at the other end of the table, someone drops their fork, and it clatters.

'Excuse me?' I swallow.

'I said...,' Mackenzie breathes, and she leans back in her chair, making sure all eyes on the table are on her. 'Did you really think you were going to be able to steal Nicky away from me?'

All eyes shift to me. I feel my cheeks burning up. It's so quiet that you can hear the water lapping into the pool filter. 'I don't know what you're talking about,' I manage.

'Oh, no? Did my eyes deceive me, Elle, or was that not you throwing yourself at Nicky first thing this morning on the tennis court?'

'I gave him a hug, that was all,' I choke out.

'Sweetie, I'm not blind. I know a pathetic little girl giving Nicky a kiss when I see it. You're like one of those desperate, virginal autograph hunters, all enamoured with him. But I will tell you this for free, Elle. He might be taken in by your stuck-up British accent and your mediocre cuisine. He might think he loves little Elle Callaway getting up for him at night and fawning over his every word. But Nicky, Elle? Nicky is *mine*. He has been all along. You seem to have conveniently forgotten that. So don't kid yourself by thinking you can take him from me.'

I push my chair back, getting to my feet, backing away. 'I don't have to listen to this.'

I glance up. Every pair of eyes scrutinizes me. Syd looks shocked, questioning whether she's missed something. Libby has covered her mouth with her hands. Ben Salco glowers in my direction. Ragnar's look, though, is the worst. It's like he doesn't know if he can trust me anymore.

'Can you believe this girl, Lib?' Mackenzie says, looking to Nicky's mother. 'Oh, don't leave on my account,' she continues in a melodic tone, turning back to me and getting out of her chair, following me. 'Don't tell me. Nicky was your first crush? Was it love at first sight? Did you imagine him visiting your room in the night after you'd given him some food?'

Tears spring to my eyes, my breathing ragged. At the table, they're holding their collective breath. I want to tell her that he *has* been in my room. I want to tell her about the things her fiancé has done to me in secret.

'Nicky cares about me,' is all I can think to say, my words tripping over one another.

I try to walk away.

'You're just the *help*, Elle,' Mackenzie mocks me, her tone changing once more, this time to an aggressive one. 'Get over

234

yourself. You are the last woman Nicky Salco would be interested in.'

I wipe my eyes. I feel ashamed, yet I stand my ground. 'Try asking him that,' I state resolutely, in a low tone.

My words cause the rage to explode from Mackenzie's chest. With a vicious cry, she comes at me. 'You *bitch*!' she blazes at me. Before I know it, I feel the hot sting of Mackenzie's palm as it fires low across my cheek, the edge of her expensive watch catching my bottom lip. As she makes contact, my head whips to the side and I almost lose my balance. Heat rushes to my face, my neck and cheeks turning a shade of puce as I hear the chorus of horrified gasps from the seven remaining members of the table. I clutch my face, realizing she's drawn blood.

'You're hardly one to talk,' I hiss with every inch of courage I can muster. 'What about you and Bryan Dabrowski?'

'How *dare* you!' Mackenzie hollers, coming at me again as I stumble back, my feet tripping on the water's edge. 'Bryan Dabrowski is my *associate*!'

With her last words, she thrusts against me, arms outstretched, her nails digging into my neck, her other hand striking directly into my chest. I let go of my face, feeling my world tilt as I fall headlong into the pool.

Chapter Twenty-Four

Cold, chlorinated water hits me. For a brief moment, I am fully submerged, bubbles rising, the rushing sound in my ears all around, blotting out Mackenzie's screeching, though it's still there.

I twist, my clothes getting caught up in the water before I kick my legs, coming up for air to find Tag is leaning down, holding out his hand, shouting my name. I realise the others are all now on their feet. Mikhail is holding his daughter back. She is still shrieking in my direction.

'Get out of this house!' she screams. 'You are fired! Get your things and leave! I never want to see your face again! You're a nothing! A nobody!'

I am trembling as Tag helps me out of the water, my clothes drenched. Glancing back, I witness several pairs of disapproving eyes on me, Ragnar's included.

'This way, I'll get her a towel,' Sydney mutters, as I feel the weight of Tag's arms go around my shoulders as he escorts me towards my room. I am dripping everywhere, and there's a small trail of watery blood. Humiliation rolls over me in waves. I needed Nicky here to stand up for me; to tell the truth. Mackenzie seems to believe it's all a fantasy, and that I'm the one living in a dreamworld.

Tag ushers me inside my door. He lets me go. 'Are you alright?' he breathes, Sydney bundling through the door behind us. I wander forward, my mind racing. I hardly know what to think.

'What the hell just happened?' Sydney blurts, closing the door behind her. 'Elle, what the hell was that? Did you kiss Nicky?'

They're staring at me expectantly, and all I can think is that I want to run. To get out of here immediately.

I turn, still in a haze, looking around for a bag, locating my backpack. My clothes drip water all over the floor as I move. I go to my bedside, grabbing my passport and the letter Lonzo wrote for me from the drawer. I grab my copy of *Jane Eyre* and my phone. I go to the wardrobe, grabbing a few pairs of underwear and some clothes straight off their hangers. I go into the bathroom, seizing my make-up and a toothbrush.

'Did you know about this?' Sydney is barking at Tag.

'No I didn't know about this!' Tag's voice rises behind me. 'What was that?'

'Elle, what the hell just happened? Bryan Dabrowski's a realtor. He's helping Mac locate new store premises in South Beach. They're not—'

I pause, questioning whether I'd gone too far, implying there was something inappropriate about Mackenzie's relationship with her so-called *associate*. Still, I was angry. 'I need to go,' I mutter, shaking my head, zipping up the bag and feeling worse that I'm now causing arguments between Tag and Sydney. 'I need to leave, right now.'

'Elle, what are you doing? You at least gotta change outta those clothes. Nicky'll be back soon, we can straighten all this out. He can explain to Mac that there's nothing goin' on between you two.'

I stop still, staring at her, water dripping from the tips of my hair. The look that I give her tells her everything she needs to know.

'Hell to the no,' she chokes. 'There *is* somethin' going on between y'all?'

'I can't stay,' I tell her.

'Elle, wait for Nicky, please,' Tag implores me. 'You've gone pale. And you're bleeding.'

237

I touch my lip. 'What? And suffer some more humiliation? Have Mackenzie throw me in the pool again?'

Tag steps forward to grip me, but I avoid his grasp. 'Let me get you some ice, at least,' he says.

I push past him. 'I need to get out of here,' I say.

Out in the garden, it's quiet. As I move, I glance to my right. Ben and Libby Salco are next to the lunch table. Mikhail and Sara Scheffler are with their daughter, seemingly trying to calm her down. My wet clothes are chafing my thighs as I head left past the driveway towards the gate. Sydney comes rushing up behind me.

'I'm calling them now, Elle. They should be in the car back from Jupiter. Please, just hold on one second.'

'I can't stay, Syd,' I say, reaching the end of the path. 'Please, just let me go.'

I open the gate. Mackenzie's voice cuts through the air. 'Good riddance!' she shrieks. 'And don't even think about coming back!'

I see Sydney swallow, her forlorn look as I turn and leave the grounds.

Outside on the pavement, I reach for my phone, my heart still hammering hard in my chest. I scroll quickly to the name that I want.

'Elle?' Oliver answers after a couple of rings. 'How are you?'

I swallow tears. 'Are you free?' I ask. 'Could you come and pick me up?'

'Where are you?'

'I'm leaving Gables by the Sea. Can you come quickly?'

'Sure, of course, I'm just in Coconut Grove. I'll hop in the car now. Everything alright?'

'No,' I tell him, and a sob escapes my lips. 'No, no, it's not.'

~

It's dark outside. I'm warm and dry, my bare feet tucked under me, on a sofa at a house in Brickell that belongs to Oliver's parents. It's a gated property off South Miami Avenue; the small, private garden lined by palm trees. I'm wearing a warm, black hooded-top with a Miami Heat basketball logo on the front, the sleeves so long they cover my fingers, and a pair of Oliver's mother's pyjama bottoms. My wet clothes are in the tumble dryer, in a utility room at the back of the house. My hair is still damp, but drying. My lower lip is swollen, a little encrusted with blood, where Mackenzie's watch sent my teeth into my own flesh, before I ended up in the swimming pool. I still have scratch marks on my neck.

Two hours ago, I waited in the shadows for Oliver's car, my heart beating so fast I could hardly breathe. When he arrived, he'd leaned over, opening up the passenger side door so I could duck inside.

'Holy shit,' he'd said furiously when he saw me. 'What the hell happened? Did Salco do this you?'

'Mackenzie Scheffler,' I'd replied, closing the door. 'Please just drive.'

He'd put his foot down, almost running a red light in the process. I'd given him minimal details, though he knew that Mackenzie was the one to shove me into the pool. I told him that Nicky wasn't there. He'd brought me back here, running me a warm bath. Alone, I'd sat on the toilet with the seat down and cried. Silent sobs, because I didn't want Oliver to hear me crying, when a large part of me knows I've brought this on myself.

'Sydney is calling me,' Oliver says as rest my head against the back of the sofa.

'I switched my phone off,' I mumble in response.

'Do I answer?'

'I can talk to her.'

'You're sure? You don't have to tell them where you are. You're safe here.'

The phone stops ringing. Oliver unlocks his handset, then hands me his phone. I call her back.

'Oliver, it's Sydney Swanson—' I hear her say as she answers immediately, an urgent tone in her voice.

'It's me,' I say, though my voice emerges as a kind of croak.

'Elle? You're with Oliver? Thank god. Are you alright?'

'I'm alright,' I say.

'I've got Nicky here; he wants to talk to you. Will you talk to him?'

I go quiet for a moment. I can hear his voice in the background, asking Syd to speak to me. Before I can reply, I hear Nicky's deep voice.

'Elle? Where are you? I can come get you.'

'I'm in Brickell,' I say in a muted tone.

'Have you got the address?'

I go silent.

'Syd told me everything,' he breathes. 'Elle, I'm so sorry.'

'I don't want to go back there. Not now.'

'Then I'll come to you. Please.'

I raise my eyes to Oliver. He glowers at me, as though warning me against having anyone come here. I give him a nod, telling him it's alright.

'94 South West 22nd,' he says, and I repeat the address to Nicky.

'I'm getting in the car now,' he says. 'I'll be there soon.'

My heart starts to clatter in my chest when Nicky's 4x4 rolls up outside. Oliver opens the gate remotely, allowing him to park in the driveway, stark headlights shining through the windows at the front of the house, sending shadows chasing across the room.

'Is she here?' I hear Nicky say with some urgency when Oliver opens the front door. I can only see Oliver. He says nothing in response, regarding our visitor with distain, lifting his chin in my direction.

'Elle?' Nicky says as he enters, turning the corner. Laughably, I find he's still wearing golf gear, somehow a world away from Nicky's usual wardrobe.

'That's far enough,' Oliver says behind him, in a warning tone, closing the door.

A low table with a lit candle separates us. Nicky stares down at me, his expression filled with concern. Perhaps because the lights are low, he can't see the full extent of damage to my lip.

'You can kiss my ass, Davenport,' Nicky snaps, 'If you think you're in some kind of position of power in this situation. This is between me and Elle.'

'I'm just looking out for her,' Oliver snorts. 'Which is more than I can say you did.'

I watch Nicky's Adam's apple bob up and down, as though Oliver's touched a nerve. He doesn't respond, his gaze coming back to me. I can barely look at him.

'Are you alright?' he asks me as Oliver backs off a little to the hallway.

'I am now.'

'Sydney called whilst we were in the car. I drove so fast I'm surprised I didn't get pulled over by the cops.'

'You needn't have bothered,' I reply drily. 'Mackenzie had already pushed me into the pool by that point.'

'Sydney told me what Mac said to you. What she saw this morning, out on court. Elle, what she said to you was unforgiveable. I spoke to her as soon as I got home. I think it's safe to say the conversation didn't go as she'd figured it would. I told her I couldn't marry her. That the reason was because I'm crazy about you.'

I let my shoulders drop. Until a few hours ago, those words would have been everything I'd wanted to hear. But at this very moment, they land with a hollow thud, arriving too late.

'It took her a moment, I think. To believe what I was telling her. Because the whole time she'd been worried about you stealing me away somehow, when the reality was that she'd lost me a long time ago.'

I look away.

'There was a lot of screaming,' he swallows. 'I should have talked to her sooner. I should have broken off the engagement straight after Long Island. I know that now.'

'Is your lip alright?' he ploughs on. 'Does it hurt? I wouldn't blame you if you wanted to press assault charges against her.'

He's stopped looking at me, as though my not looking at him has dented his confidence, his jaw clenching and unclenching. 'Elle, please. Say something. I know you're pissed at me because I wasn't there.'

I inhale and shake my head. 'You promised me this morning you'd end things with her, but instead, it seems, you went to play a round of *golf*.'

'My agent insisted. There was a potential sponsor there. What did you want me to do?'

I purse my lips, sending another jolt of pain through the injured one. 'Oh, I don't know, prioritise your personal life for once? I may not like Mackenzie, Nicky, but she's right about one thing. It's all about the tennis with you.'

'That's not true,' he argues shakily.

'It is true. Tennis is your whole life. Everything else is second. I was humiliated today.'

His eyes snap up when I use that word, like he's surprised that I've said it.

'Mackenzie hitting me aside… then literally *shoving* me into the swimming pool, you didn't see the way they were all looking at me. They automatically assumed I was the one in the wrong. Like I was some kind of lowlife predator who'd tried to come between you and Mackenzie. And they didn't even know the real truth of the situation.'

'They know it now. They all do. And Mac knows it's completely over between us.'

I say nothing. I look at him, raising my chin and pulling down the neckline of Oliver's hoodie. 'I have scratch marks on my neck.'

'I am so sorry,' he whispers again, his voice pained. 'I should have been there.'

'Well, you weren't. I guess we'll have to live with that.'

'I wish you'd waited for me,' he says at length. 'Why did you run to Oliver?'

'I didn't have anyone else to run to. And you don't have a phone.'

'Will you come back with me?'

'No. I won't. Not tonight.'

Nicky let's out a sigh, laced with frustration. 'Tomorrow then. I'll come back for you.'

'No, Nicky. I need time to think about my next move.'

It's a moment before he speaks. The candle on the table flickers. 'What does that mean? Is this a break? I don't understand.'

I hug my waist even tighter. 'It's not a break if you were never together in the first place.'

In the shadows, I watch his Adam's apple bob up and down again, his throat tight with emotion.

'I messed up,' he says. 'I'll do anything to put things right again. Please, Elle.'

When I say nothing, he nods his head, as though accepting that there's nothing further that he can say to convince me for now. After waiting for a long time, perhaps giving me the chance to change my mind, he backs away, defeated, and Oliver goes to open the front door for him. He pauses before he walks outside.

I watch him leave, hearing the snarl of his engine as he starts the car, the headlights illuminating one side of my face as warm tears I've held back for the last fifteen minutes come splashing down onto my cheeks.

In the morning, I wake early enough to watch the sunrise from Oliver's balcony, a lead weight lying heavy in the pit of my stomach, my eyeballs hollow inside my head.

I could go back. Ask Oliver to drive me.

Except when Oliver emerges from the shower, I ask him if he can drive me to the airport.

Chapter Twenty-Five

In the mornings, I can walk from Josie's apartment on Calle de Casanova down the road to buy, in my humble opinion, the best croissant Barcelona has to offer at La Pastisseria. The desserts there are award-winning and I find myself gazing in awe through the glass cabinets at the chefs' intricate creations. It's a twenty-minute round trip, and each day I enjoy watching a city come to life. Josie has a balcony, where I can sit with the sun on my face, sipping coffee and watch the traffic go by.

Today is sunny, yet I've completed the walk at snail's pace. As I unlock the door to the apartment, Josie starts yelling at me about how famished she is.

'Sorry,' I say as she snatches the cardboard box from me, opening it, the kitchen filling with the delicious aroma of freshly-baked pastries.

Outside it's only nine degrees, cooler than Florida. I peel off Josie's coat, the one I've borrowed for the last week, and let out a woeful sigh.

'Exactly how many more of those am I going to have to endure?' Josie groans at me, putting croissants on plates and reaching for the butter dish. She eats quickly as I know she has an online meeting to get to.

'I didn't know there was a threshold on me sighing,' I say.

'There's no threshold,' she says with her mouth full, a smattering of croissant crumbs on her lips. I pull out a chair. 'I just think if you're sighing that much, you should get on a plane back to Miami. Unless you want to lecture me about a certain fictional character again.'

'Jane Eyre left Rochester not because she didn't love him,' I blurt, watching as Josie's head falls back in her chair, slack-jawed in anguish, 'But because she drew a line in the sand. She wasn't prepared to be Mr. Rochester's mistress. She wasn't prepared to compromise.'

'And as I pointed out to you *yesterday*,' Josie argues, '*And* the day before that… you would not be Nicky's mistress. Look at the headlines for god's sake. His engagement is off, the marriage isn't going ahead. He told you he wants to be with you. You could have everything you want, on a plate with a sprig of garnish. But, no, you're here. In Spain. Moping around my apartment and lecturing me on a hundred-and-seventy-year-old work of fiction!'

I reach for the butter dish and a half-empty jar of English marmalade. 'You didn't see their faces. You didn't see the way they were all looking at me! I would never shake how we started off. That's how people would know me. *Pro tennis player has tawdry affair with personal chef*.'

Josie ploughs on, shoving the last of her croissant in her mouth and trying not to spray crumbs everywhere. 'What does it matter what anyone else thinks? Or what the headlines say? Surely it only matters what Nicky thinks? Okay, he should have been there when Mackenzie pushed you in the—'

My eyes shoot up accusingly, raising my hand unconsciously to my neck, where the marks Mackenzie left behind are almost gone. My lip is fully healed, but I hate re-living that moment: the scrape of Mackenzie's nails against my flesh, her slap, and the shock as I entered the water. It's what I remember over Nicky's apology.

Josie swallows the last of her breakfast. 'Meanwhile, Nicky Salco keeps calling my office daily, asking if I know where you are.'

His persistence has taken me by surprise. I don't know that I expected that reaction from him. It has certainly put a dent in my initial resolve. 'He knows I needed some time.'

Josie rolls her eyes. 'I imagine he thought you meant a couple of days licking your wounds at Oliver's house. I'm not sure he expected you to get on a plane and leave Miami.'

I'd asked Oliver to call Sydney, but not until my plane was about to take off. I haven't spoken to Oliver, so I don't know how the news was received, only Nicky started calling an unaware Josie immediately after, and I was forced to pass a message that I was safe once I'd landed in Spain. I imagine the only way he could track her down was via the wonders of the internet, because no one had her number.

'Me telling him that you are alright is hardly enough to placate a man who's just dumped his fiancée in front of his family and coaching team and told them he wants to be with you instead. At least have another conversation with the poor boy.'

Josie never refers to Nicky as a man. Only ever as a boy. I chew my croissant assiduously, thinking back to our conversation at Oliver's house. I'll admit, I was cold with him.

'Did you turn your phone on yet?' Josie asks.

'No,' I respond in a subdued tone.

'It's been a week. Don't you think you should?'

'I will. Eventually, I promise. I appreciate you letting me stay. I'll send an email to the agency in London later today.'

'Elles,' she says, getting up from her chair, placing her dirty plate beside the sink. 'I'm not kicking you out. You can stay here as long as you like. I only want your happiness. And despite his shortcomings, I think you and Nicky Salco are well-suited. Believe me, I never in a million years thought he would end things with Mackenzie. Makes me think he must be in love.'

I shake my head. He hasn't said so. He could have done, but he didn't. I think that I was hoping he would, and wonder if I would have got on a plane if he'd said the L word.

'Even if he does love me,' I murmur, 'I can't start a relationship on that basis. How can I? I'd always be the other woman. No, I should go back to London. Find another job.'

Josie goes back to her laptop.

'Errrr, Elle?' she says at length from the other room.

'What is it?' I question, still finishing my croissant.

'You might want to see this,' she says, her tone unsteady.

I wander through to the living room, where Josie keeps her desk in the corner, her laptop on it. She always keeps track of the celebrity headlines.

'I'm so sorry.'

I come up behind her and she turns the screen so I can see.

'Seems you were right about one thing anyway,' she exhales.

The article is on a well-known gossip website. The headline reads:

Nicky Salco's Ex Hints that Tennis Star's Cheating was Behind Cancelled Engagement as She Moves on with Miami Real Estate Tycoon.

I frown. There's a picture of Mackenzie, looking stunning, a broad smile on her face, in a low-cut top and red lipstick, holding hands on a Florida street with Bryan Dabrowski, a second image of them kissing.

Underneath is a video clip. My throat constricts.

'Do I play it?' Josie asks.

Part of me doesn't want her to, but I give a single affirmative nod.

She hits the play button. The footage is taken by a paparazzi camera, following Mackenzie as she strolls with Bryan in what looks like South Beach.

'Mackenzie, what happened with Nicky?' a male voice shouts off screen.

'Ask him what he was doing at midnight with his personal chef,' Mackenzie trills back, all sweetness and light, Bryan moving photographers protectively from her road.

It cuts out. Josie reaches for my hand and squeezes it.

'So, you go back to Miami. You make up with Nicky and you get photographed with him. Balance is restored.'

'And every news outlet in America refers to me as the woman Nicky Salco cheated on his fiancée with. Oh goody. I told you, Jose, I'm going back to London.'

In Josie's spare room, I dig out my phone from my bag, one of the few things I brought with me from Florida. I cradle my handset in my palms, dreading what I'll find there once I switch it on. As the screen comes to life, I chew my now-healed lip. Josie's given me her wifi code; as I punch in the secure combination, my heart starts to thump in my chest.

Once it connects, several messages arrive in a flurry.

Ninety-five percent of them are from Sydney.

My fingers tremble as I open them; slumping down to the bed and reading them from top to bottom with a lump in my throat.

> Elle, where are you? We can't find you. Nicky went to Oliver's but no one answered the door. Are you there?

> We can't find you. I'm worried you've gone.

> If u get this, please please call. I'm so sorry. Should have wrapped my arms around u yesterday. I'm sorry for what Mac did to you. Should have asked if u were OK. I was in shock is all. Pls 4give me x

> Oliver called. I'm so sad you've gone to Spain. Nicky's desperate. I've never seen him like this. He just wants to talk to you.

Wanted u 2 know that Mac has now moved out
and gone back to her parents. All of her stuff is
gone from the house. Nicky knows he messed up
by not being here for you. Nobody blames you,
Elle. We're on your side xx

You were right about Mac. She's been seeing
Bryan Dabrowski. Nicky thinks for some time. He
told me last night that he stopped sleeping with
Mac before he first kissed you in Cincinnati. I had
no idea. You guys hid everything so well. I'm
heartbroken for you two. Come back?

When I finish reading, I wipe my eyes. A sense of hopelessness
washes over me. Can I undo what I've done? Should I have
held on, waited for him to come back to Oliver's the next day?
What would that make us now, had I stayed? A happy couple?
Would I have slipped my feet into Mackenzie's shoes before
they were even cold? Stolen her exquisite lace wedding gown?
Would Nicky have moved me from the pool house into his
bedroom? And I'd do it all with a smile fixed on my face?

I switch off my phone again. I think back to my years with
Jamie, years that feel wasted to me now. I had no love for myself,
or self-respect. I was trodden on, cheated on, taken for granted.
Until I walked into Nicky Salco's life, I did not care for myself.
And my sister is right, it doesn't matter what anyone else thinks
of us, or how we started out. I can be that other woman, the
one who stole away his heart in the midnight hours. I could go
back there tomorrow.

Yet I know that I'd never be able to live with myself if I did.

–

'I have something for you,' the woman from the agency tells
me over the phone as I stare out across a dank, grey day in

south-west London. She's the same woman who got me the job with Nicky in the first place.

I left Josie's Barcelona apartment after ten days. I've been back in England for three, living in a rented room in shared accommodation, above a barber shop on Garrett Lane.

'Location-wise,' she continues, 'I know you said you wanted to avoid Wimbledon, but it's a great little family-run Spanish tapas bar. It's a sous chef role, providing cover for someone who's broken their leg in three places. They need somebody for a few months at least.'

'When you say Wimbledon…' I say quietly.

'Wimbledon Village. Right on the roundabout where Church Road meets the High Street. Rosalie is the name of the owner. She'd like to offer you a tryout for this afternoon.'

She's right. Location-wise it's not where I want to be. It's a little too near the All England Lawn Tennis Club for my liking, only because it makes me think about last year's championships, but this is the only offer I've had so far.

'What time?' I ask.

'She'd like you there by three p.m. Can you make that?'

I can practically walk it from Earlsfield, as my new place is on the Wimbledon side, far from the flat I shared with Jamie.

'Of course. I'll be there at three.'

Rosalie is in her late fifties, with reddish curly hair and a kind face, though her demeanour suggests that she wouldn't take any crap. She wears a wraparound dress and sensible heels, a loose-fitting cardigan on top. I'd forgotten how cold British winters can be, and have had to buy myself a new coat. The restaurant has marine blue tiles on the outside and is called 'Boca Chica'. From what I can remember of the Spanish Lonzo taught me, it translates to 'Little Mouth'. They specialize in tapas and steak.

For my tryout, Rosalie's tasked me with making some simple tapas from the restaurant's menu. The first dish is chorizo and potato croquettes, followed by garlic prawns, and lastly *albondigas*, or pork and beef meatballs in a paprika spiced tomato sauce. She also wants me to cook steak, which I've never been much good at, though I cooked them for Nicky on occasion. She's provided me with all the ingredients required. The kitchen is modest-sized, clean, well-equipped, with, oddly, a TV hung in one corner at ceiling height. There's a comfortable amount of space to work, but she watches me closely as I go about my tasks, occasionally asking me to explain what I'm doing.

She's seen my CV and my written reference from Lonzo.

'It says here you were a personal chef until recently,' she says. 'Can you tell me a little more about that?'

I clear my throat, carrying on working. 'I've working for a tennis player for the last eight months.'

'Oh? That must have been interesting. Why did you stop?'

'His coaches… they changed his routine. It turned out he didn't need me anymore.'

'And how did the job come about?'

'Um. Wimbledon, actually. Last year. It was through the agency.'

'So, they were a professional player. Am I allowed to ask which one?'

I force a smile. 'Nicky Salco.'

At the sounds of muted gasps, my eyes are suddenly drawn to the double doors that separate the kitchen from the main restaurant. Two heads appear above the window pane belonging to two dark-haired, pretty girls, their eyes like saucers.

'Girls!' Rosalie turns and snaps.

They duck down again, but one of them sticks her head out, into the kitchen.

'Sorry, but did she just say Nicky Salco?'

Rosalie turns her eyes to me. 'Elle, I must apologise. These are my daughters, Livia and Adriana. Tennis mad, these two.'

Both girls shuffle out into the room. My guess is both are in their late teens, with dark hair and eyes. One is wearing a dress and a pair of Converse trainers, the other in ripped jeans and bare feet.

Pausing, I say, 'hello.'

They beam at me. 'Did you just say you worked for Nicky Salco?' the younger of the two blurts.

'Livia!' Rosalie snaps. 'I am trying to conduct an interview.'

'Oh, please, Mum! Can't we just hear her answer?' the one called Adriana begs.

Rosalie cocks her head to one side and rolls her eyes.

'I did,' I say, and this time my smile is genuine.

'You were Nicky Salco's *personal* chef?' Livia marvels at me.

'What's he like?' Adriana adds.

My memory is of his kisses. 'He's nice. I mean, he was mostly out on court. I didn't interact with him too much.'

The truth would hardly be appropriate at this moment in time.

'Why did he break up with his fiancée?' Adriana asks, and I worry that they've seen the articles online.

'Girls!' Rosalie snaps, clapping her hands. 'Out! Ask your questions later!'

Both girls let out a grumbled moan and file out of the room. I smile as Rosalie offers her apologies, and continue making tapas.

When the tryout is over, I remove my apron.

'Thank you, Elle. Everything was delicious. I would be delighted to take you on if you would like to come and join us here?'

'Would the head chef not want to speak to me?'

Rosalie looks to the floor. 'My husband, Marco, he used to be the head chef here. Until he passed away suddenly a few years ago. Now his brother, Bernardo, is head chef.' She levels her gaze to me. 'But, as he well knows, I run the show.'

I nod. Working in the same place as two tennis-crazy teenagers, who clearly both have a massive crush on Nicky is probably a bad idea, yet something about this place appeals to me.

Existing in this limbo, grappling with the consequences of my decision to leave Miami, I still haven't worked out how this story ends.

–

As it turns out, it's a lot of change to get used to. Boca Chica is a popular restaurant, and the pace doesn't allow for much conversation. For most shifts, it's get-your-head-down-and-cook. Bernardo is not what I would call charismatic, lacking Lonzo's sense of humour or culinary flair. He barks orders grumpily at me, yet most of the time he looks bored.

I still feel guilt for not having bid my favourite Cuban chef goodbye. I wonder if he misses me, in the same way that I miss him teaching me Spanish and laughing at my getting things wrong. I wonder if he judges me for getting involved with Nicky.

I try not to think about Nicky Salco, but he's always there, at the back of my mind. Livia and Adriana have grilled me enough times about him, not that I've ever given anything more than the smallest detail away, but they go away giddy to feed off the information they've gleaned from me. They know he's called off his wedding. They relish in the knowledge that he's a single man. If they know about the cheating rumours, they're not saying.

I know he missed the Rio Open, which journalists speculated was due to the train wreck that was his personal life. It makes me feel guilty, that even in my absence I'm furthering this idea that I'm a problem; that Nicky's tennis game is suffering because of me.

The restaurant is closed on Mondays. I'm clearing up after the Tuesday lunch rush when both girls come into the kitchen. Adriana is chewing gum; Livia sucking on a lollipop. Bernardo and Pete, the junior chef, have gone into the alley at the back for a smoke.

Livia reaches for the remote control for the TV, up on a high shelf. She switches it on, flipping through numerous channels like she knows what she's looking for.

'Indian Wells started yesterday,' she says. 'Nicky Salco had his opening match.'

She stops on the Tennis Channel. I find myself looking at Nicky for the first time in almost a month. My stomach does a somersault. He's in California.

'He looks awful there,' Adriana comments. 'He really doesn't suit the facial hair. Must be really cut up about breaking up with the fiancée.'

I'm still staring. I disagree with her about the just-there facial hair, but she's right. His face is drawn, and he looks exhausted. He's lacking his usual vigour out on court.

'Did he make it through?' I ask.

'Got knocked out first round,' Adriana says with a tepid shrug.

I cringe inwardly.

'*Again*,' Livia adds. 'He should really dump his coach.'

'He's not as good as he used to be. But he's still my favourite. We thought you might want to watch the highlights.'

They remain with me for a while before peeling off. Livia has school exams to prepare for. I watch and listen as the commentators tear apart Nicky's performance, every negative comment a pin prick to my heart, and once more I find myself questioning why I didn't stay.

Arriving back in my room at midnight, after a short bus ride, I decide it's time to switch on my phone again.

There have been no more messages from Sydney, just a couple from my sister, which I reply to. My thumb hovering over the screen, I send Sydney a message. I know whatever I say will get back to Nicky.

Are you free to talk? I type.

Thinking she probably won't receive the message for some time, I start getting ready to collapse into bed. To my surprise, she calls me immediately.

254

'Elle?' I hear Sydney say, my chest tightening at the sound of her voice. She sounds so far away.

'Where are you?' I ask.

'I'm in a hotel room in California. We fly back to Miami later on. You?'

'I'm back in London,' I respond, pacing.

'London? Can you tell me *where* in London?'

I pause. 'It's probably for the best that I don't give that away,' I respond quietly.

She also goes quiet for a moment, then sighs. 'Girl, I am so sorry. We were all stunned when Mackenzie did what she did. Nobody had even picked up on the fact that there was something goin' on between you two. But I was not expecting that.'

'You weren't the only one.'

'When Nicky came back to the house after that golf game, he had a face like thunder. He took Mac into a room. Moments later, she's screaming the house down, then Nicky comes out and announces the whole wedding's off, that he's in love with you.'

'He—' I begin, realising that this would have been before he came to see me at Oliver's house. 'He actually said that?'

'Said he was done hiding it. That he was sorry to Mikhail and that he appreciated his patronage and his sponsorship *yada yada yada*, but that he'd fallen headlong in love with you and that it was only fair to sever all ties with Mackenzie.'

'What did Mikhail say?'

Sydney puts on a deep voice, imitating Mackenzie's father. '*You'll never see another dime of my money, you jackass.*'

'What did Nicky say?'

'He said, '*look around you; I don't need your money anymore*'.'

'Yes, but that's not strictly true, is it?'

'The sponsor, the one at the golf game? That deal is worth *ten mil*. It's all signed off. Nicky's gotta do some ads for cologne. I mean, they don't seem to care that he's not winning, anyway.'

'I'm glad everything's working out for him,' I say quietly.

'Girl, what planet are you on? All Nicky wants is you. Back in his life. And in case you hadn't noticed, he ain't winning shit. The man is fraught. He's broken. It's like he's lost all purpose. Like, he doesn't even care about the tennis anymore. He's just going through the motions. Tag is losing hope. The Miami Open starts in a week and a half, and Nicky's walking into it like he's lost all interest. And it's his favourite tournament.'

A lump has firmly lodged itself in my throat at her words. My shoulders slump and I start telling myself again that it's my fault.

'I'm sorry, I'm sorry,' she says. 'I didn't say all that to make you feel bad.'

I wipe tears. 'Yes, but I don't think I'm exactly helping either.'

'Tag thinks Nicky's been in a spiral. He couldn't focus properly on his game because he was grappling with being in love, and it knocked him for six. He met you and it's like he reverted back to being in eighth grade.'

I listen, Syd's words making my chest swell. I still don't know where it leaves me. A large part of me wants to throw everything in a suitcase and get on a plane. To go to him.

'He just wants to talk to you, Elle. But he knows he can't force you. He knows he messed up.'

I can't get any words out to respond. Exhaustion washes over me.

'Can I tell him I spoke to you?' she asks.

'Yes,' I whisper.

'You want me to pass any messages?'

'No,' I choke out. 'Syd, I'm so sorry, I need to go.'

I hang up, tossing the phone down onto the bed. I cover my face with my hands and sob into my palms. I can't make sense of my thoughts. I thought I had my reasons for leaving, but even these seem unclear to me now.

Chapter Twenty-Six

Every day, I get up, I go to work, and robotically I make tapas and steaks to the best of my ability. I keep my head down. Bernardo occasionally acknowledges my existence. Rosalie appreciates my hard work. Her daughters flit around the kitchen like butterflies, getting under everyone's toes whilst they talk to me about tennis, bombarding me with questions about Nicky Salco, oblivious to the truth behind our relationship. I hate their attention and love it in equal parts.

In mid-March, when the Miami Open is due to start, Livia and Adriana insist on having the TV on during the dinner service, because Miami is five hours behind Wimbledon and it's 7 p.m. when Nicky's opening match starts at 2 p.m. local time on the Tuesday. My knife hovers over the chopping board, and I'm in danger of slicing off one of my fingers due to my eyes constantly flipping up to the screen, waiting for him to appear. I realise now, in my work place, that he is the distraction now. He's the one affecting *my* game.

In the studio, the main commentary team is cheesily American, Miami palm trees the back drop to their studio.

'Let's talk about Nicky Salco,' the female commentator says, and I can see Bernardo glare at me when my back straightens and I stop working altogether. 'He's got home advantage here in Miami, is he gonna be able to convert that to success on the court?'

'This guy...' the first male commentator snorts into his microphone, shaking his head. He's got the most ridiculously white set of teeth. 'He's not made it easy on himself the last few months, has he? His personal life has been splashed all over the tabloids, his focus hasn't been on point, he's produced a lot of unforced errors. I really hope he can turn it around here, because Nicky Salco has had more than a year now of people questioning his ability, as well as his choice of coach. His last few tournaments have been lacking in any kind of finesse that we know he's so very capable of. It's a real shame.'

'There's nothing wrong with his coach,' I mutter under my breath, going back to my chopping board, ignoring Bernardo's glare of disapproval.

Adriana and Livia are leaning against the counter top when Nicky finally walks on court to rapturous applause. It's clear the affection Miami has for him, their local boy. Livia and Adriana immediately start swooning. I keep working because the orders are coming thick and fast, but I steal a glance. What I see makes my heart flip, because it's clear to me, today is a day when Nicky has morphed into the so-called 'Triple Salco'. I can see his mood simmering already. Some small thing will have upset him, and his frustration is palpable. It's the part of Nicky I've never quite come to terms with. This is maybe when it hurts the most, because he no longer feels mine. He feels like a stranger. And being far away from him, it hurts even more.

'Oooh, he's looking grumpy today,' Adriana says flippantly, studying her nails.

'Grumpy Nicky,' Livia sighs, adding, 'But still sexy Nicky,' and I have to bite my lip.

The match is a disaster. Nicky looks like he's not even trying. The commentators have a field day. He even gets booed by the crowd at one point. I keep my eyes on six filet steaks I need to cook to perfection, because Bernardo will be glaring at me for weeks if I don't, but it hurts to see him play that way when I know the kind of tennis he can produce. Yet once again, he crashes out. And the worst thing is; he doesn't even look bothered by that.

'Nicky emailed me two tickets to his opening match at the Madrid Open. Or rather Sydney did on Nicky's behalf. Do I go?'

A couple of weeks' later, Josie calls me early on my day off, waking me from a deep slumber.

'Do you like tennis?'

'Elle, be serious.'

I squint. The light peeks through my curtains. I can hear the pitter-patter of rain. 'I'm not even awake yet. Go if you think you should go.'

'And what if he tries to talk to me?'

I sit up in bed. It feels like I can't bury my head anymore. That enough time has passed.

'Then talk to him if you think you should talk to him,' I croak.

'You are in an infuriating mood.'

'Actually, I feel better. Stronger.'

'So, if I happened to let slip where you were, that wouldn't be a bad thing?'

'It wouldn't,' I say, despite my fears. 'I think it's time.'

–

The Monte-Carlo Masters takes place before Madrid. It's a tournament played on clay, Nicky's least favourite surface. Once more I find myself juggling tapas, stakes and snatching glances at the TV screen mounted on the kitchen wall. Nicky scrapes through the first round, wearing his favourite navy blue and a sweat band that pushes the hair from his eyes. The idea of him being in Europe sends pulses down my spine.

I'm clearing up that night, the restaurant closed, when Rosalie enters the kitchen. The TV is still showing the tennis highlights. When I see her, my back straightens, and I reach for the remote to switch off the unit.

'Don't switch it off on my account,' she says.

'It's fine. I'm really not interested.'

'In the tennis; or just Nicky Salco?'

I stiffen, swallowing hard.

'I see the way my daughters look at him. Like he's a gift to their looks-obsessed, adolescent minds. And then I see the way you look up at him on that screen. Like you can see underneath all that. The girls talked about him breaking up with a fiancée. I looked up the articles. The news came out just before the time that you came to see us. The rumours about...'

I grip the tea towel I've been holding, twisting it in between my fingers, looking to the floor.

'Elle, I meant nothing by it. You don't have to tell me anything. I just wanted to reassure you that you are very welcome here.'

—

Josie doesn't tell me if she goes to Madrid or not. Yet I know the dates like they were tattooed on the insides of my eyelids. I know the time of his match, who he's playing, who his next opponent might be. On the TV, with the volume turned higher than usual, I search for my sister's face in the crowd. Instead of glaring, Bernardo just rolls his eyes at me due to amount of advanced prep I've done for today. He's grateful. Outside, it's sunny. The lunch shift only just started and chits are already coming in. I sneak glances up at the TV but it takes everything in me not to down tools and stare at the screen.

—

It happens on a Wednesday.

I arrive at work by ten thirty, grappling to find the keys to the restaurant door at the bottom of my bag. There's a car parked on the curb. I pay it no heed, until the back door opens and the person who emerges almost makes my knees buckle.

It happens almost in slow-motion, my world blurring at the edges. I'd forgotten how tall he is. How lithe his movements are. How athletic he looks. He's wearing navy blue again, his hair tousled, as though he just got out of bed.

For a split second I question whether I'm imagining what I'm seeing.

When Nicky walks towards me, all I can do is stand there, my heart about to implode inside my chest. My inward reaction tells me one thing: that I am still very much in love with this man.

'Hey,' he says, stopping on the pavement in front of me.

It's a calm 'hey'. A composed 'hey'. A casual I-just-dropped-by 'hey'. Possibly with a touch of fragility or nervousness. Without a racket, he doesn't seem to know what to do with his hands, and I realise that it was the same at Oliver's house.

I stare at him, unable to get any words out. I cannot believe that he's here, in the flesh, standing on a pavement in south-west London.

'Shouldn't you be in Madrid?' I blurt.

He lets out a shaky breath. 'I took the first flight out this morning. Bought my passport and wallet, that's it. I'm booked on a flight back over later on.'

'Alone?'

He swallows. 'Rag had a fit. I told him I had to see you. How are you?'

I ignore his question, shake my head. 'Don't you have a match tomorrow?'

'I should still make it. Unless the crazy budget airline I flew over here with cancels my flight.' He shrugs. 'Guess if that happens, I'll forfeit.'

I can't believe the words coming out of his mouth. It's no wonder Rag hit the roof. My voice comes out as a squeak. 'You saw Josie?'

He nods. 'She came down courtside at the end of the match yesterday. I was signing some autographs when I hear this very

261

British sounding woman yelling my name at the top of her lungs, mad as hell with me.'

I look to the pavement with a broken smile. 'That sounds like my sister.'

'Made my heart sing. The sight of her. 'Cause I was prepared to get on my knees if she didn't tell me where you were.'

His words still me. 'I'm here,' I say. 'This is where I am.'

He nods, his gaze raking over me. It takes a moment for him to speak. 'Are you alright?'

I indicate to the restaurant. 'I work here now. I cook steak and tapas all day.'

He gives the building a cursory glance, distracted, perhaps by his own thoughts. He lets out a shaky breath. 'I kept going over in my head on the plane what I was going to say to you if I tracked you down. Elle, I messed up. I should have done what I promised I was going to do that day. I should never have gone to that golf game. And I took it for granted that you would still be at Oliver's the next morning. When I realized you'd gone...'

I shake my head. 'I didn't know I was going to leave. I was awake at lot that night. Thinking about everything. I didn't want to go back to the house. Not after what Mackenzie did.'

'I thought you'd be pleased when I broke things off with Mac.'

I raise dubious eyebrows at him.

His shoulders slump. 'Alright, it was too little, too late, I get that.'

I take a breath, steeling myself with words I've been practicing in my head, to say if I ever saw him again. 'Nicky, you weren't honest with me at Oliver's house. Sydney told me what happened. That you ended things with Mac and you told everyone that you were in love with me.'

His eyes flash. He takes another step forward and my stomach lurches. 'Which is true. I am in love with you, Elle.'

'Then why didn't you tell me that? If you'd told me you'd loved me, maybe I wouldn't have got on a plane to Barcelona.'

He winces. 'I wasn't gonna get on my knees and tell you I loved you with Oliver Davenport breathing down my neck. The guy already looked like he wanted to murder me. And I was unhappy at the fact you'd run to him in the first place.'

'Nicky, your fiancée had just thrown me in your pool! I had to call someone.'

'Did it have to be him?'

'I didn't know anyone else!'

'Are you still talking to him?'

That's the moment I see a stranger over Nicky's shoulder on the other side of the road, his camera phone pointed right at us.

'Nicky, someone's filming us.'

He grimaces for a second, glancing back. 'I don't care. I want the whole world to know that I love you. Elle, please, I just want you back with me. Come with me.'

The temptation is overwhelming. I search his face. 'What if we... if *this* doesn't work in the cold light of day? What if the secret nature of it was the only thrill?'

Something in his expression alters. He lets go of me, stepping back. 'That's crazy. What are you afraid of? Is this about Oliver? Did I miss my chance because he was there for you when I wasn't?'

'This has nothing to do with Oliver.'

'Then what? I love you, Elle. I can't function without you.'

'Everyone will look at me like I was your dirty little secret that whole time. Ragnar specifically asked me not to distract you.'

'You were never my dirty little secret. I should have just had the balls to break up with Mac last summer when I wanted to. No one is gonna look at you that way. And when I told them all I was in love with you, Rag looked more pleased than anyone. Elle, when I saw you that morning on the tennis court, everything clicked into place. I knew that I wanted to do things differently. It took you coming into my life to make me realise

I'd never been in love. Until you walked into that house last summer and turned my life upside down.'

He's back closer to me again; my face in his palms, so close he could kiss me. 'Please, Elle, I'll do anything.'

Then he does something I don't expect. He drops to his knees. I am horrified, my gaze flitting to the stranger with his mobile phone who still appears to be filming us.

'What do I have to do to have you back in my life?' he begs. 'Tell me. I miss you so damned much.'

'Nicky, what are you doing?' I hiss at him. 'Get up. Someone is over there. This will end up being some viral video.'

'Don't care,' he states. 'Tell me what I've gotta do. Tell me what I've gotta do and I swear to God, I'll do it.'

I stare down at him. His eyes are pleading.

I'm breathless. How have we reached this point? Him being here makes me question exactly what it is I want. I don't know where the words come from, but they're out of my mouth before I can stop them: 'Win a Grand Slam.'

It takes a moment for the words to sink in, for his shoulders to drop again. I feel my chest tighten. I'm so shocked at myself I can't even un-say it.

'Is that supposed to be a joke?' Nicky chokes out.

I could flip it on its head, make out like it's supposed to be funny. Except that I don't. I steel myself, remembering that before this experience, I barely had an ounce of self-worth. 'You once told me you never back away from a challenge,' I say quietly.

He's still on his knees on the pavement. The man filming us is moving closer now. Nicky is aghast. 'Is that your way of saying you're through with me? That we're done? You have seen my game recently, haven't you?'

He gets up, hands in his hair.

'I believe in you,' I whisper, though I'm not sure he hears me. 'You told me that winning another Grand Slam was what you wanted. So, win another major tennis tournament. Go after what you want.'

He looks like he might cry. Instead of tying my stomach in knots, it further steels my resolve. He gets to his feet. 'I *am* going after what I want,' he snaps. 'Why do you think I left a goddamned tournament to come here? *You* are what I want, Elle. Just you, I don't care about anything else.'

'That's just it, Nicky. There are two very separate things that matter here. Tennis and your personal life. You've never treated tennis like it's your job. You live it, you breathe it. You care about it more than anything.' *Take your soul out of it*, I want to add, but I don't. 'You've bought into this idea that the Triple Salco exists. But it doesn't, only in your mind. There is only one Nicky Salco, Nicky. One beating heart. The rest is... it's not relevant.'

His broad shoulders continue to droop. I feel like I'm not making any sense. He shakes his head, pacing, the conversation clearly not going as he wanted it to. He raises his hands, resting them on the back of his head, his expression one of disbelief.

'So that's it?' he questions. 'I don't get to have you unless I win a trophy first? What you're asking, it's...'

He exhales hard. 'I gotta get outta here,' he mutters, his voice breaking as he backs away, hands in his hair again, unable to make eye contact with me.

'Nicky, I—' I begin but he's striding faster now. 'Nicky!'

He doesn't look back. My chest constricts. He's back at the car door, opening up the back, disappearing from view. I watch his car as it speeds away. The man on the other side of the street films me until I offer him my middle finger, then he scarpers.

When the car is gone, I locate my keys and open the door to the restaurant, fumbling with the lock.

In the kitchen, I stop and gasp breaths. I sink to the floor and wonder if I've just thrown away the only chance at happiness I'll ever have.

The worst thing? I didn't even tell him I loved him back.

Chapter Twenty-Seven

'*Wait-a-minute, wait-a-minute, wait-a-minute*, you said WHAT to him?' Josie exclaims over the phone, whilst I stand in the back alleyway behind the restaurant, next to the rubbish bins, massaging my forehead.

'He asked me what he could do to win me back; I said win a grand slam,' I repeat, my voice trembling.

'You mean you didn't just… *forgive* him?'

This time, my voice cracks. 'I realise how it sounds *now*.'

'He got on a plane for you! The moment I told him where you were he was asking Syd to book him a flight. Armed gladiators could not have stopped him, Elle.'

I've already paced. Hyperventilated. Wiped sweaty palms on my chef's apron. I pinch the bridge of my nose. 'I don't know why I said it. I told him he needed to separate tennis from his personal life.'

'Elle, you could still have pointed that out *and* taken him back. You didn't need to give him some warped ultimatum at the same time!'

'May I remind you that this is the same man you told me that I was insane to get involved with?'

'Yes, but he did the one thing I never thought he would do. He ended things with his fiancée. For *you*. When I saw him in Madrid, all he could talk about was you. *My* sister. How much he wanted you back in his life, what a mess he'd made of things. I thought you loved him, Elle. I don't understand why all of a sudden you are pushing him away.'

266

I go quiet, chewing my thumb nail. 'I told him I believed in him.'

'Oh well that makes *all* the difference. Somebody hand that man a trophy!'

She sobers. 'I'm sorry, Elle. I'm on your side, you know I am. I was just expecting this phone call to be you telling me you had reconciled and were blissfully happy or whatnot. What if he never wins another major?'

There's a lump in my throat. Bernardo appears in the alleyway with his hands on his hips, before clicking his fingers at me.

'Jose, I have to go. I'm sorry. I'll call you later.'

Minutes later I'm back in the kitchen, prepping tapas for the lunch service. I can't concentrate. I've blamed my throwaway comment to Nicky on temporary insanity. I think about calling Syd and begging to speak to him. Take it all back. *Can I take it back?*

Josie's words stay with me. *What if he never wins another major?* Will I be stuck waiting for each of the four Grand Slams to come around, year on year, whilst meanwhile Nicky meets someone else, gets married and has babies, and I live with my ludicrous ultimatum? Will the memory of me fade? Will he realise that he never really loved me in the first place? Will he come back and beg that we forget the whole thing? Should I do that?

I try to ratify my actions. Jane Eyre goes back to Mr. Rochester on her own terms. She inherits money. She's still passionate about her man.

Jane Eyre doesn't tell Rochester he has to win a Grand Slam tennis championship in order to win her heart.

What kind of idiot am I?

When lunch is over, Rosalie enters the kitchen, flanked by Adriana and Livia, both of whom seem twitchy. She's holding a copy of a newspaper folded in two.

'Berni, Pete, could you give me a minute with Elle, please?'

He nods as I eye the newspaper, a sense of dread looming over me, remembering the stranger on the other side of the street who was filming my conversation with Nicky.

When the other chefs are out of the room, she unfurls the paper. It's a copy of the *Evening Standard*. On the front page is a headline about imminent train strikes, but underneath is a photograph. I recognise the marine blue of the outside of the restaurant instantly, the sign 'Boca Chica' visible at the top of the picture. Below it, Nicky kneels in front of me, his face visible, looking up at me. Underneath, the caption reads '*Nicky Salc-uh-oh…*' I can hear him asking what he can do to win me back. I taste bile as I recall my response.

Win a Grand Slam.

I feel sick.

'I suppose I ought to be thanking you for the free publicity,' Rosalie says with a dry smile.

Both girls look like they might explode. 'Is it true, Elle?' Adriana breathes. 'Nicky Salco was standing outside *this* restaurant *this* morning?'

'Why was he here?' Livia echoes. 'What did he want?'

I look into Rosalie's eyes. They seem to bore into my soul. 'I'm sorry,' I whisper. 'I didn't know he would come here.'

'Elle, you've no need to apologise to me.'

I gasp out loud, covering my mouth. I can't stop the tears. I turn and dart into the pantry, holding onto one of the wooden shelves as sobs make my shoulders quiver.

Behind me, I hear Rosalie say something to the girls. They seem to object before she dismisses them outright.

In their family home, above the restaurant, she pours me a glass of wine and offers me a seat on her sofa. I've looked at the newspaper article, which says very little. A caption at the bottom asks 'Do you know this woman?' followed by a phone number. Over the next half an hour I confess to her the details of my relationship with Nicky, ending with what I told him this morning. She listens, seemingly without judgment, with the occasional nod of her head.

268

'I shouldn't have said it,' I say, my wine virtually untouched for speaking. 'But now I don't know if it's something I can take back.'

It is a few moments before Rosalie addresses me.

'What would your life be like now, do you think? If you hadn't run. If you had stayed with him in Miami.'

'I—' I begin, trying to picture it. 'I don't know. We would be together, I suppose.'

'Would you have been happy with your position, do you think?'

'I think I would always be worrying what people thought of me. That they would think I stole Nicky somehow from Mackenzie. My insecurities would have probably have eaten me up. I would have felt like I didn't deserve him.'

'You know, you have to respect yourself, Elle, before you can have mutual respect in a relationship.'

I nod. Because I know she's right. Because I never have before.

'Today you asked Nicky to start anew. So that you may start your relationship on an equal footing.'

I slump back into the sofa cushions. 'But what if he never wins a major tournament?'

'Do you believe that he will?'

'Maybe not straight away. But I believe that he will eventually, yes.'

'And are you willing to wait for him until he does?'

Tears sting my eyes, because how long is a piece of string? It could take years, yet still I nod my head.

'Then you've given him a reason to fight. You must have faith in your own conviction. And faith in him to succeed.'

'But can I go back on my statement?'

'If you get on a plane to Spain tomorrow, I won't hold it against you. But if you do, I warn you, you may well find Adriana and Livia hiding in your suitcase.'

It's raining when I step off the bus in Earlsfield. I can't face retreating to my quiet, lonely little room. Nicky will probably be back in Madrid by now. It's hard to believe that only twelve hours have passed since I saw him in the flesh. I duck into a local pub, the windows fogging up with the number of bodies pressed inside, forgetting for a moment that my face has been on the front of every single copy of today's *Evening Standard*. I push through to the bar, ordering myself a vodka tonic. Nobody seems to pay me any attention.

I take a seat at the end of the bar, next to the wall, the only one that's free. Further towards the front, there's a rowdy group of men and women making a racket. As my gaze settles on them, I see Jamie is among them, relaxed into the contours of a sofa, his arm slung around the shoulders of a young, brassy-blonde female. He's laughing brashly with his friends, paying her no attention despite their physical contact. She looks miserable and bored. I watch as her eyes dart around the room, perhaps wondering if she can make her escape, or if she can talk to someone else. I realise that less than a year ago, that woman was me, my self-worth flatlining, my self-belief hovering just above zero. And I realise that if Nicky was in here with me, his eyes would be on mine, and his attention on no one else on me.

And he loves me.

I take out my phone, thinking I will look up flights to Spain. If I go tomorrow, it might not be too late to take back what I said.

There's a message on my phone from Syd. I open up the screen to read it.

Girl, I don't know what you said to him, it reads, *but whatever it was, you've lit a fire.*

I stare at the words. My heart swells. I take a drink and press my back up against the wall.

I remind myself that yes, I do believe in him, and that all I can do at this point is just that.

Believe.

–

The next day, I watch Nicky's second round match in Madrid during the lunch rush, six fillet and two sirloin steaks lined up and ready for me to griddle on a cast iron skillet. When Nicky appears on court I stop still, my stomach performing a somersault.

He looks exhausted. More than exhausted. Drained. Weary. His movements are sloppy. He's unfocussed. The commentary team makes some disparaging comments about him being photographed in Wimbledon in London the previous day, and how he doesn't look well-rested. The last I remember seeing him like this on the TV screen, even his mother knew that he wasn't going to have a good day. She called him *wild Nicky*.

'Elle!' Bernardo yells at me and I squeal. The first steak is burning in the skillet. I move it, catching the handle, causing it to flip, sending the dish, an oil slick and the half-burnt steak clattering to the floor. To make matters worse, the nearby smoke alarm goes off. Adriana comes running in, followed by Rosalie, my cheeks reddening under their stares. Rosalie looks up to the television, the camera zoomed in close on Nicky sat in his chair beside the umpire, his expression thunderous.

In the same moment, Bernardo starts yelling at me in his native Spanish, shooing me out of the room, calling Pete to come over and clean up.

I walk outside to the back alley, burying my face in my palms, trying to stop the barrage of hot tears threatening to spill over onto my cheeks.

'Excuse me?' a voice says, and I glance up. A man I don't recognise lingers, wearing an overcoat over an unkempt suit. 'Were you the girl yesterday pictured with Nicky Salco?'

'Who are you?' I gawp at him.

'I'm from the Evening Standard. Are you Elle Caraway? Would you care to comment on the nature of your relationship with tennis player Nicky Salco?'

The way he asks the question sends alarm bells shooting through me. He must be a journalist. 'No, I would not care to comment!' I shout at him. 'Leave me alone!'

Before he can say anything else, I dart back into the kitchen, mortified.

The TV has been switched off. Pete is cleaning up my mess with a mop. Bernardo is standing over a clean skillet, monitoring two steaks sizzling in the pan.

Bernardo snaps his fingers in my direction. '*Salsa brava*,' he clips, before pointing over to a pan. I swallow, trying to compose myself, then walk over to the sink and wash my hands. I mouth an apology to Pete and he offers me a wobbly smile in return.

When the lunch shift is over, Rosalie invites me upstairs.

'Bernardo isn't happy,' she states.

'Of course,' I nod my head in return.

'He's asked that the TV remains switched off whilst you're working.'

'I understand.'

'I don't mind you ducking outside every once in a while, to check the live score. But I can't have you burning the steaks, Elle, I'm sorry.'

'I'll apologise to Bernardo. It won't happen again.'

Nicky crashes of the Madrid Open.

'I watched the match,' Josie says to me that night over the phone. 'Did you see it?'

I sit on my bed in my rented room, hugging my knees, and recount my burnt-steak story, explaining that I'm no longer allowed to watch any tennis at work.

'Does this Bernardo guy know what's going on with you and Nicky?'

'Even if he did, I don't think he'd care.' Then I sigh, before adding, 'I think I've made things worse.'

'How have you made things worse?'

'Nicky getting beaten. I shouldn't have said what I said.'

'You think you being there would have made things any easier for him?'

'Maybe? I don't know.'

'Well, it's too late now,' Josie sighs. 'I'm not sure you can take it back.'

Later, when I'm in bed, on the cusp of sleep, I receive a text message from Syd.

> Girlllll, Tag told me what u said to Nicky.

It's followed by,

> Sheesh.

Under the sheets, I curl up into a ball and wish for some invisible force to come and swallow me up.

Chapter Twenty-Eight

Over the next few days, I come to wholly regret what I said. I can see now why Nicky thought it was my way of telling him I didn't want to be with him. Yet the small voice in my head begs me to give him to chance, to continue to believe in him, so I do nothing. I get up, go to work, cook steaks and make tapas under Bernardo's endless scrutiny, then go home and go to bed.

I tell myself I can wait. I can wait for him to win a Grand Slam.

When I remind myself that I may have to wait more than a year, I start checking prices of flights to Rome, where Nicky is about to compete in the Italian Open.

On the day of his opening match, I keep my head down. The lunch rush is manic, Rosalie coming nervously in and out of the kitchen and checking that service remains brisk. A late lunch booking means we're still cooking steaks at three p.m.

Adriana enters the kitchen just as I'm adding another sirloin to the griddle. I glance up at her and she gives me two very enthusiastic thumbs up. When I frown at her, she motions hitting an invisible tennis ball. I take it she means that Nicky has won.

When the shift is over, and Pete and Bernardo are outside having a smoke, I pull out my phone from my pocket.

See? Josie has messaged me. *Maybe you just have to have faith.*

I type out, *Why do you say that?*

A moment later, she replies, *Didn't you see? Nicky just won his match 6-0, 6-0, 6-0.*

I turn and locate the remote control for the TV. It's still on the Tennis Channel since my burn-a-steak moment.

I wait patiently for highlights, drumming my fingertips against the metal counter top.

I'm still waiting when Bernardo re-enters the kitchen. I scramble to switch the TV off, yet he presses his thick fingers down on my shoulder.

He nods his head, gives me a half-smile. 'Rosalie told me. So today, I don't mind.'

I feel my cheeks burn. I don't have to wait too much longer for the highlight reel. I only get a short glimpse, but it's enough. He's wearing a green top with white shorts. He obliterates his opponent. He seems… composed, punching the air with every winning point. I am reminded of something Syd said to me last year. *Nicky is in annihilation mode.* He's sharper. More focussed. Hungry, almost. His determination makes me smile.

It fills me with a new kind of hope.

–

On a Friday afternoon in mid-May, I am sat on the carpet in Rosalie's living room with Adriana and Livia, waiting for Nicky's match to begin in Paris at Roland Garros. He's back in navy blue.

It's a semi-final of the French Open.

The narrative of the commentary has changed. For so long now, all the commentators could talk about was Nicky's disastrous form. His not-so-great temperament. His losing streak. His turbulent personal life. *Triple Salco.*

In Rome, he reached the last four. *No one would have expected Nicky Salco to be in this position*, one commentator said. *He's really turned things around here*, said another, before he was knocked out by the number two seeded player.

I've been watching him. I see his focus. His relative calm. His confidence. I see the man he knows he can be. When something doesn't go his way, I see him shrug it off. He no longer looks across the net with a furrowed brow. Something has lifted. The commentators can't get enough. In the press conferences, despite the barrage of questions, he remains stoic.

Adriana and Livia tell me that this is all my doing. That this is Nicky's response to my challenge.

I keep quiet, and guard my heart. Watching makes me ache for him. The fear inside me is always there, but it no longer has influence.

I glance down at my phone at the message from Josie. I'm watching, she says. I picture her in her living room in Barcelona, a freshly made jug of Sangria on the same table she's resting her bare feet on, Gideon still grumbling because he had to have the Tennis Channel added to his digital TV subscription at his girlfriend's behest, and now it's costing him an extra twenty-five Euros a month for a beefed-up package.

Nicky's opponent is French, an experienced player, a top seed with home crowd advantage. Nicky is very much the underdog.

Rosalie brings me my own glass of Sangria.

When Nicky takes the first set, the camera pans to Ragnar, Tag and Sydney in the crowd. Seeing them ecstatic propels me to my feet. After that, I can't sit back down.

I pace behind the sofa, hands in a prayer position. When he takes the third set, and the match, Adriana and Livia shriek, leaping to their feet and jumping up and down until their mother tells them the floor will give way.

'He's done it! He's in the final!' they continue to scream, racing over to me and smothering me with hugs, shaking me.

I sit, stunned, watching through the gap in their bodies as Nicky waves to the crowd, shaking his French opponent by the hand at the net. I feel my phone vibrate.

OMG!!!!!!!!!!!!!!!!!!!!!!!!!! Josie's message reads.

When I sit back down, I feel Rosalie's fingers grip my knee. 'Maybe you should go to Paris,' she sighs.

My eyes widen. 'You think I should?' I breathe.

She looks over at Livia and Adriana, who are still twirling in excitement. 'I do. He'll play again on Sunday, no?'

'You could manage here without me?'

She shrugs, offering me a wry smile. 'We can manage. Don't worry yourself about that.'

Josie sends me another text, as though she's been listening to our conversation all along. *I think you should go to Paris*, she says.

Back downstairs in the kitchen, preparing for the dinner service, my fingertips hover over the keyboard on my phone.

I need to see him, I type out to Sydney, deliberating before I hit the 'send' key.

Her reply is virtually instantaneous. *How quickly can you get here?* she asks.

Tomorrow, I type back. *Tell me where to meet.*

Josie insists on accompanying me to Paris. The following day I take the first Eurostar from London; she flies early into Charles de Gaulle. We are staying in an Aparthotel called Maison le Bac, one of the few venues that had available space on the day of the ladies' singles final at Roland Garros. Josie talks endlessly about nothing in particular, trying to keep my mind off seeing Nicky, insisting we take a walk around town, buying French-style hot dogs in a baguette from a vendor outside the Louvres, then taking selfies on the Pont Neuf with a ton of other tourists who are clearly only in town for the tennis.

'Are you nervous?' Josie asks me, as we make our way on foot from Concorde metro station to the Hôtel de Crillon, my rendezvous point with Nicky. Syd's asked me to report to reception.

I'm so excited I could sprint. I'm also terrified. I've washed my hair, shaved and plucked everything, put on a simple layer of make-up and had my nails done at a salon in Wimbledon, just squeezing in before closing time. I want alone time with him. I want to tell Nicky I love him, no matter if he wins or loses. I want to feel his lips on mine again.

I should probably put on a show of being calm and collected, but the fact is I'm thrilled for him. This is his first Grand Slam final in more than six years, and I know how much it will mean to him and the team. Plus, if he wins, he's fulfilled my ridiculous requirement and I can free myself of my self-imposed shackles.

'I'll wait here,' Josie says to me once we've admired the elegant foyer, when the French receptionist has directed me to lifts to get to the room.

'Are you sure?' I breathe with a shaky smile.

'Don't need to see Nicky Salco sticking his tongue down your throat. Once was plenty enough.' She grins at me. 'Good luck.'

We embrace and I squeeze my eyes tightly shut.

'He's the luckiest man alive,' she whispers in my ear. 'Wish him luck for tomorrow from me.'

As I get into the lift, I stand next to a woman who looks like Anna Wintour and feel underdressed. I'm wearing white cut-off trousers and a fitted denim jacket. I smooth my hair, feeling my heart flip as the lift reaches my floor.

Outside suite 404, I knock my knuckles together. I try to listen for the sound of his voice. My heart's thudding when I finally rap on the door.

Sydney answers. I offer her a huge grin, throwing myself into her arms. When she pulls back, her smile doesn't match my own. It's... taut. Fake, almost.

'Come on in,' she says, like something's jammed in her throat.

I enter the room with half excitement, half trepidation. When I turn the corner, I come to a halt, crushed.

'Ragnar,' I swallow.

Ragnar stands with his hands behind his back in a military stance, in the same tracksuit he always wears, the grey one with the red stripe. His look is serene, with maybe a hint of an apology behind his gentle eyes. He's not looking as stern as I'm used to.

'Hello, Elle,' he smiles drily.

Sydney, having shut the door behind me, comes back round to stand next to him. When I glance at her, her bottom lip seems to tremble. 'I'm sorry,' she mouths, shaking her head.

My shoulders droop. 'Nicky's not here, is he?' I swallow, trying to stop my own tears.

'No,' Ragnar states simply.

'Does he know I'm in Paris?' I ask.

'No,' Ragnar clips again. 'I'm sorry.'

This time, it's me with the trembling bottom lip. To come all this way, expecting to see Nicky, only to find the only person I'll get to see is Ragnar, feels like a cruel joke. Except, I remind myself, this is all my own doing, and I could have been in Nicky's arms weeks ago, which makes me feel worse.

'Elle, I wanted to speak to you. And Nicky will of course be angry with me when he finds out, but he is on the cusp of something. I can't have anything interrupt his concentration right now. Look at how far he's come in a few short weeks.'

I look to the floor, still trying to curb the flow of tears.

He steps forward, his normally severe eyes twinkling. He grips my forearms. 'No, no, Elle, please don't cry. Don't you see? You've given me this gift. You've given Nicky a gift.'

'What gift did I give you?' I breathe.

He laughs. 'Singular focus. Extraordinary, unparalleled, remarkable focus. You've cleared his mind of everything but you. You've achieved what I never could. Everything that cluttered his mind until you gave the command that he win a Grand Slam.'

I wipe my tears, shake my head. 'It was never meant as a command.'

'Well, he took it as an instruction. A decree. And I am coming to understand… what I didn't see before. What I was stupid to not see before, that he worships you, Elle. He would do anything for you. The lengths he will go to.'

'But I need to ask you,' he continues, stepping back. 'I want to ask you… please… let me have this time with him. I know

279

he can win tomorrow's match. But if he doesn't, I know he can win the next final, or the one after that. I believe that he will make it. And I know that you believe in him too.'

I nod my head frantically, in case there was ever any uncertainty, but I'm still bursting with sadness.

'You will get your wish,' Ragnar finishes with. 'I just need you to be patient.'

I offer him a shaky smile, despite my disappointment.

Syd steps forward. 'I did my best to get you and Josie tickets for tomorrow. There was nothing left, I'm so sorry. I can get y'all ground passes. There's a big screen you can watch the match on inside the venue. If Nicky wins...'

I'm not sure how I'm going to sit through this next match. 'I'm grateful, Syd. I really am. I wouldn't want to take anything away from him. I'll find somewhere to watch it with Josie. Then if he wins...'

I can't finish my sentence. 'If he wins, I will be hunting you down, girl, like a goddamn mountain lion. You bet your life on it.'

On the Sunday, Josie finds us a British pub, just behind the Champs Elysees, that is showing the tennis finals and that's walkable from our hotel. She orders us both a greasy portion of fish & chips and a pint of Guinness, mainly because being in France isn't helping her desire for British comfort food. I never drink Guinness but it matches my current mood.

'Honestly, I'm still annoyed with Sydney,' Josie says once we're settled at a table near a TV screen.

'Don't be, it's not her fault,' I sigh. 'She made the mistake of telling Tag I was coming to Paris. He was the one who wanted to consult Ragnar first. She's still pissed off with him for that. She said she's buying Nicky a smartphone the first chance she gets.'

Josie's cackle breaks the spell and I laugh with her. Me not being able to speak to him direct is like something out of an old-fashioned film.

On the TV, Nicky and his opponent are announced to raucous cheers from the packed crowd. The sun is out, the roof of the stadium wide open. Carrying his bag, the camera films Nicky as he climbs a staircase up to the court, lit both sides in white neon. He's in a yellow top, the first time I've seen him in that colour. While he waits, he performs several knee tuck jumps, which I've watched him do with Tag back in Miami. Seeing him on screen makes me regret not taking Sydney up on her offer of ground passes to Roland Garros. Sitting in a bar, on the other side of Paris, I feel like I could be anywhere.

When the match begins, I lose my appetite, pushing my plate away.

The first set goes to a tie-break, Nicky on the defensive. He fights hard, but loses 10-8. Ordinarily, a loss like that would derail him, yet he doesn't flinch, and I see only a man with singular focus sitting alone and waiting for the beginning of the second set. The crowd seems to be coming round to him too. A set of spectacular rallies back-to-back has the crowd on its feet, and Nicky scrapes through to take the second set. Both the next two sets go with serve.

The fifth set I mostly watch with the heel of my hands pressed into my eyeballs; my elbows rested on the table.

'Come on, Nicky,' Josie whispers under her breath.

The crowd cheers. I peek. Nicky's on court, his right hand hanging limply at his side, tapping his racket against the side of his knee. He's closed his eyes and is talking to himself. At one point, I think I see him wipe a tear from his eye.

I look at the score. It's not gone his way. I want to tell him it doesn't matter. That I'll be there, no matter the ending. Except he has no way of knowing that, and I'm heartbroken to witness Nicky's first Grand Slam prospect in years slipping from his grasp.

In the end, a badly-timed double fault ruins his chances.

I return to England that evening, alone, and with a heavy heart.

Chapter Twenty-Nine

In south-west London, the sun is out. It's Tuesday, and today is the second day of the Wimbledon Tennis Championships. I am back in the kitchen with my apron on, preparing a pile of filet steaks, listening to the sports commentary on the radio.

'...*He's poised, he's sharp, he's composed. These are not words you usually associate with Nicky Salco. If you watch the American's performance from a few months' ago, you would think they're two different people. His attitude, his demeanour, his focus. People have been questioning his choice of coach for months, but to give credit to the Swede, Ragnar Norddahl, he's really turned things around here. Suddenly, Nicky Salco is looking like a serious threat, and it's all anyone's talking about. Semi-finalist at Queen's, finalist at the French Open, it's going to be exciting to see what he can do here at Wimbledon this year. He's definitely the man to watch.*'

There's a smile on my lips, an ache in my chest that hasn't gone away since Paris. I know from Syd that they are staying back at the house on Parkside Gardens, agonizingly close to my current location. Yet I've stayed away. I know all I can do is watch and wait.

According to Rosalie, Adriana and Livia left at 4 a.m. to go and queue up for tickets outside the All England Lawn Tennis Club grounds. I wish I could have gone with them.

Towards the end of the lunch service, Rosalie comes into the kitchen when I'm cleaning up.

'There's a young couple outside who would like to compliment the chef on their steaks,' she smiles.

Bernardo looks up. I've done all the steaks today. He gives me the side-eye and goes back to what he's doing.

'Should I go out?' I ask, keeping my apron on.

She gives me a wink. 'They asked for you especially.'

I frown, suddenly wary of who she can be talking about. I hope it's not a journalist trying to get a comment out of me. I check my watch. Nicky's opening match starts at 2p.m., one hour from now.

I emerge into the restaurant, a broad smile stretching across my face. Tag and Syd are at a table beside the wall, both grinning in my direction.

Tag gets to his feet, wrapping me in a warm embrace. I haven't seen him since the night I left the house in Miami. Sydney follows suit, giving me a bear hug.

'That was the best steak I've had in forever,' Tag says. 'Reminded me of how much I miss your cooking.'

Rosalie makes eyes at us, indicating that we should go outside to talk.

'I'll get the bill, you guys go head outside,' Syd says.

'You sure?' Tag asks, taking her hand, and I smile at the affection between them.

'I got it, don't worry,' Syd says, looking to Rosalie.

Outside on the pavement, I look around, checking nobody is filming. Tag puts his sunglasses on, cocks his head to one side, as though in sympathy. 'How are you doing?' he asks.

I can't look at him. 'I'm… still wishing I'd never said what I said.'

Tag shakes his head. 'No, no. Elle, with those four words… You've altered his destiny. You've lifted his game. You've changed the way he thinks. He can win this thing. It's just a matter of…'

'Seven matches?' I smile, the fluttering sensation returning to my chest.

'Seven matches,' he repeats. He shrugs. 'It's a walk in the park.'

'I believe in him.'

'I know you do. He knows you do.'

'He does?'

Tag nods his head. 'He doesn't say it. But I know he doesn't want to let you down.'

I look to the pavement.

'You know he's kicked his nighttime eating habit?'

'Yeah? Finally,' I laugh.

'I welcomed him to the world of being an adult. He says he doesn't even wake up anymore.'

I nod again, because it's a positive development. A part of me still wishes I could cook for him after midnight. 'Will you tell Nicky that you've seen me?' I ask.

'I might make it sound like we bumped into you.'

'Then could you give him a message from me?'

'Of course.'

I pause. 'Tell him I love him and I can't wait to see him.'

A smile pulls at one side of Tag's mouth as Sydney emerges from the restaurant. He nods his head. 'I'll tell him.'

'Elle, I'm sorry, honey, we gotta go,' Sydney blurts. 'We're meeting Nicky and Rag at the venue. I got you this.' She reaches into her bag and pulls out a white envelope which I take from her.

'What is it?' I ask.

'Open it.'

I tear open the envelope. Inside is a single ticket for the Championships, for the day of the Men's Singles Final on Centre Court.

'I'm hoping you'll have a reason to use it. Since I failed to get you one in Paris... you know, I thought I'd be optimistic.'

'Thank you, Syd,' I breathe, hugging her, as tears spring to my eyes.

'Don't thank me too hard, I think it's near the top at the back. Was the only ticket I could get my paws on.'

'If he gets through, I'll be there.'

We say our goodbyes. I wave to them down the street before I watch Sydney running back towards me, Tag waiting for her in the distance.

'I forgot to show you,' Sydney grins, holding out a key on a pink, fluffy keyring. 'Ta-da!'

'What is it?' I ask, confused.

'Only the keys to a three-bedroom apartment, in Coconut Grove, purchased by one Tag Holström, for he and I to move in together! The divorce is final, baby!'

We let out a mutual squeal on the pavement, throwing our arms around one another and jumping around in circles.

'Amazing! I'm so happy for you,' I grin, holding onto both her hands, and offering Tag a double thumbs up. He laughs at the spectacle we're making of ourselves on a South-West London street.

Sydney pokes me playfully in the chest. 'Girl, *I'm* happy for me. Now I just wanna be happy for *you*. Then all my stars are aligned.'

I nod my head. I'd be lying if I say I can wait for much longer.

I watch Nicky's opening match in Rosalie's living room, hugging my knees. It's odd seeing him on the screen, knowing he's there in person, barely half a mile down the road, behind the secure walls of the All England Lawn Tennis Club.

He's playing on Court 12, all in white. It takes me back to one year earlier. Over the warm-up, he removes his cap, ruffling his hair before replacing it. Watching him, I crave his touch. He wins the toss and chooses to serve. He isn't sulking or looking angry. He seems... quiet. Determined.

The male umpire calls for quiet. When he announces 'play', Nicky is ready. His first serve is an ace. A ripple goes through the crowd. The camera cuts to the wall-mounted speedometer, which reads 149 miles per hour. I can see spectators exchanging whispers. Nicky walks calmly to the other side, a ball girl passing him his next ball.

'Quiet please,' the umpire says.

Then he does it again, at the very same speed.

This time the crowd's applause is magnified.

On the third ace, I concede a smile.

On the fourth in a row, as he takes the game, I feel pride surging in my veins.

In my lap, my phone buzzes.

Start as you mean to go on, Josie says.

Rosalie has drafted in additional chefs for the next two weeks. I have three junior agency chefs looking to me for instructions because Bernardo refuses to deal with them. After a busy dinner shift, Adriana drags me upstairs because 'Today at Wimbledon' is on the TV. As it turns out, they managed to get tickets in the crowd for Nicky's match, which he won in straight sets, serving a total of forty-five aces. I sit down on the sofa just as they are showing highlights from the press conferences.

'Nicky, you breezed through your opening match, how would you describe your performance today?' a journalist asks.

He looks handsome. Handsome yet stoic. Like this is a business transaction to be completed. He looks like a man in full control of his emotions. He doesn't crack a smile, just gives a slight shrug.

'One down, six to go, you know? I'm well-versed in first round matches. It's the latter stages I want. I want the challenge of the final. I want that Centre Court place. And if I want that, I gotta earn it, I gotta raise my game. So today was a warm-up. Give me the next one. And the one after that.'

'You've had quite the transformation recently. Do you credit your coach with turning things around?'

'Not just my coach, no,' Nicky sighs. He takes a breath, looking away from the camera. 'There've been other influences. Some home truths. A wake-up call, I would say.'

'What kind of a wake-up call?'

Nicky takes a moment to answer. 'That it's not all about the tennis.'

A week later, the wait between matches is killing me. By the quarter-finals, Nicky hasn't even dropped a set. He's making all the sports headlines, his big serve and high return rate featuring heavily in the newspaper sports pages. That and his personal life, he's all anyone is talking about. There are articles that show pictures of Nicky with his shirt off, Nicky and Mackenzie – alluding to their break-up – and some that mention me by name as his former personal chef, with question marks over our public relationship. It takes every ounce of resistance I have not to finish my shift, sprint up to Parkside Gardens and hammer on the door just to throw myself into his arms. Technically, the only thing stopping me is my ultimatum, which the press doesn't know about, and the small matter of it apparently propelling Nicky to win matches. I don't want to jinx anything, so I wait, in agony, to see whether he progresses through the rounds.

When he takes the quarter-final in a similar fashion, the crowds go wild.

When the semi-final plays out, I hide behind the sofa, my nails all bitten to the quick.

When I hear one of the commentators say, 'He's done it! He's in the final!' my heart threatens to shatter into a million pieces.

Chapter Thirty

Sunlight streams down onto the well-manicured grass of Centre Court. The roof is open.

It's Sunday, the day of the Wimbledon Men's Singles Final, and I've barely slept. I'm too tightly wound. It's my first time inside the All England Lawn Tennis Club, and I fast-walked all the way to queue up outside. There's a slight breeze under a cloudless sky: optimal tennis conditions.

From my green, fold-down seat – part of a block on the third tier up, close to the south-west corner, on the right-hand side of the umpire – I take in the view. There is a lot of dark green. Every seat is taken: almost fifteen thousand of them. People have dressed for the occasion. The atmosphere buzzes. The Royal Box is full. The women's game already has their champion: now it's the men's turn. Everywhere there is excitable chatter. The spectator to my left has an ear piece, which he seems to be sharing with his wife, presumably so they can listen to the commentary.

The line umpires are already in position. I'm on an end seat beside some concrete stairs, on one of the furthest away rows nearer the back, though I am not quite relegated to the rows behind me, right at the top, in the shadows of the court's outer roof.

I close my eyes, listening to the hum all around me, and when I think back to a year ago, this feels like a dream. Like I'm an imposter. Except I now know that I have more reason to be here than anyone, and that, apart from the players themselves, I am the person with the most riding on this match. Yes, there might be those who've taken a flutter on Nicky's victory, or bet on his opponent triumphing in straight sets. But I'm the only one here whose heart is on the line. Whose future will be decided by two men thrashing out rallies across a battle field made from possibly the most valuable portion of turf on the planet.

Before the players arrive, I spy Sydney walking to the area set aside for Nicky's family on the far side of the Royal Box to my right, above the score board, near the middle. Tag is there, as is Ragnar and also Libby and Ben Salco. Sydney is looking up in my direction, but not in the right place.

I can't see you, I watch her text me. *What are you wearing?*

I get to my feet. Standing up on the end by the stairs, I text her back. *Red skirt, white top, denim jacket.* It took me forever to decide what to wear. In the end I went with the colours of the U.S. flag.

Syd clocks me and waves. I wave back.

How is he doing? I ask.

Calm, she texts back. *Got a job to do.*

Does he know I'm here? I type.

He asked if I was able to get you a ticket, she responds. *I told him unfortunately not.*

I'm glad, I say, because the last thing I want to do is distract him.

Nicky's opponent in the Wimbledon final is a twenty-four-year-old Croatian named Luka Kuzmanić. He's the third seed, the only other player in the tournament so far other than Nicky not to have dropped a set. He's lithe, nimble and light on his feet, very fast, and, like Nicky, has a solid return of serve. He won the Australian Open back in January, meaning they've each won one Grand Slam, only Nicky's victory in that tournament was six years ago. On paper, Kuzmanić looks good, plus he's younger, though he has a reputation for acting a little superior. With his improved attitude of late, Nicky therefore has massive crowd advantage, and a vast, enthusiastic female following, all of whom appear to believe he is single and available. No more journalists have visited me, so, apparently, I was a passing phase.

My heartbeat accelerates as the players are welcomed out on court, applause gently rippling through the crowd before building to a loud cacophony of clapping and whooping. Kuzmanić walks out in front. Both men carry their own bags. Nicky looks calm. His hair's shorter. I watch him get ready in his chair to the left of the umpire, knowing that I'm too far away for him to see, but for a moment willing him to look behind him in my direction. The rational part of my brain knows that it's best he doesn't know I'm here, but my heart wants him to see, that I'll support him no matter the outcome.

A few minutes later, following warm-ups, the umpire announces that Kuzmanić has won the toss and elected to serve first. I sit and chew what is left of my nails, just about able to hear the commentary from my neighbour's earpiece.

Kuzmanić's opening serve is out. I squeeze my fist. It's a good sign. Nicky once spent half an hour at two a.m. explaining to me why a first serve is crucial, whilst eating his way through a hearty bowl of pasta.

As I watch the match, I knot my fingers together, resting my lips against them, my elbows on my knees. The score remains close, the two men matching one another shot for shot. But Kuzmanić takes the first set on a tiebreak, 8-6.

Tag says this is the best tennis he's ever seen Nicky play, Sydney texts me during the break.

I'm so tense I cannot reply. It's all too much to bear. Nicky is on his feet before the break is due to end, and I burst into applause, shouting his name.

'Nicky Salco fan?' the spectator in the seat to my left comments wryly.

'Just a little,' I reply with a polite smile, but in my head, I'm screaming, *he's mine*.

In response, Nicky storms through the second set to rapturous applause, taking it 6-4. In the third set, he's also successful, taking it 6-3. Kuzmanić looks flustered, and at one point is given a verbal warning for throwing his racket. I admire Nicky's level of calm, knowing that he's the one who has lived out his career being hot-headed. Even the commentators I can hear pick up on it.

In the fifth game of the fourth set, Nicky overreaches, taking a tumble and skidding on the grass surface. He holds onto his knee, wincing in pain. Play is stopped so he can receive medical attention. I can see Rag and Tag leaning forward in concern. My heart is thundering inside my chest and I grip the sides of my seat to stop me running down the staircase to where the medic has his stretched out on the grass turf.

My phone vibrates. It's Josie. *This ultimatum thing*, she writes. *I think it's gone too far. You should just throw yourself at him, whether he wins this match or not.*

I exhale, craning my neck to see Nicky nodding his head, giving a thumbs up to the man in charge of treating him. *It's not over yet*, I type back.

Nicky's knee is strapped up. He gets up to more applause and continues to play, though loses the fourth set on a tie break.

The opening of the fifth set brings the biggest cheer. I've never heard anything like it, the ground under me vibrating with the noise. It's more akin to a football stadium. Nicky is still the favourite, the crowd willing him on to win. My knees jig up and down with nerves. It's level pegging.

Kuzmanić opens with a disastrous double fault. Nicky seems to seize the moment. When it's his turn to serve, he dishes out four top speed aces in a row: a love game to more euphoric applause. He is a man on a mission. I watch him raise his eyes to Rag and Tag; Tag on his feet, shouting at the top of his voice, punching the air. Just when Kuzmanić looks like he is clawing things back, Nicky smashes down a lob close to the line, breaking Kuzmanić's serve. Nicky pumps his fist in Rag and Tag's direction. This time, both are on their feet and my chest floods with hope.

I've never wanted anything so badly in my life.

At 4.45pm on the Sunday afternoon, Nicky earns his first ever Wimbledon Championship point. The crowd holds its collective breath. I close my eyes and pray.

It's a huge serve, but Kuzmanić has lightning quick reflexes, managing to return it back over the net. Nicky thwacks the ball back, Kuzmanić stretching but making contact. Nicky thunders it back down the sideline, Kuzmanić backhanding it over the net. It's a low drop shot but Nicky makes it, sending Kuzmanić into a sprint. Kuzmanić catches it between his legs, a lob going up high before Nicky smashes it down into the central service line.

Kuzmanić doesn't stand a chance.

I'm on my feet in an instant, my eyes on Nicky as he collapses to the ground, dropping his racket, rolling onto his back, his hands covering his face. He remains like that for some moments. The applause that echoes around the stands is deafening. Rag and Tag are embracing; so are Nicky's parents. The man next to me is clapping. He glances at my tearful grin.

'He won,' he says.

'He did,' I reply.

He seems surprised to see the tears that are falling uncontrollably down my cheeks.

'Goodness, you really *are* a fan,' he notes.

'You have no idea,' I breathe, more to myself, the lump in my throat so taut I can barely speak.

My phone is blowing up with messages from Jodie. I watch as a beaming Nicky shakes hands with Kuzmanić at the net, then with the umpire, before putting his arms in the air for the crowd. Another wild surge of applause and cheers sounds out. Nicky covers his head with his arms, as though he can barely believe it. Moments pass before he is heading across the court to see Rag, Tag, Sydney and his parents.

I watch as the guards guide him as he jumps over a short wall to the left of the scoreboard, climbing up towards a commentary box, before someone guides him up to the next level, where spectators pat him on the back. His parents he hugs first. Then Rag, who slaps him hard on the back. He shares a bear hug with Tag. Finally, I watch as he hugs Sydney before I see her say something in his ear.

And that's when Sydney points in my direction.

Nicky's turned around. His eyes are searching, but he doesn't see me. Then he's on the move, back down to the court, back the way he came. I can hear through the commentary that people are questioning what on earth he is doing. I track him as he re-enters the court, crossing swiftly towards the umpire, with his hand on his hips scanning how and where he can get access to the crowd. Applause continues, all eyes on where he's going.

'What's he doing?' the wife of the man sitting next to me mutters, as more and more people get out their phones.

I watch as Nicky easily hops up over the dark green barrier that separates the crowd from the court. Then I lose sight of him, before I see him use his powerful arms as leverage, pulling himself up to the next tier to reach the stairs. My eyes are swimming, so at that moment all I can see is a white blob approaching. Blinking away my tears I take one step to my right, so that I'm standing in the centre of the concrete stairs. When he looks up and sees me, I see him smile, quickening his pace. My heart swells, and I lose track of how many people are filming him on their phones as he races upwards.

When he reaches me, stopping slightly below me, there's a jaunty smile on his face, as though nothing's ever changed between us. It's like he's walked into the kitchen to find me cooking something in the middle of the night, except he's a little more sweaty than usual.

'Hi,' he says, and I'm vaguely aware that absolutely everyone surrounding us is filming, the entire crowd continuing to applaud him.

'Hi,' I breathe back, my heart pummelling my rib cage.

'I didn't know you would be here,' he says over the din.

'Just dropped by,' I smile and the tears are falling again. 'You did it.'

He steps up one more step, so that our faces are level. He gently wipes my tears. 'I did. All thanks to you.'

'No, no. You did that. That was all you.'

He brushes my cheek with the tip of his thumb. 'You never left my mind.'

'I know,' I smile.

'I love you,' he says.

'I know,' I manage, the lump lodged in my throat again. 'I love you too.'

The noise of the crowd is deafening. At this moment, there's nothing more to say. He sweeps me into a kiss, our lips meeting with equal intensity, the passion that I feel for him exploding in my chest, my arms moving around the back of his neck as he crushes me to him. Within a few seconds we've both realised that the whole world is watching him kiss me. Nicky pulls away and I feel my cheeks burn, glancing to my left and right, seeing only a thousand smartphones raised high in the air, pointed right at us. At this moment, that we'll probably ended up plastered all over social media doesn't bother me in the least.

'Come with me,' Nicky says, leaning his forehead to mine.

I raise my eyes to him. 'I don't think I'm allowed.'

'You're with me,' he whispers back. 'And I just won this thing.'

His hands are in mine. I never want to let him go again. I hang on tight and nod as he turns, taking in all the camera lenses, then takes a step down, leading me with him. I glance back and give a wave at the couple who'd been sitting next to me, both of them now aghast, the wife grinning inanely in my direction.

Nicky grips my hand tight as he leads me down the stairs, checking I don't fall. A steward shows us the way so we don't have to climb over any walls, though I have to navigate one last barrier that takes us onto the court. Nicky sweeps me into his arms and lifts me over, to approval from the crowd. When he puts me back down, I look down at my feet on the soft green grass of Centre Court and part of me can't quite believe this is happening. I picture Adriana and Livia's faces at this moment. The applause from down at this level is ear-splitting. Officials are watching us with trepidation. Nicky waves to the crowd as he holds my waist, walking me over towards the other side of the court, below where Rag and Tag are sitting. Together we go back up again, following his original route, until he can deliver me to Sydney, his parents and Rag and Tag. Before he lets me go, he pulls me in close.

'Promise me you won't go anywhere,' he says over the sound of the crowd, his lips hovering against my ear. 'There's so much I need to say to you.'

I nod my head frantically and he gives me a big smile. 'I promise I won't go anywhere,' I say, my stomach doing somersaults. 'I'll wait.'

He lowers his lips to mine one last time before handing me over to Sydney. She's pushed past the others to be the first to throw her arms around me. I glance back because Nicky is still holding my hand. Reluctantly, he lets go, and I watch him back away, heading back down towards the court before being approached by a suited official to receive instructions on the award ceremony.

It's a while before Syd stops squealing, and I realise I'm crying again. So too is Libby, who holds onto me so tightly I feel my lungs might burst. There's an awkward moment where Ben Salco gives me a light hug, but it's short-lived because Rag and Tag seem to both want to embrace me at once.

'You did this, Elle,' Tag grins at me as we absorb the atmosphere, which is electric. 'You changed everything.'

Ragnar squeezes my shoulders and, in this moment, however painful the wait has been, I know it's all been worth it.

After the awards ceremony, an interview and photographs, Nicky signs autographs on court, doling out some of his kit from his tennis bags to waiting fans. He's then escorted by an official out of sight. And it's all over.

Chapter Thirty-One

'What happens now?' I ask Syd, still wiping tears as we prepare to leave the court, the crowd starting to thin out. My ears are still ringing from all the applause.

'He'll be escorted outside to the balcony for the crowds outside to show their appreciation, then I think he gets shown the winners board, because they add the names immediately. Then I'm not sure, but he'll shower then go straight into a press conference. Then we'll head back to the house for a little down time before it's the Champions Dinner tonight. Nicky's expected to escort the winner of the ladies' final from yesterday, Sabine Jelenski. So… you're gonna have to share him for just a little longer.'

Sabine Jelenski is young, blonde, and incredibly talented, with legs up to her neck.

'I picked you out a few dresses just in case. Hopefully something will fit.'

'Wait, I can go too?'

'Honey, do you not know me by now? I do the groundwork. I plan ahead for any contingency. Sabine Jelenski might be his official date, but girl, I think I know who Nicky's gonna want on his arm.'

My lips twist. I wipe more tears. 'Thank you for thinking of everything,' I say.

Making our way off court, Libby takes my elbow. Ben Salco hangs back, and I'm still not convinced he thinks that Nicky made the right move by choosing me. But his wife is another story.

'Oh, I prayed for you to come along,' Libby hums ecstatically, looking to the sky, as I cover her hand with my own. 'When Nicky got engaged to Mackenzie, I took him to lunch the next day and I said to him, sternly, "Are you sure you love this woman?" and he said to me, "Of course I do, Mom, why d'you think I proposed to her?" But I knew. I knew he'd never really been in love. All he thought about was tennis. So, I told him, "Nicky, one day a girl is gonna show up who you're not gonna be able to live without." Two years later, you walked into his kitchen and my prayers were answered.'

We wait inside a room, whilst Nicky is ushered into a press conference, watching on a screen close to the conference room as Nicky is flanked by a backdrop of the familiar Wimbledon colours: green and purple. He's freshly showered, his hair still damp and tousled, raked through with his fingers. He's wearing a long-sleeved white top with a zip up the front. Yet he has the look of being on cloud nine.

A female spokesperson makes an introduction, asking journalists to state their name and organisation before asking their question.

'Nicky we're not used to seeing you smile so much,' the first journalist says. 'Your first Wimbledon Championship, tell us how you're feeling.'

Nicky exhales, rubs his chin, still smiling. 'Honestly? It doesn't feel real. It feels amazing. Better than amazing. I gotta lot to smile about. I've been saving them up.'

'Nicky, the crowd was on your side today. Did that help your game?'

He laughs. 'Usually, the fans are getting frustrated with me, and I'm getting frustrated with myself, so yeah, it's been nice having the crowd support me for a change. The atmosphere out there today blew me away. Especially at the end.'

'Nicky, you've said before today that you've been pushed to raise your game recently, would you care to expand on that?'

He's quiet for a moment. 'I would say that someone helped me lift my game, yes.'

'And not just your coach Ragnar Norddahl?'

'Ragnar and Tag Holström have been instrumental in helping me improve my game, yes, but sometimes you need someone to really challenge you and make you realise what's important.'

'Are you talking about Elle Callaway?'

In front of the screen, I stiffen, shocked that my name has been brought into proceedings. Sydney looks at me, eyes wide and brimming with excitement. Tag gives me a friendly nudge. On the screen, Nicky leans forward, nearer the microphone.

'It's Caraway. Like the seed, not the golf equipment,' he says. 'And yes, I'm talking about Elle.'

'I think the whole world wants to know, was she the woman you were... uh... celebrating with at the end of the match?'

'Ladies and Gentlemen, could we please keep the questions tennis-related?' the spokesperson interjects.

'I'm happy to take the question,' Nicky smiles at her, his eyes twinkling. 'Yes, it was. And just so we're clear, she's also the woman I was photographed with recently. She's also the love of my life. She challenges me like no one else does. She made me realise if I take all that emotion out of the tennis, the better I play. She also makes the best cheesecake you'll ever taste in your life. So, the quicker we can wrap things up here, the quicker I can get back to her.'

A ripple of laughter follows from the press pack. There's a grin on my face and warmth in my heart as Nicky is bombarded with yet more questions.

We continue to wait around in the reception room. Tag goes to check on Nicky's knee. The next time I see Nicky is in an underground car park, where a black Range Rover and a people carrier are waiting to escort us off the premises. The All England Club has an entire network of underground tunnels that the public are not granted access to, which, as someone who only recently started to follow the game of tennis, wholly amazes me.

He's waiting beside the Range Rover with his hands behind his back. The moment he sees me, his gaze settles on mine. Everyone else hangs back as I approach, and I'm wrapped in his embrace, and we kiss like nobody is watching, my arms snaking up around his neck.

Behind me, Sydney is still organizing everyone. I am to travel in the back of the Range Rover with Nicky. It has tinted windows. Everyone else will be travelling back to the house in the people carrier.

Once we're alone in the back of the car, Nicky and I watch one another, our faces close, like neither of us can believe this is actually happening: that we're here, together — legitimately — and that he just won a Grand Slam. I don't even notice when the car moves. I glance down at my fingers entwined with his.

'I came to Paris. Before the final,' I tell him.

He frowns. 'Wait, what? You were in Paris?'

'I told Syd I wanted to see you before the match. Only when I got there, it was Ragnar waiting for me.'

His eyes narrow. 'Did they all know you were there?'

I bite my lip. 'I think so.'

'They are so fired. All of them.'

I reach up, stroking my palm along his cheek. His frown dissipates. 'Rag believed in you. He didn't want me to disrupt your focus.'

'That's all very well, but I didn't win in Paris.'

'I was so desperate to see you,' I breathe and Nicky pulls me in, kissing me with wanton abandon until our poor driver is either blushing or nauseated.

'Tag gave me your message,' he says when he pulls away, stroking my hair, his breath shaky. 'Before the first match a couple of weeks ago. I knew I had to go out there and win seven matches in a row. There was no other option for me.'

I suppress a smile. 'Did you have a plan for if you lost today?'

'Yes. I figured I'd march on out of there, straight down the road to your restaurant, get down on my knees again and double down on begging you to take me back, no matter how many people came to film me. Because I couldn't wait any longer.'

I laugh, and his hands move to around my waist. 'Me neither. Don't worry; you wouldn't have needed to go anywhere. It would have been me on that staircase, rugby-tackling the security guards just to get to the court so I could take back what I said.'

'Now that I would have paid good money to see.'

We're kissing like lovesick teenagers again, his hand on the back of my head, his lips warm and inviting against mine. I'm vaguely aware that we've left the All England Club and we're travelling along the residential Bathgate Road, lined with expensive gated properties. I think that our driver must be thanking his lucky stars this is a short journey, such is the slushy display of amorousness on show.

When we reach the house, the others are all already waiting. The sight of the building brings back memories of my first day, when I took the job of being Nicky's personal chef. It seems like so much has happened in that time. In the driveway, Nicky's father wraps him in a bear hug, slapping him on the back, before he embraces his mother. I watch as he laughs with Rag, and along with Tag, they share a group hug. Finally, Nicky stands before Syd, his hands on his hips.

Sydney's eyes widen. 'Oh god, what?' she exclaims.

Nicky tongues the inside of his cheek. 'Elle came to Paris, huh?'

Syd's right arm shoots out towards Ragnar. 'Talk to your coach about that. I was the one who wanted to get you guys together. Bruh, I've been shipping you all this time.'

He smiles before offering her a hug. 'Because you're so amazing, you're completely forgiven.'

'Oh, so you wanna pay me more of them Benjamins for a little more of that something amazing?' Syd winks as she embraces him and I smile.

'I think you'll definitely be getting a raise *and* a bonus,' Nicky concedes. 'Now how long do we have before we gotta go to this Champions' Ball thing?'

Syd checks her watch. 'I think we can stretch it to forty-five minutes of down time if you can get ready in twenty minutes? Cars arrive at seven fifteen. We got champagne inside on ice. Or, by that, I mean I put it in the fridge just in case.'

'Garden celebration it is,' Ben Salco nods and Ragnar agrees with him enthusiastically.

Inside, Nicky takes my hand. 'We'll be right out,' he says. 'I just need five minutes alone with Elle.'

'She deserves a little longer than five minutes, don't you think?' Tag laughs and Nicky shoots him a look. The others head through to the kitchen. To my right is the dining room, where I first laid eyes on Nicky's face.

We take the stairs. I realise that, when I was living here, I never saw the upstairs bedrooms. Suddenly my heart is racing.

On the landing, we turn right, to the master bedroom at the front of the house. Nicky holds the door open for me as I enter. When he closes it, we're alone for the first time in a very long time, and it's not even after hours. People know we're here. Together. It takes me a brief moment to adjust my mindset.

I look at him and bite my lip. I can feel the electricity that runs between us. He takes a step closer, and then another, like this is some kind of mating ritual. His eyes are on my mouth. I tilt my head upwards a fraction, as though in acceptance. His hands go to my waist, easing me against him, until I can feel the full extent of his arousal pressing into my abdomen.

'I missed you,' I breathe, my hands going around him, my fingers sliding into his hair, tipping his head toward me, craving his touch.

'I missed you more,' he says in response. When he lowers his mouth, the kiss is tentative at first, brushing his lips over mine, until my tongue loses patience and nudges forward and it's all the reassurance he needs. A low groan escapes his throat as he crushes me to him, his kisses turning white hot, hungry and insistent. My hands are on him, remembering him, sliding over the contours of his back and chest through his clothes, unrestrained and reckless, desperate to absorb him somehow, as he in turn devours me, his fingers splayed out over my waist, my back, my bottom, pulling me so tightly to him that I lose breath. Until, from outside, there is a thumping sound on the staircase and Sydney cries out 'Nickyyy!', causing him to raise his head.

'Not now, Syd!' Nicky groans, but there's already a hammering on the door.

'Nicky!' Sydney shouts again.

'What is it?' he shouts back.

'Phone call,' she says. 'Can I come in?'

'Hold up a sec,' he says, glancing down. His eyes come to mine, his thick length still pushing into me, making its presence known. 'I can't answer the door,' he whispers. 'Not like this.'

'I'll go,' I smile, making a point of looking down where our bodies are pressed together before we part.

I open the door. Nicky's had to turn his back on Syd, raking a hand through his hair.

'Sorry to interrupt y'all but the President's on the phone,' she blurts, holding up her handset, eyes wide.

'As in *the* President?' I repeat in surprise.

'The very same,' she grins, carefully passing me the handset. 'He wants to congratulate Nicky.'

'Right this minute?' Nicky asks.

'There's a guy in the White House waiting to connect you,' Sydney says. 'Right this minute. He's a tennis fan, remember?'

'You'd better take this,' I say as I go back to Nicky and hand him the phone. Sydney backs off, closing the door as she goes.

Nicky looks non-plussed, flustered almost. 'Hello?' he says into his phone, massaging his forehead as he does so. I hear a deep voice speaking at the other end, confirming that Nicky is being connected. A moment later, my eyes widen as the actual

President of the United States begins speaking. I recognise his voice. Nicky is polite, thanking the Leader of the Free World for his congratulations, with his unoccupied hand brushing the tip of his thumb over my lips. I dart out my tongue, tasting his flesh, kissing it, and Nicky tries to stop the smile that's creeping onto his lips, giving me a look that all he wants to do is hang up on the President and ravish me. From what I can hear, the President is droning on about his grandmother, and how she introduced him to the sport.

Enjoying this new power that I wield over the man I love, I let my hands drift lower, to the hem of his tennis top, sliding my fingers underneath, grazing against the elastic waistband of his sports shorts. Nicky moves the phone away, the President still talking, and draws a shaky breath, his eyes going to mine, as though inviting me to proceed. As my fingers begin to explore the hard contours of his abdomen under the material, I feel Nicky flinch at my touch. He's so warm. My lips twist into a smile as Nicky attempts to break down the highs and lows of his Championship match, with his free hand grabbing a fistful of my top and yanking me closer, until his lips brush against my neck, all the while the President yabbering on the end of the line.

I back away from him, feeling confidence in my veins. I close the blinds, dim the lights, then kick off my shoes and take my jacket off, allowing the latter fall to the floor. My skirt comes next as I slither out of it. It lands around my ankles. I pull my top over my head before it's discarded. Nicky watches me, his gaze roving appreciatively over my body, a smile playing on his lips.

'Thank you, Mr. President, Sir, I would really love that. And thank you again for calling,' he swallows. 'You have a wonderful day.'

With that he ends the call. I'm kneeling up on the bed in front of him wearing only my underwear.

'You're killing me,' Nicky breathes, backing away to the door and opening it a fraction.

'Syd?' he calls out.

'Yeah?' she says from downstairs.

'I'm leaving your phone out here. You might wanna warn whoever is organising this dinner that we're gonna be late.'

'How late is late?'

Nicky looks back at me, his eyes ablaze. I offer him a light shrug. He's already kicking off his shoes.

'Late,' he calls out to Sydney and closes the door again.

Within a second, he's yanked both his tops over his head, tossing them aside. The shorts and socks follow just as swiftly and I feel the mattress shift under his weight as he kneels opposite me. His hands clasp my waist.

'I didn't think we would go this fast,' he whispers, a smile on his lips.

'I can put my clothes back on if you'd prefer.'

'Oh-ho, let's not be too hasty,' he smirks, sliding both his palms up my lower back as he reaches the clasp on my bra. 'Can I?' he asks.

I give a slight nod and the lace material falls away. I love the feel of his chest grazing my nipples as he guides me closer, one hand moving to cup my breast, his thumb teasing the taut bud until I'm breathless for his kiss.

'I don't have anything,' Nicky breathes against my mouth. 'As in I didn't bring any birth control.'

I raise my eyes to his. 'It's alright. I'm on the pill. And in the last year I've only had one sexual partner. You might know him.'

I can see his frown up close. He grits his teeth. 'You mean… you and Oliver…'

I pull a horrified face. 'Oliver? I had one date with Oliver, during which, I might add, I confessed to him that I was in love with my boss.'

'But in Miami… when we were in that club—'

I bite my lip. 'He offered to try and make you jealous.'

'Yeah, well, it worked. One hundred per cent.'

305

'Oliver is my friend. I've never slept with Oliver, Nicky. Not even close. He kissed me once.'

Nicky presses me to him, resting his head on my shoulder. 'You have no idea how happy you've just made me,' he whispers. 'Just the idea of it has tortured me.'

We remain like that for a moment, holding onto one another, my fingers sliding into his hair at the nape of his neck. 'I didn't know it, Elle, but I've been in love with you for a long time,' he sighs.

I pull back, searching his face. I've never seen him look so vulnerable.

'I fell in love with you in this house,' I tell him.

My admission elicits a gentle moan from him, pulling me to him, his lips capturing mine, kissing me with an intensity that turns my insides to liquid, sending a pulse of electricity direct to my core, feeling his thick length press into my stomach. I kiss him back with each of the emotions that are exploding in my brain: relief, love, desire, desperation, and everything in between. I want to feel him. All of him, in every way. Forever.

In a single motion he's shifted me to my back. I let out a gasp as Nicky moves lower, taking my nipple in his mouth and sucking hard, flicking his tongue across the tip until I'm arching my back. When he moves to the other, I feel liquid dampen my underwear and I moan. It's a loud moan, and I don't care who hears it.

'Let me hear you,' he rasps, his voice laced with flagrant desire, his lips grazing the contours of my breasts, before he's back to me, our mouths colliding again, and his fingers are guiding my lace underwear down my thighs. His body shifts then, and in an exquisite moment I feel his full weight on top of me, naked, warm and hard, his arousal pressing against my sex, pulsating and wet and ready for him. He slows his kisses, settling between my legs, our bodies fully entwined. He raises his head, his breathing ragged as he looks down at me, brushing his fingers against my swollen lips, stroking my cheek.

'Christ, how I've missed you,' he says, his tone hoarse with emotion. 'Since we've been apart, you're all I've thought about.'

'I love you,' I whisper, skating my fingertips along the line of his jaw. 'Every night I pictured us like this. With you inside me.'

He kisses me again, tenderly, taking his time, yet I'm panting with the anticipation. I want to feel his fullness inside me. I feel his biceps tremor at holding himself up and I'm reminded he's completed a gruelling five-set match barely an hour before.

I break the kiss. 'Wait,' I whisper. Using my right thigh as leverage, I lift my hips and he allows me to turn him, until he's lying on his back and I can straddle him. I scrape my nails down his chest. His gaze captivates me. Reaching down, lifting myself up, I run my fingers along the underside of his shaft, stroking him, hearing his satisfied sigh.

'I'm going to take my time, if that's alright,' I smile.

'When it comes to you, anything is alright by me,' he says.

I guide him closer, sliding his enlarged tip down my slippery folds, soaking him with my wetness, until he's probing my entrance. Nicky closes his eyes, and I love that I'm doing this to him. I dip him inside me, just an inch, my body opening up to him, welcoming him, then withdraw him again, and I relish the sound of the groan on his lips, his head going back. When I hear my name on his lips, I can't wait anymore, and I feed him into my body, swollen with need as I expand around his substantial length, sinking my hips downward, so that he's buried deep. When we're fully joined, Nicky's eyes drift open, we let out a sigh of mutual satisfaction, fire igniting my insides. He caresses my thighs, encouraging me, his hips twitching beneath me, and when I begin to move it is unhurried at first, rising and dropping back down, arching my back, embracing my own sensuality, experiencing this exquisite fullness, my mind swirling in a haze of heady pleasure. Until Nicky, I'd never had a sexual experience like it. I increase my speed, upping the tempo of my rotating hips, relishing my control as I ride him, the friction creating delicious sensations that fizz up and down my spine. Nicky slides his palm down across my belly, his fingertips continuing on the same path, until he takes my fingers in his and guides them to the point where our bodies meet. He's encouraging me to touch myself, and whilst a year ago the thought might have filled me with mortification, today I can't wait to put on a show for him. My fingertips obey his request, and when I graze against my wetness in a circular motion, my body judders in reaction, and it almost sends me over the edge.

'That's it, Elle,' he murmurs. I love the sound of my name on his lips. I love everything about him, this man that I've fallen so hard for. I want him to know that I've never felt like this before. Loved, worshipped. I lean down, our mouths crashing together, and Nicky's fingers cover mine, increasing the pressure against my pleasure spot. The loudest moan escapes my lips, into his mouth.

'Right there,' I whisper and I slow the rotation of my hips, the pleasure of both our fingers sliding against me, 'Oh god, Nicky,' I whisper, 'Mmm, I'm so close.'

'Let yourself go,' he whispers, and I'm flying, that blissful moment before I'm about to crash over the edge. My fingertips keep to a steady rhythm but with Nicky increasing the pressure, just by a fraction, the resulting rushing sensation is enough to make me cry out, my orgasm exploding around him like a fireworks display, long and slow spasms of my vagina contracting along his full length. My head goes back. He rides out my climax with me, keeping up the pressure against my fingertips until I collapse onto his chest, gasping for breath. Holy hell.

It takes me a moment to realise he's still fully engorged inside me. I raise my head a fraction, placing two hands against his chest and push myself back upwards, feeling him pulse and throb inside me. I take power from having him between my thighs, where I can control the tempo of my movements. I grind my hips forward and his head goes back again. I'm so wet that I feel him slide in and out of me. I rise up, so he's almost out of me, before plunging him back inside. I love watching what it's doing him, driving him wild. Soon he's writhing with me, bucking his hips, arching his back, craving his release, the bed frame starting to move, hitting the wall as we move. And before long, his hands clamp down on my thighs, steadying me as he comes with my name on his lips followed by a string of loud curse words.

Nicky's arms fall away, splaying wide across the mattress. We're both sweaty, out of breath. Slowly, I clamber off him, feeling the same arms go around me as I lay my head against his chest, listening to the sound of his racing heartbeat.

'Elle?'

'Mmm?'

He turns his head, kissing my forehead. 'In the cold light of day, this is going to work. You know that right? We're going to work.'

'I know,' I breathe, because I don't doubt that it's the truth.

He's quiet again. 'And, Elle?'

'Mmm?'

'You know I love you. Will you move back to Miami with me?'

I raise my head. 'But what about my job? I like my job. I like it here in London. You can come and visit me and I can come and visit you. We'll do the long-distance thing.'

He stares down at me, blinking, as though lost for words.

'I—' he begins and I grin.

'I'm joking,' I giggle, pinching his side and he exhales, laughter in his throat, his arms going round me again.

'Jesus, thank god,' he groans, rolling me onto my back, pressing our sticky bodies back together.

I stroke his face. 'Of course I'll come to Miami with you. My contract already ran out at the restaurant two days ago. I swear if I ever have to griddle another steak, it'll be too soon.'

He's showering me with kisses again. 'For a minute there I thought I was about to lose you again.'

'You'll never lose me again, I swear it.'

He kisses me deeply and I've never loved him more. 'Good, because I'll never let you go.'

I look down at our naked bodies entwined, suddenly feeling sorry for Syd. 'We're very late; we should probably get showered.'

'Can't I just stay here with you?'

'Negative,' I laugh, sitting up and swinging my legs over the side of the bed. 'I've been stuck in a kitchen for four and half months. I want to get dressed up and go to the ball.'

We're late to the Championship Dinner, Nicky apologising to the terse-looking women's Wimbledon Singles Champion, Sabine Jelenski, whose boyfriend looks positively terrified of her. Once the official photographs have been taken, Nicky is able to enjoy the night.

In the morning, we're back in bed, naked, Nicky's warm body pressed into mine from behind, our evening clothes strewn in heaps along the carpet, all the way from the door.

I am woken by the sound of my phone vibrating.

'Hello?' I say groggily, as Nicky stirs behind me, one arm draped around my middle.

'Put me on speaker,' Josie's voice demands down the line.

'What?' I grumble.

'Just put me on speaker,' she says again.

I lay the phone flat on the sheet, squinting at the screen to switch on the speaker.

'Okay, you're on speaker,' I say hoarsely.

'Good morning, Nicky,' Josie purrs.

'Hey, Jose,' Nicky responds, his voice also thick with sleep.

'Congratulations,' she hums.

'Thank you.'

'You realise you're both on the front page of every British newspaper this morning. Even some of the Spanish ones.'

'Jose, we're sleeping,' I groan.

'Yes, well, I'm sure you haven't had much of that either. I just wanted to remind Nicky of his promise to me.'

Beside me, Nicky starts shaking with laughter. 'Wow,' he says. 'I might have known you wouldn't forget about that, Josie.'

'What promise?' I question.

'When I saw Josie in Madrid, I promised her if she told me where you were, I'd grant her use of a pool house in Miami anytime she needed it.'

'And…,' Josie hums down the phone.

Nicky leans up, rubbing his eyes, looking down at me. 'And your sister played hardball. She said if she told me if we got back together as a result of her telling me where you were, she wanted a whole pool house. That I had to give one to her. Like, hand over property deeds and everything.'

'Josie!' I blurt.

'Hey,' Josie says, 'I was angry with him. I wasn't just going to give him your location for free, Elles.'

'I said yes,' Nicky says. 'So, I guess now your sister is the proud owner of a pool house.'

'You don't have a spare pool house to give her.'

His eyes twinkle. 'Yes, I do. She can have yours.'

'That's my pool house, Jose! You'll have to fight me for it,' I say to the phone.

'You get to share the big house… with me,' Nicky laughs.

'It's the principle of the thing,' I shoot back.

'Prime real estate. Miami vacays, here I come,' Josie sings, but I can tell she's trying not to laugh. 'Let me know when the honeymoon period's over. I can't have you two fawning over one another whilst I'm working on my tan.'

'Bye, Josie,' I sulk.

'Love you,' she trills. 'You'd better take care of my sister, Salco.'

'I will, Caraway. That's a promise.'

I hang up. Nicky turns me into him, wrapping his arms around me, giving me hangdog look. 'I'll build you another pool house. A bigger one.'

'Give her Ragnar's. That one never gets any light. We'll dig a hole in the garden and fill it with water. That can be her pool.'

He laughs and strokes my hair. 'Are you saying you never want your sister to come visit us?'

'My sister is tolerable only in very small doses.'

'I would have given her the house.'

'What?'

'I'm serious. I would have given her the house. I would have lived in a tent on the tennis court if it meant I got one shot at seeing you again.'

I can't help but smile, resting my hand against his cheek. A year ago, when I took a job as a personal chef, I could never have foreseen that I'd be lying here with the man of my dreams, and that he'd be someone who'd offer to give up his house for me. I never dreamed I'd be this happy.

'I knew in my heart that you would do it,' I whisper to him. 'I will never stop believing in you.'

He kisses me again. 'And I will always be grateful for you,' he says. 'You are the best thing that ever happened to me.'

POST-MATCH COMMENTARY

We've been back in Miami for two weeks. We talked about going somewhere, but in the end, we wanted to stay at home. Because it's ours now. Our home.

The doctor told Nicky to rest his knee, so he hasn't picked up a racket since we touched back down in Florida. Tag has flown to Sweden with Syd to meet his parents; and Ragnar has gone to visit his new American girlfriend, who he's being incredibly coy about. Lonzo has been given paid time off and is with his family in the city's Little Havana.

In London, following his win, I took Nicky to meet Rosalie. Livia and Adriana were there too, quaking with excitement and nervousness as he entered the room. Nicky was the perfect gentleman, of course, and I now suspect their crushes on him might have increased threefold. Bernardo grunted at me in a goodbye, glad that he had his old chef back, someone who didn't like tennis or insist on switching on the TV. I promised Rosalie I would drop by when I was next in London.

On our return, Nicky bought a new double sun lounger with a canopy for beside the pool: the pool that I now refuse to associate with Mackenzie's furious outburst towards me in January. We've spent significant portions of time exploring one another's wants and desires in every room in the house, several times over, including on the sheepskin rug, which seems to be Nicky's favourite place to make love, my days of faking a climax gladly behind me. Other than that, we've barely left the lounger, except to eat meals or to go inside if it rains. At night, we sleep together in my pool house, because Nicky moved in there when I left, as he says to feel closer to me. We've hired an architect to re-model the interior of the house, to be able to start afresh. We're open and honest with each other, and our silences are comfortable.

It's almost the perfect set-up. Almost.

If I don't work for Nicky, I can't work. As per my visa rules, it's not permitted. I can cook to my heart's content – which I do – but financially, I am reliant on Nicky for everything. Despite his insistence that I pay for nothing, he knows it bothers me that I can't contribute.

On a Thursday morning, we're on the sun lounger, our legs entwined, a copy of *Wuthering Heights* lying face down in the sun whilst Nicky showers me with lazy kisses. I'm trying out some other classic romance novels, yet the book has been abandoned, and I'm currently in danger of going under, the flames of desire licking at my insides.

'I should think about making lunch,' I hum when Nicky's mouth moves to my neck.

'Surely lunch can wait,' he murmurs, his fingertips gliding up my thigh, under the hem of my bikini bottom. 'I've replaced food with sex.'

My laugh is slow and languid. 'I thought you'd replaced tennis with sex.'

'I have. But sex also trumps food. Sex with you wins every time.'

He comes back to my mouth, kissing me into oblivion until we're interrupted by the bell at the entrance gate to the garden.

Nicky lifts his head. 'Who the hell can that be?' he mutters.

On our return, he'd spent a long day doing press, following his win. Tag and Sydney are not due back until Saturday, and Ragnar not until Monday. Nicky's parents are in Orlando seeing friends.

'I'll go,' I say, getting up from the sun lounger and pulling on my denim shorts.

'It's probably just kids selling cookies,' Nicky mumbles.

'Then we can buy some,' I say over my shoulder with a jaunty smile.

When I open the gate, a woman is standing there who I don't recognise. She has chin-length blonde hair, and wears fitted jeans, sunglasses and a light-coloured blazer.

'Can I help you?' I ask.

She takes off the glasses and gives me a friendly smile.

'Hi, I'm looking for Lonzo Cabrera.'

'I'm sorry, he's not here right now. Can I pass on a message?'

She cocks her head to one side. 'You wouldn't happen to be Elle, would you? Lonzo said you would be here.'

'I'm Elle,' I say warily.

Nicky comes up behind me. He's put a shirt on, though is still in bare feet. He wraps his arms protectively around my bare stomach. The woman clearly recognizes him.

'Oh, I see now what Lonzo meant,' she smiles knowingly. 'I saw you both on the TV for Wimbledon. Congratulations on your win.'

'Thank you,' Nicky states in a low tone. 'And you are…?'

She holds out her hand to me and I shake it. 'My name is Violet Morano. I run a boutique wedding planning business for south Florida based out of Westchester. I just lost two of my wedding cake designers to a competitor. Lonzo sent me some pictures of the wedding cake you made, and I have to say, I was very impressed. I wondered if you'd be interested in discussing working with me.'

I look at her in surprise. 'I would love to talk to you, but did Lonzo mention that I don't have a green card? I'm not an American.'

She waves her hand dismissively. 'Sweetie, I'm the wife of an immigration lawyer. My last cakemaker was from Switzerland. I mean, he was married to an American woman, which helped, but I'm sure we could fix you right up with the correct visa if marriage isn't on the cards just yet.'

I feel Nicky flinch behind me, his arms tightening around my waist.

Violet gets out her business card and hands it over. 'Listen, there's no pressure. From what I saw, your work is incredible, just the style I'm on the lookout for. So, think about it, and if you wanna hear more, call me, let's grab a coffee sometime.'

I glance down at the ornate card, offering her a smile. 'Thank you,' I tell her. 'I'll do that. Thank you for stopping by.'

'Don't thank me, thank Lonzo. He's the one who sent me the pictures.'

She bids us a friendly goodbye. I make a mental note to send Lonzo a message. When the gate is closed and I turn around in Nicky's arms, he has a wry smile on his face.

'Don't say what I think you're going to say,' I chide him, as I wriggle free, and he follows me back to the sun lounger, holding my hand.

'What do you think I'm gonna say?' he asks.

'You cannot marry me so I can get a green card. It's too soon to be talking about marriage.'

'Why is it too soon to be talking about marriage?'

I sit back down on the sun lounger beside the pool, looking at the details on the business card Violet's just given me, drawing my knees up to my chest. I plan to call her. 'You shouldn't feel an obligation to marry me, just so I can get a job in the U.S.'

Nicky slides back down next to me on the lounger, watching me. A moment passes, before he says, 'Okay, but what if I want to marry you?'

'Is that a proposal?' I shoot back.

'No. But consider it a warning that I plan on asking you one day.'

'Weren't you already engaged to someone else six months ago?'

Nicky sucks air through his teeth. 'It takes a really bad thing to know when you're on to a really good one.'

I feel it's my place to challenge him. 'We've been together, like, two weeks.'

'Best two weeks of my life, and not if you count back to the first time we kissed in Cincinnati. If you look at it like that, it's been ten months. And when you know, you know.' He lowers his head, brushing a feather-light kiss against my lips. 'And I know,' he whispers.

He pulls away and I look across at him, trying hard not to smile. He twists his body to face me.

'Okay,' he says, 'Let's put it this way. I'm not gonna marry you so you can get a green card. I'm gonna marry you because I want to grow old with you. I want to have little Salco babies with you. I want to share my life with you. I want to worship you because you're my goddess, and I can't get enough of your heavenly body. I want to marry you because I love you, and no one will ever hold the same power over me that you do, Elle Caraway. I am a slave to your existence. Plus, you make a mean cheesecake that no man in his right mind can resist. Except you're mine. And nobody else's.'

His confession breaks me. There are tears in my eyes. I cling to him when he kisses me, because I ache for him. I think I always will.

'And none of this long engagement business either,' he says when he finally lifts his head. 'If we get engaged, I'd want to get married straight away. Within a month.'

'A month?' I giggle against his lips. 'Nicky, do you know what it takes to plan a wedding?'

'I do, actually, and we don't need any of it. Just us, here, and some witnesses, our family and close friends. And a very special wedding cake that you've made.'

'A month, though? I think I'm going to need another Grand Slam for that.'

He raises his eyebrows. 'You challenging me, Callaway?'

'I might be.'

His lips push forward in a pout and he's frowning. 'Alright. If I win the U.S. Open in September, you have to marry me within a month.'

I straighten, and hold out my hand. We shake on it.

'You got yourself a deal,' he says with a grin.

'And if you don't win?'

'You doubting me now?'

'Not for a minute. I just need to know the terms of our agreement.'

He thinks about it for a moment. 'If I don't win, you still marry me, but you get all the preparation time you need.'

'Doesn't that constitute a long engagement?'

'Guess I've got my work cut out for me, then.'

He lies back, and I snuggle into him. He presses another kiss against my forehead.

'What are you thinking?' I say, after a moment of silence.

'I'm planning my proposal. What are you thinking?'

I bite my lip, giving him a squeeze. 'I'm thinking of how much I love you, and that I hope you win the U.S. Open.'

And, Reader... he did.